Rad... ... ...for the women's section about feminism, sexism and everything in between.

She grew up in London but has worked in Chile and Barcelona. She studied English Literature at University College London, followed it up with a Masters in journalism at City University London, and now spends most of her time writing.

Her debut novel *Virgin* was published in 2014, and *Not That Easy* is the eagerly awaited sequel.

Twitter: @radhikasanghani
Instagram: @radhikasanghani
Facebook: Radhika Sanghani (author)

Not THAT EASY

RADHIKA SANGHANI

Published in Great Britain 2015
by Mills & Boon, an imprint of Harlequin (UK) Limited,
Eton House, 18-24 Paradise Road, Richmond, Surrey, TW9 1SR

Not That Easy © 2015 Radhika Sanghani

ISBN: 978-0-263-91536-5

97-0915

Harlequin (UK) Limited's policy is to use papers that are natural, renewable and recyclable products and made from wood grown in sustainable forests. The logging and manufacturing processes conform to the legal environmental regulations of the country of origin.

Printed and bound by
CPI Group (UK) Ltd, Croydon, CR0 4YY

To anyone who has ever felt like their life is a total mess

Chapter 1

'Ellie, you're single. You should take the single room.'

I stared at Will in shock. He couldn't be serious.

'The rest of us are all seeing people, so we need the double bedrooms,' he continued.

'Please tell me you're kidding,' I said slowly.

Will stood up tall and went straight into accountant mode. 'I'm not trying to be a dick,' he said diplomatically. 'I just think it makes sense for us three to take the big rooms because Emma is with Sergio, Ollie is with Yomi and I'm with Cheng. You're single, so you should have this room. Logically, you don't need the double bed.'

I looked around the tiny room at the others. Emma was shuffling awkwardly on her black-wedged heels and avoiding eye contact with me, while Ollie was inspecting the laminated floorboards. He ran his hand over his short bleached hair and blinked at me innocently with his bright blue eyes. I forgave him immediately.

'It won't be that bad. You can pay slightly less rent,' said Will.

He was serious. He was actually serious. I stared at Emma and Ollie again, waiting for them to stick up for me.

Ten seconds later, I was still waiting.

This was a trap. A coup de whatever in my own bloody home. 'Are you fucking kidding me?' I cried out.

Will's tweezed eyebrows settled themselves into a familiar frown and he crossed his arms.

'Emma?' I demanded, as I turned to face her. 'Do you agree with Will? Are you a part of this blatant singleism now?'

She shook her short blonde hair. 'No, of course not, babe, but I do kind of really need a double bedroom. Serge will stay here loads and he's six foot six, El. I don't think he'll fit in a single bed.'

I gave her a withering look before turning to Ollie. 'Ollie? What about you?' I asked, hoping my eyes looked more doe-eyed than rabid.

'Ah, I'm really sorry, Ellie,' he said. 'It's just that Yomi will stay with me whenever she's down visiting me from uni in Bristol.'

I sighed. Of course the perfect almost-doctor girlfriend was going to visit him whenever she had time off from saving people's lives.

'Come on, Ellie, it's the easiest option,' said Will with a look of faux sympathy on his annoyingly symmetrical face. 'If you had a boyfriend, it would be different, but you don't really need all that extra space. If you're worried about wardrobe space, we can all give you sections in ours, can't we?'

Emma nodded fervently. 'Of course! You can put whatever you want in my room and borrow my stuff whenever. Even my thigh-high leather boots.'

Oh God. Was this actually happening? Were my friends really consigning me to the single bed and a life of single-dom? Even my BFF, Emma, was siding with them and slowly losing the second *F* from her acronym.

I had to try to stop this or I would die alone in my child-sized bed.

'I cannot *believe* this,' I finally spluttered. 'You can't just relegate the smallest room in the house to me like I'm some kind of unwanted spinster aunt. I'm part of this household too, and we're going to live together the whole year—I'm not staying in this shoebox the entire time.'

'I guess we could switch halfway?' Ollie offered. 'I mean, I dunno if I could, but maybe you could, Will? You're not in a serious relationship with Cheng, are you? If you split up, maybe you could swap with Ellie?'

'Whoa,' I said, holding up my left hand. 'First, stop talking as though I have agreed to taking the smallest room, because I haven't, and second, Will, what the fuck—Cheng isn't even your boyfriend??'

Will looked uneasy. 'We're not exclusive,' he admitted, 'but we do spend most nights together. And if I'm not with him, let's face it, I'm shagging someone else. I need the double for when I bring guys home.'

'But what if I want to bring someone home?' I asked.

He snorted and Emma suppressed a laugh. The cow.

'Ellie, I love you,' said Will, 'but after hanging out with you a fair bit this summer, I think I can safely say you're not the kind of girl to bring a guy home.'

'That's so unfair!' I cried. 'Just because I didn't sleep with any strangers over the summer doesn't mean I never will.'

He raised the perfectly arched eyebrows at me. 'Ellie, have you ever even had a one-night stand?'

I flushed and felt my face heating up. This was a very sore topic. I couldn't lie because I'd sworn to stop covering up the truth about my—limited, very limited—sexual history, and besides, Emma knew everything anyway. If I lied, she'd just think I was pathetic.

'Fine,' I growled. 'I have never had a one-night stand, but if you give me this shitty little room, I never will.'

'You could go back to theirs?' suggested Ollie.

'What?' I asked in exasperation. 'How is this even a conversation? I am twenty-two years old. I am clearly capable of casual sex, and if I want to do it, I will. I'm not taking this room on the basis of being single because that is...'

Shit, what was it?

'That is outright discrimination,' I declared. 'We live in a democracy and we're...we're going to pick names out of a hat.'

'Ellie, stop acting so childish. We can reach an agreement like adults,' said Will.

'I dunno, it seems fair to me,' said Ollie. I flashed him a look of utter gratitude. 'Shall we just do rock, paper, scissors?'

'Meh, fuck it,' said Emma, shrugging her shoulders and sticking her right hand out into the air above the bed.

On the other corner of the bed, Will rolled his eyes and stuck his fist out. Ollie did the same and, from the one remaining corner, I placed my trembling arm out so our hands met in a charged square.

I had to win this. If I wanted to live the life of a young professional graduate in London, I needed the right setting.

I couldn't go on dates if I didn't have anywhere to bring them back to.

'OK, on the count of three,' said Ollie. 'One…'

Please, Julius Caesar, help me out here, I prayed to my own personal hero. God had never really done it for me—which broke my Greek Orthodox mother's heart—but the Roman conqueror had helped me out once before, and he could do it again.

'Two…'

Oh shit, I had to pick one. Um…rock. The strongest one. Caesar would pick the strongest.

'Three.'

There were two rocks and two pieces of paper in front of us.

Will scowled at me. 'OK, Ellie, it's between you and me now,' he said, as Emma whooped with joy and Ollie high-fived her. It was fine. I hadn't actually lost. Caesar had helped me out. The rock was clearly a keeper. I would play it again.

'I'll count,' offered Ollie.

Will and I faced each other across the bed and I stood with my legs wide open. This was it. Roman luck was on my side; I could squash this Gallic peasant.

'One…two…three.'

My pale rock lay in the shadow of a triumphant palm paper. Will grinned smugly at me. Bollocks. Just like my hero I'd forgotten the cunning of Brutus's betrayal. *Et tu, Brutus.*

'I knew you would go for a rock again, Ellie,' said Will. 'You're so predictable.'

My face dropped and Emma reached out across the bed to squeeze my limp fist. My Ides of March had begun.

* * *

I looked around my room. I'd covered the bed in a floral bedspread and hung scarves from the ceiling to give it an Aladdin's cave vibe. There were fairy lights around the window, and photos of me, Emma and Lara taped onto the walls. If I stood on the bed, I could touch all four walls and reach pretty much any item in the room.

The bed, for lack of other options, was pushed up against the non-double-glazed window. It meant condensation was slowly dripping onto my Primark cushions. I sighed. Throughout my three years of university I'd lived in halls of residence and constantly dreamt about living in a proper flatshare with friends. This was not what I'd expected. A room of my own it may be, but I bet even Virginia Woolf would be seriously unimpressed with it.

'Nooo, get off me!' squealed a high-pitched voice.

I thumped the wall behind me with my fist.

'Nope, not me,' called Ollie from behind the wall.

I rolled my eyes and stood on my bed to hit the ceiling.

I could hear suppressed giggles before Cheng yelled, 'Sorry. We'll keep it down.'

Will's low voice murmured something and then the squealing came back. I sighed and collapsed back onto my bed. We'd been living here for only forty-eight hours but I—quite literally—knew the ins and outs of Will and Cheng's relationship. Thanks to the shitty plaster walls I also knew every loving word Ollie said to Yomi whenever she was visiting. The only person whose relationship I couldn't overhear was Emma's because her room was down the hall, but she told me every detail about her sex life with Sergio every time we hung out anyway.

As fun as it was living in the youngest—and cheapest—

part of London, I had never felt more single. I opened my laptop and logged onto Facebook to see how great everyone else's lives were now we had graduated.

Kara was back in a relationship with Tom and working for a publishing company. Belgian Marie seemed to have five boyfriends who all looked like varying versions of Burberry models, and my arch-nemesis, Hannah Fielding, was working as a writer for *Tatler*. Ugh, she was even tagged in a picture with Kate Moss. That was just so bloody typical.

I looked around my tiny room, where the mould was growing over the landlord's cheap paint, and I felt an urge to start crying. Instead, I decided to tech-harm.

I reached out slowly for my iPhone, knowing I would regret what I was about to do. I tapped open the screen and, feeling pre-emptively sick, opened up Instagram. The sepia-filtered world burst into life and I scrolled down the feed to see photos of my uni friends dating beautiful people, working for high-powered companies and sunbathing on the rooftop of Shoreditch House in white bikinis with retro sunglasses. I could feel self-pitying tears pricking my eyelids when the door burst open.

'Ellie, we're having a major crisis,' gasped Will. He was standing in my doorway wearing red boxers patterned with tiny yellow cars. Were those mini Noddys sitting in the yellow cars? I craned my head forward. 'Stop staring at my penis and help me,' he snapped.

'Oh, right, sorry. What's up?'

'No one in the house has any lube,' he declared.

I snorted. 'Oh, right, and you think *me*, the single flatmate with the single bedroom, is going to be the one to help you out with that?'

He raised an eyebrow. 'Please, I'm not that deluded. But

I just wondered if you have any more of that Aussie miracle conditioner you use.'

I stared at him. 'Um, no? I need to go to the supermarket. Why do you want to wash your hair now anyway?'

'It's not going on my hair, babe. At least, not for the hair you can see.' He smirked.

'I literally have no clue what you're talking— OH MY GOD. You want to use my £4.49 conditioner for lube?!'

'Well, that's what I've been using for the past week until you ran out. You don't mind, do you?' he asked.

'Yes, I bloody mind,' I cried. 'I can't believe that's why I've had to buy double the amount I normally buy. I thought I just had really…knotty hair lately,' I finished lamely.

He rolled his eyes at me. 'I'll go and ask Emma.' His Noddy boxers retreated down the hallway until he paused to face me.

'Hey, were you crying?' he asked.

'No, 'course not,' I cried. 'Why would you think that?'

'You have Facebook open on your computer and Instagram on your phone. You only do that when you're miserable, Ellie.'

'Will, you've lived with me for less than a week and only known me for a few months. That doesn't mean anything,' I replied tartly.

'How about the fact you have mascara running down your face, then?'

Bugger.

'Oh, fuck off, Will,' I yelled, as he laughed and walked off.

I pulled the duvet over me. I felt as single as my bed. It wasn't that I wanted a boyfriend per se, it was more that everyone else was so ahead of me in the romantic—well, sexual—stages of life. Hell, they were shagging with conditioner while I was watching them on Instagram.

The problem was that everyone I'd grown up with had lost their virginities aged fifteen to seventeen. At school, all my girlfriends had gone out with the boys at the school next door, and after a year of climbing up the bases, they'd eventually 'done it'.

But because I was the frizzy-haired Greek girl with thick eyebrows and ill-fitting jeans, no one had been particularly interested. My only sexual encounter during my school years happened when I was seventeen and it was so bad that my friends nicknamed it a 'bite job'. So, while I was still recovering from the humiliation of biting James Martell's penis, they were sharing sex stories in the sixth-form common room. Even my best and oldest friend, Lara, had got involved.

It was worse at uni. By then, everyone had already had a couple of relationships, peppering the gaps with drunken one-night stands and the odd inappropriate fling. They carried on shagging throughout uni, boasting about it in drinking games. Only, as always, I either had to listen with a fake smile on my face or—the less awkward option—make up a sexual past of my own. Because I'd been a virgin until the ripe old age of twenty-one.

It wasn't out of choice. All I'd wanted to do was break my hymen, but no one vaguely attractive had offered. In my final year of uni, I'd been so desperate to lose my V-plates that when freckly, twenty-six-year-old graphic designer Jack Brown asked me out, I practically threw myself at him. He didn't protest, and after a few dates, he deflowered me. I thought my happiness would never end.

Until a week later, when he abandoned me on the streets of Shoreditch with chlamydia.

It had been a shit end to a shit year, but I'd spent the summer getting pissed and taking my anti-chlamydia pills, so I was now well and truly over my STD and Jack Brown. The only problem was that he was still the only person I'd had sex with, and I hadn't even orgasmed the one time we'd shagged. The only orgasms I'd ever had happened solo in my bedroom with my £14.99 bullet vibrator.

No one really played sex drinking games any more, but I still couldn't join in when Emma and Lara discussed anal and sixty-nines. It just meant I felt left out. I'd spent all summer batting my eyelids at every average-looking male— aged under thirty, naturally—in sight, but none of them had done anything but snog me. I had become officially unfuck-able. Now being shoved into this single room and labelled the sexually inactive housemate was just like being a virgin again. No matter what I did to try to keep up, everyone was always ten steps ahead of me. It wasn't even for want of trying.

I lowered my head into my hands and let out a pathetic moan. I was twenty per cent of my way through my twenties. I had only eighty per cent left before I'd be at a child-bearing age and seriously in want of a husband. I should be out having wild, passionate no-strings-attached sex with dreadlocked men on motorbikes before meeting The One, but instead I was lying alone in my mouldy bedroom.

It wasn't fair. Emma had slept with about thirty people. Lara had shagged about nine. Why hadn't I managed to get anywhere near that? I was average-looking and just as fun as them. I'd always thought that my virginity was the obstacle and, as soon as I lost it, it would be easy and I could start having casual sex.

But that hadn't happened. Maybe it was because I hadn't tried hard enough. Or because I was just doomed to be different—the podgy girl with dark body hair destined to have below-average sex and bite jobs. I'd always felt like the awkward teenage Greek girl who didn't really fit in anywhere.

I wasn't anything like my cousins or family friends—the thought of getting married to someone 'from the community' made my skin crawl. I'd die of claustrophobia and boredom, and that's if any guy ever agreed. I wasn't exactly the pretty, tanned girl they dreamt of. All my cousins loved dressing up and wearing lip gloss, while I'd rather kick about in Chucks and old leggings. Dream daughter I was not.

And I wasn't like anyone at school either. I didn't have the natural confidence that the girls had—that came from knowing they were beautiful, privileged and loved. I hadn't exactly had a tough background, but I never saw my dad and my mum was pretty overbearing. She was always different to the other mums as well—she still spoke with a thick Greek accent and it would never occur to her to watch *The OC* with us as Lara's mum did.

Maybe it's why I was always so much more insecure than the others, and maybe my mum's strictness about boys was why I didn't get involved with them for so long.

Or maybe there was just something wrong with me.

Even now that I'd figured out eyebrow threading and finally made some amazing friends, I still felt like little Ellie Kolstakis, aged fourteen, the girl no one wanted to dance with at the school disco. I knew it was stupid. I was twenty-two now, with a cool internship, living in an East London flatshare. But when all my flatmates were going on dates, bringing people home and sharing a lifestyle that eluded me no matter how hard I tried? Yeah, sometimes I still felt pretty fucking shit.

Chapter 2

Emma and I had met Will and Ollie in the last week of uni. I was still recovering from the joint shock of losing my V-card to a wanker and getting an STI. Emma had taken me out to the Student Union to drown my sorrows in £1 vodka shots. We were £10 in when we met Will and Ollie.

I fell head over heels in love with Ollie. He was half-black, with impossibly blue eyes, and his short hair was dyed peroxide blond. He looked like an Urban Outfitters model. In my vodka-fuelled haze, I realised he was the only man I had ever wanted, the one I was destined to meet after being betrayed by the de-virginiser, and…he was talking to Emma about his girlfriend. The romantic music scratched to a halt in my head as I realised he was firmly out of bounds.

'Ellie?' called out Emma, as she waved her hand in front of my face. 'This is Ollie, he just graduated in Philosophy from SOAS, and Will, who's studying accountancy at King's. They were in the same halls as Amelia.'

I put on a fake smile and we spent the rest of the night

getting drunk together. Emma charmed the group with funny stories while I subtly tried to take selfies with Ollie so I could sigh over them in the morning. When Will saw what I was doing, he dragged me to my feet and made me dance to music with no words. The DJ was just about to switch from the drum and bass to music I actually knew when Will started snogging the hottest guy in the club. I went to the loo and starting throwing up the 'vodka', which was rumoured to be paint stripper. When Emma and I tottered onto the night bus at 4 a.m. with Ollie, Will and Cheng in tow, we realised we'd found our new housemates.

* * *

Four months later, we were all living in our Haggerston home with paper-thin walls and rent we couldn't afford. I was still partly in love with Ollie, but resigned to his love for the beautiful but intimidating Yomi, and semi-scared of Will and his financial speak. Emma was the same as always, but now that she was loved up with Sergio, I was down a wingwoman and more single than ever. It was time to call Lara.

'Why haven't you invited me round yet?' she demanded, as she picked up the phone. 'We're meant to be best friends, but suddenly you're all edgy living in East London and can't invite me over?'

'I've been here for four days, Lara. We only got a sofa yesterday. The fridge arrived this morning.'

'I can't believe you think I'm so high-maintenance I need a fridge and sofa to come over.'

I laughed. 'Shut up, you know you're welcome whenever. In fact…do you want to come over this weekend? I miss you.'

'I miss you too. Oxford is so boring right now. My feminism society is obsessed with bringing down the Bulling-don Club and I'm so over it.'

'You do realise I have no idea what you're talking about? But if you're bored, please get the train down this weekend. We can go out with the hipsters in Hackney.'

'By hipsters do you mean your flatmates?'

I snorted. 'They wish. Actually, I guess Ollie is naturally pretty cool. He's been wearing skinnies since before they were in. But Will is definitely a wannabe.'

'Mmm, it does feel like he tries quite hard to fit in,' she agreed. 'Last time we all went out together, he got really drunk and admitted he consciously tried to get rid of his Leeds accent. He accidentally used the word "brew" and almost had a breakdown.'

'Shit. I had no idea he cared that much. It explains why he loves you though—he probably thinks you're really posh because of the Oxford thing.'

She groaned. 'People really need to get over those stereo-types. Half the students here are as posh as I am, as in total plebs. Anyway, how are you?'

'Meh. Spent the whole morning tech-harming.'

'Ellie. I've told you to delete Instagram off your phone. Did you do it with Facebook as well?'

'May-be.'

She sighed. 'We've been through this before. None of them actually have perfect lives. If we Instagrammed the coolest things we did, we'd have perfect lives too.'

'I know, I know. But some of them are just like golden people. I feel like the pale people watching them on stage.'

'Stop making *Tender is the Night* references. You know what happens to Dick Diver at the end. And look at *The*

Great Gatsby. Do you want someone to shoot you in your swimming pool?'

'At least Gatsby had a swimming pool. I'll never even get a mortgage at this rate.'

'Join the club,' she said. 'We're the real lost generation. Screw the 1920s modernist kids—it's totally us.'

I nodded wisely until I remembered she couldn't see me. 'Totally. The generation of unpaid interns.'

'How is that going?' she asked sympathetically.

'Maxine is still a bitch. I've spent the past month just getting her NFLs and she still won't let me write anything even though that's why she hired me—because she allegedly liked my vlog and uni columns. Today she made me work till 7 p.m. I'm so tired.'

'NFLs?'

'No-fat lattes.'

'That is so stereotypical. Who does she think she is— Anna Wintour?'

'You say that, but apparently the *London Mag* makes more money than *Vogue.* So Maxine has decided she is the Devil Who Wears Whistles and is hell-bent on ruining my unpaid existence.'

'Well, when I'm a high-flying lawyer who doesn't have time to do anything, I'll let you live in my penthouse and fetch me NFLs. I'll even pay you.'

'Fuck off, Lara.'

'Love you too. Anyway, so this weekend…'

'Yep, you're coming over?'

'I can do on Saturday. But if you're free on Friday night, some of the girls from school are getting together for a dinner.'

'Oh my God, no. Lara, you're the one that's still friends

with them, not me. I haven't spoken to them for years and I'm absolutely fine with that. We don't need to change that.'

'Ellie, stop being so dramatic. These are the girls we grew up with, not mass murderers. I think it will be fun for you to come. You know, mix it up a bit.'

'But their lives are so perfect. I'll have to hear about how it's so difficult maintaining a size-six figure and juggling life as a hot blonde lawyer with going out to fancy restaurants with perfect boyfriends.'

'You know I'm blonde and going into law?'

'Do you want me to hate you too? Stop reminding me.'

'Ha ha. But, honestly, El, what are you so worried about? We're not the same people we were at school.'

'It's just whenever I'm around them I feel like teenage me, and all the insecurities come flying back. Like, I can't join in their sex stories, their rich stories, their success stories… It's too much.'

'Even though you're no longer a virgin, you're confident and hot, and you have the coolest internship ever?'

'Well, when you put it like that…'

'Exactly, so what's the problem?'

'I don't know. I guess I just feel weird lately. I think it's just moving into Haggerston, and the fact that my job is kind of a nightmare. I felt really good all summer, but now it's sinking in that all the others are in relationships, and not only has no one asked me out since Jack, but I'm unpaid and relying on my mum—who hates every life choice I make and wishes I was married to a Greek estate agent.'

Lara snorted. 'I can't imagine you being with anyone like that, much less married.'

'Exactly! I'd be the worst wife ever.'

'But, honestly, El, I think coming to meet the schoolgirls

will be good for you. They'll all be super impressed with what you're doing, you'll realise they're not the "Mean Girls" you thought they were in Year Ten, and it will distract you from everything else that's going on.'

'Oh fine. So long as you promise to still come round to mine on Saturday for commiseration drinks? I'll get Emma on board.'

'Deal.'

* * *

I walked into Chotto Matte in Soho feeling as if I should be waiting tables rather than eating. My skinny jeans and oversized jumper may have looked casually chic in the office, but now I felt underdressed and frumpy. Especially when I followed the waiter down to our table and saw fifteen models sitting there.

'Oh my God, Ellie,' squealed Maisie. 'You look amazing. It's so good to see you. I can't believe how long it is!'

She pulled me into a hug. 'You look great too,' I said lamely. 'Really nice to see you.'

The rest of the girls turned around and enveloped me in turn, so I had to repeat the exact same small talk fifteen times. By the time I got to Lara, I gave her a death stare. I was an idiot for ever thinking this would be a good idea.

We sat down and I gulped at the prices on the menu. There was a sharing option that started at £40 per person. Without drinks—of which I would be needing many to get through this dinner. Fuck. Maybe I could just get a side and feign being full from a large lunch?

'So, how have things been?' cried Polly. 'It's been forever. I hear you're working for *London Mag* these days—that's pretty cool. Is it amazing?'

'Um, yeah, I guess so. Minus the psycho boss, the long hours and the fact that I don't get paid for it.'

'Shit,' she said with a momentary frown crossing her Botoxed face. OK, it wasn't Botoxed, but no doubt it would be in ten years.

'How are you anyway?' I asked.

'Oh, amazing,' she said, the frown disappearing. 'Like, obviously it's so intense working in law, but the work is so great, and I love the people. Also, Alex works for Goldman Sachs next door, so we basically just share cabs home the entire time, and he lives round the corner in this amazing penthouse apartment his parents got him, so it's ideal.'

'Wow, that's, um, amazing,' I said.

Lara caught my eye and snorted.

'So how did you meet Alex?' asked Lara. 'I've seen pictures on Facebook, but I haven't met him yet. It sounds like it's all going well though?'

'Yeah, it's so good. I'm so lucky. We actually met through mutual friends at uni, but we didn't really get together until this summer. He's really nice. You'd like him. I think he knows Jez actually—are you two still hooking up?'

Lara groaned. 'Sadly, yes. I do plan on ending it soon, but the sex is just so good… I mean, he's a commitment-phobic idiot, but we're having fun, so I guess it kind of works for now.'

'Ah, I know what you mean,' said Polly. 'We've all been there, don't worry. I reckon as soon as you find someone new, you'll totally forget him.'

'Yeah, maybe I'll meet an incredibly eligible lawyer when I start my training,' said Lara.

'What? No, you cannot date your colleagues,' cried Polly.

'Trust me. That's a recipe for disaster. Hey, what about you, Ellie, are you seeing anyone?'

'Um, no, not right now.'

'Oh, right,' she said, eyes glazing over.

'But I did have a thing with someone at the end of uni,' I continued.

'Oh my God, tell me everything!'

'Well, it was just this guy called Jack. He was an artist, quite a few years older than me. We were dating for a while, we slept together, and it was all good.'

'Um, and then what?' asked Lily. I realised that by now the whole table was listening to me. 'Oh my God, did you lose your virginity?! Shit, Ellie, that's huge!'

I smiled weakly. I'd forgotten how gossip-hungry everyone at school had been. Considering I'd been one of the few girls to graduate with my virginity, the state of my hymen was clearly pretty big news.

'Yep,' I said. 'Jack took my V-plates.'

'Ahhh!' everyone shrieked in excitement. 'OMG, congrats, Ellie. How was it? That's amazing—tell us everything.'

This was why I'd never send my daughter to an all-girls school—no question was off limits. At one point we'd even known each other's period cycles.

'It was good. I mean, we only did it the once, but it was fine. It didn't really hurt.'

'Oh my God, amazing. So then what happened?' asked Katie.

Oh shit. Now I had to tell them that Jack hadn't really cared about me and then gave me 'the clap'. So much for trying to come across as new cool Ellie who has her shit together—this just proved I was the same girl who managed to bite a guy's penis.

I glanced at Lara. She wouldn't care if I lied. I looked at the girls. They were all sitting open-mouthed, waiting for the next instalment. I don't think they'd ever been so interested in me when I was the virgin at school. Maybe I should go with the truth—if they wanted gossip, I could definitely provide that.

'So…a few days later, we went for coffee and he told me how much he believed in true love, and that he'd never felt this way before.' The girls gasped collectively. 'Only, then he said that "Luisa" had changed his life. It turned out he wasn't talking about me—he was talking about someone else.'

'Oh my God, no way. That's insane,' said Lily. 'I can't believe that actually happened.'

'Do you know what's even worse?' They all shook their heads. 'Luisa had chlamydia.'

'Wait, do you mean…?'

'I got chlamydia from the one time I had sex.'

The girls burst into laughter, and I grinned with them. I'd never had a sex story to make them laugh before. Normally, it was me sitting there open-mouthed listening to their stories, but being the centre of everything was definitely more fun.

'That is so funny, Ellie,' said Maisie. 'I mean, he sounds like a total wanker, but at least you got a good story out of it.'

'Yeah, a story and an STD in exchange for my maidenhood. Not a bad deal.'

She laughed in response. 'Exactly. Hey, Cass, didn't you get chlamydia twice at uni? That was hysterical.'

'OK, it wasn't as bad as it sounds. It was from the same guy.'

'I'm not so sure that makes it better, Cass,' said Lara.

'But if it makes you feel better, I once did something even worse. I broke Jez's penis.'

'What?' I cried. 'How have I not heard this story?'

'Shit, did I never tell you?' she said. 'God, it was a couple of years ago now. I think you must have been away. It was so funny though. I was on top, and I think the angle was weird, because suddenly he screamed. I got off him and his penis was, like, bent in half. We had to go to hospital and it turned out that I'd given him a penile fracture.'

'Oh my God, that's hilarious,' cried Lily, after we'd all stopped laughing. 'Reminds me of when I ripped Max's foreskin in Year Nine after a pretty vigorous hand job.'

'And that time when you got caught giving him a blow job by his mum! That was amazing,' said Cass. 'Ooh, look, the food's here. We'd better stop being so filthy or we're going to get kicked out.'

I looked up and saw plates of tiny dishes being served out. There were dozens of them. Seeing as the cheapest thing on the menu was about £7, this was not good. 'You already ordered?' I asked uncertainly.

'Oh yeah, we just got a massive selection of stuff though. We figured it would be easiest,' said Polly. 'Doesn't it look incredible?'

Guess I wasn't going to be eating a side for my main, then.

* * *

'I cannot believe we ate all of that,' I said to Lara as everyone else chatted around us. 'I feel a bit sick now.'

'I know, right? Especially when Tania decided it was a really good idea for us all to tell our grossest sex moments. Cass's one is still making me feel a bit ill.'

'Ugh, yes. Now that's a new fear for me—remind me

not to have period sex. I really can't handle the thought of him withdrawing and blood splattering onto the white walls. I feel so sorry for sixteen-year-old Cass. Must have been mortifying.'

'Oh, it was,' said Cass, leaning over to us. 'It looked like a scene from *The Texas Chain Saw Massacre*. There were these red dots on the walls. We had to wipe them off afterwards and they left brown smudges.'

'Ew, Cass!'

'But you know what?' she continued. 'Weirdly, I had the best orgasm of my life two seconds before bloodgate. Who knew?'

'Hilarious.' Lara laughed. 'I think my best ever orgasm was with this guy I met in my gap year. He had the most gifted tongue I have ever come across. I swear his girlfriend must be the luckiest person in the world.'

'Oh my God, that is such an important quality in a guy,' said Cass. 'I once broke up with someone who refused to go down on me unless I'd showered two minutes before. I think he had hygiene issues.'

I laughed with them and then slipped away to go to the loo. It was fun chatting with the girls—I'd forgotten how funny they could be—but I was starting to feel weird. I knew it wasn't a big deal that I couldn't join in with any orgasm stories. Everyone knew I wasn't exactly experienced and they didn't really care, but I hated feeling as if I was on the outside of the conversation. It just made me feel left out. They were all having ridiculous amounts of fun having orgasms and casual sex, and I was categorically *not*.

It made me feel as if we were back in the school common room with everyone sharing funny virginity-losing stories while I still hadn't even been kissed. I knew things were different now, but it was still shit to not feel part of the main events. I still had no idea what it was like to do a walk of shame, or have period sex, or even get licked out by a guy.

I wanted to have that fun. Now I wasn't a virgin, why couldn't I be out there getting with guys? It was fine having orgasms alone in my room, but I wanted to understand the euphoria that girls in movies had every time a guy went down on them. I wanted to know what was so good about sex.

I knew I'd be good at it too. I loved talking about sex and imagining it—if I just had the chance to partake in it a bit more, I bet I'd be a natural. I wouldn't be the kind of girl who just wanted the guy to marry her in the morning. I'd be more than happy to keep it casual. Hell, I wouldn't even need to get their number so long as they gave me an orgasm instead.

I stared at myself in the toilet mirror. I could do this. I didn't have to just spend my twenties dreaming about this lifestyle—I could make it happen. All I needed to do was stop moping, and up my game.

If I wanted to know what it felt like to have orgasm-filled casual sex, well, there was only one thing for it—I had to start having more sex.

As of tomorrow, I needed to start slutting it up.

Chapter 3

It was Saturday night and Lara and Emma were sprawled across me on the sofa. I'd explained my plan to them with generally positive receptions, and now we were figuring out a way for me to meet my prospective sexual partners.

'Ow, Ellie, move your elbow, I can't see the screen,' said Lara. I shifted my elbow, splashing rosé on the new third-hand sofa.

'Oops,' I said. 'I should probably clean that up.'

'No! This is the reason we got a black sofa, remember?' said Emma. 'Ignore it and type in the website already.'

'OK, OK,' I said. 'But shouldn't I be getting Tinder instead of going on a dating site? I feel a bit old-fashioned.'

'Noooo,' cried Emma. 'I don't care what everyone says—Tinder is still a sex app.' Lara opened her mouth, but Emma ignored her. 'I *know* that's how everyone met their new boyfriends or whatever, but every guy I know still thinks of it as a way to get quick hook-ups. Like, you don't even have to fill in any info on it. It's totally judged on your looks. At least with an online site you have to make a bit of an effort.'

'But I'm OK with casual hook-ups,' I pointed out. 'That's kind of why I'm doing this.'

'Oh fine, get Tinder.' Emma sighed. 'Just do this as well. Please? For me?'

'Fine,' I said. 'Tinder can be my backup if this fails. So which online site shall I join?'

'Definitely OKCupid,' said Lara. 'I've heard Plenty Of Fish is more of a sex-only site. Besides, I'm on OKC and I've seen so many normal people on there. There's an option where you can search for people who have degrees—it's amazing. One week I only searched for people who have PhDs.'

'Exactly,' cried Emma. 'On Tinder you have no idea what anyone does, so you could end up going on a date with some old perv, or a chav with shaved eyebrows who works in construction.'

'What's wrong with construction workers?' I asked, semi-offended. 'One of my uncles in Greece is a builder.'

'Oh my God, no, I don't hate all builders,' said Emma. 'I love when the hot ones go topless. But I'm talking about the sexist ones who yell out "Oi, sexy" at girls on the street. You know?'

I shook my head at her. 'You do realise that's, like, the most ancient stereotype ever, and you're just as bad admiring their abs?'

'No, I get what you mean, Emma,' said Lara. 'You want to date someone on your level, which is why OKC is great.'

I raised an eyebrow at her, wondering when my friends had got so snobby. I'd be happy shagging a homeless guy so long as he was hot and chlamydia free.

'I mean, I still get my fair share of messages from chavs

with topless selfies who spell "your" and "you're" wrong,' continued Lara. 'And quite a few just asking me when I'm free to fuck them… *But* I've also seen so many people I know on there, and loads of them went to uni, which makes me think we would at least have stuff in common.'

'So have you gone on any dates?' I asked her, knowing she would have already told me if she had.

'Well, I'm still casually seeing Jez, but I started panicking I was wasting my prime years by dating a weed addict with commitment issues, so…I went on three last month,' she replied.

'Oh my God,' I shrieked. 'Three dates and you didn't tell me? What the fuck, Lara?' She hadn't told me about breaking Jez's penis either. Why was Lara hiding things from me?

She blushed. 'I guess… Oh, I don't know, I was kind of scared you'd judge me for being on a dating site.'

'Judge you?! Hello, I'm the girl who stuck a bottle of bubble bath up her vagina and didn't know you could get chlamydia from blow jobs.'

She snorted. 'Yeah, fair point. Have you got rid of the chlamydia by the way?'

'The doctor gave her some pills. She's fine,' interrupted Emma. 'Anyway, I'm done with talking about STIs. Lara, tell us your dating stories.'

'No, wait! First, tell me why you thought I'd judge you,' I said, ignoring Emma's frustrated sighs. I still felt weird Lara hadn't said anything about all this. Oh God—maybe it was because she felt she couldn't because I'm so virginal and new to sex?

Lara fidgeted on the sofa. 'Oh, I don't know, I guess just because most people who use dating sites are old, so I was a bit nervous you'd all think I was desperate or that it was a bit weird. But it just makes so much sense to date online,' she said. 'Like, you don't have to bother with the cringeness of going to a bar and hoping you meet someone, then being depressed if you don't. Or the pathetic hope that every cute guy on a park bench will come and ask you out.'

I nodded in support, trying to prove that I was exactly the sort of person she could have told all of this to earlier. 'Totally. This is definitely the way I'm going to find my next shag as well. I don't even have to leave my sofa or dressing gown to find a man. This site was made for me.'

'So you really only want one-night stands and not a boyfriend?' asked Emma.

'Yeah, I think so. It took me so long to lose my virginity that now I just feel like I have all this lost time to make up for. I want to get out there and have amazing sex with different people. I like sex—well, the little I've had of it. But it wasn't particularly fun, and I'm so ready for that. I feel like it's God's gift to us, to get orgasms and have a bit of fun while global warming is tearing the planet apart.' The girls looked baffled. 'I just want to have my slutty phase already.'

'Slutty phase?' asked Lara with a raised eyebrow. 'You know how I feel about the word "slut", Ellie. It shows the double standards society has for men and women. He's a player, she's a slut, etc. You know how it goes. Can't you find a different word?'

'No,' cried Emma. 'It's all about reclaiming the word "slut". Like, it essentially means someone who has sex a lot, so why is that a bad thing? It shouldn't be gendered, obviously, but we can just use it for men and women. If we call ourselves sluts, it loses its negative meaning. We need to re-appropriate it so it's a positive word for someone embracing their sexuality and their, like, libido.'

'Um, I'm lost,' I said.

'OK, like, if I start saying "Ah, that girl is so slutty" with admiration instead of judgement, it gets rid of all the connotations the word has. And even better if we start calling guys sluts too.'

Lara looked impressed. 'I had no idea you were so passionate about this, Em.'

She grinned. 'Well, as a former slut, it's a topic that's pretty close to my heart. I heard enough guys calling me a slut growing up, and each time I let it hurt me, before I realised I could just make that word mean whatever I want. When I decided slut meant "hot, sexually confident, empowered woman", it didn't hurt as much.'

I nodded enthusiastically. 'I did the exact same thing with "virgin". Like, it used to make me feel frigid and ugly and left out. Until I had sex and then I realised it didn't have to mean that. It could just be a factual word for not ever having been penetrated.'

'Um, I think that's how most people already use it, Ellie,' said Lara.

'No, what about "you look like a friendless virgin"?' I asked. 'Or "oh my God, you virgin weirdo". Those are insults. It's the same as "slut". Emma's so right, we should totally redefine it.'

'Yeah,' cried Emma. 'Being a slut doesn't have to make you feel any of that patriarchal bollocks where you're cheap and dirty. It can make you feel powerful, carefree and in control. Fuck it, Ellie, go be a slut.'

'Oh, I fully intend to. I want to meet up with these OKC dates and start shagging my way across central London.'

Emma cried out, 'Ah, you're making me so nostalgic for my single past. I miss the days of waking up and trying to figure out how to get back home from whatever bit of London I was in. I used to love the crazy stories. Did I tell you I once got a tattoo during a one-nighter?'

Lara and I exchanged shocked glances. 'Um. No?'

'I met him in a club.' She grinned. 'Just some random guy, but his flatmate was a tattoo artist. We biked back to Dalston—I sat on the handlebars. We were so fucked on MDMA that when we got back to his and his flatmate offered to give me a tattoo, I agreed.'

'Well, where is it?!' I demanded, trying to ignore the twinge of discomfort I felt whenever my friends discussed drugs. It was the one thing I would never try—along with anal because there's another perfectly good hole millimetres away—and it always made me feel distant from my drug-taking friends. Thank God Lara was as uncool as me and didn't take MDMA either.

'So, it was a tiny star that I got on the sole of my foot,' she said. 'But that bit of your skin is really rough, so it doesn't really work for tattoos and they disappear over time. If you squint you can kind of see the outline though.' She thrust her bare left foot in our faces.

'Oh yeah,' said Lara. 'Holy shit, that's crazy.'

Emma nodded wistfully. 'Isn't it? Those days were fun. Not that I don't love being with Sergio, obviously. He's great and I love him.'

Lara and I nodded along with her, still transfixed by her surprise tattoo. 'Anyway,' continued Emma. 'Lara, you're not getting out of sharing your dating stories.'

'OK, but I'm going to need more wine to relive these,' she said.

Emma filled up our glasses and I closed the laptop screen. 'Spill,' I said.

'OK, so it started with SafariLover,' she said. 'And, no, I don't mean he liked animals. He was actually called Jake, but he worked for Apple doing some techie stuff. We went for drinks in Farringdon on our first date but he spent the whole time discussing fucking *bitcoins*. On a plus note, he was as attractive as his pictures and at least six foot, but it was just the bitcoins...' We nodded sympathetically and she continued. 'Obviously I still snogged him, but then I didn't reply to any of his texts after that. Then I moved on to date two. He was Juanderful.'

'Wonderful?' asked Emma.

'Nope. JUAN-derful. That was his OKC username. He was Spanish, thirty-five and very, very attractive. Unfortunately he lacked brain cells and was basically just there to improve his English. So that didn't work. We had an amazing goodbye kiss though—I was seriously tempted to go back to his but couldn't handle doing dirty talk in another language.'

'I can't even do it in English,' I said.

'You just need the practice,' said Emma reassuringly. 'So, what about date three?'

'Averagecupid56.' She grinned.

'There are fifty-five other average cupids?' I asked with a raised eyebrow.

'Can't imagine any of them being like Mr 56 though. He turned up on a bicycle for starters.'

'Wow, guess he wasn't planning on getting lucky,' I said.

'That didn't stop my tattoo guy.' Emma grinned.

'It wasn't so much the bike that bothered me, it was more the fact that he was sitting in the corner of the pub waiting for me with a copy of the *Guardian*.' We groaned. 'Oh no, it gets worse. He took me to a restaurant where he ordered quinoa and then spent the entire time discussing his gap yah and dream to volunteer for that Médecins Sans Fron-tières thing. He was definitely the fittest of the three and clearly intelligent but he was the biggest stereotype ever. It was kind of off-putting, but—'

'But you still snogged him?' I interrupted.

She gave me a withering look. 'What do you take me for? I shagged him.'

ELK123
22, London

My self-summary:
I live in East London and work in the media but am not the typical stereotype—I promise. I don't wear plas-tic glasses, I hardly ever wear vintage, and I'd much rather be travelling around the world with a backpack. OK, maybe I am the stereotype…

What I'm doing with my life:
Interning. Generally involves fetching lattes, crying in the loo and wondering why I bothered going to uni.

I'm really good at:
Making my friends laugh. Generally at me, not with me.

The first things people usually notice about me:
My 36Ds.

Favourite books, movies, shows, music and food:
The question has put these in the wrong order—food comes above all these things. Will eat pretty much anything.

Love romcoms, old Disney films and trashy American TV.

Listen to everything from old-school rap to Taylor Swift.

My favourite books have to have a female protagonist because not enough of them do. And I just prefer reading about women, you know?

Studied English Lit at uni so am a bit of a bookworm.

The six things I could never do without:

My friends

Black clothing (am not a goth. Black is just my colour)

Tortellini (only thing I can cook)

Cheese (ditto)

The internet

Support bras

I spend a lot of time thinking about:

Being a woman and a feminist in the twenty-first century. Very challenging when people think it means you're a hairy lesbian.

On a typical Friday night I am:

Passed out drunk in an alleyway. Normally with my friends lying on top of me.

The most private thing I'm willing to admit:

I was a virgin until twenty-one.

I'm looking for:

Whatever you can give me.

You should message me if:
You read to the bottom of this and still want to date me.
N.B. Bonus points if you can spell

'So, what do you guys think?' I asked. There was a four-second silence while Lara and Emma looked at each other.

'Um, it's…very honest,' said Emma slowly. 'The virgin thing is particularly, uh… Ellie, *why* did you put that in?'

'Because I want to be honest. I feel like this is a chance for me to meet guys who like me for me, and respect me. I just want to make sure I end up sleeping with someone who doesn't care that I only just lost my V-plates.'

'Yeah, you're going to have to take that out,' said Lara bluntly. 'And—support bras? You want to seduce these men, not scare the shit out of them. Also, the 36Ds? Ellie, that's just cheap, as is the fact that you're looking for *whatever they can give you.*'

'That was flirty,' I said hotly.

'Is the fact that you can only cook pasta and are clearly having an existential crisis flirty too?' she asked.

Emma nodded in agreement. 'Babe, they don't need to know all this stuff up front. Maybe just tone it down a bit?' She looked at my crestfallen face. 'I mean, I love that it's so *you*, but I'm not really sure it works. Like, the passed out drunk in an alleyway part sounds a bit…wrong.'

Lara snorted with laughter and I turned to her angrily. 'It isn't *wrong*. It's just *funny*. I said I'm good at making my friends laugh and I was trying to prove my point.' They were now both laughing hysterically into their glasses of rosé. 'Ugh, whatever. If you think you can do better, why don't you take over?'

'I thought you'd never ask,' said Lara, grabbing the laptop. 'Come on, Emma, let's fix this.'

ELK123
22, London

My self-summary:
I live in East London and work in the media. Studied English at uni and am now wondering why.

What I'm doing with my life:
Interning for a high-profile online magazine.

I'm really good at:
Making my friends laugh.

The first things people usually notice about me:
My smile.

Favourite books, movies, shows, music and food:
Love romcoms, old Disney films and trashy American TV.
Listen to everything from old-school rap to drum and bass.
Favourite authors range from Jane Austen to Jack Kerouac.

The six things I could never do without:
My friends
Clothes
Alcohol
Coffee
Novels
Saturday nights

I spend a lot of time thinking about:
How fun last weekend was.

On a typical Friday night I am:
Out drinking with my friends.

The most private thing I'm willing to admit:
I've never been on a dating site before.

I'm looking for:
Whatever happens.

You should message me if:
You want to.

'What *is* this?' I cried out. 'Message me *if you want to*? I sound like a fucking PROSTITUTE. And you both know I hate Jack Kerouac. This is… This is all lies,' I spluttered.

'Nooo, it's not lies,' said Emma. 'It's more of an air-brushed version of the truth. We kept in some of it anyway, like…the bit about music?'

'Drum and bass? Do I look like the kind of person who wants to take E and jump up and down to music without words?' I shrieked.

'Babe, you don't really *jump* to drum and bass,' said Emma, before catching sight of my face. 'OK, OK, if you hate it, we can change it. But, honestly, I think this would work a bit better than your one. I mean, would you rather your future date sees you as self-deprecating and awkward—which we love about you—or sexy and fun?'

'Exactly,' said Lara. 'You'd exaggerate your CV, so you

may as well do the same for this. Just think of it as a dating CV. It's like, um, an online portfolio.'

I frowned at them both and then broke into a grin. 'Wait, so do you guys really think I have a good smile?'

'We wrote that?' asked Lara. 'Oh yeah. We figured it was better than drawing attention to the mass of hair on your head or your massive tits. Besides, smiles sound sexy.'

'But this isn't me being myself. It's me trying to be the kind of girl guys like.'

'Exactly,' said Emma. 'Guys will like it.'

'Uh, what happened to you being a feminist?' I asked. 'One boyfriend and you're all "pretend you like Kerouac and drum and bass" to get a guy.'

'It's just playing them at their own game,' replied Emma, waving her hand at me. 'They do it too—how many of these guys really like half the stuff they say they do? The ones who put "looking for friendship"? Utter bollocks. All they want is a casual fuck, but they can't say that or no one will click on them. It's just the game.'

'Well…that's shit,' I said. 'I thought *The Game* was an anti-women self-help book for men to pull girls by ebbing away at their self-esteem.'

'Yeah, it's that too,' said Emma. 'But I was talking about the concept not the book, babe.'

'Either way, it sounds like crap,' I said. 'It's so old-fashioned. I'm so over the game. In fact, I officially opt out of the game.'

Lara raised an eyebrow at me. 'So, you're going to use your original profile, then?'

I threw a cushion at her. 'Oh, fuck off, you both know my attempt was shit and I'm using your version. But you don't have to look so smug about it.'

They grinned at each other. 'Knew it,' said Emma. 'As much as we hate the game, it's just gotta be played.'

'OK, this is it,' said Lara. 'I'm clicking save, and…it's done! Now we've just got to hope that this mass of lies gets Ellie laid.'

Chapter 4

Forty-eight hours had passed since the creation of ELK123 and I was yet to get laid. However, I had just checked my phone and there were FOUR messages waiting for me. I was well on my way to slutdom.

Hey, sexy, can I come on your face? How about Tues night?

I blushed and dropped my phone onto my keyboard. I looked around the office furtively, but Maxine was yelling down her phone and no one else was in yet. It was only the unpaid intern who was expected to be in at 8 a.m.

I clicked on HotDog69 and gagged. His profile picture was a topless selfie and his beer belly—covered in sparse pube-like hairs—was glaring at me. I quickly exited his profile and went back to my inbox. There were three more messages. My heart beat in trepidation as I read the next one.

Hey, hun. u ok. I hope we could become mates and get to know each other.

My names percy. I gotta say you are the definition of beautiful and got beautiful eyes. I hope we have the chance to become good mates and maybe more. I think we would get along well and ill always be here for you whenever you need someone to talk to. I will never ever judge you no matter what and i always try to be a good mate xx

I stared at the message in confusion. He wanted to be there for me? He didn't even know me. And were the spelling mistakes intentional or could he really just not use punctuation? I hesitantly clicked on Perce69's profile—I was noticing a username theme here—and was met with a picture of a sweet-looking guy with a receding hairline and blue eyes.

He didn't look as horrid as HotDog so I scrolled down. OK, he worked in sales, was twenty-nine, lived in North London, and…the most private thing he was willing to admit was that he had a sex addiction. Ew. At least he thought I was beautiful and would never judge me. Feeling more confident, I looked at my third message.

I would hug a cactus, then swim through shark infested salt water to the arctic to do battle with an angry mother polar bear on a 2x2 foot iceberg for the chance to share a Nandos half chicken with corn on the cob with you on a webcam over a dial-up connection. X

Right. At least that was original. Everyone liked a Nando's half chicken—but if we were sharing, shouldn't we get a full chicken? Not only was Marcus1986 clearly a nutter, he was also stingy. I didn't bother clicking on his profile and moved on to my last message. *Please be normal,* I prayed. It was from someone called JT_ldn and there was no 69 on the end of his username. This looked promising.

Hey, Elk, your profile seems cool. So what kind of media work do you do? I live in East London too. Have you been living amongst the hipsters for a while or are you a new kid on the block?
JT x

Oh my God. It was an actual message from a normal person who had read my profile and wasn't just spamming me with perv-mail. OK, so he had mistaken my initials for my name, but that was easily done. There had to be a few people out there called Elk.

I clicked on his profile and was instantly impressed. JT was HOT. He was also twenty-nine—exciting; from Ireland—sexy accent; and worked at Marc Jacobs—shit. Gay??? I quickly scrolled down and breathed out in relief as I saw he worked in the IT section of Marc Jacobs. That was promising, as was the fact that he was six foot three and loved nights in with red wine and film noirs. If you swapped it for carbs and romcoms, that was my ideal night in too.

Hey JT, nice to (virtually!) meet you. I'm 'working' for an online magazine, which is pretty cool except for the fact it's unpaid. I'm new to East—what about you? Amazing you work for MJ. Do you get free stuff?
Ellie x

I tapped out the message quickly so that I could edit it afterwards. The awkward 'virtually' joke would probably have to go. I ended it with a kiss, which felt weird considering I'd never met him but decided it would be rude not to after he'd given me one. It was probably just internet dating etiquette. Come to think of it, HotDog69 was quite rude for not putting a kiss on his.

'Ellie, what are you doing?' screeched Maxine. I dropped my phone onto my desk and realised with horror that I'd pressed 'send'. Why had I put in those cringe attempts to be flirty?! There was no way he'd reply now.

'Just booking the restaurant for your lunch meeting with Clara,' I said brightly, as I turned to face my boss. Her dark hair was piled onto her head in a messy bun, but her red lipstick immaculately framed her snarling mouth.

'Good—make it for 2 p.m.,' she said. 'Now, we need someone to write a feature about London stereotypes.' Oh my God. Was she finally about to ask me to actually *write* something for her? 'So, do the research, then send it over to Camilla and she'll write it.'

My heart sank. Typical. 'OK, sounds great,' I said. 'What kind of thing are you thinking?'

She sighed theatrically and replied in the same exasperated tone she used whenever I asked her a question. 'You know…a North London girl who buys Cath Kidston wellies and the Brixton girl in flowery skirts and Doc Martens, blow-dries in Notting Hill.'

I nodded rapidly as I scribbled down what she was saying. It sounded like exactly the sort of thing I had read multiple times on various websites and could write in my sleep. But instead I'd have to do all the work, then send it on to the star writer who would just move a few words around and stick her name on it.

'Send it to her by lunch,' barked Maxine. 'I'm off out.

When you get a minute can you also sort out the stationery cupboard and do me a cuts search on that latest socialite? I'm doing an interview with her.'

'Um, who?' I asked nervously.

'Oh God.' She sighed. 'You know, the eyebrow one? The model?'

'Cara Delevingne?'

'Exactly. Next thing you'll be asking me what a cuts search is,' she said, as she grabbed her camel jacket.

I fake-laughed. 'Right, as if I didn't know it was…general research?'

She looked straight at me. 'Ellie. Newspaper clippings. The username and login is on the whiteboard.'

'Thankyousomuch,' I garbled in relief, and she shook her head at me in despair.

I threw on my leather jacket and grabbed my blue canvas tote bag. It was 6 p.m. and I had only ten minutes before Maxine came back. If she saw that I was still there, she would inevitably give me more tasks to do, so I was taking my chance to leave.

It had been a long Monday. As always my colleagues just ignored me as they discussed their dates on the Kings Road, and what happened at Annabelle's on Saturday. I'd been left with the hard work, and they'd buggered off at 5 p.m.

Today Camilla had even made me source the photos for her article, so I was now officially late to meet my mum. The only thing that had kept me going all day was the fact that JT had replied. He'd told me that he did get a discount, he loved East London and he knew loads about media. He'd confused 'your' with 'you're' only once, and he hadn't called me Elk again.

My phone beeped. I tapped it open and saw the bright pink OKC app icon. I opened it, grinning in anticipation of a reply from JT.

Hello Elk
How are you this morning? I like your profile. I wondered how you felt about discreetly humiliating a man that secretly wears tights and using him for your benefit?
   I hope you don't mind me asking!

The picture was of a pair of shiny silver leggings and I could see the outline of Superman69's squashed penis.

'Aghh,' I shrieked, as I crashed into my mum.

'Elena, about time,' she said, rubbing dirt off my coat. 'Do you have to run like that? I could hear you thudding all the way down the road. And you shouldn't walk looking at your phone. Someone could steal it.'

The subtle criticisms had begun already. I told myself to take deep breaths and stay calm. I was a grown-up now. I had my own flat, £30,000 worth of debt and a job. Well, an internship, but still. I was an adult and I could handle one weekday dinner with my mother.

'Nice to see you too, Mum. Shall we go inside the restaurant, then?'

She made a non-committal sound, so I walked into Pizza Express and let the waiter guide us to a table.

'So, this is nice, isn't it?' I said brightly.

'Is that jacket new?' she asked, eyeing up my new Topshop purchase.

'It's just Primark, Mum,' I groaned in exasperation.

'Does Primark do real leather?'

I forced my face into a calm smile. 'Mum, what's with all

the questions? It's just pleather. But if you like it that much, you can borrow it!'

Her eyes narrowed. 'You know I'm not asking because I want to borrow it, Elena. I'm just wondering what you're spending my money on.'

'Mum, why don't we just order first before we get into all that? Shall we get dough balls to share? I bet I know what you're going to get—the avocado and goat's cheese salad, right?'

'The cannelloni. Maybe you should get the salad?' she asked.

'Are you kidding me? Salad isn't real food. I'm famished,' I announced, ignoring the fact that she was staring pointedly at my stomach. 'Dough balls to start, then a pepperoni pizza and probably a dessert too.'

'Right, OK,' she said and looked back down at her menu.

'What does that mean, Mum?' I asked. I could feel irritation rising up my oesophagus and tried to take deep breaths.

'Nothing,' she said. 'I just said OK, but…maybe you shouldn't be eating so much.'

'ARE YOU KIDDING ME?' I shrieked. All hopes of staying calm and rational had fully evaporated. 'Do you want me to be ANOREXIC? I can't believe you would even bring up my weight—I'm a size ten slash twelve slash fourteen. That is *healthy*, Mum. God, I can't believe you're trying to give me an eating disorder.'

'Elena,' she hissed. 'Will you keep your voice down? You know I just want you to be healthy and look good. Obviously you're not fat, but if you carry on as you are…'

'Oh. My. God. Are you saying you think I'm going to get fat? That is *so* typical of you. I work ten-hour days, and I don't have an income. All I can afford is pasta and cheap food that just happens to be unhealthy. I don't have time to go to the gym, and I couldn't even afford a membership if I did. Do you even know how much vegetables cost these days? This is just not my fault.'

She sighed. 'I wish you wouldn't buy cheap rubbish like pasta the whole time. When are they going to start paying you at your work?'

'Don't know,' I mumbled moodily.

'Why can't you just get a job that pays?' she asked.

I felt a twinge of guilt. She was asking the question that ran through my head on a daily basis, but it was too depressing to deal with. If I wanted my dream writing job, I had to work unpaid for months and then I may or may not get a permanent position with a salary at the end of it. That was just how it worked. The only way to get a typical paid job was to go back in time and do a law degree.

'Mum, I've explained this to you, like, a hundred times.' I sighed. 'Everyone who wants to work in media has to work unpaid for a few months. Just be glad I'm only doing a two-month internship—Emma's friend worked unpaid for nine months before she got a job at *Tatler*.'

'Doesn't that girl we met at your graduation have a job at *Tatler*? She told me she was starting immediately.'

Fucking Hannah Fielding. 'She is a complete bitch, Mum,' I cried. 'Besides, she only got the job because her parents know people. It's pure nepotism.'

My mum sighed. 'OK, Elena, do your unpaid work, but I'm only helping you out for now. Next month I'm not going to pay your rent any more.'

'Sure, that's fine,' I said confidently. 'I'll definitely have a paid job by then.' I crossed my fingers under the table. It could happen. Probably. 'But in the meantime…' I gave her my most daughterly smile.

'Yes, OK,' she said wearily. 'You can have one hundred pounds on top of your rent and bills.'

My mouth dropped open. 'Mum, I can't survive on a hundred quid a month! I'll starve to death. Or—even worse—I'll end up just buying reduced ready meals, then I'll get a really high salt intake and cholesterol will build up in my arteries and I'll probably get diabetes. And acne. Then no one will ever fancy me.'

She looked alarmed. 'Elena, you have to eat well. Can't you buy couscous and quinoa? They're not expensive if you buy in bulk and you can just cook them with fresh vegetables.'

'Quinoa is very expensive these days,' I said authoritatively. 'So is hummus. And tzatziki.'

'I've taught you so many times to make your own dips, Lena,' she said. She had used the name she called me as a baby. I grinned to myself—I knew I'd win her over by name-dropping Greek food. 'Will two hundred pounds help?'

Chapter 5

We had exchanged fourteen messages in three days and JT still hadn't asked me out. I was officially confused. Surely he was messaging me because he wanted to go on a date and shag me? In which case, why hadn't he suggested a date already?

The thought crossed my mind that maybe he was just enjoying getting to know me, but then I remembered Emma's words: *They all want to fuck you—it's just a game.* He was probably just trying to play it cool so he didn't come across as too keen. But I didn't care about that—I just wanted to be, well, wanted.

The girls thought this whole thing was about me trying to reach double digits by the time I was twenty-five, but there was more to it. Sex with Jack hadn't really felt like sex—it was just a few minutes of breaking my hymen. Now I wanted to do it properly and enjoy it. Em had amazing sex with Sergio, and even though Jez was a bit hit-and-miss, Lara always had fun in bed with him. Wasn't it my turn to get that?

I knew I hadn't ever met JT and he could be a total disaster, but he seemed like the ideal candidate to help me out there. And it was a two-way deal. We'd both get some fun out of it. It would be mutually beneficial if all went to plan, and if worst came to worst, I'd leave in the morning and never see him again. I'd get my chance to live it up and figure out womanhood, while he'd get a shag and an orgasm. Come to think of it, hopefully I'd get one of those too. I just needed some help.

I barged into Emma's room in my purple dressing gown patterned with white stars. 'Ems, I need help.' She was lying in bed resting her head on Sergio's tanned, hairless torso. 'Oh crap, I should have knocked, sorry. I didn't know you were here, Serge.'

'It's fine, come in,' he said and patted the duvet. I walked over and sat down with them.

'I don't know what to do about JT,' I moaned.

'How many messages has it been now?' asked Emma without moving her head off Serge's hot bod. This was not helping my self-esteem. 'Twelve?'

'Fourteen. Surely that's a bit excessive now?'

'Why can't you ask him out?' asked Sergio.

'But…won't he think I'm desperate? What about the game?'

Emma scrunched up her face. 'I don't know. I think the whole point of online dating is that it evens out the playing field. Like, obviously it's so sexist that society says men have to ask out women, but it is kind of ingrained. When a woman asks out a man in real life he's like, she's either desperate or a slut. But online…well, it's kind of the norm, isn't it?'

'Huh, maybe,' I said, as Sergio started covering Emma's face in tiny kisses.

'I didn't think you were desperate or a slut when you wrote your number on that receipt,' he said.

I rolled my eyes at them. 'Can you get a room already?' He raised his eyebrows and gestured at Emma's purple fairy lights, leopard print and fur. 'You know what I mean,' I said. 'Anyway, Emma, do you really think it's more acceptable for a girl to ask out a guy online?'

'Yeah,' she cried. 'It's way more equal on there. In fact, I think women actually have more power than men on online dating sites. Because girls will get more messages than the guys and then when a guy does get a message, there's more of a chance he'll reply. Girls have more choice.'

I nodded slowly. 'That makes sense. But what if he rejects me?'

'Who cares? He hasn't even met you—you're just pixels. It's like when Oxford University rejected my UCAS application before even meeting me. You can't get upset because they don't even know who you are. They're just rejecting a piece of paper, or a bunch of words on a website in your case.'

'Yeah, you're so right,' I said. 'You know what? I feel way more empowered. Thanks, Em. I don't give a shit if JT rejects me any more. My personality comes through in person not pixels. I bet he'd never turn down a one-night stand with me IRL, so who cares if he does online?'

'What's this IRL?' asked Sergio.

'In real life,' replied Emma and I automatically.

'Anyway, you can get back to having sex now,' I announced, as I walked out of the room. 'I'm off to ask out a man.'

I sat in the living room staring blindly at the TV. JT still hadn't replied. The message I'd sent kept flashing up in my head:

So I was wondering if maybe we should meet in person?
How about a drink?

It had been, like, two hours and he still hadn't replied.
I'd managed to fuck it up with a guy without even meeting
him. I was seriously doomed.

'Hey, El, how's it going?'

Ollie walked into the room and sat on the sofa next to
me. I quickly pulled my leggings down so he wouldn't see
my unshaven legs. 'Oh fine,' I said. 'Only, I just messaged
a guy online and he hasn't replied. Such is my life.'

'Oh yeah? You know, I can't believe you're doing online dating.'

'What, why not?' I asked, feeling semi-offended.

'I just wouldn't have thought you'd need to.'

Was that…a compliment? 'Oh really? That's so nice.'

'Well, you're twenty-two. I would have thought that's a
bit, like, young.'

'It is not too young,' I cried. 'Hello, we live in the Tinder
world. This is just what everyone does. How else are you
meant to meet someone?'

'Yeah, but Tinder seems more legit. Why didn't you just
do that?'

'Because it still feels like a sex app and I like the idea
of knowing someone's basic details and thoughts before
meeting them.'

'So you're not looking for sex?' He grinned, showing
his little dimples.

I blushed. 'Well, I mean, I am. But I'd rather do it after
a date, and not just in the loo of a bar.'

'Don't. You're making me nostalgic for my single days.'

'You had sex in a loo?'

'A girl went down on me outside the uni student union once. Pre-Yomi, obviously.'

'Jesus,' I said, trying to ignore the fact that I was suddenly seriously envious of this blow job girl.

'I know. It was fucking fun.'

'Sounds it. So, Yomi straightened you out, then?'

He grinned at me and I tried to not stare into his eyes. 'I've still got my dirty side.'

I laughed. 'Ew, you sound so pervy.'

'I try. So, who's this guy who isn't replying to you?'

'Ah, he's called JT. Seems normal, hot and interesting. We've been messaging, but then I asked him out and he didn't reply.'

'You asked him out?'

'Should I not have? Is that weird? Oh God.'

'No, calm down. I think it's really cool. I don't think there are many girls who would do that. In fact, I'd be fucking thrilled if a girl asked me out.'

'Really?' He nodded and looked into my eyes. Oh Christ. I really had to stop fancying my flatmate who had a GIRL-FRIEND. 'I don't think Yomi would be,' I said, bringing the conversation back to the perfect doctor.

'Fair point. But she doesn't like a lot of what I do, so…'

Did this mean there was trouble in paradise? 'Really? What kind of stuff?' I asked.

'She doesn't really like my mates from home, which kind of bothers me. It's because most of them didn't go to uni, and I guess she finds them hard to relate to. But they're all really good guys. And she works so hard she's rarely up for going out. I know she's under a lot of pressure with her finals, but it's just difficult, you know?'

I nodded, trying to pretend I was au fait with relationship

problems. 'Yeah, that sounds difficult. It's why I don't want a boyfriend right now—I can't handle the compromises.'

'Ha, I know what you mean. We're too young to stop being selfish.'

'Exactly.' I grinned. 'Maybe Yomi needs to remember to be younger.'

'Yeah, maybe. Hey, do you mind if I change the channel? Tottenham are playing.'

'Go for it. I, um, need to do something upstairs anyway.'

'Cool. See you later.'

I went up to my room with my heart fluttering. He was so insanely attractive, and if he and Yomi broke up, then Caesar would be answering all of my prayers. But in the meantime, he'd still given me an idea. I'd been so wrapped up in my profile that I'd forgotten I was competing with hundreds, nay *thousands*, of attractive single women online.

I needed to check out the competition. I went to OKCupid.com, logged out of my profile and clicked 'create profile'. Select gender: male.

I quickly made a basic profile (Tim201) and started searching. I wanted women aged twenty to twenty-nine. The list came up and my mouth dropped open in surprise. These profiles were nothing like my modest-but-flirty attempt. All these girls looked like part-time models, porn stars or Abercrombie & Fitch employees. I was doomed. Utterly doomed.

I clicked on Ange_xx. Her doe-eyed pose won me over immediately and I was semi-seduced by her pouting selfies. Oh God. Why would JT_ldn want to date me if there were girls like Ange_xx out there? I was officially fucked.

I scrolled back to my own profile and stared at the pictures in misery. They all looked like me. This was not going to work. Wasn't the whole point of online dating to make yourself look better than you really do? I needed to slut up my pics. ASAP.

My first port of call was Facebook. I went straight to my photos from sixth form. I sighed in relief as I flicked through them and realised I was right; my boobs were on show in every single one. I was caked in make-up, my curves were forced into minuscule dresses, and I looked sexy enough to take on Ange_xx.

I selected one of the most blatant pictures and, ignoring the twinge of self-disapproval I was feeling, quickly made it my new profile picture. I knew Emma had said online dating was a feminist tool, so I probably shouldn't have gone for such a tacky man-catching ploy, but if everyone else was doing it… Besides, I bet it wasn't just the girls. JT_ldn was probably four inches shorter and five years older than he promised.

Fuck, what if he had lied?!

My phone beeped. There was a message from JT.

I'd love to. Think we should do it soon before you get a whole line of dates with your new profile picture. Very hot by the way.

I screeched out loud. OK, it was kind of embarrassing he had noticed my photo ploy—but he also thought I was hot and wanted to go for drinks, and I had successfully asked out a guy!!! I was a woman of the future and a feminist in action. No one had to know I'd used a photo of my tits to do it.

Chapter 6

I was standing at the entrance of Angel tube station trying to swallow the stress-induced gags my stomach kept
heaving up. It was 8.03 p.m. and I was about to meet JT in
person. I glanced around weakly but couldn't see anyone
who looked six foot three with crinkly green eyes and dark
blond hair. My watch said 8.06 p.m. Oh God. Was he about
to stand me up?

My phone vibrated. Fuck, fuck, fuck. It was from him.

Hey, just inside next to the ticket machine. Wearing a red
scarf. Holding a book. See you soon!

I sighed in relief that he hadn't stood me up—and then
realised with a jolt that this was actually happening. I was
about to have an actual internet date. It was too late to run
away. Oh God.

Feeling sicker than ever, I wrapped my jacket tightly
around me and slowly stepped into the station. The ticket

machine was on the left. As promised, there was a tall man standing next to it. I quickly ducked behind a *Big Issue* seller and peeped out over his shoulder to spy on JT. I couldn't see his face but he was wearing a black woollen coat with a maroon scarf. I breathed out in relief; he looked hot from behind.

I stood up straight and boldly walked over to him. My blood was pounding, but I forced myself to keep going. When I was inches away, I cleared my throat. He turned around to face me and the smile on my face plummeted.

JT WAS ANCIENT.

He had wrinkles, greying hair, and, oh my fucking God, was he missing a tooth?! I felt a stream of bile rise up into my mouth and I gagged audibly.

He opened his mouth to speak but before he could say a word, I whirled around and ran out of the station. When I was outside I started breathing slowly. It was OK. These things happened but at least I was in public and the elderly JT couldn't attack me. I was safe.

'Ellie,' called a voice behind me. Oh my fucking God. It was him—he'd found me and now he was about to attack me. I quickened my pace and ran past benches full of staring passers-by. I turned my head to check if he was following me and fell flat on my face onto the pavement.

'Are you all right?'

I looked up in pain and saw an attractive blond man smiling above me. His dark green eyes crinkled as he smiled and there were no wrinkles to be seen. It was JT_ldn. The real one.

'I…don't understand,' I said. 'You look like your picture.'

'Erm, should I not?' he asked with a raised eyebrow. My eyes flew straight to his neck. He was wearing a bright red scarf, three shades lighter than the maroon scarf I'd just seen. With a wave of relief, I realised that this was the JT I'd meant to meet and the other man was just an awful, awful coincidence in a maroon scarf.

I had officially fucked up.

'No, no, it's a good thing, trust me,' I said, as I pulled myself off the kerb.

'Right, and do you always run away from your dates? This is the first time I've had to chase after someone on a date, you know.' He grinned.

I felt my cheeks flush as I realised what I'd just done. I had just run away from the hottest date I'd ever had. And then tripped on a jagged pavestone.

'So, um, about that,' I said sheepishly. 'The red scarf thing kind of threw up a bit of confusion.'

'Go on...'

I sighed. 'Well, there's a forty-year-old, fat, unattractive man wearing a red scarf down by the ticket machine. I thought he was you, or you were him, or I don't know...'

He threw back his head and howled with laughter. I noticed in relief that he had all his teeth. 'That's hilarious. You thought I was some paedo?'

'Essentially...yeah.' I winced. 'Sorry. I'm so embarrassed.'

'Don't be, this is a great story to tell the grandkids.' Grandkids?! We hadn't even held hands yet. 'I'm kidding,' he added.

'Yeah, obviously.' I laughed nervously. 'Sorry, I'm still all over the place from the whole paedo thing. And then the running away bit. Can we start over?'

He smiled and held out his right hand. 'Sure, I'm JT. Good to meet you.'

'I'm Ellie. Nice to meet you too,' I said, shaking his hand.

'Great, so now we've got the formalities out of the way, how about we go and grab some food?' I nodded happily, ignoring the weighted lump of undigested pasta in my stomach reminding me I had just eaten a whole pack of tortellini. 'So there's a fun Chinese buffet place up the corner. You keen?'

'Buffet?'

'Yeah, but you do have to be pretty hungry to get your money's worth, so if you're not that hungry, we can always just get tacos or something elsewhere,' he suggested.

Tacos sounded perfect—but what if he thought I was one of those anorexic girls who couldn't handle buffets? My appetite was the one positive attribute guys loved about me. All my male friends were terrified of dating skinny dieting girls who only ordered salads and counted calories—they'd all told me this was my niche. Considering I didn't have that many, I knew I had to work it.

I mentally said goodbye to the light, refreshing tacos and prepared myself for a second carby dinner. 'Buffet sounds great.'

'Are you sure?' he asked. There it was, my get-out card. I just had to say no and we could get tacos.

'Yeah, definitely. I'm starving.'

'Cool, it's just down here,' he said, gesturing as we started walking down the high street. 'So, how has your day been?'

'Um, pretty uneventful until the past ten minutes,' I said.

'Same.' He laughed. 'I can't say I imagined I'd be running down the street behind my first OKCupid date.'

'This is your first time too?' I asked.

'Yeah, I thought I'd give it a try and do something new.' He shrugged. 'Everyone kept raving about it at work, so I figured I'd give it a shot. What about you? What made you take the virtual leap?'

'Um...' I racked my brains for an appropriate response that didn't have the phrase 'slut' or 'one-night stand' in it. 'Pretty much the same as you, really. Just something different.'

'Yeah.' He nodded. 'I guess I'm just looking for whatever happens, really. Whether that's a relationship or just...casual fun.' He looked straight into my eyes and I felt a tingle run up my spine. Thank God I'd shaved my legs and trimmed my bush—one-night stand, here I come.

He looked at me questioningly and I realised I'd stopped walking. 'Yeah, I'm the same,' I said. 'Just looking for whatever life throws at me.'

He raised an eyebrow at me. 'Are you quoting my dating profile?'

Oh fuck. I was unconsciously reciting the 'Looking for' section of his profile. I knew I shouldn't have read it so many times. 'Um, unintentionally?'

He laughed. 'Well, at least you've done your homework. Gotta be safe, eh?'

'Exactly.' I grinned. 'So, uh, is this the restaurant?' We were standing outside the fanciest Chinese restaurant I'd ever seen. Stone lions were wrapped around the columns at the front and the words 'Red Dragon' were written in a non-tacky gold.

'This is it,' he said. 'Hope you're hungry.'

My plate was heaped with Ma Po Tofu, steamed aubergine, egg fried rice and crispy seaweed. The whole thing cost £18.99 and I'd eaten only three chopsticks' worth.

'This is so good,' said JT, as he finished his first helping. 'Do you not like it? You've barely eaten a thing.' He looked discerningly at the mound of food on my plate.

'Oh God, no, it's amazing. I'm just pacing myself.' I raised my chopsticks to my mouth and forced myself to swallow. It was the nicest Chinese I'd had in years but I was so full of £1.99 tortellini I couldn't eat it. Typical. 'Anyway, tell me more about you,' I said. 'You work for Marc Jacobs, right? Are you going to get me freebies?'

'You're not the first person to ask me that, but no, I'm sorry, those are strictly for me. Shit, that makes me sound very camp doesn't it?'

'Yeah, just a bit.' I smiled. 'Honestly though, I was pretty relieved when I saw on your profile that you work in IT and not fashion.'

'Bit more manly, eh?'

'Totally,' I replied, wishing I could think of something witty to add. Instead, I reached for my chopsticks and forced more mouthfuls down me.

'So I know you're interning for some crazy boss, but what exactly is the magazine? Is it a fashion one?' he asked.

'Uh, it's more just a bit of everything. It's the *London Mag.* Have you heard of it?'

'Obviously,' he said, leaning back in his chair. 'It's the new online one that's getting bigger each week. I'm impressed.'

'Yeah, except you forget I'm not actually getting paid for it.'

'This is some extensive hinting that you can't get the bill, Ellie,' he teased. 'I would have paid anyway, you know.'

I blushed and looked up at him through my layers of mascara in an attempt to look like Ange_xx. 'I would never expect a man to pay for me.'

He laughed. 'You're hilarious. I'm so glad I said yes to this date with you.'

I had no idea what I'd done that was so funny, but if he was enjoying the date, who was I to say otherwise? 'Me too,' I said.

'I was kind of surprised when you asked me out though,' he admitted.

'What, why?' Shit—maybe Emma was wrong and it was still desperate to ask someone out online?

'I guess I'm not used to forward girls,' he said.

Forward?! I wasn't FORWARD. I was a virgin at twenty-one, for Chrissake.

'Right.'

'No, it's not a bad thing. It's…sexy. I like it. In fact, I like it so much that I'm going to get the bill and rescue you from that plate of food that you clearly don't want to eat.'

Oh my God, I didn't have to eat my cold Chinese. This was it—he was officially the one. You could fall in love with one-night stands-to-be, right?

Chapter 7

I crossed my legs and flicked my mass of hair over my shoulder as I laughed demurely at JT's joke. I was perched on a bar stool in the poshest wine bar—OK, only wine bar—I'd ever been to and I was determined to act as elegantly as was required.

'Another glass of Muscadet?' asked JT. I nodded enthusiastically and almost toppled off my stool. 'Careful,' he said, as he steadied me with his arm.

The only problem was that it was getting quite difficult to act the height of sophistication when my date was plying me with drinks. Was this glass number...four? Five?

I ignored the sensible voice in my head screeching at me to order a tap water and graciously picked up the wine glass the barman put in front of me.

'Why thank you,' I said.

'Anything for the lady,' said JT. He looked straight into my eyes and I swallowed a laugh.

'I'll just have a tap water as well, please,' I told the barman.

'Water already?' asked JT.

'Oh, just to stop me from getting absolutely pissed and embarrassing myself,' I said.

'I don't think you could embarrass yourself,' he said.

I stared at him. 'Um, are you kidding me? You do realise I started this date by running away from you because I thought you were a paedophile? And, last week—'

He interrupted me mid-sentence by leaning in and planting his lips on top of mine. I spluttered in surprise before my brain whirred into action and I kissed him back. Lara and Emma were so wrong—my embarrassing stories *were* seductive.

He stood up from his stool and came closer to me as we kissed. I leant against him and he started rubbing his tongue against mine. I reciprocated to the best of my abilities and put my hands on his face. He grabbed my arse and pulled me in towards him. I gasped out loud at how X-rated things were getting, but JT seemed to interpret it as a sound of pleasure and started snogging me at double the speed.

I held on to the bar to steady myself, and out of the corner of my eye, I saw the barman shake his head in disgust. The British prude inside of me tried to break away, but JT pulled me in closer towards him and squeezed my boob.

'You're so sexy,' he murmured in my ear. 'I'm just going to go to the bathroom and then I'm taking you home with me.'

I nodded mutely and he winked at me before turning around and walking away. I let out the breath I hadn't realised I was holding in. This was it. I was going to have my first ever one-night stand.

'Excuse me,' said the barman.

'Oh, I don't want another drink,' I said. 'Thanks, but we're off now.'

He raised his eyebrows at me. 'I was actually going to say, I think you have something on your face.'

I stared at him in confusion and then reached out to touch my face. It was damp. Oh, how embarrassing, it must be saliva, but…how could he see that? I lowered my hand and squinted at it in the purple UV light. It was covered in a dark liquid.

WHAT THE FUCK WAS ON MY FACE?

I stood up and rushed towards the mirrored walls of the bar. My entire left cheek, and parts of my forehead, were covered in this brown liquid. Had I rubbed against some paint? Was it red wine?!

I whirled around to look at the barman again. He was hiding a grin. 'I think it might be blood,' he said.

Blood?! Why was my face bleeding?? Then it slowly dawned on me. It wasn't my blood. It was JT's. He had nose-bled on my face.

My hands jumped to cover my face instinctively and I ran blindly towards the loos. I pushed past the queue of surprised girls and raced to the mirror. Under the bright yellow lights I could see my face was covered in blood. I looked like a Halloween midwife.

I turned the taps on full and began washing it off my face. It slid off along with half my make-up. After furiously scrubbing at my skin with paper towels, I was blood free. Thank God.

Then I realised I had to go back outside to JT. God, I couldn't go home with him now—I couldn't even face him. What were you supposed to say to the guy who nose-bled on you mid-snog? Had he known all along that he was bleeding on me? Or did he realise only when he went to the loo? Surely he had seen it on my face—why the fuck hadn't he told me??

I couldn't deal with this right now. It was just too embarrassing. Maybe I could just hide out in the loo stall for a few minutes, and once JT had got the message and left, I could go home. I glanced over to the loo cubicle but then as the main bathroom door swung open, I saw the inside of the bar. I could vaguely make out JT skulking in a corner. I ran straight into the nearest cubicle and slammed the door shut.

'Hello? Lady?'

I jumped in alarm. I was sitting on a toilet seat with my head in between my legs and there was someone banging on the cubicle door. Oh my God, JT. The blood. I was hiding in the loo. Had I been here all night?!

I cautiously unbolted the loo door and peered out. The toilet attendant had her hands on her hips and looked seriously pissed off.

'You've been in there twenty minutes, lady. We have a no drugs policy. I've called the manager.'

Drugs?? Surely I could have just had a bad stomach? I looked around the loos and realised there was still a queue of girls. The bar hadn't closed and JT could still be outside waiting for me. The bathroom door opened and the barman from earlier was standing there.

'You again.' He grinned.

'I wasn't doing drugs, I promise. I…fell asleep on the loo.'

He hid a smile and I realised he was kind of attractive. Even though he was only about an inch taller than me, he had an impressively symmetrical face, three-day stubble and short blond dreadlocks.

'Was that after you were cleaning blood off your face?' he asked.

I briefly closed my eyes. Did he really have to remind me of the humiliation?

'Anyway,' he said. 'You know your boyfriend's been waiting for you this entire time out there?'

'Oh fuck, is he still there?' I cried out. 'I thought he'd have gone by now.'

He raised an eyebrow at me. 'You're hiding from your boyfriend?'

'Oh, you know he's not my boyfriend,' I snapped at him. 'He's my first ever online date, and after he nose-bled on me, I didn't fancy seeing him again.'

'Oh, obviously,' he said. 'That's how all my dates go too.'

I was about to snap at him again when I noticed he was grinning at me. 'Yeah, this hasn't been one of my best.'

'Hey, how about I help you sneak out of here without seeing your guy?' he offered.

'Ohmigod, would you really? I would literally love you for life.'

'OK, calm down,' he said. 'Just…follow me.'

I followed him out of the toilets and through a door marked 'Private'. We walked up the stairs and then found ourselves outside. I breathed a sigh of relief.

'Thanks so much.'

'Hey, don't mention it.' He shrugged. 'You've drastically improved my night on the comedy scales anyway.'

'Hopefully I'll find it as funny tomorrow. So what's your name?'

'Pete.' He grinned. 'And the damsel in distress?'

I looked at him blankly. 'Ohhh, right. Ellie. I'm Ellie.'

'Nice to meet you, Ellie,' he said. 'Well, get home safe,

and feel free to bring any more of your online dates here. I'll help you out with an escape route whenever you need one.'

'Wait, really? Because that would be kind of incredible.'

He laughed. 'Let's do it. This can be your regular bar for dates and I'll help you out when they bleed on you.'

'OK, deal.' I grinned. 'Anyway, I'm sobering up and I reckon I'd better get the bus home, so...I'll see you around.'

'See you.'

Chapter 8

'Ohmigod, ew, what the fuck is on her face?'

'It looks like...dried blood.'

I pulled the duvet over my head. 'What's happening?' I groaned.

A bright light seared through my eyes as my duvet flew off me.

'And she's naked,' a male voice said.

I clutched my boobs and looked around me wildly as my pupils slowly dilated and my room came into focus. Emma was sitting on my bed scratching her nails, Will was dramatically shielding his eyes with my duvet, and Ollie was politely looking at his battered Nike high-tops at the far end of my room.

'What are you all doing?' I asked with as much dignity as I could muster with my hands over my nipples.

'Babe, do you wanna put some clothes on?' asked Emma. 'We thought we'd all wake you up and hear the goss about your first online date, but then we saw this...blood on your face.' She held up her sparkling green nails at me, and I saw flakes of JT's dried nose-blood on the tips of her talons.

I sighed loudly. 'Right, OK,' I said. 'Why doesn't everyone turn around and I'll put my dressing gown on?' Obligingly, my housemates turned their backs to me and I grabbed my fluffy dressing gown from the floor and wrapped it around me. 'OK, we're good,' I said.

'Thank God,' cried Will, as he lowered my duvet from his face. 'I was starting to pass out in this thing. When did you last do a whites wash?' He saw my face and switched topics. 'Anyway, never mind about your washing. How was JT?'

'And...the blood?' asked Emma.

I looked at Ollie's face and sighed. He was never going to see me the same way again. Not that it really mattered. I took a deep breath and began.

'So, I got to Angel and looked for the man in the red scarf, but he was forty and wrinkly with a beer belly.' There were shocked gasps and I smiled proudly, knowing my date horror story was worse than any of theirs. 'So, naturally, I ran away. But whilst I was trying to get away, I tripped on the pavement.'

'Oh my God,' screeched Will.

'So I was lying on the pavement, terrified, when someone came up to me. It was JT—only, the real one. He was normal aged with a slightly different red scarf, and the first JT was just a massive mistake.'

'Oh,' said Will. 'I thought you were going to say the blood was from some kind of perverted sexual assault.'

'Um, no,' I said slowly. 'If that had happened, I would have called the police and would not be telling you this so casually.' He shrugged and I carried on, ignoring my pounding hangover. 'Anyway, JT was gorgeous and normal and I even ate a second dinner for him. Then we went for drinks and he paid for everything and we snogged loads. Only, then he went to the loo and the barman told me I had stuff on my face and…it was blood. Because he nose-bled on me.'

All three of my flatmates stared at me in revulsion.

'Fuck me, that's disgusting,' cried Will.

'Oh yeah? Coming from the guy who uses conditioner as lube?'

Ollie grinned. 'Shit, Ellie, that is one hell of a date story.'

'Thanks, I guess.'

'It's hysterical,' he said. 'But…did you go home with him after?'

I paused as I tried to remember what happened next. The rest of the night was a warm fuzzy blur of—

'Oh God,' I cried. 'I went to the loo to wash it off, then I hid in there from him and fell asleep. Until the hot manager came and took me out the secret fire escape.'

Emma and Will started howling with laughter, but Ollie stared at me. He looked kind of impressed. 'A hot manager?' he asked. 'Shit, your night sounds pretty wild.'

I shrugged, hiding a grin. My night did sound dramatic. So much for 'single Ellie with her single bed'—I so almost had a one-night stand. 'Yeah, I guess it was. Does it make you miss your single days?'

He stared straight into my eyes and I felt my knees go tingly. 'Sometimes,' he said softly.

'That's fucking ridiculous,' gasped Emma. She was rolling on my bed with Will, still snorting with laughter. 'It reminds me of the time you got with the only emo in Mahiki.'

'Emma, you weren't even there that night,' I snapped.

'And then you slipped on your friend's come in your bath,' she gasped.

Will sat up straight. 'Come…or conditioner?' he asked and then collapsed with laughter again.

I rolled my eyes at them. 'Guys, get over it. We've all had bad dates.'

'Uh, yeah, but I've never abandoned mine after they bled on me,' cried Will. 'Mainly because they've never bled on me.'

'EWWW, the blood,' shrieked Emma, as she remembered it was on her hands. 'I'm covered in a strange man's blood. OHMIGOD, AIDS!!'

'Fuck,' I cried in panic. 'You don't think…?'

Will groaned loudly. 'You're both so fucking stupid sometimes,' he said. 'AIDS is a severe form of HIV and you're not going to get it from his nosebleed unless it's gone into an open wound on your face. Do you have a cut on your face, Ellie?'

I raced over to my full-length mirror and examined my face. 'OK, no,' I admitted.

'Then, my darling, you are AIDS free,' he said. 'Congratulations.'

I hobbled downstairs to the kitchen to find breakfast and stop my hangover. My head was banging and I needed carbs to soak up the alcohol. But all I had was Sainsbury's own-brand Crunchy Nut Cornflakes.

Forlornly, I tipped the packet into a bowl and reached for the milk. I was pouring it in when I realised there were small black lumps floating in my bowl. What the fuck were they?! I grabbed a spoon and lifted a few out to examine them closely. They looked like rabbit poos, only smaller.

Then I froze. There were sounds coming from my cornflakes carton. I took a deep breath and moved towards it. I held on to the sideboard to steady myself and hesitantly peered inside. There was a tiny grey lump moving in my cornflakes. I opened my mouth and screamed.

Will walked into the kitchen. 'Seen a mouse?' he asked nonchalantly, as he pushed past my trembling body to get to his cupboard.

'IT'S IN MY CORNFLAKES!' I shrieked.

'Yeah, there's a few in here,' he said. 'I saw a bunch running out of the bin bags last week.'

I stared at him aghast. 'Are you fucking kidding me? You've seen mice in here, and you didn't think to tell anyone?! What's wrong with you, Will? We need to buy traps and…and poison.'

'Ellie,' he said, 'we live in London. Obviously we're going to have mice. Besides, we have a four-bed in Haggerston with a living room and only pay £550 each. We're lucky we just have mice.'

'As opposed to?' I asked. 'Oh fuck, do you mean RATS?'

'Calm down.' He sighed. 'You can't have mice and rats at the same time.'

'They're…mutually exclusive?'

'Exactly,' he said. 'Anyway, are you going to eat those cornflakes? I'm starving.'

'There is a mouse in the box,' I said slowly. 'Do you not get this?'

'Whatever.' He shrugged. 'I'll just take the mouse out.'

I stared at him in incomprehension and backed out of the kitchen quickly, straight up the stairs to Emma's room.

'Em,' I cried, as I pushed open her door. 'There's loads of mice and Will doesn't care. What do we do?'

'Ugh, I know,' she said, as she paused the programme she was watching on her laptop. 'I've just been getting Serge to bring me food or staying at his more.'

'Right, well, some of us don't have a boyfriend to rely on, so...shall we buy some traps and try to get rid of them?' I asked in frustration.

'Meh, I don't think they really work,' she said. 'Besides, it's not like they're rats.'

How was my best friend OK with mice living in our cereals? I shook my head at her and went straight to Ollie's room. I knocked and waited for him to reply.

'Come in,' he called.

I pushed open the door and walked into his room. It was all grey, and the only effort he had put into decorating it was a collage of pictures of him and Yomi stuck onto his wardrobe. They were both so attractive that they looked like a celeb couple. She had massive green eyes and a weave that made her look like Beyoncé. Ugh.

I walked straight past her smiling face and sat down on his bed.

'What's up?' he asked.

'Mice,' I announced. 'Apparently they live with us and I found one in my cornflakes.'

He laughed. 'Shit, I can't believe they got into your food.'

'I know. Who knew mice love own-brand cornflakes?'

'Glad to see we don't have middle-class mice. Maybe we should name them,' he suggested.

'Or,' I said, 'perhaps we could, um, exterminate them all?'

He scrunched up his face at me and I stopped myself running over to touch it. 'How do you propose we do that?' he asked.

'Traps? Poison? Pest-killing men?'

'I think the men only come in for rats and stuff, and I reckon they'd be pretty expensive, but I guess we could try the others. The only thing is that poison means the mice will eat it, then die wherever they are. We could have dead mice living in our walls.'

'Ohmigod, ew.'

'Exactly.'

'OK, so traps?' I asked.

'Two options—lovely humane cages that just catch them without hurting them but cost loads, or cheap traps that snap their legs and get blood everywhere,' he said.

I groaned and collapsed back onto the bed. It smelt musty but in a sexy kind of way. Ew, it was probably his and Yomi's sex smells. I sat up again. 'You don't want to do anything either, do you?' I asked him.

'The others want to leave the mice alone too?'

'Yeah, and I can tell you do as well. Am I the only one who wants to eat food that's not contaminated by mice poo?'

'I think so,' he said. 'But, hey, if we keep the house extra clean for a bit, they'll go away on their own. Or, at least, there'll be less of them.'

'OK.' I sighed. 'And there was me thinking that living in an East London flatshare would be glamorous.'

'Nothing glamorous about earning the minimum wage in our twenties,' he said.

'But at least you have an actual job,' I said. 'Doesn't advertising pay well?'

'Not in your first year, and not when every graduate in London is willing to do it for free as an internship.'

'Ah, yeah, that would be me.'

'Don't worry. I did my fair share of interning too. And journalism is way cooler than advertising, so I reckon it will pay off in the long run.'

'Mmm, maybe,' I said. 'Anyway, on less depressing topics, how's stuff with Yomi?'

'Yeah, good,' he said. 'But, I guess…well, four years is a long time to be together and long distance is hard at the moment. It will be easier when she's not still up in Bristol and she's back here in London.'

'Yeah, definitely.' I nodded, as though I was highly experienced with long-term, long-distance relationships. 'I'm sure it will get easier soon.'

'I hope so,' he said. 'It's getting to that weird time where I'm twenty-five and I've had the same girlfriend for four years. I kind of miss playing the field.'

Oh my God. My dreams were coming true. Ollie wanted to break up with Yomi. I forced myself to breathe calmly. I couldn't suggest they break up or it would look bad. I had to be subtle.

'Maybe you should?' I asked. Subtle was overrated.

'Ah, who knows what will happen. You're lucky you don't have to deal with any of this crap.'

'Mm, yeah, so lucky that no one wants to date me. They just want to bleed on me.'

He laughed. 'That's more action than I've got all week. Anyway, are we going to go clean this kitchen or what?'

'Let's do it,' I said. 'Maybe my man-repelling powers will work on these mice. Fingers crossed they're male.'

'What if they're gay mice? They'll be all over me.'

'Ha ha. They'd be over Will more like.'

'Hey, I'm not that bad.'

'I know. I mean, I, uh… Kitchen?'

He grinned at me. 'Kitchen.'

Chapter 9

'Would anyone like a tea?' I asked.

There was silence. I stood up and leant across my desk so I was facing my colleagues. 'Guys, tea?' I repeated.

The three writers all ignored me. Hattie, the youngest, shook her head, but Jenna and Camilla didn't even bother to look up. I sighed to myself and walked through to the mini kitchenette alone. The more I tried to be friendly to the other office workers at the *London Mag*, the more they ignored me. Maybe if my next online date belonged to their Chelsea circle, I might get the occasional greeting.

I pulled out my phone as the kettle boiled. There had been no word from JT ever since I had abandoned him in the Holly & Ivy. Which was fair enough, really. But there had also been a categorical silence from anyone semi-normal on OKCupid. Perhaps JT had sent round a warning email putting everyone off me—even though he was the one who'd bled on my face. I couldn't even find a sluttier selfie to attract the swarms to my profile.

I went to the search section of the site and selected my filters. I wanted someone over six feet, with a degree so we had stuff in common, and...ooh, it would be nice if they spoke a foreign language. And worked in...finance/banking/real estate. Then they could afford to pay for my dinner.

I pressed 'search'. Five results came up. They were all above the age of forty. Two were female. I sighed and deleted all my filters. Then I selected 'aged 23–30' and 'male'. Foreign languages and degrees would have to wait.

A couple of the men looked attractive. If only these guys would ask me out instead of all the creeps, but they never did. Unless...I asked them out first? It had worked for JT and Emma was right—it didn't really feel like rejection when they were just pixels. Besides, they could be lying and secretly be seventy-year-old perverts.

Without giving myself a chance to change my mind, I tapped out a message to Ben84.

Hey, how are you? Been on here long?

It wasn't Pulitzer Prize winning, but it wasn't as if any of the men sent me well-crafted witty messages. I may as well just send the same message to multiple men. I'd sent it to eight different people when I felt someone hovering over my shoulder.

'Maxine,' I cried out. 'Sorry, I...uh, didn't notice you there. Would you like a tea?'

'Hmm, the kettle boiled about five minutes ago. What are you so engrossed in?' she asked, narrowing her carefully made-up eyes at me.

'Oh, it's, um, nothing,' I mumbled. 'Just personal messages. Sorry, I shouldn't look at them at work.'

'It looked like a dating app to me,' she said. I stared at her in shock. Was she spying on me now? As if it wasn't enough that I worked unpaid fifty hours a week and acted as her personal assistant most of the time. 'Well, don't look so shocked, Ellie. You're not the only one using them—they're huge at the moment. I want to do a feature on them. Maybe you can collate your experiences as research for Camilla to write up.'

'Or I could write it myself,' I suggested boldly. This was my chance. I could write about JT and go on more dates and interview people using it. It would be my first proper feature. It was perfect for me. I could—

'No,' she said. 'I'll get Camilla to message you about it later.' She poured the water I had just boiled into her mug and walked off.

* * *

'I'm so glad you're here,' I cried, as I sank my head into Lara's fur scarf. 'Work is so rubbish, we have mice at home, and my date nose-bled on me.'

She pulled my head up by my ponytail. 'Right, OK, can you get out of my scarf, please?' she said.

'Sorry,' I mumbled and shifted away to sit on the chair next to her. 'I'm just so tired.'

'Yeah, how are you, Lara? How is it being in your final year of uni? What's going on with Jez? Have you been on any more online dates?' she asked herself loudly.

'Fine, I'm sorry.' I sighed. 'We'll start with you. What's up?'

'Ellie, I am on track to get a first in Law from one of the best universities in the country. I am attractive, smart and cool.'

'Um, where exactly is this going?'

'And yet, and yet, I am still semi-obsessed with a pathetic

man called JEZ—which isn't even a real name by the way—who prefers weed and KFC to me. What the actual fuck is wrong with me?' She groaned and threw her head into her perfectly manicured hands.

I stroked her head sympathetically. She had a point. Jez was a waste of space who was so below Lara's league that it was embarrassing.

'Excuse me, please, can we get a bottle of the house red and a baked Camembert?' I called out to the waiter. 'Actually, let's make that two.'

'Two bottles or two cheeses?'

'Cheese, obviously.' I turned back to Lara. 'Anyway, maybe you're obsessed with him because…the sex is amazing?'

'Yeah, it is good that I come every time, but that's only when he is sober enough to get it up.'

'Why don't you just end it, Lar?' I asked. 'We've been through all these pros and cons a million times and each time we just get to the same conclusion—you're so, so, *so* much better than him.'

'I know.' She sighed. 'But we aren't exclusive, so I can date other people and I'm not technically tied down to him, which makes me think that it's not a big deal and I may as well have fun with him while I'm waiting for someone better to come along.'

'It does sound perfect,' I admitted. 'But I'm guessing you're so involved with him that you don't actually feel that single?'

'Exactly,' she cried. 'I'm so hung up on him that I don't even want to see other guys, and whenever I try to stop seeing him, I miss him too much to last more than a week.'

I stroked her arm sympathetically. 'I'm sorry, it's such a shit catch-22. Hey, is this cashmere?'

'My mum's. Yeah, it's shit. I guess I just have to resign myself to a life of depressing misery and…'

'Occasional fantastic sex?'

'Exactly.' She sighed loudly. 'Anyway, your turn. Mice and Maxine?'

'Don't even,' I groaned. 'She is awful and is apparently now spying on my dating life—but refuses to let me write about it.'

'She never lets you write anything,' said Lara. 'Why is this such a surprise?'

'It's not, but it doesn't make it any less shit.'

'Have you stood up to her?'

'Yes! It's so frustrating. I don't know what to do any more. It's my own catch-22,' I said woefully.

'How's it going with Ollie?'

'What about him?' I asked innocently.

'Ellie, every time I mention his name you basically swoon. Everyone—including Ollie—knows you love him.'

'Oh fuck,' I said, feeling the blood rush from my face. 'Really?'

'Yes, you idiot. Even Yomi probably knows.'

'Ugh, whatever,' I said, deflated by the mention of the girl-friend. 'It's not like it's even an option. It's just a stupid crush. It doesn't mean anything. I just like looking at his face.'

'I reckon you like a bit more than his face.'

'I may have bumped into him in the hallway a few times in his towel post-shower.'

'Was his body as good as you'd imagined?'

'Let's just say I've now changed my shower schedule to increase my chances of bumping into him topless. Any-way, Miss Three-Dates-In-A-Month, I need your help with my dating life.'

'Oh yeah, Emma told me all about you camping out in the loo post-blood.' She grinned.

'Great, glad to hear my love life is providing so much entertainment for you all. But, seriously, Lara, I need a second date. I feel like everyone's lives are amazing and mine isn't just crap, it's, like, PG-rated.'

'I guess,' she said. 'But you do have a tendency to get a bit, um, not obsessed per se, but...stuck on certain things. I'm sure it will happen naturally if you let it.'

I stared at her blankly. 'Lara. Do we sit back and wait for jobs to offer themselves to us? Do we wait to win the lottery? No. We apply for jobs, we earn salaries, and we take action. I'm not going to *wait* for some guy to ask me out on a date and have sex with me—I'm going to find as many men as I can and make it happen for myself. In fact,' I said smugly, 'I've already messaged eight men on OKC today. So, I'm sure I'll have another date coming up soon.'

'Show me, show me,' she cried, grabbing my phone from my hands. 'Oh, wow, you've got a reply from one of them. Ben84. He looks attractive.'

'You don't need to sound so surprised.'

'And he works in graphic design, has a degree in philosophy, and he's five foot eleven. Not bad.'

'Are these the first things you look at? You don't read their sections?'

''Course not,' she said. 'I don't care what their favourite books and TV shows are. I just want to know their job, height, background and looks, obviously. Online dating is just like online shopping—you just scroll through looking at pictures and specs. Then you pick one and you either like it or return it. Easy. Oh, good, the cheese is here.'

By the end of my evening with Lara, I had a date lined

up with Ben84. We were going to go for drinks in Islington and I had the perfect bar in mind, complete with affordable wines and a handy escape route.

I leant my head against the glass window of the night bus and closed my eyes. It had been amazing catching up with Lara, discussing every miserable detail of our lives and flicking through men on the app. The only thing was I hadn't really been able to tell her that I was, well, nervous. Like, I was obviously really excited to go on this second date, and Ben84 did look promising. There was a strong chance I'd end up back at his.

It was all what I wanted, but it was also kind of terrifying. As fun as it was planning one-night stands, it kind of reminded me of the time I tried to lose my virginity to a stranger in a club and secretly knew it was a horrible idea. The idea of being totally naked in front of some random guy was terrifying. He'd see my lumpy body, my awkward tan lines, my pubes... What if he judged me? Worse, what if he rejected me?

Lara and Emma didn't really ever have to worry about that—they were both gorgeous in that typical, generic way. They waxed their pubes and they were size eights. If you got them naked in bed, you'd be getting exactly what you expected. With me, it was different. I could scrub up OK, but nothing could hide my cellulite and dark body hair when I was spreadeagled on a bed. I was scared of getting to a guy's bed and having him look at me with disappointment.

I tried to imagine what the girls would say. They'd just tell me I was ridiculous and looked fine naked, which is why I never told them this. I didn't need to hear that standard rubbish girls always spouted at each other to make them feel better. Besides, it was too embarrassing even for me to admit that I was also secretly frightened I had a gross vagina that smelt weird.

It was fine—I could cheer myself up. Boys didn't care about all that crap, right? They were excited just to have a naked girl opening her legs up for them. It was what I wanted too, for a number of reasons. Like…

1) *I've only been waiting my whole life for a chance to date and have multiple men and fun sex and actually* live *my life.*

2) *Everyone does it. Can finally see what all the fuss is about.*

3) *Haven't had an orgasm during sex yet. This is ideal way to have lots of sex and try out different things without being embarrassed.*

4) *Boys do it without a stigma, so I should too. Feminists would approve.*

5) *If it all goes to shit, I can run out of his house in the morning and will never have to see him again.*

I breathed out in relief. I was right—the pros of having one-night stands were endless. Con-wise there were hardly any issues.

1) *May fall in love with them.* But—very unlikely. Especially if stranger off the internet. Will hardly know them.

2) *If they don't call me again, I might get sad.* Fact of life—bad things happen. You'll get over it, Ellie. It's not like you haven't been rejected before.

3) *Might feel dirty and slutty.* Fine, but remember— other people think being slutty is bad but you can

choose the meaning you want it to have. Slutty is not necessarily a bad thing.

Five pros against three cons. I felt better. Fuck my body anxiety—I could just turn the lights off. It looked like Ben84 was going to get lucky.

Chapter 10

The past few days had passed in a blur. Maxine was still a bitch, Emma was with Sergio, Will was off shagging any-one and everyone, and Ollie was up in Bristol visiting Yomi. But it was finally Friday afternoon and I was going to meet Ben84. The only problem was that I wasn't sure where.

I pulled out my phone, hoping it would shed some light on where I should be in the next couple of hours. Thank God—there was a text from Ben. We had finally progressed from OKC messages to real life texting, aka the second-base equivalent of online dating.

Hey, so I know you have a bar in Angel in mind. But do you want to just meet me in the Waterstones bookshop on the high street first? I'll be in between Wittgenstein and Jung. 6pm.

What. The. Fuck.
He not only wanted to meet inside a bookshop, instead

of outside the tube station or the bar like a normal person, but he was going to be in…the artist aisles? Who even were these people?! I Googled them.

Ludwig Josef Johann Wittgenstein was an Austrian-British philosopher who worked primarily in logic, the philosophy of mathematics, the philosophy of mind and the philosophy of language.

Ah, right. So Wittgenstein was a philosopher not an artist. I was pretty sure Jung was another kind of communist like Marx but I Googled just to double-check.

Carl Gustav Jung, often referred to as C. G. Jung, was a Swiss psychiatrist and psychotherapist who founded analytical psychology.

Oops. Well, at least now I knew he was definitely going to be in the philosophy aisles. It kind of made sense because he studied it at university, but on no other level did I understand it. At all. It had to be a joke—no one could be that pretentious. I forwarded it to Emma for a second opinion. She called back.

'Emma,' I whispered, 'what the hell does it mean? Does he actually want me to go to the philosophy aisles of the bookshop to meet him?'

'Oh God, are you hiding in the loos at work again, Ellie? You can talk to people from your desk, you know?'

'Um, maybe at your chilled, cool PR firm, but not here. Anyway, Ben's message. What the actual fuck?'

'He's got to be kidding. No guy would ever write that seriously.'

'But his pictures were quite hipster. He wears thick glasses and skinny jeans.'

Emma scoffed. 'Babe, Justin Bieber fans wear hipster glasses. It means nothing any more.'

'Maybe, but either way, what do I reply to him?'

There was a long pause and then a loud shriek. 'Ohmigod, I've got it. I'm a genius. You need to text him back with something equally as witty.'

'Right. That's all very well in theory except for the teeny tiny obstacle that—'

'That you're not witty?' she interrupted. 'Do not worry, my young friend. I've got it.' The line went dead.

I sighed and got up off the closed loo seat and walked out of the cubicle. Maxine was standing there with her arms crossed.

'So, this is where you hang out on your lunch break, is it?' she asked, raising her recently threaded brows.

'Um, I just needed to make a quick personal call,' I mumbled.

'Yes, I gathered,' she said. 'So your next date is potentially a hipster who wants to meet in the philosophy section of a bookstore?'

I stared at her in silence. She arched her eyebrows higher and I coughed on air. 'Um, yes,' I eventually managed.

'That, Ellie, is very *London Mag*,' she said with a small smile. 'You're going to write about it for me. A column. The single life. I want minuscule details, I want embarrassing facts, and I want honesty. Brutal, painful "ohmigod, her life is horrendous" honesty. Got it? And can you shut your mouth, please, you look like a goldfish.'

Obediently, I closed my mouth. Then I opened it again.

'Hang on, I…haven't got it. You want me to write a column? On being single in London and dating?'

She nodded. 'Exactly. Now, do I have to repeat myself any more or are we all good here?'

'Um…how many words?' I asked.

She grinned. 'Finally, a real question. Four hundred words for each Friday. So I want it by Tuesday so you have time to edit it. Make it funny. We can call it "NSFW", like "Not Safe For Work". It'll be fun. You can start with this philosophy date, or the one that nose-bled on you last week.'

I choked again. 'How…how do you know that?'

'Please, Ellie, I know every tiny little thing that goes on in this office. And next time you want to complain about me, please don't use the office email system. Your personal one will suffice for those purposes, I think, don't you?'

I nodded mutely and she turned around on her Russell & Bromley brogues.

Had Maxine just given me a column? To write about myself? I stared at myself in the mirror and grinned maniacally. I was basically a twenty-two-year-old version of Carrie Bradshaw without the shoes or annoying habits. Everything was finally going my way—except had Maxine mentioned money? Oh fuck it. Writing experience was probably more important than a salary anyway.

This was amazing. I could have a cool anonymous column, write all about my dates in total detail, and then I'd be a mysterious insta-celeb with a portfolio of past work. She'd have to pay me eventually and I could stop feeling guilty about spending my mum's money. I looked at myself in the mirror, smiling at the frizzy-haired reflection. Who knew I'd turn out to be so successful?

I pulled out my phone to send a message to the girls. I

was going to send one to my mum too, but then decided I'd better save that for when the salary was confirmed.

The phone beeped immediately with a reply from Emma. I opened it with a grin, waiting for the inevitable emojis and exclamation marks.

6pm sounds good. You'll find me in between *Twilight* and *The Hunger Games*.

I laughed out loud. That was definitely more useful than a congratulatory message. Maybe I should just forward it on to Ben. Hopefully he would see that it was an obvious joke, and if not, it would just be great fodder for my new anon column.

He replied within seconds.

Ha ha. We'll see who comes to find who first...

Right. Well, that didn't shed any light on where we were actually meeting. And what if *Twilight* was actually really far away from *The Hunger Games*? Which one would I stand near?? Why the hell was dating so *complicated*?

Oh fuck it. We lived in a modern age, and if he couldn't find me next to some popular teen fiction, he could damn well call me. Besides, I was going to be an actual, published writer.

* * *

I was standing in Waterstones and had no idea where Ben was. This was the most humiliating rendezvous I had ever experienced. I was so stressed that even the thought of my new column couldn't cheer me up. My day-to-night outfit—a midi-length black dress with ankle boots and leather jacket—no longer felt sexy. I'd gone between the philosophy and teen fiction aisles so many times now that I had rivers of sweat dripping down my cleavage.

I pulled my phone out hoping he had messaged to say exactly where he was but…nothing. I walked over to the philosophy section again and stood there with my arms crossed. If he wanted to go on this date, he could come and find me right here.

Five minutes later, I was back in the teen fiction section searching for him. It was 6.15 p.m. and I was no closer to finding my date. Then I felt a tap on my shoulder. I whirled around and finally came face-to-face with Ben84.

'Ellie?' he asked. He had floppy brown hair, was exactly my height—which meant the five foot eleven thing was a definite lie—wore cute black-rimmed glasses and was dressed in grey jeans with a checked shirt. He looked relatively attractive but, more important, was not seventy years old.

'Hey,' I said nervously. 'You found me.'

'Yeah. Sorry about the whole bookshop thing. I just saw on your profile that you like reading, so I thought it could be cute. I didn't really think about the logistics though, so that backfired a bit.'

I smiled back at him with a new rush of affection and hoped he was thinking that I looked exactly like my pictures too.

'You know,' he said, 'you don't look like your profile picture.'

The smile dropped off my face. 'Sorry?'

'No, don't worry, you look better than your pictures. More…my style, I guess.'

'Right,' I said slowly. 'Cheers?'

'No worries. So shall we go to this bar, then?'

'Yes, definitely,' I said, resisting the urge to wipe the sweat away from my cleavage. 'Let's go.'

'Well, hello there.' Pete-the-barman grinned. 'You're back. And there's another one.'

'Another what?' asked Ben.

I let out a bark of laughter. 'Oh, nothing. I was here last week with some friends and met Pete.'

'Cool. I'm Ben. Nice to meet you.'

Pete reached out across the bar to shake Ben's hand and gave me a not-so-subtle wink. I rolled my eyes and dragged Ben across to the other side of the bar.

'Let's just order here,' I said. 'What are you getting?'

'Just a pint, I reckon. You?'

'A glass of white wine, I think.'

'OK,' he said and leant across to order our drinks. I looked around the bar idly and found myself staring at Pete. I couldn't figure out if I was attracted to him or not. He was definitely flirty, but was he actually good-looking? His dreads looked kinda dirty. 'Here you go,' said Ben.

'Oh God, thanks. Sorry, I was totally in my own world there. Shit, have you paid?' I asked.

'Yep, don't worry about it,' he said, as I started reaching for my purse.

'Sorry, I didn't even notice. I'll definitely get the next ones,' I promised.

'Cool,' he said. 'Cheers.' We clinked glasses and then he looked at me expectantly. 'So, tell me about yourself.'

'Wow, OK. Um, that's a pretty big question. I don't even know where to begin.'

'How about you just start with what you do for a living,

and what you like doing in your spare time, and all that standard crap,' he suggested.

'Excuse me, Ben, are you saying you didn't read any of that "standard crap" when it was all nicely laid out on my profile?' I asked in mock-horror.

He grinned. 'OK, you've got me. I just saw your picture and figured that was all that mattered. Have you been on any dates from it before, then?'

Should I tell him that on my first attempt someone bled on me two metres from where we're standing, or should I pretend I'm a total novice? Honesty. Always total honesty.

'Just one, but it was pretty uneventful,' I said. 'No spark. What about you?'

'Yeah, I've been on quite a few. Well, not that many, but it's just a really cool way to meet people, you know? And it's chilled. There's not that many expectations and you can kind of just see how things go.'

'Yeah, I get that.' I nodded. 'So, you work as a graphic designer, right? And how old are you?'

'Oh, so now it's your turn for the twenty questions, eh? But, yes, I'm a graphic designer. Have been for a few years. I'm twenty-nine now. Studied philosophy at uni and, as you can probably tell, I'm still quite keen on it.'

'Wittgenstein?'

'And Jung, obviously,' he said with a grin, pronouncing it with a 'Y'. I silently congratulated myself for not having attempted to say it. 'How about another drink?'

'Sure. Can you make mine a large?'

A few hours and too many glasses of wine later, I was kissing Ben as though my life depended on it. I saw Pete watching us out of the corner of my eye, but after snogging Ben for about fifteen minutes, Pete was long gone.

'Ellie, do you… Do you want to come back to mine?' asked Ben shyly.

Oh my God. It was happening. I was about to have my first ever ONS. Was I wearing matching underwear?

'Sure,' I said. 'Cab? Night bus? What works for you?'

He looked a bit taken aback, then grinned. 'A cab will get us there quicker. Let's go outside and I'll call us one.'

'Perfect. I'm just going to run to the loo first, and then I'll come upstairs and meet you there. Plan?'

'Yeah, great,' he said. 'So long as you don't do a runner!'

I smiled weakly. 'Would I ever do something like that?'

He got up and left the bar. I rushed to the loo and inspected my reflection. I had done smoky-eye make-up earlier, which meant that the more it smudged, the more it just looked as if it was the effect I was going for. My hair was getting a bit poufy so I pulled it into a tight bun, and put on another layer of lipstick. My lips were chafed from rubbing against Ben's stubble, but I didn't care. Because I was about to have *sex*. With a semi-stranger. In his flat in… I made a mental note to ask him where he lived, so I could text Emma and Lara. Safety first.

As I exited the loo, I bumped into Pete. 'Oh, hey,' I said.

'I see this date is going noticeably better than the last,' said Pete. 'Although, again you're in the loo and he's not here. Do you make a habit of abandoning your dates?'

'Never! What an audacious sushestion,' I cried. Maybe I was drunker than I'd realised.

'Well, I'm glad your date's gone,' he said. 'Because I wanted a moment alone with you.'

Oh God. Was he…coming onto me? Could I kiss two men in one night—especially with my date upstairs waiting to take me home and fuck my brains out? I felt a grin spread uncontrollably across my face. Of course I could.

'You did?' I asked him, trying to make my eyes wide and sexy.

'Yeah,' he said nervously. I opened my lips apart slightly and angled my head to the side, so he would know I was willing to let him kiss me. He looked straight into my eyes and leant towards me. This was it—I was going to snog the barman while my date ordered a cab. This was such great material for 'Never Have I Ever'. Shame it hadn't happened in time for university.

I closed my eyes as Pete came nearer, waiting for his lips to touch mine. Instead, I felt something nibble my cheek.

'OW,' I screeched, wrenching my eyes open. 'What the fuck? Did you just…bite me?!'

He backed away and laughed awkwardly. 'No, I, um… Yeah. Yeah, I guess I did,' he said, looking firmly at the floor.

I stared at him. 'But…why?'

'Just, um, thought it would be fun,' he said with an embarrassed shrug.

'Right. What? I… Sorry, am I missing something here?'

'No, it was just a little bite.'

I stared at him in incomprehension. What the fuck was happening?? He looked down at the floor. I shook my head. I would deal with this in the morning.

'OK,' I said. 'Well, I'd, um, better get going. So, bye?'

'Wait, can I have your number first, Ellie? Please?'

'Um, yeah, fine,' I said, taking the phone he was holding out to me. I tapped my number out, then gave it back to him, vowing to never, ever return to this bar again. 'I'd better go, but, um, have a good night.'

I walked quickly out of the bar without looking behind me. I had no idea what had just happened, but all I wanted to do was call Lara. Instead, I had to go home with an internet date who liked Wittgenstein. This was not a good sign.

'Ellie, hey,' said Ben, as I walked out of the bar.

I reminded myself that he was more attractive than Pete, didn't have dreadlocks and, most important, had not bitten me. I greeted him back with a long kiss.

'Well, hello.' He grinned. 'The cab's here.'

'Oh yeah, where are we going?'

'Hoxton.'

'Oh, perfect, near me,' I said, climbing into the back seat of the cab. It was a battered Honda with tape across one of the windowpanes. *Please be a registered minicab,* I prayed. *Are you listening, Caesar? Or even you, God? I don't want to die without having a real orgasm.*

Chapter 11

'It's this one,' gasped Ben, as we stood snogging in the hallway. He pushed me into his bedroom and straight onto the double bed in the middle of the room. We had kissed non-stop for the fifteen-minute cab ride to his, and now we were both ready to fuck. 'God I've wanted you all night,' he breathed into my neck.

I couldn't think of anything to say, so I chose not to reply. Instead, I used all my energy to focus on not throwing up whilst snogging him.

He pinned my arms up above my head and pulled my dress off in one swift move. He had definitely done this before. I tried not to think about my tummy being on show and quickly undid my bra so he would be too distracted by my boobs to notice my lower lumps.

'You're so sexy,' he said, nuzzling into my cleavage. I giggled in response, wondering what I was meant to do when his head was nowhere near my face. I settled for rubbing my hands across his back, but he took this as an invitation to lower himself down the bed, further away from my face. He pulled off my tights and knickers.

I lay on his bed stark naked with my trimmed pubes on show. I forced myself to breathe calmly. I did not care that he could see my pubes. I was a feminist. I didn't believe in pulling out every hair. I had tried shaving, hair removal creams, waxing, and all had ended in painful humiliation, so I had opted for scissors. It was fine, normal even.

He took his glasses off and came up close to my vagina as though he was inspecting it. Then he pulled apart the lips and gently slipped his tongue out onto my clitoris. I gasped. It was not in pleasure.

I never knew what to do when someone was licking me out—even though it had happened only once before—and all I could think was that he was licking the little trimmed hairs on my labia majora. Besides, what if it smelt badly? I'd been at work all day; it was probably really sweaty down there.

I pulled him up towards me and began snogging him again. 'Wait, I've got something in my mouth,' he said.

Oh my God. A pube. It had to be. I must have missed one and he had a long strand in his mouth.

I sat frozen as he pulled something out of his mouth. We squinted at it in the dim light. It wasn't a pube. It was a white little wad of...paper?

He'd found loo roll inside my vagina.

I wanted to scream, but instead I sprung into action. I grabbed it from him, flicked it away and said, 'Oh, looks like some random fluff.'

He shrugged. 'Weird.'

I breathed out in relief. He hadn't figured out what it was. I flung my arms around him and distracted him with kisses. He closed his eyes and snogged me back. The crisis was averted. Thank fuck he hadn't realised that while he'd been licking my clitoris he'd also been licking old loo roll. God, how long had it been there?!

The thought of urine-stained toilet paper was not helping me get in the mood for sex. I had to focus. This was more important than a minor paper mishap. I needed to get Ben naked. I started trying to undo the buttons on his shirt, but he rescued me from my fumbling efforts and pulled his shirt off. He did the same with his jeans until they got stuck around his ankles.

'Are you OK?' I asked.

'Fine,' he grunted. 'For fuck's sake, these jeans are so bloody tight sometimes.'

'Yep, guess they're called skinny jeans for a reason,' I quipped.

He ignored me and pulled them off with a triumphant tug, taking his boxers with them. I tried to sneak a look at his penis, but he was angled away from me and it was dark.

I lay back on his bed, nervous. Oh God. This was finally about to happen. I was officially terrified. 'Do you, um, have a…condom?'

'Shit, I don't know,' he said. 'Can we do it without?'

I sat up straight in the bed. Without?! Did he want me to give him my leftover chlamydia? Or give me his?? I opened my mouth to categorically tell him no we could not, but no words came out. *Pull yourself together, Elena,* I yelled at myself, using the name only my mother ever used. The thought of my mother jolted me into action. She would kill me if I got AIDS.

'No,' I said firmly.

He sighed and started looking around his room for a condom. 'Got one.'

'Great.'

I smiled nervously as he started slipping it on. He came closer to me in the dark and lowered his body on top of mine. We kissed gently and I ran my hands over his body. He was so toned, and his muscles rippled as he groaned. I lowered my hand towards his penis. I felt his snail trail and followed it down. That was funny...the hair leading down his tummy to his penis was spiky. And it was in a very thin line.

I got out my other hand and touched the line down to his penis. It carried on all the way. But where were his pubes?! Frantically, I searched across his groin, but I couldn't feel any pubes. It was all smooth except for the thin line going down. If he were a woman, I'd say he had a Brazilian landing strip.

I jolted up and pushed him off me.

'What's wrong?' he asked.

'Oh, nothing,' I said. 'Just, um, can we put the light on for a sec?'

'Sure.' He grinned. 'Sorry, I thought you'd be like most girls and prefer fucking in the dark.' He flicked a light switch and suddenly I was face-to-face with his naked body. His pubes were shaved so that he had a thin line, about two millimetres wide, going down from his belly button to his penis.

It was a boy Brazilian. I stopped myself from crying out in shock. I had to stay calm. Boyzilians were probably a thing, and I just hadn't seen enough penises to come across one before. It was fine—we could still have sex. I was so close to getting what I wanted and finally doing what everyone else did. I had to keep going or I'd never find out what all the fuss was about.

'Ben, I'm so sorry.' I sighed. 'I just… I'm not sure I can do this.'

'What? Why not?' he asked.

'Just, um, I don't feel great.'

'Fine, whatever,' he said, clearly pissed off. 'Are you… uh, bussing it home, then?'

I stared at him in shock. He wanted me to leave his flat. In the early predawn hours. He didn't want me in his bed and I would have to walk through a council estate to get home. How was any of this happening? *He* was the one who'd ruined this with his pubes.

'Bussing it?' I cried out. 'Excuse me? It's, like, three in the morning.'

'Sorry,' he said, looking guilty. 'I didn't mean that. I just meant you don't have to stay if you don't want to.'

'I think it's probably best if I just stay and leave in the morning,' I said slowly. I knew I should probably get a cab home—especially as he was basically kicking me out—but I didn't really want to pay for one and there was no way I was getting a night bus alone. As humiliating as it was, I was staying right there.

'OK,' he said, turning the light off and getting into bed. I lay down next to him and he put an arm over me and squeezed my boobs. I was tempted to push him off me, but if we weren't going to shag, he may as well get to hold my 36Ds as a consolation prize.

When he started snoring gently, I eased his arm off me and searched frantically for my phone. I had to tell the girls what had happened. I opened WhatsApp.

Me: He has a Boyzilian. As in, shaved and trimmed pubes in a thin line. His man garden is neater than mine.
Me: Also. Oh God. He found loo roll in my vagina. With his tongue.

I sent the message to Emma and Lara, but neither answered. They were probably asleep. I closed my eyes and tried to do the same, but all I could think about were his manicured pubes and my filthy vagina. How, *how* had I managed to find the only man in London who had neater pubes than me?

It was so embarrassing. But at the same time, I was kind of relieved we hadn't slept together. As much as I wanted to start having casual sex, I didn't want to be repulsed by the person I was shagging—if I wanted to orgasm with them, it was probably a good idea if I actually liked the guy. Not enough to crave a relationship and second date, but just to feel some kind of…connection.

Ben and I didn't have that. It wasn't even just the Boyzilian—he was also kind of dull. And weirdly pale. In a strange way, he reminded me of Jack the Deflowerer. I shuddered.

No, this failed one-night stand was definitely a good thing. There was no point shagging someone I didn't like. I deserved better.

Chapter 12

I woke up in a panic. I was lying in a bed with no bed sheets. I could feel the scratchy material of the mattress and duvet against my bare skin. Ohmigod—my bare skin. I pulled the duvet off me and looked down. I was totally naked. I scanned the bed for any other signs of life, but there was nobody next to me.

I felt something soggy stuck to my leg. I reached down and found the unused condom from last night attached to me. I yanked it off, flinging it across the room, and then lay back down in the bed with my eyes shut as everything flooded back. Ben. His Boyzilian. Loo roll. Hoxton. Pete biting my cheek. Oh God.

I needed to get the fuck out of there.

I tiptoed down the hallway in last night's black dress, with my jacket slung over my shoulder. The walls were covered in a peeling paint and the floorboards had nails poking out. I heard sounds in the kitchen and poked my head round. Ben was in there wearing tight white boxers. He had his back to me and I could see the defined muscles in his arse. I felt a pang of lust and then remembered his man garden.

'Ben?' I called out. 'I've got to, um, get home.'

He turned to face me, holding two mugs. Oh God. It was looking at me again. The skinny Boyzilian. In the cold light of day I could see how dark the hairs were against his milky-white skin. I felt like gagging. 'What, already?' he said. 'I was just bringing us tea. I remember your profile saying you love Earl Grey.'

'Um, thanks,' I said, trying to avert my eyes from his Boyzilian. 'But, honestly, I have to leave.'

'Oh, right.' He put the teas down looking pissed off. 'Guess I'll show you out, then.'

'Cheers.'

We walked in silence to the front door. 'So it's just down the stairs, then you turn right to the nearest bus stop.'

'Cool, thanks,' I said. He looked straight into my eyes and leant in to kiss me. I moved my head so his lips brushed against my cheek. I could smell last night's food on his breath. 'Bye, then!'

'I'll call you,' he cried out, as I raced down the stairs.

Who knew I'd ever be the kind of girl who had guys wanting to call her? In spite of everything, I felt a warm glow of pride. I'd turned down a guy. I hadn't exactly achieved my sex goal, but I'd made a sensible decision and now I had a not-hideous man chasing me. This was so *Sex and the City.*

* * *

'Fuck me harder,' moaned a male voice. I stood frozen outside of the living room. It must be the TV. Was someone watching *Basic Instinct*? Or maybe a 10 a.m. porno? I edged the door open and peered round.

'Is this hard enough for you, you filthy bastard?' said Will.

I screamed. Will was standing behind a guy, thrusting his penis into him. He was waving a black whip in the air. The guy was on all fours moaning loudly. They both turned to look at me.

'Ellie, get the fuck out of here,' shouted Will, as he carried on thrusting himself into his partner. *Why* was he continuing when I was right there?? I tried to leave but found I was paralysed to the spot. 'What are you even doing here?' he asked. 'You're meant to be on a one-night stand.'

'I left,' I said. 'Why are you, um, shagging in the living room?'

'Sorry, we thought everyone was out,' said the guy on his knees. 'I'm Raj by the way.'

'I'm Ellie, nice to meet you,' I replied automatically. Raj moaned in response and I jolted back to life. I spun on my heels, running out of the room and slamming the door as I left.

'Ah,' I screamed, as I crashed into Ollie. 'Oh God, sorry, I didn't see you. I just… I walked in on…'

'Will and Raj? Don't worry, I did the same thing about five minutes ago.'

'What is wrong with them? Can't they just do it in Will's room?'

He shrugged. 'I wish I knew. Tea?'

'Please.' I followed him into the kitchen and sat down at the table. 'I'm so shattered.'

'Same. I went out with the boys and it got pretty messy. I think I might still be drunk.'

I laughed. 'I wish I was still drunk. I'm depressingly sober.'

'Did you just get home? What were you doing last night?'

'Oh, don't ask. I had another online date. I went back to his, and it didn't go so well.'

He put down the kettle and turned to look at me. 'Yeah?'

'We didn't sleep together. I kind of…decided not to.'

'Why not? You stayed at his though, right?'

'Yeah, I just don't think I fancied him in the end. We were really close to doing it, but then I figured that I wanted more. You know? Like, he was fine. It would have been OK. But it just didn't feel right, and as much as I want to get laid, I want to enjoy it.'

'Hey, good on you,' he said, plonking a mug down in front of me. 'I wish I'd thought like that when I was single.'

'You didn't?' I couldn't imagine Ollie ever sleeping with someone unattractive or regretting it. Surely he'd just shagged the hottest girls at uni?

'I dunno. I've had a few regrettable one-night stands, but I haven't really done the whole dating thing. I met Yomi pretty early, and, yeah.'

'You're lucky. Dating is shit.'

He laughed. 'I don't know. Sounds like you're owning it. Turning down guys who are into you, and constantly lining up new dates.'

'You're making it sound a lot better than it feels,' I said, grinning at him. He may have had zero sleep but he still looked effortlessly hot. If Ben had looked like him, I definitely would have shagged him—Boyzilian or no Boyzilian.

'Hey, is that your phone?' he said.

I pulled my eyes away from his light stubble and picked up my phone. 'Oh God. Please can this text not be from Ben. I really can't deal with that right now.'

Unknown number: Hey, sorry about the weirdness last night. Would love to take you for dinner to apologise. I think you're really cool, and I maybe have a bit of a crush on you… Pete.

I burst out laughing. 'No way.'

'Who is it?' asked Ollie. 'Is it Ben?'

'Um, so I kind of left out a bit of my story of last night… I went back to the bar I went to with JT. And the same barman was there. We had a weird moment where I think he bit me? And now he wants to take me for dinner "to apologise".'

Ollie shook his head laughing. 'See? You've got all the guys.'

'I do not,' I said.

But he had a point. Pete was the second guy in less than twenty-four hours who wanted me. I mean, I wasn't sure if I fancied him, and I was still weirded out by the *Twilight* moment, but it did feel good.

'So are you going to say yes?'

'Huh. I really don't know. I mean, he's attractive, and he's pretty cool. I think he'd be a really fun date. But…'

'He has vampire tendencies?'

'Well, yeah. But, also, I'm not sure I'm feeling it. I mean, there are, like, shitloads of men online. I don't really have to say yes to Pete just because he ticks a few boxes. I can probably find someone better online. I don't want to settle, you know?'

'I do,' he said, staring at me. Why didn't guys who look like Ollie ask me out? 'So what are you going to say to him?'

'Oh God. I've never written a rejection text before. Can't I just ignore him?'

'What, and miss out on your first ever rejection text? No way. And do you know how it feels to be the guy and not get a response? It's shit.'

'What, like that's ever happened to you?' I scoffed.

'Yeah, of course it has. I'm a guy. I ask out girls. Sometimes they don't respond. And I always wish they'd have the courtesy to actually say no instead of leaving me to wonder if they've lost their phone or whatever.'

'Wait, you actually think that? I thought that was a girl thing.'

'Nope. Boys get it too. So, do me a favour and let this guy down properly.'

I laughed. 'OK. How about…this?' I typed out a response and showed it to Ollie.

Hey, Pete, thanks, but I don't really feel the same way… Sorry. And maybe next time, don't bite the girl you fancy.

'Ouch. I'm starting to feel pretty sorry for this Pete.' Ollie grinned. 'I'd hate to get turned down by you, Ellie.'

'Well, you know…' I laughed awkwardly. Little did Ollie know there was no way in hell I would ever reject him. Even if he bit me and had a Boyzilian.

Chapter 13

NSFW

Dating in London is hard. Really, really hard. It doesn't even matter if you're not looking for a long-term relationship—it's hard enough to get some casual fun. I know because that's exactly what I'm trying to do.

Now, before you start imagining me as a sex-starved, middle-aged woman with warts, let me tell you that I am twenty-two years old and wart-less. I am at the age where everyone assumes I should be having wanton flings and going on a different date every Saturday night.

I am not.

But it isn't for want of trying. Now that I've graduated from uni, I don't meet new people constantly. Instead, I spend most days at work, and see my closest friends on weekends. It is rare for me to meet new, single and interested boys.

Which is why I started online dating. I figured it would

be the perfect way for me to meet new guys without even having to take off my dressing gown or shave my legs. So far, I have been on two dates.

Date 1: Tall, attractive and nice. We met in central London and went for a Chinese dinner. Unfortunately I had already eaten dinner, so he probably thought I was one of those dieters who never lose weight. But things went better from there. We headed to a bar, got drunk together and ended up kissing.

Until he nose-bled on me. Then I hid in the loo till he was gone, and exited via a fire escape.

Date 2: A cute hipster who wanted to meet in a bookshop. This was stressful. I couldn't find him in the philosophy aisles and he couldn't find me by The Hunger Games. *I have vowed that from now on I will meet my dates in more concrete places.*

I took him to my bar with a fire escape. I should have used it. Instead, I ended up back at his and came face-to-face with his manicured pubes. He had a landing strip and I didn't. I fled.

These are my dating experiences so far. But I will not give up hope, dear readers. I will battle on through the blood and Boyzilians to find my dream date. And, more important, I will tell you every detail of my escapades...

'Good,' said Maxine.

'Just…good?' I asked her.

'Don't push it, Ellie,' she snapped. 'It's good and doesn't need much editing. But I'll send you my edits later. I'll put it online on Friday.'

'Awesome.' I grinned. 'I wonder if people will guess who it is.'

'Well, they won't have much guessing to do because it will have your name right at the bottom with a photograph,' she said, tapping away at her keyboard.

'What?' I cried out. 'I thought it was going to be anonymous.'

Maxine snorted. 'Please, Ellie. No one wants to hear the confessions of some nameless twenty-two-year-old. They want a name to Google and a picture to judge.'

'But…but I spoke about his *pubes*. And I said I'm not sex-starved. But I kind of insinuated that I am. Oh my God, my MOTHER,' I shrieked.

Maxine looked up from her Mac with a sigh. 'Can you take this existential breakdown elsewhere, please? I'm doing you a favour publishing this with your name. It'll be good for your career in the long run.'

'Yeah, if I want to be the next Belle de Jour.'

'I think you have a way to go before you get there, Ellie,' she said, dismissing me with a wave of her hand.

I stared at her aghast before slowly turning around and exiting her glass-walled office. This was not good. I had essentially given Maxine a carte blanche to publish my innermost secrets. For free.

I grabbed my coat and wallet. This justified a non-instant coffee. I speed-dialled Lara as I ran down the stairs of the office and straight into Pret.

'Not at work, then?' she asked.

'Minor, minor crisis,' I said, mid deep breaths, trying to practise yoga in the middle of the queue. Omm. Omm.

'Bitten? Bled on?'

'More that I just wrote about all of that for a column for Maxine.'

'Oh yeah. How did it go?'

'Well, I thought I was doing it anonymously. And I'm not,' I finished. If I sounded calm, maybe I'd feel it.

'Holy fuck,' screeched Lara. 'It's going to be all over the internet with your name?!'

'And a photograph,' I replied twitchily. Her reaction was not conducive to my attempted yogic state.

'So, everyone, as in literally every single person we know including your mum and my grandma, is going to hear about your dates. And your unsuccessful love life,' she said.

'Yes.'

'So just to reiterate, it's—'

'Yes!' I shrieked.

I took a deep breath. 'Sorry. I'm just a bit stressed about it and I'm trying to stay calm.'

'But, Ellie, couldn't this possibly be very damaging for your career? Like, not just disastrous for your friends and family, but it might stop you ever working in a really serious job. How can you be a war reporter if you've been writing about Boyzilians?' she asked.

'I know,' I said in a tiny voice. 'I always secretly thought it would be quite cool if I reported in Syria or something. And maybe saved a child's life while I was there.'

'You need to tell Maxine this isn't an option,' she said.

'Well, I tried, but you know what she's like. She flat-out refused.'

'Ellie, I'm studying law. This is so illegal. Not only is she making you work as much as a full-time paid employee, but now she's exploiting your rights. You could take her to tribunal. You could sue her.'

'Yeah, like I'm going to sue a magazine that earns millions of pounds each year. Actually, do you think I could earn millions by suing?'

'Well, probably not,' she said. 'But you should stand up to Maxine anyway.'

'But then she'll just tell me to resign. And then I won't have anything. Besides, maybe, like possibly, this is a really good thing to happen. If my column is really successful, then I could actually be the new Carrie Bradshaw. Except a less irritating, younger, poorer version.'

'I guess,' said Lara doubtfully. 'But is this the kind of journalism you want to do?'

'I don't know. I suppose I'm better at it than I would be at court reporting. But if I'd known she was going to name me, I would have just taken out the most explicit stuff.'

'I think that's the stuff that's going to make it popular though, Ellie. Otherwise it's just the vague thoughts of a twenty-something-year-old.'

'Ugh, why is our society so obsessed with *sex*?'

'Are you actually kidding me?' she said. 'Out of everyone I know, you are by far the most obsessed with anything sex-related.'

'But I barely even have sex.'

'And how often do you think about it?'

'Every ten minutes. But that's normal, right?'

'For a teenage boy going through puberty,' she declared.

'Oh, sod off,' I said. 'I'd better go and get myself a coffee before Maxine wonders where I've got to.'

'Good luck.'

I hung up and bought myself a flat white. This was fine. Absolutely fine. I would just become a famous columnist. It couldn't be that hard. I just had to be funny, honest and amazing.

Oh God, I was fucked. My column would crash and burn

and I would forever be the cringe girl that tried to write humorously about Boyzilians and failed. I sipped my drink and burnt my tongue. Bad omen number one, tick.

Chapter 14

I walked into the living room and collapsed onto the sofa. Then I remembered Will and Raj shagging in the middle of the room and went up to my bedroom instead. I was exhausted. Maxine had made me edit my column about four times and my eyes were searing from reading the words that would soon be published worldwide. All I wanted to do was curl up in front of a shitty TV show and turn off my brain.

'I'm a survivor and I'm not gonna give up...' It was the ringtone Emma had chosen for herself on my phone.

'What's up?' I sighed.

'OK, please don't hate me and I will love you for life if you do this, and you're amazing and—'

'Get to the point, please,' I interrupted. 'I have a *Hollyoaks* omnibus and a large Aero with my name on it.'

'Oh no,' she wailed. 'The thing is, Ellie, I wouldn't normally ask but you know tonight is mine and Sergio's anniversary?'

'You've been together a year?' I asked, creasing up my

forehead. How did that work? I swear they hadn't known each other for a whole year.

'It's our official eight months,' she said. 'Anyway, I've come to his house to surprise him with dinner. I've made it all and I've got it with me, but I left the keys in my room. And he's coming soon and I don't have time to come back and get here again, and…'

I sighed loudly. My evening plans were slowly ebbing away. 'Fine, I'll do it. He lives in Islington, right?'

'Yes, ohmigod, I love you so much, you're incredible,' she cried. 'The keys are in my room, in the top dresser, in the drawer with the lube.'

''Course they are. OK, I'll jump on the bus and be with you soon.'

'Would you, um, possibly mind getting the overground instead? I just think it will be quicker.'

'Fine.' I sighed, mentally trying to work out how much more a train journey cost. 'See you soon.'

'Thankyousomuch. I owe you majorly.'

I walked across Highbury Fields to Sergio's flat. It didn't take me long to spot Emma outside. She was wearing her trademark leopard-print fur coat and was surrounded by two huge bags. I couldn't help smiling as I approached her. She threw herself fully into everything she did. It was my favourite thing about her.

'Ellie,' she cried. 'Thank you so, so, so much for this. I love you.'

'No worries,' I said, waving the keys in front of her. 'So, what's the big plan, then?'

'Well, I have a Spanish feast cooked to perfection inside these two bags.' She gestured to the large Ikea bags at her feet. 'Gazpacho, then a tortilla and then flan for dessert.'

'Whoa,' I said, genuinely impressed. 'When did you find the time to make them all?'

'Oh, over the weekend,' she said, waving her hand. 'I froze it all. I know Serge works late on Wednesdays at the moment, so he won't be home until 8 p.m. Which is perfect for me, because I can set out the dinner and then when he gets here it will be a total surprise.'

I grinned in spite of myself. Her enthusiasm was infectious. 'Very cute,' I said. 'Now, can you open the door already so I can pee?'

'Oh, right, yeah. Grab a bag, will you?' She opened the door and we climbed up the stairs to Sergio's studio flat. 'Here it is,' she said, as she fumbled with the key. 'Ta-da!'

The studio flat was quite large. It had a big living room/ bedroom with a small kitchenette on the side with a little table. The floor was wooden and there was a big white bed in the middle of the room. It was moving.

I turned to look at Emma. Her face was pale as she stared at the moaning mound on the bed moving rhythmically. I tried to take her hand, but she brushed me off.

'Sergio?' she said.

The mound stopped moving. 'Fuck,' it said. The white sheet slowly dropped off it to reveal Sergio lying on top of a pair of legs. He turned to face Emma as the woman underneath pulled the sheet over her.

'Emma... I'm so... What...what are you doing here?' he stuttered.

'It's our eight-month anniversary,' she said with tears in her eyes. 'I'm here to surprise you with a dinner.'

'Eight months?' cried the voice under Sergio. 'You told me you were ending it with her. Not celebrating a fucking anniversary.'

'I'm sorry,' he breathed out. His normally olive face looked pale. 'Emma, I feel so awful.' He stood up, fumbling for his clothes. He pulled a pair of jeans on. 'I didn't want you to find out like this.'

'Find out what?' asked Emma bravely. I gulped. I should not be here. This was awful. Awful. The worst thing ever and I was here watching it. I stepped back into the shadows of the hallway and looked at Emma with tears in my eyes. She was so brave. She lifted her chin in the air and stared determinedly at her boyfriend. 'What exactly *is* this little sordid situation? I'm guessing it's not just a one-time fuck. So how long has it been happening?'

'Um, I think, maybe, a few weeks,' murmured Sergio. 'I'm so sorry, Emma.'

'Why? Just...why would you do this?'

'I don't know,' he said, running his hand through his hair. 'I just felt things were getting a bit...stale. And then I met Hannah at work. And...I fell for her.'

'You love her?' Emma's voice was getting more strangled now.

'I think so,' he said, looking down at the floor.

'Right,' she said. There was a moment's pause when Sergio tried to speak again, but Emma held her hand up to him. 'Sergio, just shut the fuck up,' she said. He closed his mouth. Emma turned to face the woman. She was a brunette with huge boobs and lots of make-up. She looked older than us. 'So you knew about me?' she asked.

The woman scowled. 'He told me he was ending it.'

'But why didn't you wait till he ended it? Why did you help him cheat? Love?' she asked.

'I thought if we started fucking he would see how good

it is and end things with you,' the woman said. I winced on behalf of Emma, but she didn't move.

'Sergio. You are a complete cunt, and I will never forgive you for not being honest with me. If you stop loving someone, you tell them. You don't cheat on them. Because...' Her voice started breaking. 'Now you've hurt me so much more than you could have ever imagined.'

Sergio had the decency to look devastated. 'Emma, I did love you,' he said. I saw her go pale at the past tense.

'I will get over you, and I will be OK,' she said. 'And one day, I'll be a million times stronger because of this. While all you've done is show me how pathetic you really are. I have... I have zero respect for you.'

She turned around and walked past me to go down the stairs. I grabbed the bags and stared at the half-naked pair standing frozen in the room. 'I'd just like to reiterate that you're a complete cunt, and I think you're an evil bitch,' I said, before slamming the door shut.

We sat on the grass surrounded by the bags of food. 'Lucky you can eat Spanish food cold,' said Emma, as she shoved tortilla into her mouth. She'd stopped crying and now she was determined to eat all of the food she'd made for Sergio. 'Pass me the Rioja.' I passed her the bottle of wine and she poured half of it into her mouth. 'Much better, thanks,' she said.

'Em, you were incredible in there,' I said softly. 'I'm so proud of you for being so calm and not losing your shit. I feel like it was the best you could have done in that...that fucking horrible situation.'

'What else could I have done, El?' she replied wearily. 'If I broke his shit and attacked him, he'd just think I was a typical crazy woman. If I yelled at the woman, I would have just given him an opportunity to protect her.'

I nodded and squeezed her shoulder. 'You're amazing. Just to make that totally clear. He is a pathetic useless wanker and you're the best person I know.'

She started crying again and I hugged her. 'Ellie, it just hurts so much,' she sobbed.

'I know, Em, but you're going to be OK. Just like you said, you're going to be stronger for it and your life will be fantastic and his will shrivel up just like his penis did when we walked in.'

She giggled through her tears. 'I guess it's one way to lose a hard-on, huh? Having your girlfriend walk in on you fucking someone else.'

'Totally, and, oh my God, that woman he is with. She's so fucking tacky,' I cried. 'I swear she was actually wearing blue eyeshadow. Who does that?'

Emma nodded. 'I know she was hideous, and old, but that just makes me feel shitter. He must really love her. It's not just a fun sex thing.'

'If he does, then he wasn't and isn't and never will be the right guy for you,' I said. 'You deserve someone so fantastic they're going to put you first at every opportunity and never even look at someone else. Because they'd be fucking moronic to do that when they have you to go home to at night.'

'Thanks, babe.' She sniffled. 'I know it will get easier. It just… It's just so fucking *shit*. I want to get fucked. Totally completely off my face and go out and fuck my problems away.'

'We'll do whatever you need to do,' I promised her.

'Even if we have to do it every night for a month?'

'Um, that might not go down so well at work but who

cares, they're not even paying me. Of course I'll come and watch you, um, fuck your problems away.'

'Thanks, babe. I really need to spend time with you and my girl friends. You're the ones who never let me down. I should never have trusted the slimy European bastard.'

'Let's not get racist now,' I said, but one look from her glowering eyes forced me to switch tracks. 'You're right. The dirty, sombrero-wearing, tortilla-loving Spaniard.'

'Sombreros are Mexican, Ellie.' She sniffed. 'But thanks for the sentiment.'

'Any time.' I grinned as she passed me a slice of tortilla. 'Here's to hos over bros.'

We clinked tortilla slices and shoved them straight into our mouths. 'Sisters over misters,' she said with her mouth full.

'Gals over…balls?'

'Chicks over dicks.'

'Tits over…the shits?' I suggested. Emma started crying. 'Babe, what's wrong? Did I say something? You're not a tit, you're amazing.'

'No, it's just…the *patatas bravas* remind me of him,' she howled. 'I miss him so much, Ellie. It hurts so bad.'

I put my arms around her, hugging her tight. I wished I could break Sergio's slimy little body for what he had done to my normally bubbly, huge-hearted friend. The cheating bastard deserved a life of utter misery. I hoped he'd choke on a sodding *patata brava*.

Chapter 15

It was a Thursday night and instead of finally having my night of shit TV and junk food, I was wearing five-inch heels and lipstick.

'Um, I can't really walk in these,' I said, tottering around the room. Lara, Emma and Amelia ignored me. They were all gazing at their reflections in the different mirrors scattered around Emma's room, putting on layers of make-up.

'So, what's this night we're going to, then?' asked Lara, as she finished touching up her mascara.

'It's called Drop and Pull,' said Amelia. She was one of Emma's closest friends and painfully cooler than the rest of us. Her hair was cut into a pixie crop with dark green highlights and she was wearing heeled, velvet Doc Martens. 'My friend throws it every week in Storm. It's really fun.'

'What's Storm?' I asked.

She turned to look at me with a creased brow. 'Ellie, it's, like, one of the biggest clubs in East London at the moment. I swear I have no idea how these things pass you by.'

Lara raised her eyebrows at me. 'Even I've heard of it and I don't live in London.'

'Yes, well, you spend enough time here, don't you?' I grumbled at her.

'Most of it helping you out with a crisis of some sort,' she snapped back.

'OK, girls, can we focus on why we're all here, please, and ditch the bickering,' intervened Emma. She turned away from the mirror to face us and we stared back in response. She was wearing black leather jeggings, a loose grey top and red lipstick. It was the most un-Emma outfit I'd ever seen but it was incredibly sexy.

'Um, you look fucking hot,' said Amelia.

I nodded fervently. 'This new look is definitely a keeper.'

'Really?' asked Emma anxiously. 'It's not as tight or sparkly as my normal stuff. I just don't feel that sparkly at the moment. I want to be a bit...I don't know, darker, I guess.'

'Don't go getting all goth on us now,' said Lara. 'But I'm with Ellie. This *really* suits you.'

'Thanks.' Emma grinned. 'And now, people, can we please refill my glass. I'm meant to be getting over Sergio tonight, and to do that, I need to be totally and utterly *fucked*.'

'I've got you a little treat that will help with that,' said Amelia with a wink. Emma grinned and they slid off to the bathroom.

Lara and I were left alone in the room. 'I'm glad you don't do drugs too,' I said. 'It's weird we both don't do them, isn't it? Maybe it's because we had the same school experience and didn't know that many people who did them.'

'Yeah, I guess.' Lara shrugged as she carried on putting

on her mascara. 'Although I do sometimes take the odd pill, or mandy.'

I stared at her. 'What? Seriously? Why did you never tell me?'

'I dunno. I didn't really think it was a thing. It's just once in a while at uni, if I feel like it.'

'But how come you never mentioned it?' I cried.

'El, chill out. Why do you care so much?'

Why did I care? For a start it was another thing I'd just discovered about Lara that I never knew before. And if Lara took drugs, then it meant I was the only one who didn't. I didn't even have a proper reason for not doing them; it's just I got so drunk so quickly and I was semi gluten intolerant, so I figured I'd just be the kind of person to react really badly to them. Besides, *Trainspotting* had pretty much put me off for life.

'It's fine. I don't really care,' I said, trying to ignore the panicked feeling in my tummy. 'Obviously. I was just surprised. Are you, uh, going to do any tonight?'

'Could do,' she said. 'You don't mind, do you?'

YES, I MINDED. Now I'd be the only one not taking drugs. What if they all got really high—do drugs make you high? Wasted? Off their faces?—and I was all sober on my own? I'd feel so left out. Maybe, maybe I should just join them? It wasn't as if I was particularly anti-drugs; I was just a bit scared of them.

Emma and Amelia walked out of the bathroom giggling. 'Ah, step one to getting fucked,' said Emma. 'Do you want any, Lar? I couldn't remember if you like mandy or not.'

'Meh, maybe later,' she said. How was she so casual?!

I fidgeted awkwardly, simultaneously embarrassed that no one had asked if I wanted any and relieved that I hadn't had to say no. Sometimes I felt as if I wasn't just a bit behind with the whole sex thing—it was in every aspect of life. I just felt so bloody Pollyanna sometimes.

Well, fuck it, I could be dirty too, and I didn't need to take MDMA to do it. I'd just stick to my one-night-stand plan, and then I'd feel more like a normal graduate.

* * *

'So this place is pretty, um, hardcore,' I said, as we walked into the bar. It was split into several rooms and each had a separate 'love' theme. There were people wearing fur, sequins, face paint and leather bikinis. My jeans and top combo suddenly felt very PG.

'Isn't it?' shrieked Amelia happily. She was already snogging her on-off girlfriend in the DJ booth. 'You guys go on ahead. I'm gonna help Lou with her set.'

Emma rolled her eyes and dragged Lara and me off to the bar. 'I love Meely, but she is the worst person to go out on a rebound night with.'

'Unlike Lara and I.' I grinned, wrapping my arms around both of their necks.

'Speak for yourself,' said Lara. 'The second a hot DJ comes to find me, I'll be ditching both of you faster than you can say "tequila".' She slammed three tequila shots down in front of us. 'Come on, girls.'

We dutifully grabbed a lime, dabbed salt on our hands and grabbed a shot. 'I am seriously going to regret this tomorrow.' I sighed.

'Ah, come on, we're only young once,' said Lara. 'YOLO?'

I rolled my eyes at her. 'You don't have to be at work with a psycho boss at 9 a.m. tomorrow.'

'Excuse me. No more work talk,' said Emma. 'Here's to being young, fun and impossibly hot.'

We clinked glasses, licked the salt and downed the tequila.

'Gahh,' I cried, as I sucked my lime dry. 'That was awful. Next round is on me.'

'Let me,' said a male voice.

All three of us whirled around to look at him, praying he wouldn't be fat and old. He was young, normal-looking, and had two friends. All three of them were tall, good-looking and well dressed. I exchanged glances with Emma and Lara and knew what they were both thinking: *Jackpot.*

'Hey, I'm Myles,' he said. 'And this is Cosmo and Nick.'

Myles was staring intently at Emma. He was tall with dark hair and perfect teeth. Cosmo was dark-skinned with the most symmetrical face I had ever seen. He was grinning at Lara, who was fluttering her fake eyelashes so much I worried they would fall into her drink. Nick, the last one, was tall and skinny with curly blond hair. He was wearing an expensive-looking shirt with black jeans and suede loafers. He wasn't the type of guy I would normally go for but he was definitely attractive.

The only problem was that he wasn't looking at me. At all. He was staring at a blonde girl gyrating on the dance floor. Typical.

We each took one of the shots Myles bought and downed them. Emma and Lara separately turned around to chat to their prospective men and I was left with Nick, who still hadn't acknowledged me.

'Hey, I'm Ellie,' I said, smiling up at him.

'Hi. Nick.' He turned to look at me and then turned away again. I stared at him in surprise. That was unnecessarily rude. But then again, he was wearing a tiny gold ring on his little finger. I couldn't really expect much more from a pretentious guy like that.

'Well, you're friendly, aren't you,' I remarked. 'I didn't really want to get stuck talking to you either.'

'What?' he asked, looking up at me.

'You know, you can stay facing me,' I said. 'She isn't going to disappear the second you stop staring at her. Besides, it's kind of creepy how obviously you're watching her.'

The sides of his mouth turned up slightly. He was hot when he almost-smiled. It showed off his tan, hazel eyes and chiselled side profile. I couldn't help but notice that he was seriously out of my league looks-wise. 'Sorry. It's my ex. It's, uh, pretty recent.'

'Of course I get stuck with the guy looking for a rebound,' I muttered to myself.

'Did you just say what I think you did?' he asked, looking at me strangely.

Shit. I hadn't thought he'd hear me with the loud music. I shrugged my shoulders, pretending I'd meant for him to hear me. 'Meh, you'll never see me again. I may as well be honest.'

He stared at me for a second and then changed the conversation. 'Hey, what if they become a thing?' he asked, gesturing behind me.

Emma was standing there snogging Myles. I couldn't see Lara because Cosmo was wrapped around her.

'Shit. That was fast,' I remarked.

'They're both pretty smooth workers,' he said.

'How do you know them?' I asked.

'Oh, we're all friends from back home. We were at uni together, then decided to move over here.'

'Where's back home?'

'Auckland.'

'Sorry?'

'New Zealand,' he said, raising his eyebrows at me. 'Auckland is—'

'The capital city. I know. I just didn't hear you earlier,' I retorted.

He laughed. 'That would be Wellington. But Auckland is the biggest city if that's what you meant.'

I blushed. Thank God he couldn't see the red patches on my cheeks in the dark light. 'It is. So, how long have you lived here? Long enough to have a long-term girlfriend I guess?'

'Well, a year, but she came over with me from NZ. We were together for a couple of years but split up about six months ago.'

'What?! Six months ago and you're not over it?' I cried.

'It's not that long,' he replied, looking miffed. 'Besides, she cheated on me.'

'Well, she got cheated on yesterday and she's already pretty over it,' I said, gesturing to Emma.

'Shit,' he said. 'I guess I'm a bit behind, then, huh?'

'A bit? Hey, you should probably be on your next relationship by now.' I grinned.

'Is that an offer, then?'

'Oh, I'm just offering you friendly advice. Why would I get involved with someone who loves his ex-girlfriend, stalks her and is rude to girls in bars?'

'Because you're very drunk?'

I clutched my drink towards me. 'You do realise you sound like a bit of a pervert? Have you put anything in my beer?'

'Your Peroni is safe,' he said. 'Sorry. I was trying to flirt. Didn't realise I was so out of practice.'

I grinned. He *was* trying to flirt with me. This was progress. Now I could snog the third least interestingly named New Zealander while Emma and Lara got off with theirs. 'So you haven't been with anyone since…Blondie?'

He raised his eyebrows. Crap, maybe continuing to discuss his ex wasn't the best flirting move. 'Sara,' he said. 'And nope…no one has been special enough to tempt me.'

'Until…?'

'Until what?'

'Oh, nothing,' I said. 'Anyway, um, what do you want to do?'

'We're in a club. I guess we should get some more drinks, or we could dance?'

Dance? Couldn't he just snog me already? 'We could do, or…we could take a leaf out of our friends' books?'

He stared at me in surprise and then grinned. 'Well, OK, then.' He pulled me towards him and began kissing me. I snogged him back happily. I couldn't believe I'd been so out of character and forward, but, honestly, I couldn't be bothered to wait around any more. Besides, it was about time I ditched my Pollyanna complex. Out of the corner of my eye, I saw Emma wink at me while Lara gestured at her mobile.

'Sorry, one sec,' I said to Nick, as I pulled out my phone. My WhatsApp was flashing.

Emma: I'm going home with him! Who knew my rebound would happen so quickly?!

Lara: Good for you! Tempted to go back with mine…but feel bit bad cz of Jez.

Emma: Fuck Jez!! Go home with your hot guy.

Lara: Maybe later!

I rolled my eyes. We'd been in the club for about half an hour and Emma was leaving. Lara was probably off any minute soon.

'You OK?' asked Nick.

'Fine,' I said. 'Although it looks like my friends are bailing on me for your mates.'

'Oh yeah? Well, you know you could do the same.'

I wrinkled my eyes at him. 'I don't really fancy a threesome, or a fivesome, if that's what you mean.'

'Uh, I meant you can come home with me if you want.'

Oh my God. A spontaneous one-night stand. With a hot foreign man wearing posh shoes. I stared back at him. Could I do this? Like, really go through with it? He smiled at me tentatively and a dimple appeared on his right cheek. I felt my vagina throb with lust and knew it was getting wet. My body wanted this and…so did I.

'OK,' I said in a small voice. 'Wait a sec.'

I tapped out a reply to the girls in our group thread. Within seconds it was vibrating with their responses.

Me: Maybe I'm going home with mine too.

Emma: Ahhh!!! Good for you!!!!

Lara: OMG.

Emma: How cool wd it be if they all lived together??

Me: They don't ☹ already checked. God, can't believe having actual first ONS.

Emma: So excited for you.

Me: Stop being excited for me. This is YOUR 'get over the wanker' night.

Lara: So true. Over him yet?

Emma: Not till I get under Myles…

Me: Ha ha. Have fun.

Lara: El, you're not leaving yet are you??

Me: Fuck no. I'm way too sober. See you at the bar, babe!

'All good?' asked Nick.

I looked up at him in surprise. 'Sorry, got a bit, um, distracted. But, yeah, all good.'

'Sweet,' he said and grinned at me. 'So, do you want to get out of here?'

'Already?'

'If you want. Or we can get another drink.'

'I don't think I'm drunk enough yet,' I blurted out.

He laughed. 'Cheers. Didn't realise you needed to be off your face to be able to come home with me.'

'I didn't mean it like that.' I grinned. 'I just… One more drink?'

'Let's do it,' he said. 'I'm not the kind of guy to ever turn down more beers.'

Chapter 16

'SE1, five Lighthouse Road,' said Nick to the cab driver, before turning to me and grabbing my face. He pulled me towards him and started kissing me. I closed my eyes and let myself fall into the drunken swirl of my mind. The one beer had turned into several and now it was gone midnight and we were in a cab back to Nick's place. The spontaneous one-night stand I'd been trying to orchestrate on my online dates was about to happen—but it looked as if I was too drunk to enjoy it. Bollocks.

'Where do you live?' I asked Nick, breaking away from our kiss.

'Waterloo,' he said. 'It's not too far from here. And, bonus, I live alone.'

'You do? What do you do again?' I asked him. I'd spent the past few hours drinking with him but knew absolutely no details about his life. It was pretty much the opposite of my online dates where I knew the basics before we'd even met.

'I'm a banker,' he said.

I gulped. I was going home with a banker. He didn't even live in East London. He lived in Zone 1. No one I knew lived in Zone 1.

'Here you are,' said the cab driver. I looked up in surprise. We were outside a glass block of flats. I could see the London Eye and we were just by the Thames.

Nick handed the driver two banknotes and opened the door. I followed him out of the cab in a daze. I was now officially terrified. He probably brought a girl back here every night and I would just be the sexually inexperienced one who could never compare to the others. He steered me into the lift and I gaped in surprise.

'What's wrong?' he asked.

'Your lift has mirrored walls,' I squeaked. 'It's like…a hotel.'

He laughed. 'Yeah, I know it's pretty fancy. My work paid for me to come over here from New Zealand, so they've hooked me up with this sweet pad.'

'How old are you?'

'Erm, twenty-nine, why?'

'Just… No reason,' I said nervously. He was so out of my league. He was an actual grown-up man with a legit job that paid for him to have the kind of flat I could only dream of.

'Please tell me you are over eighteen,' he said.

I looked at his four reflections in the mirrors and clutched my head. 'Ow, the mirrors hurt. And yes, of course I am.'

'How old?'

'Guess.'

'Twenty-two?'

'No,' I said, annoyed that I looked my age. 'I'm twenty-three.' I had just lied. Why had I lied? One year didn't even make a difference. If I was going to lie, I should have at least pretended I was twenty-five.

'Oh,' he said. 'At least you'll age well, eh? Anyway, this is it. Home sweet home.'

He pushed open the door and my jaw dropped in amazement. The living room/dining room area had a huge glass window that looked on to the Thames. You could see the entire London skyline lit up. It was beautiful.

'Oh my fucking God,' I gasped. 'This is insane.'

'Isn't it? But the best part…is the bedroom.'

I followed him eagerly into the bedroom expecting a revolving bed and mirrored ceiling. But it was an ordinary double room with some wardrobes and a TV. I turned around with raised eyebrows and Nick pulled me towards him with a kiss. This was it—finally, *finally* I was having my ONS. I pulled my top over my shoulders and undid my bra quickly. My jeans and knickers followed suit.

'Oh, hello,' he said. I realised he hadn't even removed his jacket and I was standing in front of him stark naked. He was looking at my body appraisingly. I stood up tall and realised I felt very sexy being in a strange, hot man's glass penthouse. OK, it wasn't actually on the top floor, but it was still very high up.

I kicked off my heels and walked backwards away from Nick. I felt like the confident French girl in a film noir. 'Um, where are you going, Ellie?' he asked.

I ignored him and walked into the living room. I stood up against the window imagining how attractive my silhouette must look against the London skyline. I turned my head slowly over my shoulder to look back at him, craning it to the side.

But he wasn't there. I turned around in annoyance. What

was the point of me acting sexy if he wasn't going to be there to enjoy it?

'Nick?' I called out. There was silence. 'Nick??'

'Here,' he said, as he walked out of the bedroom. 'What are you doing?'

'Oh, just looking down at the city,' I said in a breathy, light voice. I imagined it was how Brigitte Bardot spoke when she was trying to seduce someone.

'Nice,' he said, running his hands across my naked body. I threw my head back hoping I looked as sexy as I felt. I parted my lips waiting for him to kiss me. He took his hands off me and peered out of the window. 'It really is fucking high up, eh?'

His accent was starting to irritate me and why was he looking at the view not my naked body? 'Yeah, no shit,' I snapped.

'So I've got an idea,' he said, turning to face me with a grin. 'Let's chuck eggs out of the window.'

'What?' I cried out. How had my sexy routine resulted in him wanting to egg London?

'It will be fun. We can try to hit stuff.'

'Nick. That's really dangerous. We could hurt someone walking on the street.'

'I guess,' he said. 'But it's pretty late. The streets are kinda empty.'

'Maybe we should just go into the bedroom.' I sighed. My film noir was slowly turning into an American teen lad movie.

'Cool.' He grinned. We walked into his bedroom and I lay down on his bed. This time he took off his clothes too and lay on top of me with his boxers on. We started kissing slowly, and then faster, and then he pulled his boxers off.

I felt his penis harden against my vagina. It rubbed against it and I moaned in pleasure. 'Ow,' he cried out.

'What?' I asked in surprise.

'Nothing, just a bit spiky,' he said and carried on kissing me.

'Sorry?' I said in a strangled voice. He thought my pubes were spiky. They hurt his penis. My mother*fucking* pubes were ruining my life yet again.

'They're just a bit coarse. I don't care. I think a little bit of hair is sexy.' He grinned at me and I felt mollified. At least he wasn't into hairless fannies.

He rubbed his hands over my coarse pubes, and his penis came closer to my vagina. I wondered if this was it. Was my vagina going to get penetrated for the second time? Oh *fuck*, what if he had a Boyzilian?!

I pushed him off me and stared at his groin. He had trimmed pubes just like me, and no sign whatsoever of a Boyzilian. I breathed out in relief and then grinned to myself. We were pubic kindred spirits.

'Fuck me,' I said. Oh my God, where was this coming from? Perhaps I'd been a *femme fatale* in my past life. 'Now,' I commanded.

'Um, I need a condom first,' he said.

Oh shit. I'd forgotten the condom. I must be drunker than I thought—which meant this would be the perfect moment to brazenly admit I had one with me. 'Oh yeah. I've got one if you want,' I said, as casually as I could.

'Cool,' he said. I walked over to my bag with a grin and rifled through my purse until I found Emma's condom.

'Here you go,' I said nervously, holding it out to him.

He barely glanced at the packaging and just ripped it open. He slid the condom over his penis. I breathed out a sigh of relief that he hadn't expected me to do it for him. The last time I'd tried was during PSHE lessons at school and the tip of the practice banana had gone through the top of the condom.

'Now I'm going to fuck you,' he said. 'Get on your knees.'

Ooh, dominating. Exciting. I obeyed and got on all fours on his bed. He knelt behind me and grabbed my hips. I felt his penis rubbing against my lips as it searched for my vagina. He took his left hand off my right boob and guided his penis inside me. I gasped as the rubber chafed against my barely used vagina.

He pushed himself back and forth, thrusting his penis inside me. I cried out in excitement.

'You're so tight,' he cried out. 'It's amazing.'

I flushed with pride as his balls thwacked against my vagina. I hoped they weren't getting itched by my spiky pubes.

He thrust faster. I gasped out loud. I could feel it now. I imagined someone watching us. We probably looked like a scene from a porno. Me on all fours on his bed, him fucking me from behind, and his hands on my tits. I moaned loudly. I threw myself into my one-time role as a porn star and began moving my body with his.

He gasped loudly, slapped my arse and then went silent and stopped moving.

'Um…' I said. 'Have you, um…'

'What?'

'Come?'

'Yeah,' he said. 'Sorry. I just comed.'

'Came.'

'You came?'

'No,' I said slowly. 'You came. You didn't "comed".'

'What?'

'It's "came" not "comed",' I cried out in exasperation. 'Your grammar's wrong.'

'Oh, OK,' he said. He slid out of me and a lump dropped out of me onto the bed. I craned my neck around in alarm and realised it was just the condom, weighted down with semen.

I collapsed onto the bed in exhaustion. It felt as if I'd just done a four-minute press-up. Nick fell on top of me and rubbed my boobs. 'That was so good,' he said, snuggling his head into me. Were one-night stands meant to be so…cosy?

'Yeah,' I said ambivalently. And then I realised—I'd done it. I'd just had a one-night stand. I had to text Emma and Lara. 'One sec.' I grinned. I leant across him and found my phone lying on the floor. It had new messages.

Emma: Oh my God, his penis was huge. Done it three times. Exhausted.
Lara: Jealous. Cosmo was so dull I abandoned him. Getting drunk with Meely and her gf.
Emma: Wooo!
Me: Well I just had my first ever ONS.
Me: We had the same pubic situation. No Boyzilian in sight.
Me: Didn't come but still feel pretty damn euphoric.

Chapter 17

I woke up yawning. The sunlight was streaming onto my face and I could see Big Ben through the window. Wait. Big Ben. I didn't live near Big Ben. I bolted upright and looked around me.

Nick was lying next to me, snoring. I closed my eyes slowly as everything came back to me. The downside of living a slutty life meant that I was now spending a lot of time waking up in strange places. But this was the first time that I'd woken up next to someone so attractive.

Even when he was passed out and hungover, he looked good. His dirty blond curls were mussed up, his skin had the kind of tan I couldn't even find in a bottle, and he actually had dimples. Symmetrical ones. I seriously couldn't believe he'd wanted me.

I contemplated taking a selfie with him while he was sleeping to show the girls, but figured it was too risky. How could you explain getting caught with a camera in his face? Instead, I yawned again and stood up. My head was banging. Repeatedly. I felt my nipples harden and looked down. I was stark naked.

I walked over to a chest of drawers and began rooting through them. I found a white T-shirt and put it on, then absent-mindedly picked up my phone and walked into the next room with the huge window looming down at me. With a wince, I remembered my film noir escapades. Hopefully Nick was too pissed to remember them. I collapsed on the sofa and pulled out my mobile.

It had a bunch of new messages. And some missed calls. I looked at the calls and my heart stopped. Five missed calls from Maxine. Why was she calling me on a Saturday?

Then it hit me. It wasn't Saturday. It was Friday. And it was…10.25 a.m. Which meant I was an hour and twenty-five…oh, now twenty-six minutes late for work.

Oh fuck.

I called her back immediately. Right, I needed to come up with an excuse. Something plausible like E. coli or—

'Ellie, how nice of you to call,' she answered.

'I'm so sorry,' I gushed. 'I just woke up feeling absolutely awful. I've been, um, throwing up all morning.'

'Late night at Drop and Pull?'

'What?' I asked in shock.

'Your friend Tweeted it and mentioned you.'

'Oh fuck,' I breathed out.

'Fuck indeed,' she said. 'You'd better have got me some new material for a column.'

'I do,' I cried out, knowing there was no way in hell I could write about my one-night stand on the internet. 'Loads.'

'Good,' she said. 'Well, because your latest one already

has five thousand hits I'll let you off. Take today off and come in on Monday with your next column done.'

'Oh my God... Really?'

'Yes. But I'm not going to make a habit of it.'

'Thank you so much, Maxine,' I started saying before I realised she had already hung up. Who knew my boss had a heart? I snuggled into the sofa deciding I would deal with the issue of my next column later in the weekend. SHIT—MY COLUMN.

I pulled up the home page of the *London Mag*. It was right there at the top. *NSFW. By Ellie Kolstakis*. I let out a breath I hadn't realised I'd been holding. It looked amazing. I smiled in spite of myself. I was an actual real columnist. I clicked on it. My words were there on the page, and there was a picture of me at the bottom. Ohmigod, there were comments too. I clicked on them excitedly.

Who is this moron? No wonder she's single.

A Boyzilian? Sounds made up to me. And nothing wrong with a nosebleed. Abandoning someone is a bit drastic.

Oh. Perhaps there'd be some nicer ones on my Twitter? I checked my account and my blood froze.

Really nice you blogged about our date. Classy stuff. Didn't realise my pubes were so offensive to you.

It was from a Benjy84. My hand flew to my mouth. He had seen it. Why hadn't it occurred to me that he would see it?! Please could JT have not seen his. It was so much worse that I'd abandoned him post-nosebleed. I scrolled through my messages but there were only general hate comments. Clearly I was not a modern-day Carrie Bradshaw. The only Carrie I was emulating was the psycho prom girl from the horror movie.

I exited Twitter and flicked to my WhatsApp.

Emma: Weird but congrats. Glad you enjoyed, babe.
Lara: Yeah. God, so knackered, not at all envious of you both at work.
Emma: Ugh, I know so exhausted at my desk.
Lara: You made it to work Ellie?
Emma: OMG, El, my colleague just showed me your column!! Congrats, girl, it's amazing.
Lara: So proud of you. Ignore the comments. They're all fuckers.
Lara: Ellie? Why haven't you seen these messages?

They had sent the messages at 9.30 a.m. because unlike me they had clearly set their alarms. I was an idiot.

Me: So I didn't quite make it to work… But Maxine gave me day off because she's so impressed with my column. Unfortunately no one else is.
Lara: ?
Me: Ben84 Tweeted me his disgust at my column.
Emma: Ha ha. You've made my day. Can't believe you didn't go to work.
Me: I know. Hanging out on the sofa at Nick's place.
Emma: Aw. Very coupley.
Me: No, I'm alone.
Lara: That's weird. Go into the bedroom.
Emma: Seconded. Go wake him up with a blowie.

I rolled my eyes and tucked my phone under a pillow. I turned on the TV and saw Kate Winslet standing up on front of *Titanic*'s deck with Leo's arms behind her. 'I'm flying,' she gasped. I curled up in a blanket to watch it. Benjy84 was irrelevant—I was hanging out in my one-night stand's flat and Leo was on TV.

It was now almost noon and Nick still hadn't woken up. I had finished *Titanic*, redone my make-up after crying most of it off, and now I was starving. I had even considered poaching the eggs he had wanted to throw out of the window but decided that was a step too far.

I padded into the bedroom and looked at the bed. He was breathing deeply. The duvet was covering most of his body but I could see his tanned torso peeking out. It wasn't as toned as Ben84's, but then it also didn't come with a Boyzilian. Thank God.

I wasn't quite sure what to do now. Did I leave? Shouldn't I wait for him to wake up so we could have breakfast together, and then I could do my FIRST EVER ACTUAL walk of shame? I knew I would never see him again, because it was a one-nighter, but that just meant I was extra keen for a morning together.

I coughed loudly. He didn't move. I sat on the bed and prodded him. 'Mmm,' he groaned. I prodded him harder. 'Ow,' he cried and rubbed his eyes.

I quickly positioned myself seductively on his bed and mussed up my hair. 'Oh, hi.' I smiled. 'How are you?'

'Hey.' He yawned. 'What time is it?'

'Midday.'

'Fuck,' he cried out and jumped out of bed. This was not the morning kiss I had been expecting. 'Why didn't you wake me up earlier? I need to get to work.'

'Oh, sorry,' I said. 'I…thought it was Saturday. Then my boss gave me the day off and I guess I assumed you had a day off too.'

'No,' he said grimly, as he grabbed his mobile. 'Luckily, I don't have any meetings today, so no one important will notice I've been gone half the morning. I'm just going to jump in the shower. Do you want to go in after me?'

'Um, no, it's fine. I'll shower at home,' I said.

'Cool, see you in a sec.' He walked past me with a towel slung over his shoulder. I sat on his bed and sighed. Clearly my morning brunch was not going to happen today. I would have to spend my day off alone. I didn't even have any money to spend on retail therapy.

I started picking up my discarded clothes from various locations around the room. My knickers had ended up in the hallway and one of my socks was well and truly lost. I squeezed my bare feet into my heels and winced in pain as they rubbed against my blisters and I stood up tall. Why hadn't I worn flats?

All dressed up with nowhere to go, I treaded around Nick's room. He didn't have any pictures on the walls, any photos of friends or a single personal artifact. It was a bachelor's pad to the max. The only personal item I could see was a packet of developed photographs on the dresser. Could I…? The shower was still running, so I quickly opened the envelope and pulled out the pictures. They were of Nick and a bunch of his friends. Boring.

I kept on shuffling through the pile until I found a photograph of the blonde ex-girlfriend. Sara. She was totally naked and sitting astride a chair. She had no pubes whatsoever. Her body was *Playboy*-perfect.

Slowly, I put everything back as I had found it. I shouldn't have snooped. Now I just felt very, very inadequate. Of course my tight vagina hadn't lived up to Sara's incredible non-spiky body. Nick had slept with me only as a rebound from Sara. It was a fact; he had told me. I grabbed my bag and walked up to the bathroom. I had to say bye and get out of here immediately. My cheeks were flushing with shame and I didn't want to be here any more.

'Nick?' I rapped lightly on the bathroom door.

It swung open to reveal Nick standing there in his towel grinning at me with wet hair. 'Hey. Sorry I took so long.'

'No worries,' I said. 'I'd better go anyway. So…just thought I'd say bye.' I stood fidgeting with the strap of Emma's studded clutch bag.

'Oh, OK,' he said. 'If you just wait five minutes, I can come with you to the Tube.'

'No it's fine, honestly. I'm not feeling too great. Hungover.'

'Yeah, me too. Anyway, it's been great, Ellie. We should do this again sometime.'

'Mm, sure,' I said. He leant towards me and gave me a quick peck on the lips. 'Bye, then.'

'Wait, give me your number,' he said. I sighed. He wasn't going to call me, so why did he need my phone number? The amount of men over London who had my number and would never use it was depressingly high. I tapped my number into his phone. I supposed there was no real harm adding one more man to the list. 'I've just missed-called you so you have my number too,' he added.

'OK, cheers. Well, see you later,' I said and walked out of his flat. I let out a deep breath. I had survived my first ever ONS—and, even better, it turned out I wasn't one of those girls who fell in love with the guy immediately afterwards. I had no desire to ever hear from Nick again. It was

OK to be his rebound for the night, because I'd been using him too, but a regular thing? Absolutely not. I couldn't be a slut and up my numbers if I kept shagging the same guy.

I exited the lift and stumbled down the street in last night's clothes. I could feel tourists staring at me and I grinned to myself. They were probably subtly taking photos of the typical London girl leaving her eligible one-night stand's apartment at midday. I hoped my face was aglow with post-coital hormones. Only, I was leaving sans orgasm. Could your face still glow if you hadn't come the night before?

That was frustrating. All I wanted was to orgasm from penetration but my dream was still eluding me. As exciting as it was getting all the other elements of an ONS, that was the one I really wanted. Maybe there was a reason it wasn't happening? Like, maybe something was wrong with me? I felt a wave of anxiety at the thought. It was definitely possible that I was part of the tiny percentage of women who couldn't orgasm from penetration. I might even be unorgasmable.

Chapter 18

NSFW

I thought there was nothing worse than being the rebound girl. But it turns out there is: being told *you're the rebound girl. Suddenly you can't blame the gut feeling on your paranoia or lack of self-esteem. Your inferior status as someone who will never live up to the person the guy really loves is validated—by the guy himself.*

That was my Thursday night. I went home with the rebound. It didn't matter that his apartment was exactly the sort of thing a chick-lit hero would have, because I wasn't a chick-lit heroine. My romcom was more American Pie *than* Love Actually *and my one-night stand took me home only because it seemed more enjoyable than stalking his ex.*

I let him do this. Now I am forced to face the reality that I may be mentally deranged. Why else would I convince— nay, command—the guy watching his ex dance with a bunch of men to take me home instead?

I suppose I was using him too. I really wanted a wild night with a hot man while my friends went home with his friends. It seemed too perfect an opportunity to pass up. I don't regret it. I got my wild night. But now in the cold light of my walk of shame, I wonder if I made the right choice.

Was I making an empowered decision to go home with the guy who wished I was someone else, or was I just so desperate to be empowered and fun that I settled for someone who didn't respect me?

I gulped out loud. This week's edited, final column was nothing like the mild, PG-rated version I had sent through to Maxine. She had called me into her office and interrogated me on every detail until I realised I had told her Nick's penis looked like a courgette. She was so horrified by the level of detail that she decided it was too much even for *London Mag.*

But it hadn't stopped her putting in the fact that I wanted wild animal sex on my one-night stand. There was no way my parents would ever speak to me again. Thank God I barely had a relationship with my dad. Hopefully he would be too preoccupied with his stepkids to notice that his own flesh and blood was telling the world about her slutty Thursday-night anecdotes. It was a miracle my mum hadn't seen my first column yet.

Now I was terrified Nick would see it as Ben had. Should I just risk it and hope he would never see it, or should I somehow bring it up with him and persuade him to never, ever Google me? Maybe…maybe I could lie about my surname and he'd never be able to search for me online? Oh, who was I kidding—it's not as if there were many Ellies working for the *London Mag*. Even my mum would find it soon.

I felt a tug on my intestines and gasped out loud. My guilt twinges had been getting stronger and deeper. It was Monday now. My first column had been up for four days and with every day that passed without my mum saying anything, the guilt trebled. Deep down I wanted to just pull off the Band-Aid and tell her. Get it over and done with and never have to think about it again.

I twiddled my curly hair around my baby finger and then dropped it in disgust. I had ditched that childhood habit years ago. What was I doing reverting back to this?! I had to sort myself out and tell my mum.

Before I could think twice about what I was doing, I grabbed my mobile and my jacket. Now that Maxine was publishing explicit details of my life to the world, I was getting a lot more brazen about leaving my desk for extended breaks. She needed me. My column was the best read on the website and there was no way she would get rid of me just because I frequented Pret too often.

I asked around if anyone wanted a drink, but I was met with familiar silence. Perfect, it would just make my trip cheaper. My hands were shaking as I exited the building and dialled my mum's number. This was the hardest thing I had ever had to do. It was worse than losing my virginity and shaving my pubes combined.

'Elena?' asked my mum. 'Why aren't you at work?'

I sighed. 'I am, Mum. I'm just on a quick break. How are you?'

'Hmm, you shouldn't take too many breaks or they'll never pay you.'

'Yeah...I guess.'

'I'm having a complete disaster.'

'Really?' I asked in surprise.

'It is the broadband. TalkTalk won't let me quit and now I am paying for them and Sky. But Sky is offering me Sky-Plus and OnDemand for much cheaper, so now I want to stay with them, and they will give me all my Greek movie channels, so...'

Oh God. My mum classified broadband-provider drama as disastrous. How was she going to cope with her only daughter telling the world about her explicit love life?

'Mum,' I interrupted. 'That sounds really stressful, but while I'm on a quick break, can I just tell you something?'

'You haven't fallen out with your housemates, have you?'

'What? Why... What?'

'I just worry that they will find you difficult to live with,' she explained.

I sighed in frustration. 'My housemates love me. Anyway, what I wanted to tell you was...I've started writing a column. For the website I work for.'

'Writing? About time you did something there instead of just making the teas.'

'Mum, I never made the tea for them—they don't even drink tea. But, yes, it's cool that I'm writing. The only thing is...I'm writing about things you might not like.'

I could literally hear her eyebrows furrowing together. 'What sort of things?'

'Um...so my column is called "NSFW", which means "Not Safe for Work", so...I guess...X-rated topics?'

There was a pregnant pause on the other end of the phone. Then my mum started shrieking in Greek. 'I always knew I was doomed,' she cried. 'Ever since we left the village to come here. The others warned me you would become loose.

But I didn't think you had until you told me this. And you're writing about…SEX.'

'Mum, Mum, calm down,' I cried. 'I'm not loose!! I've barely… I mean…I just write about dating. And then, sometimes, I guess it gets a bit more explicit.' I no longer understood what my mum's high-pitched Greek meant. Especially when it was peppered with the occasional wail. 'Mum, I'm sorry.'

She breathed out loudly and switched back to English. 'Ellie, why would you do this? How can you write about sex to the whole world? Do you have no shame?'

I felt my tummy crumple up. I did feel sort of bad about doing it, but at the same time, it was so normal these days. The internet was full of stuff like this. 'I know it's kind of… out there, but, Mum, this is what I enjoy doing. I'm good at it. It's the most popular thing on the website.'

'Yes, because sex sells,' she cried out. 'It's obvious and tacky and…cheap. Couldn't you write about something clever?'

I tried to reply but had nothing to say. She had a point. Was I just selling myself for commercialism? 'But, Mum, it's meant to be kind of funny. To make people laugh, but also to make them feel like they're not alone. I want women to realise that everyone else is having awkward sex experiences too.'

'But there's so much you can do, and you choose *this*?'

I sighed. 'I'm sorry, Mum. I don't know what else to say. This is what I'm good at and what I enjoy. I'm so sorry it affects you so much. I didn't want to upset you.'

'Of course it's going to affect me,' she cried. 'What about when all our family see it? Or my friends? They're all going to talk. Oh God—the *shame*.'

I sat down on a brick wall and put my head in my hands. I hadn't thought about how this would affect my mum. But surely I had to follow my own path? What would Julius Caesar do? He would definitely betray his family and go for it. Could I do that though? 'Mum, I'm really sorry,' I said, taking a deep breath. 'But this is my dream and I need to do it. The first one is already online.'

'Why is this your dream though? Can't you aim higher, Elena?'

'I don't know, Mum. I've just realised this is what I'm good at writing and what I enjoy. It's what I want.'

'Well, then, couldn't you do it anonymously?'

'My editor wouldn't let me,' I replied pathetically. 'I tried, I really did, but then I realised it's such a benefit for me to use my name. It will help me get famous.'

'Fame? Fame?! You want to be like those loose girls in the magazines who sell themselves for—'

'Mum, chill out,' I interrupted. 'I didn't mean fame per se. I just meant…I can become well known. In the writing industry. It will be so good for my career.'

'Huh, career. I don't know what kind of career this is,' she muttered. 'Are you at least getting good money now?'

'Um…'

'Oh, Elena, what is wrong with you?' she cried.

'Sorry,' I muttered, looking at the cracks in the pavement. 'And…Mum, I really hate to do this, but can you transfer a tiny bit of money to my account? For rent?'

She sighed loudly and moaned. 'What have I done to deserve a daughter like this?'

'Mum, I'm still here. And you don't have to be so dramatic. I just need a tiny bit. Like, a hundred pounds? I want to make Greek food,' I offered, remembering how it had worked last time. 'Like falafel and stuff.'

'Falafel?' she wailed. 'That's Egyptian.'

'Moussaka. I meant moussaka,' I added hurriedly. 'Please?'

The wailing was so loud I hung up the phone quietly. Moussaka money would have to wait.

Chapter 19

Emma and I were lying on her bed gazing up at the Ryan Gosling poster on her ceiling. Our hair was tousled together on the pillow and we were listening to her 'Feminist Playlist'. For the first time since Emma had met Sergio, I realised how much I had missed just hanging out with her alone. It was so nice lying on her bed without a hairy Spaniard in between us.

'So did it help?' I asked her. 'Sleeping with Myles? Do you feel like you've moved on a bit from Serge?'

'Sergio,' she said. 'He isn't allowed any affectionate names any more. And yeah, I guess... It was nice to feel wanted again, and to know I can always get a date and a guy. But it didn't really help me hurt less. I think only time will help with that.'

I squeezed her hand. 'I'm sorry, Em. You didn't deserve this. He really is a useless pathetic moron.'

'I know. I just hate that he made me feel pathetic too.'

'You're the least pathetic person I know,' I said. 'You

have an amazing PR job, the best friends ever—though I say so myself—you're beautiful, clever and funny, and, let's be honest, we all knew you were so out of Sergio's league.'

She grinned. 'I guess I was. I convinced myself he was really ambitious and driven because he's studying for a PhD as well as working in the pub, but I think he's going to drop out so he can just stay at the pub. And as much as I like drinking, a pub mistress's life just isn't for me.'

'Exactly,' I said. 'And his English was a bit shitty at times. He didn't understand any of our abbrevs.'

'El, no one understands our abbrevs. We should carry glossaries to wear on the backs of our clothes.'

'Or subtitles.' I grinned. 'Audio description?'

'Definitely.' She laughed. 'Ah, thank God I have you. Don't go getting a boyfriend on me now, will you?'

'Oh please. I've lasted twenty-two years single. Do you really think that's going to change now?'

'I dunno… You lasted twenty-one years a virgin but that changed pretty recently. And you did just have your first ONS. Things are changing for you.'

'Huh, I guess. But don't worry, I'm still poor and un-textable. Nick said he would message me and didn't.'

'Uh-oh,' warned Emma.

'What?'

'You're not meant to fall for the ONS, Ellie. Have I taught you nothing? They take your number for three reasons but none of those reasons will ever be that they want you to be their girlfriend.'

'Relax. I haven't fallen for him. And do I even want to know what these three reasons are?' I asked her.

'No, but here goes. One, in case they need to tell you they have an STD.' I shrieked, but Emma ignored me and carried on. 'Two, some kind of man conquest thing. Put you in their little black book, etc. Three, to mind-fuck you. Plain as.'

'Surely there has to be an occasional four, in case they fall for you?'

Emma snorted out loud. 'You've been watching way too many romcoms. That does not happen in real life. The only other option I'll accept is, four, you were such a good shag that they want a booty call on speed dial. But never a girl-friend.'

'OK, got it,' I said, mock-saluting her. 'Nick isn't going to call me unless he finds out he's infested me or wants a round two—with no commitment.'

'Exactly. But, hey, if you haven't fallen for him, why do you even want him to call?'

'I don't know.' I sighed. 'I was so proud of myself for not being the kinda gal who gets carried away by those sex hormones… What are they called?'

'Oxytocin.'

'Yeah, that. Well, I didn't have any desire for him to pro-fess undying love for me—I was happy to just leave it as a one-nighter. But then he asked for my number and that threw me. Like, why would you ask if you aren't going to use it? If he'd never asked for it, I'd have no expectations and I'd be fine. Now I feel like there could be more there.'

'The classic mind-fuck,' said Emma darkly. 'They love doing it. The fuckers.'

'No hard feelings towards men, then, eh?'

'Shut up,' she said, rolling away from me. 'And why do you keep saying "eh"?'

'Oh God, Nick's already influenced me. I think it's a New Zealandish thing.'

'That's not a word. What do you call them anyway? New Zealanders?'

'I guess. Oh wait, Kiwis?'

'Is that racist?'

'I'll Google it,' I said. A few seconds later, I announced, 'Nah. They call themselves that too.'

She groaned loudly. 'Ellie. What are we doing? We're lying on my bed and Googling crap about New Zealand linguistics. This is not how I imagined my twenties.'

'Really?' I said. 'I think I kind of always knew this is how they'd end up. Besides, it's only a Monday night.'

She rolled her eyes at me. 'Exactly. We should still be hungover from Saturday.'

* * *

I lay in bed staring at my laptop. The new Danish crime drama was playing, but I wasn't really paying attention. I was thinking about Nick. I'd told Emma the truth—I didn't really ever expect to hear from him again, but the fact that he'd asked for my number had confused me. It had made me feel as if he wanted to see me again, and, well, I wouldn't be averse to it.

He'd been funny, and nice to me—and, more important, he was insanely hot. Even though the memory of a naked Sara made me feel sick, I'd had fun with him. I'd managed to flirt without coming across like a Bridget Jones with verbal diarrhoea, and he made me feel sexy. The sex had been good too. Like, obviously I hadn't achieved my end goal, but it had been more fun than sex with Jack Brown, and definitely more enjoyable than being licked out by Boyzilian. Maybe I'd even orgasm on Take 2?

Damn. Maybe Emma was right and I was falling into

dangerous territory? On cue, my door flew open and she barged in waving my phone.

'Oh thanks,' I said. 'I forgot I left it in your room. Any messages?'

'HE CALLED,' she cried. 'It must be a number four situation. He wants another go. A booty call.'

'Ohmigod.' My onesie slipped off my shoulders as I sat upright. 'Seriously? What did he say?'

'Um, I didn't answer. That would be weird, Ellie.'

'Oh, right, yeah. Fuck. What shall I do?'

'Call him back, you idiot.'

I froze. I desperately wanted to, but what if I was just falling into the classic romcom mould of being the girl who got used? I was already sitting at home wondering if we'd flirt some more and have sex again. Everyone knew that meant I'd end up getting my heart shattered. I should end it now before I got hurt.

'Emma, he's just using me as a rebound,' I said. 'Maybe I shouldn't sleep with him again. I didn't even come.'

'You're using him too though, babe. And remember, he's a pretentious wanker banker with a signet ring. It's an ideal situation. You know you won't fall for each other. It will be strictly business.'

'Isn't that kind of...slutty?'

She sat down on my bed and looked into my eyes. 'Ellie,' she said earnestly. 'We've spoken about this. We're not using "slut" in a negative way. Take that word back and reclaim it for whatever you want it to mean. Fuck what the world says.'

'You're right. It's just hard to know what to do.'

'Look. I can't tell you what to do. But just make sure you do what you actually want to do, regardless of labels and being scared of what people will think of you. M'kay?'

'Oh all right, I'm going to call him. You know, I still can't believe he actually called.' I grinned. Getting hurt was part of twenty-something life anyway. If I wanted to live, then I was going to have to deal with the bad bits too. Besides, I might get an orgasm out of it.

''Course he did, you must have been the best shag ever with your barely broken hymen. It was probably the tightest he'd ever had,' she said, walking out the door.

'Wait, where are you going?' I cried out in alarm.

'Um, to give you some privacy?'

'What? Why would I want that? Can you sit back down so I can put it on speakerphone?'

She rolled her eyes and sat back down. I placed the phone on top of a cushion and gingerly pressed 'call'.

Within seconds, Nick answered. 'Hey. How's it going?'

I panicked. I hadn't thought he'd actually answer, let alone so bloody quickly. Or that he'd sound so masculine and sexy on the phone. What on earth was I going to say to him? Emma prodded my leg.

'Oh, um, hi,' I said.

'It's me, Nick.'

'Yeah, I know. I saved your number.'

'Sweet. So, uh, how are things?'

'Yeah, good, thanks,' I said. 'Survived day one of work post-weekend. What about you?'

'Same. Had a pretty quiet weekend after Thursday night. Think I needed to recover.' I felt paranoia rising in me. Did he need to recover from sleeping with me? Was it really that bad? 'But I had lots of fun with you.'

Ah. 'Me too,' I managed to say.

'Do you want to meet up again? Sometime soon?'

'Yeah, I… That would be nice.'

'Sweet. How about Wednesday?'

'Right, sure.'

'Great. I'll text you a plan, but it will probably involve dinner and drinks. How does that sound?'

'Pretty…sweet.'

'Awesome. Catch you later.'

'Bye.'

I hung up the phone and turned to face Emma. 'OMG, you're right, my vagina must be tiny. He wants to go for drinks!'

'Get you.' Emma laughed. 'An actual date from your one-night stand. Maybe it's time I started learning from you.'

'But that was officially the most awkward phone conversation ever,' I said. 'Why didn't he just text me like a normal person?'

'I think it's cute he called. I see what you mean about the accent though. It's strong but kind of sexy. Or should I say six-y? Eh?'

I threw my pillow at her. 'Have you never heard a foreign accent before? Now get out of my room, *chica*.'

'Too soon to joke about Sergio,' she warned, exiting my room.

'Wait, Em, can I borrow your pubes trimmer thing?' I called out. 'I need to prepare for my date.'

'Ellie, can you just buy your own? It's, like, ten pounds from Boots.'

'I know, sorry, but I keep forgetting and I can't use scissors in case I cut my clit again. You know I'm paranoid about that.'

She rolled her eyes at me. 'Fine. It's on the top shelf in the bathroom.'

'Gracias, guapa.'

* * *

I ran around my room in my towel, shoving things into a bag. It was 8 a.m. on Wednesday. I had to leave for work in half an hour and I had a date in less than twelve hours. It meant I had a dilemma: should I bring a change of clothes for the next day?

If it were a weekend, it wouldn't matter. But if I stayed at Nick's place, I'd need some clothes to change into or Maxine would know I had stayed out. Only, if Nick noticed my new outfit in the morning, he'd realise that I'd assumed I was going home with him. That would be seriously embarrassing.

Oh fuck it. I'd better be safe than sorry. At worst, I could always get changed in the loo at work or a nearby café. I grabbed a black cotton dress, tights and underwear and shoved them into my bag. Was it too premeditated to pack some contact lens solution too? And some moisturiser? I chucked them into my bag before I could chicken out. I'd just have to hide them from him.

My towel slipped down as I picked up my bag and I caught sight of my naked body in the mirror. It was lumpy and pale as usual, bar the black forest in between my legs. Oh fuck—I had forgotten to trim my mass of pubes. I groaned out loud and ran back into the bathroom for a speed-trim.

I sat on the loo, legs wide open, brandishing Emma's pink bikini trimmer. One end was a typical razor and the other was a battery-powered pube trimmer. It was revolutionary. I no longer had to navigate my pubic zone with a wobbly pair of nail scissors, hoping I was cutting them to a normal length. Now I could just select one of three lengths and press 'on'.

I selected the shortest length and switched it on. It started humming and I gently steered it around my vagina. I pulled the lips up so it could cut the thick hairs short and then coasted it around the top. The only part I was still unsure about was my crack. How far down did I trim? Was I meant to go all the way up to the bum hole—and was it weird to have short hairs though? Should I just leave them, or shave them?

I groaned at the thought of shaving—I hated the hairs growing back stubbly and itchy. I couldn't wait until I actually started earning a salary, so I could go and get my bum crack waxed for a fiver in Peckham. It might hurt more, and still had the potential for full-blown disaster, but at least someone else would be accountable.

Shit, I was getting late for work. I pulled my bum cheeks open and ran the trimmer along the edges. That would have to do until Maxine gave me a salary. Hopefully Nick wouldn't mind the spikiness. He wouldn't even see it—unless he went down on me. God, I really hoped he wouldn't go down on me. I couldn't handle the stress of trying to act relaxed, or faking an orgasm, whilst constantly stressing out that the smell of my vagina might cause him to pass out. Now I was even worried he'd choke on some loo roll hiding in my labia.

I yelped out in pain. My trimmer had just caught one of the longer hairs and pulled it. I breathed through the discomfort and pulled the skin taut so it wouldn't happen again. It reminded me of the excruciating agony of getting a full Brazilian wax. Thank God I had eschewed those porn-originated pubic styles in favour of my trimmed, spiky little hedgehog. I gazed at it fondly and gave it a small stroke. Eight-fifteen wasn't too late. I definitely had time for a quick wank.

Chapter 20

I had butterflies in my tummy. Only, they felt more like a swarm of moths eating holes in my stomach lining. I was standing outside 99 Kensington High Street and felt totally out of my comfort zone. I didn't know whether I was meeting Nick upstairs or outside the door. I didn't even really know if I was in the right place—all I could see was a nondescript door opposite the *Daily Mail* newspaper offices, where I once came on an errand for Maxine.

I pulled out my phone to see if Nick had messaged. He had.

I'm upstairs.

Oh God. I would have to enter alone. I looked up to see a gaggle of girls walking past me. They were wearing tight dresses and heels. I was wearing another classic day-to-night outfit of ballet pumps, black jeans and a chiffon shirt. I looked as if I should be serving them the drinks.

They walked straight through the door and air-kissed the woman standing on the other side. She ticked something off a clipboard and the girls disappeared into the building. I nervously followed in their path and opened the door.

'Yes?' said the woman coldly. No air-kissing for me, then.

'Hi, um, I'm meeting someone in the rooftop gardens,' I said.

'Which bar?'

'Sorry?'

'Do you mean the Babylon bar?' she asked in a bored voice.

'Um, I guess?' How many bars were there in this building? All I could see was a sterile white hallway and a lift.

'OK, seventh floor.'

I walked past her to the lift and uncertainly got in, pressing 'seven'. It sped up to the top and I found myself facing another attractive woman looking me up and down.

'Yes?' she said.

'I'm meeting someone at the bar.'

'OK, just through there,' she said, pointing at the bar two metres in front of her.

'Thanks,' I said, wondering why exactly her job was necessary. I walked through, trying to hold my head up high even though I felt like throwing up with nerves. This was not the sort of place I came to on dates—hell, it wasn't the sort of place I even knew existed.

'Ellie, you made it,' said Nick. He was sitting at the bar with two drinks. 'I got you a Long Island Iced Tea. Hope that's OK.'

'Great, thanks,' I said, taking it from him cautiously, remembering my mum's advice about accepting drinks in bars. He wouldn't have put anything in it, would he? Surely I was already a definite shag tonight?

'Have you ever been here before?' he asked.

'Nope, never. It looks cool though.'

'Ah, wait till you see the outside part.' He grinned. 'Come on, let's go now.'

'Um, OK,' I said, clutching my drink as I followed him through the crowded bar. I had no idea so many people went for casual drinks on a Wednesday.

We walked through the door into the gardens. There was grass all over the terrace and flowers and bushes coming out of every corner. 'Oh my God,' I cried. 'How have I never been here before? This is amazing.'

'You just needed a Kiwi to come and show you the coolest parts of London.'

'Apparently so,' I said. 'Does this mean I have to show you somewhere equally cool on the next date?' Oh God. I had just said date. What if this wasn't actually a date, and I had just been really presumptuous assuming there'd be another date, and—

'You're on.' He grinned. I really had to stop being so weird about acknowledging we were on a date. 'You're cold,' he said. 'Here, take this.'

I looked at him in surprise. He was offering me his suit jacket. 'Seriously? I asked. 'That's, like, the most chivalrous thing anyone's ever done for me.'

'Uh, it's no biggie.'

'Yeah, sorry. Thanks,' I said, taking it from his outstretched arm and wrapping it around me. I had to keep reminding myself this was not a typical date. This was a rebound, mutual usage situation. 'So what have you been up to?'

'Oh, not much,' he replied. 'Just been working pretty long hours and trying to catch up with some sleep.'

'What did you do for the rest of the weekend that was so exhausting?'

'I was mainly recovering from our Thursday night.' He grinned. I blushed automatically. He was probably remembering my Brigitte Bardot routine. Why did alcohol always mistakenly make me feel sexy?

'Yeah that was…um, fun,' I said.

'Very. I hear your friends had just as much fun with my mates.'

'They did.' I tried to think of something else to say, but I was still so nervous I could hardly talk. Nick had already seen me naked, pretending to be sexually experienced, and he thought my pubes were spiky. Hell, he had probably even seen the hair going up my bum crack when we were doing doggy. I was way too sober to look him in the eyes.

'But we're the only pair going on an actual date,' he said. 'Even though I was the one who was rudest to you at the bar.'

'You weren't rude.'

'Yes, I was,' he said. 'You told me at the time.'

Oh dear. 'I did?'

'Yup. I was being a bit of a creep staring at my ex and completely ignoring you.'

Bollocks. He remembered every tiny detail of the night. This was not a good sign. I pushed the straw in my drink to the side and poured the cocktail down my throat. 'How is the ex situation going? Still stalking her?'

He laughed. 'Blunt, aren't you? Nah, I've quit that. Think it's just as the old saying goes—you don't get over someone until you get under someone else.'

'Classy, Nick. Thanks for emphasising the rebound factor.'

'Shit, sorry,' he said, looking mortified. 'I didn't think about what I was saying.'

'Hey, no worries,' I said, putting my hand on his arm. I hadn't thought he would actually feel guilty. 'I was only kidding. I don't really mind.'

'OK, glad to hear it,' he said, looking more relieved.

'Actually,' I said, 'there's something I should, um, probably tell you before you see it and Tweet me hate mail.'

'What?'

'Sorry. It's just, um…' Why was I garbling so incessantly? *Focus, Ellie, focus. Just tell him the truth so he can't say you lied to him. You don't really care what he thinks—he's just a casual shag. It's better he knows now than finds it online like Ben did.* 'You know I work for the *London Mag*?'

'Yeah, you intern there, right?'

'Exactly. And I've started writing a column for them. Called "NSFW". It's about my, uh… It's about women's issues,' I said.

'Shit, no kidding,' he cried. 'That's so cool.'

'Yeah, I guess it is. But the thing is, it's really personal sometimes. It's very much about girlie things—periods, etc.—and I guess, I guess I'm just trying to say it would be amazing if you promised to never Google me and read it. Please?'

'Hey, I really have no desire to read about your period or whatever—don't worry, I won't look it up,' he said.

I sighed in relief. 'OK, thank you. It's just, this guy I dated recently looked me up and read it, and he was kind of a dick about it. I write about really gruesome stuff—pubes, blood… He couldn't deal with it.'

He laughed. 'Trust me—I'm a typical bloke. I can't deal with stuff like that. I swear I'll never look up your column.'

I grinned at him. My half-lie had worked. 'Thank you.'

'No worries. I think it's pretty cool that you're a journalist with your own column. I respect that. Anyway, who's this wanker you dated? Do you need me to beat him up?'

I laughed. 'Nah, he's just a mistake I met on OKCupid. We only ever had one date.'

'You date online?' he asked curiously.

I sighed, preparing to justify why a twenty-two-year-old—twenty-three-year-old to him—was on a dating website. 'Yes, but all my friends are on it, everyone on it is normal, and I don't take it seriously,' I said.

'No, it's just…I'm on the same website.'

'No way,' I cried out.

'Yeah, I had some reservations at first, but my friends recommended it to me and then I just thought, why not? I'm new in the country, I may as well.'

'And have you gone on any dates from it? Ohmigod, is this, like, your bar you take them all to?!'

'Oh yeah, I greet them all with a Long Island Iced Tea too. And then we walk out here and talk about their online columns and dating sites.'

I laughed uncertainly.

'I'm kidding,' he said, raising an eyebrow at me. 'I have been on a few online dates though. There was no real spark or connection with a couple of them, but I did see one of them a few times. Until she got a bit needy.'

Note to self: do not be needy.

'In what way?' I asked.

'Oh, she just wanted to meet up the whole time, and call me her boyfriend, and then I started saying I was too sick to meet up, but she wouldn't take no for an answer. She said she would come over to mine with brownies to cheer me up.'

'Oh my God. She offered to bake you brownies?! On what number date?'

'Erm, I guess it would have been the fourth time I'd seen her.'

'That is not OK,' I said, relieved that his version of needy was not something I would accidentally do; I didn't even know how to bake. 'Baking brownies are, like, three months anniversary level. Maybe even six months.'

'Glad to see you're on the same page as me.' He grinned. 'Do you, uh, want to get out of here?'

I looked at the gardens in disappointment. We had barely even been here an hour and I'd had only one drink. It was the shortest date I'd had and that was with one of them bleeding on me. Then it hit me—this wasn't a 'let's get to know each other with the possibility of ending up in a relationship' date. It was a 'let's fuck tonight' predrink.

'Sure,' I said. 'Back to yours?'

'Oh, I was thinking we could go to a different bar or something. I know it's a weeknight, so I don't expect you to come back with me. I mean, could you even go to work in the same clothes?'

Why was he thinking about my clothes?! I'd figured that wouldn't occur to him and I could change into my new dress without him realising. God, this was embarrassing—did he even want me to go home with him? 'Um, they wouldn't even notice,' I said.

'Really? I couldn't do that at my work.'

'Actually,' I said suddenly, 'I have a spare outfit at work. In my gym bag. So I could change into that in the morning. It'll be fine.'

'Ah, well, in that case.' He smiled. 'Who needs more drinks? Let's go and find a cab.'

The cab pulled up outside Nick's apartment and I realised how completely and utterly sober I was.

'Come on,' he said, opening the door for me.

I smiled faintly and forced my legs to move. This would be fine. He had already seen my naked body and he wanted more. He'd asked me out on an actual date, and he'd bothered to choose somewhere cool. He liked me…right?

I followed him blindly through the doorway. A man in uniform took off his cap and tilted his head to me. 'Good evening,' he said.

I stared in shock. He had a concierge. How rich was he—and, more important, how did I miss this the other night? I flushed as it hit me the concierge might remember me and kept my head down as I followed Nick.

Everything was so much posher than I remembered; I felt so out of place. I felt a pang of nostalgia for Ben's shitty Hackney pad. He may have had a Boyzilian, but at least he lived somewhere normal.

'Here we are,' said Nick. 'Do you want a drink?' I nodded quickly. I needed several. 'Cool, wine? Whisky?'

'Oh, do you have ginger beer?' I asked. 'I love it with whisky.'

'A girl who likes whisky. Not something you see every day,' he said, looking visibly impressed. 'I don't have any mixers though. You're cool with it straight?'

Um, no, I wasn't cool with straight whisky. But he had looked so impressed when I said I liked it… 'OK.'

'Sweet, here you go,' he said. I closed my eyes and poured it down my throat. It burnt as it flew down me but maybe it would give me a bit of Dutch courage. 'I did not expect you to neck that.'

Were you not meant to drink them like shots? This was getting complicated; maybe we should just skip straight to the sex bit.

'Guess I'm not the average girl,' I said, hoping it sounded flirtatious. I walked over to him and kissed him. He put down his drink, wrapped his arms around me and started snogging me. It looked as if we were about to have sex right there on the kitchen floor.

'Let's go to the bedroom,' he murmured. I followed him into his room. He pulled his clothes off as well as mine. I risked a quick look at his pubes. Still trimmed. 'What's your favourite position?'

Fuck, what was my favourite position? I'd only ever done two. 'Um, I guess…doggy,' I said, cringing at saying it aloud. 'Yours?'

'Dirty.' He grinned. 'I like that too…but I prefer a girl being on top.'

Shit. Was that an invitation? I'd never been on top before. 'Um, OK,' I said.

He seemed to take this as an invitation and lay down on the bed, looking up at me expectantly. I tried to calm myself down. *It will be fine. They do it all the time in movies and porn, and those girls haven't even been to uni. You have a degree, Ellie—you can master this.*

I climbed onto him and put one leg on either side of his body. I sat down on his pubes and winced. They itched my bum. I guess this was what he meant when he said pubes could be spiky…

He pulled me towards him and started snogging me. I felt his penis poke around my vagina. How was it going to go inside? Should I guide it in or was he going to? On cue, he pushed it into me and I felt it slip in like a tampon.

'Ahhh,' he gasped and closed his eyes. Right, now I just had to move up and down and then it would be fine. I pushed my body up with my legs and winced in pain. It was like doing a push-up and I had no muscles—how was I meant to repeatedly do this?

I had a flashback of *Cruel Intentions* when Sarah Michelle Gellar told the virgin girl how to have sex. They were practising on a horse. There was something about going up and down and forwards and backwards. Slowly, I began to move my body up and down, wincing, then tried to move forwards and backwards. It felt wooden and very, very wrong.

Nick put his hands on either side of my hips and started moving me. He lifted me diagonally up and down, rhythmically. I gasped. This was actual sex. I was riding him like a cowgirl porn star. I was like a feminist prostitute riding the helpless man beneath me. His hands slipped off me and I jerked backwards.

I tried to carry on as before, but without his hands helping me, I quickly realised that I had no sexual rhythm whatsoever. It was embarrassing. I felt my cheeks flushing and I wished I could stop. We'd been here for about five minutes—surely it was about time for him to come again? Unless I was so bad that he wasn't even hard any more?

I squinted and tried to feel him inside of me, but it felt squishy. *Holy fuck, had he actually lost his boner?* I felt so stressed that I lost all traces of rhythm and began jerking mindlessly on top of him. I probably looked like a jack-in-the-box on speed.

'Slower,' he said and put his hands on my hips again.

I breathed out in relief. He was going to help me again—this would be OK. He slowly pulled me back into a gentle rhythm and I felt myself relax. I leant down towards him so my boobs were rubbing against his torso and kissed him.

He groaned and shoved his tongue inside me. I broke away for air and my boobs fell on his face. He made some murmuring noises and I grinned. I, Ellie Kolstakis, was making an actual twenty-nine-year-old man groan with pleasure.

Then I realised his groans were getting a bit high-pitched. I put my arms out on either side of his so I was basically doing an actual press-up and lifted my boobs off him. He gasped. 'Ah, ah, God, sorry, I just…couldn't breathe.'

I flushed with humiliation. I'd thought he was enjoying my boobs grazing his face, not being suffocated by their weight. 'Sorry,' I muttered. This wasn't the first time this had happened to me.

'No, don't be,' he said and pushed me off him. He rolled on top of me and slipped his penis back into me. I closed my eyes in utter relief as he took over and began thrusting into me. I knew missionary was boring and I didn't want to be the kind of girl who just lay there during sex—hell, I wanted to experiment with role play and whips—but it was just so much easier to not have to worry about my rhythm.

He squeezed my boobs and I yelped. It felt sore, but it was also kind of…nice. He stroked my nipples and I gasped out loud. Ohmigod, it was like having two mini clitorises on my boobs. How had I only just discovered how good this felt? Nick moved one of his hands away and my heart plummeted. I had to let him know he should keep his hand there.

I started making porn-star noises. He put his hand back and stroked. I closed my eyes in relief and let myself enjoy the actual feelings of sex instead of just being pleased with the fact that it was happening. If I wanted to have an orgasm with a guy, then I would have to totally relax and get in the zone. Ommmmm. Ommmmm.

I tried to meditate as he stroked my nipples and thrust his peen inside of me but my mind was too distracted. All I could think about was almost squashing him with my boobs, having no sexual rhythm and being shit at sex. Yeah, it felt nice right now, but how could I orgasm when he was right there on top of me?

He stopped thrusting and collapsed on top of me. I waited a few seconds but he didn't move. 'Um…are you OK?' I asked.

'Yeah, that was good,' he said. Was? So it was…over?

'Did you, erm, did you come?'

'Yeah,' he said. I sighed in disappointment. I hadn't even had time to get in the zone. My orgasm would have to wait.

Chapter 21

'Do you know what would be fun,' murmured Nick a few hours later.

'Enlighten me.'

'Well,' he said, rubbing his hand across my body, 'we could sixty-nine.'

I bolted upright in bed. 'Sixty-nine like…the sex position?'

'Yeah. You keen?'

Was I?! I'd been waiting for this since Lara drew an animated version of it on page sixty-nine of my History textbook. 'Yeah,' I said nonchalantly. 'Let's do it.'

'OK.' He grinned. 'Do you want to go on top or shall I?'

I hesitated. If I went on top he'd, have my vagina in his face, but it would be easier to give him head. If he was on top, he might squash me and my vagina would still be in his face. 'I'll go on top,' I said bravely.

'As the lady wishes,' he said, lying down on his back. We were still naked from our previous fuck, so I took a deep breath and climbed straight on top of him. The whisky hadn't really done anything except give me hot flushes, so I felt very sober as I opened my legs above his face. I was well aware that he could see my vagina in more detail than I ever would, no matter how many pictures I took of it with my SLR digital camera.

'Is this OK?' I asked uncertainly. I was doing the Pilates table pose above him. My head was hovering by his penis and my entire nether regions were inches away from his mouth—and his nose. Oh God, his nose. He would be able to smell everything and I'd pooed just before our date. I started to wonder if this was a good idea.

'More than OK,' he said, as he ventured straight into my vag. He started licking me and grabbed my arse towards him. This was really happening. I lowered myself towards his erect penis and opened my mouth. It slid straight in and I tried to remember the blow job tips I had Googled the year before.

I used my tongue as well as my lips and tried to squeeze my mouth tighter—but without letting my teeth get anyway near his dick. I was concentrating so hard on trying to hold on to his legs and give a decent blow job that I almost forgot his face was nestling inside my labia.

We carried on licking and sucking. It was eerily quiet, apart from the sounds of saliva thwacking against genitals. I wondered if it was meant to be this peaceful. But seeing as both our mouths were pretty preoccupied, there was no way we could make any sounds.

I started to speed up, pushing my head up and down faster than before. I felt his penis throb inside of me and I grinned to myself. I was doing a sixty-nine. Could I be any more grown-up? I was barely even thinking about the fact that my pubes were surrounding Nick's face and he could smell my vagina post-sex. Oh God, it must be so sweaty and sticky.

My arms were resting on the bed, on either side of his legs, and they were starting to hurt. All this sex was making me realise just how unfit I was. I readjusted myself and tried to lift up my arms so I could lean on his thighs instead. I clung on to his thighs precariously. It did not feel stable. Maybe I should move my right arm, onto the bed again, and then...

'OWWW,' I shrieked, as my arms gave way and I crashed off the bed. I had slipped off his legs so half my body was now thrashing wildly on the floor, and my arse was waving in Nick's direction.

He sat up. 'Are you OK?'

'Can you just... Can you pull me up onto the bed?' I gasped. He obligingly grabbed my torso and pulled me onto the bed. I lay there breathing heavily. I knew my face was flushed purple from the strain and my hair was stuck to my face with sweat. I also knew that I had just fallen off a sixty-nine.

'What happened?' he asked.

'Sorry, my, um...my hand slipped off you,' I managed to say.

'Right,' he said. 'I can safely say that's never happened before, but so long as you're OK it's all good.'

All good? Really? I'D JUST FALLEN OFF A SIXTY-NINE.

I rolled over and pressed my face into the duvet. Why was this happening to me? I had no sexual rhythm and not enough arm strength to maintain a fucking sixty-nine. I was a joke.

'Ellie, are you all right?'

'Mffmhm, tired,' I mumbled.

'OK, maybe we should just go to sleep,' he suggested.

I nodded and pulled the rest of the duvet over my head. I couldn't even sixty-nine—I was a sexual failure.

* * *

'Hi, one no-fat latte and one flat white with, like, two espressos in it, please.' I was in the Caffè Nero by my office, trying to suppress my continuous yawns. Nick and I had woken up at 7 a.m. He'd run straight in the shower, and we'd spent the next hour getting ready. I hadn't really had time to think about the awkward sex and now was not the time to start. 'Thanks,' I said, reaching out for the coffees.

I downed my drink before I even got into the building and walked over to Maxine's office to give her the NFL.

'Oh, thanks, Ellie,' she said, looking surprised.

I rubbed my eyes, wondering if I'd just imagined the 'thanks'. Maybe she was mellowing now that my columns were doing well. 'No worries. Is there anything particular you want me to do today?'

'Do you have any more content for another column?' she asked. 'Your last one's up and doing well.'

I shut my eyes briefly. Cue an onslaught of phone calls from my furious mother. 'Yeah, I guess I do,' I admitted.

'Great, well, why don't you just take today to write that up and then head off when you're done,' she suggested.

I stared at her in surprise. This was not the Maxine I knew and hated. It would take me only a few hours to write up the column, so I could probably leave at lunchtime. 'Great, thanks,' I said quickly, before she changed her mind, and ran out of her office. I pulled open the WhatsApp thread I had with Lara and Emma.

Me: Maxine had personality change. Can leave office at lunch.

Lara: OMG amazing. I'm in Hertfordshire at my mum's. Shall I come meet you post-work?

Me: YES.

Emma: Ugh jel. See you gals this eve though.

Lara: Want to hear details about Nick date.

Me: They're…worth waiting for.

Emma: Can't wait, you dirty stop-out. X

I laughed to myself as I imagined Emma realising I hadn't come home last night. One of my plastic co-workers shot me a frosty glance but instead of looking back down at my desk, I met her gaze. 'Just doing research,' I said, waving my phone at her. 'For my column?'

Jenna let out a tiny sigh that sounded more as if she was spitting at me and turned back to her laptop. I suppressed a victory grin and opened up a Word document. If I wanted to laud my column success over my (paid) co-workers, I'd have to actually keep writing them.

* * *

I walked up Mare Street to our house. It had been less than forty-eight hours since I was last there but it felt like longer. I was craving my bed, a long bath and some TV shows. But as I walked round the corner, I saw Lara sitting on the brick wall outside the house. She was early.

'I know I'm early,' she said, jumping off the wall as I approached. 'But I was going out of my mind at home with my mum.'

I gave her a hug and dropped my head onto her shoulder. 'Don't worry. I'm shattered but we can curl up on the sofa together. Actually, the sofa is out of bounds.'

'Dare I ask?'

'Will. Raj. I walked in.'

'OK, straight to your room?' she suggested.

'Yup,' I said, as we walked in through the front door. 'So, how was stuff at your mum's?' Lara's perfect lawyer mum had split up with her perfect lawyer husband last year, after it turned out he wasn't so perfect and was shagging his secretary. Now Stephanie was living in Hertfordshire near her sister. It was the opposite side of London to where we'd grown up, so I hadn't even seen Lara's new house.

'Ughhh, exhausting. Like, the new place is nice. It's a three-bed flat and it has a garden, and it's really cute, but it's never going to compare to our old place. And my mum is just being so weird at the moment,' cried Lara, as she collapsed onto my bed.

'Weird how?'

'Well, she's obsessed with making the house perfect and immaculate. When she's not at work, she's in Laura Ashley buying furniture and curtains. Even though the house is absolutely fine.'

'But your mum has always been pretty house proud, hasn't she?'

'It's different now though. I think she's just lonely, so she's trying to keep herself busy, but it's so tiring to be around.'

'I can imagine,' I said, as I dropped down onto the bed next to her. 'Do you think she's ready to go on any dates and find someone new?'

Lara scoffed. 'Please. She's fucking terrified. I keep telling her to go online, but she refuses. She says it's hard being single after so long, and even though she'd love to find someone new, she doesn't feel comfortable putting herself out there. Which is ridiculous because everyone's online. I even told her about you, and she's read your columns, but I think it maybe put her off more than anything.'

'Lar! I can't believe you did that. Your mum's going to think I'm such a slut.'

'Yeah, like the rest of the world, and you should be proud, remember?'

'Sorry,' I said. 'I keep forgetting it doesn't mean "filthy whore".'

'Let's reclaim that too. Whore equals awesome.'

'Like…"Oh my God, Lara, your hair looks so whorey right now I love it".'

She laughed. 'Totally. Let's make it a thing.'

'Not sure it's going to catch on, but, anyway, back to your mum. Why is she so scared? She's so lovely and successful, and, well, she's a massive MILF. She'd find someone within ten minutes of being online.'

Lara nodded. 'I know. But she's convinced she'll get rejected and she won't be able to handle it. I think the whole "Dad cheating" thing really damaged her. But your mum has been single ever since your dad left too, right?'

'Yup.' I sighed. My mum had been single for about ten years and while my dad—a total arsehole who called only to tell me to work harder—had a new family, she hadn't been on a single date since pre-millennium. 'I've given up hope with her. I think she's just too traditional to go online. And all her Greek friends are coupled up, so she does feel really lonely, but I think she wants to be with someone Greek and none of them are ever divorced. So it's a total catch-22.'

'Would she ever go online?'

'I wish. I've tried to convince her. Hell, I even made her a profile on Match.com and paid sixty quid for it. But she refused to go on any of the dates. I think she's got it into her head that only older women who look like Demi Moore can get dates. I know she wants to meet someone, but I just don't think it's going to happen unless he magically finds her and asks her out. She refuses to put any work into it.'

'Ohmigod, same with my mum,' cried Lara. 'Maybe it's a generational thing? Like, yeah, they had to work hard with getting jobs and stuff, but they didn't have to work for relationships. Men did all the work and women just waited. But with us we're so used to working our arses off just to get a job, let alone a promotion, and then work to get dates, to get sex, to get boyfriends... Nothing is easy any more.'

I nodded fervently. 'Exactly, that's why I love online dating, because it's a way to actually put yourself out there and get a date. If it didn't exist, there's no way I'd be on date four. I know I met Nick IRL but I wouldn't have had the confidence to flirt or go home with him if it wasn't for my previous online dates.'

'Fuck, I can't believe I forgot to ask about Nick,' she cried. 'How was the actual proper grown-up date?? More sex?'

'Well, he took me to a rooftop bar, where I felt so un-posh and awkward, but then we basically went straight back to his and shagged. Twice.'

'Nice,' said Lara. 'So you've had sex three times now. You're basically a pro.'

'Yeah, so that's the slightly shit bit... I don't know how to say this, but, well, I don't think I'm very good at sex.'

'El, no one thinks they're good at sex. Especially when they've only done it a few times. It will get better, trust me.'

I felt my cheeks flushing and looked straight at her. Her blonde hair was falling over her face as she smiled supportively at me. I wanted to trust her, but she was so different to me when it came to stuff like this. Her body was hairless and she was generically gorgeous. Of course she got better at sex with practice. She was probably born with sexual rhythm. Unlike me.

Oh hell. If I couldn't admit the truth to my oldest friend, who could I tell it to?

'Lar, I was so bad when I was on top though. I couldn't, like, get the rhythm right.'

She scrunched up her face at me. 'Really? I don't think I've ever had that. Don't you just get into it?'

'No, I don't,' I cried. 'See, I knew this would happen. I'm the only one who has weird sex issues. So fucking typical. I even fell off a sixty-nine.'

She stared at me. 'How?'

'We were positioned weirdly on the bed and my arms gave way so I slid off his body onto the floor. It was so… ugh…humiliating.'

'El,' she said, hiding a smirk. 'It's OK. Sex is awkward. That's the whole thing about it. That's why people like having sex with people they feel comfortable with—so they can laugh over the squelching sex sounds and getting pubes stuck in their teeth.'

I looked at her in horror. 'That happens?'

'Yup,' she said. 'And worse, I'm sure.'

'OK, fine, but how am I ever going to be able to orgasm during sex?' I asked.

She sighed. 'I don't know. I don't want to sound like a dick but I can come from penetration. I know other people find it harder. Maybe you can ask him to use his fingers at the same time? Or you can do it yourself?'

'Maybe, but it's not even that the technical skills are lacking. Like, he was good at giving me head. But I'm just so stressed about so much stuff that I can't let go and just... come.'

'Have you tried clearing your head?'

'Lara—I tried fucking meditating. I even made ommm sounds.'

'Out loud?'

'No, in my head,' I said, swatting her arm. 'You need to have more faith in me. But it didn't even work, hence I feel more doomed than before.'

'Maybe you just need to stop trying,' suggested Lara. 'You can come on your own, so you're clearly capable of it. If he's doing the wrong stuff, you can tell him what you like, and if he is doing it right, then just stop thinking.'

'It's not even just thinking, it's like meta-thinking. I start thinking about how I'm overthinking things and it just gets...too much.'

'No shit,' she said, rolling her eyes. 'Just tell your brain to shut the fuck up while you're fucking, and then maybe you'll come.'

'Maybe.' I sighed. 'Here's hoping he calls me so I get another chance to try.'

Chapter 22

NSFW

*M*y latest date wasn't an online date. I met him IRL, can you believe it? We were in a Shoreditch club, and instead of being just another hipster, he ended up being a banker who took me home.

It was my most successful encounter so far, and it's making me wonder if meeting someone in the flesh is always going to beat an online-based rendezvous. In real life you can feel the attraction, get a sense of their chav-to-hipster ratio, and it feels, well, real.

But on the internet, you never really know what you're getting. You have no idea if there's going to be a spark or not, so you just risk it and end up wasting a Saturday night or having to wash blood off your face in the loos.

I know I'm just talking about a good old-fashioned one-night stand here, but—please make sure you're sitting down *now—we have been on a subsequent date. An actual real date in a fancy bar with grass growing on the terrace.*

He is yet to bite me or bleed on my face, so it is an improvement on my online dates. Instead, he has impressed me with his flat (concierge and view of the Shard), promise-keeping (said he'd call and actually did), and the fact that he knows I'm writing this column and doesn't give a fuck.

So, dear reader, might I be changing the premise of this column soon? Will I no longer be single?

Um, of course not.

This is a casual fling, and it's exactly what I've been looking for. It means we both know where we stand. I don't have to sit here wondering if he is The One because we both know he isn't, and while he's using me to get over her, I'm using him for NSFW fun and column fodder. Who needs mutually exclusive when you can have mutually beneficial?

I woke up sweating, just as I did every Friday. Now my mum knew I had one-night stands and was someone else's rebound girl. Would she call me in a frenzied panic or would she get her terrifying older sister to do it? I reached out for my phone and reluctantly looked at the screen.

I had two Facebook notifications. My stomach plummeted as I saw that they were both from school friends. Surely they hadn't already seen the column—it was only 8 a.m.

Cass: OMG Ellie the column is hysterical. You're so brave. Holy shit.

Megan: Um, so proud of you for having your own column!! I'm going to send it to all the girls right now! Expect congratulatory messages all morning… Oh, and it's my birthday next week. Invite coming soon.

I laughed out loud. They liked it—and now they wanted me to go to their birthdays. Not just as Lara's plus one, but as Ellie Kolstakis. I mean, it was still terrifying to think of all the girls reading my column and telling me what they thought, but fuck it. They thought I was funny and they wanted to hang out with me. Maybe having a non-anonymous column wasn't such a bad idea.

My phone vibrated. Nick's name flashed on my screen and I physically balked. What if he'd read it?!

'Um, hello?'

'Good morning, you, glad to hear you're up. I felt a bit bad calling so early.'

'No worries, I'm, um, yeah, just got up.' He was being nice. Why was he being nice? Why didn't he just cut to the chase and tell me he was appalled by my column?

'Cool, so I was wondering if you're free tonight. I know it's last minute and you probably have amazing Friday night plans, but I thought you could come over?'

He hadn't read it. Thank God. I breathed out in relief.

'Um, sure,' I said. Lara and Emma wouldn't mind if I ditched them for a shag. That was in the Girl Code somewhere…right?

'Ah, cool, well, text me when you finish work and we'll figure out timings then. Maybe I can even pick you up from work?'

'Does that work? Can we get the Tube to yours together?'

'Well, I was probably going to jump in a cab home, so…'

'Oh! Yeah, I mean, that would be amazing, thanks.'

'Hey, I might not be English but I am a gentleman. You don't have to sound so surprised.'

'Next thing you're going to tell me you want to cook me dinner.'

'What's wrong with that? Sounds like your past boy-friends didn't know how to treat you well.'

I laughed awkwardly. 'Past boyfriends' wasn't really applicable to my life. But if Nick wanted to give me cabs and food in exchange for sex, then who was I to complain?

'Sounds good to me. See you later.'

* * *

'You're in early, Ellie,' said Hattie, as she swanned in half an hour after I'd got into the office. I raised my eyebrows. This was the friendliest she'd ever been to me.

'Yeah, thought I'd get a start on all this.' I smiled falsely, gesturing to the pile of papers on my desk.

She gave me an approving nod. 'I did the same when I was an intern a few years ago. The only way to get them to keep you on is to prove you're willing to go above and beyond.'

I looked at her in surprise. Hattie had been an intern? I'd just assumed daddy dearest had sorted the job out for her. 'I didn't know you were an intern here,' I said.

She snorted. 'Don't be ridiculous. I interned for *Tatler*, and then they offered me a job and, after a couple of years, Maxine poached me to work here.'

'Oh,' I said. 'How did you get the internship at *Tatler*?'

'I emailed the editor. She was really impressed with me taking my own initiative and told me to come in.'

I stared at Hattie in surprise. How could I have misjudged her so badly? She hadn't just got here through nepotism—

she'd worked her ass off for it, just as I was trying to. 'That's… really cool, Hattie,' I said.

'Yeah, it worked out. So, I liked your column.'

'Really? Um, thanks.' This was the only compliment I'd ever received in this office. What exactly was happening right now?

'So your date took you to KRG the other week. I think some of the girls were there that night.'

I stared at her blankly. 'Sorry?'

She sighed. 'Kensington Rooftop Gardens? Your column?'

'Oh, right,' I cried. Note to self: start abbreving posh bars. 'Yeah, it's gorgeous there.'

'Hmm, I never had you down as the kind of girl who'd go out round there,' she said, eyeing up my comfort clothes. I looked at her immaculately tailored trousers, cream blazer and thick gold jewellery and wished I'd washed my hair that morning.

'There's a lot you don't know about me,' I said, sticking up my chin.

'Yeah, are you going out with that guy, then?' she asked.

'Oh, no, it's just casual,' I said with a little shrug. Hattie looked impressed. 'What about you, seeing anyone?'

'God no,' she said. 'I just ended things with my ex because he was getting, like, so needy, so now I'm just dating.'

'Anyone special?' I asked.

'Just a couple of Chelsea guys,' she said.

'Naturally,' I said sarcastically.

'Yeah, exactly,' she said seriously. 'Hey, you should come out for drinks with us. Maybe next week?'

Oh my God, my work colleagues were finally accepting me. Who knew having an active sex life meant so many different social groups would want to start hanging out with me?!

'Yes!' I said. 'Um, that would be good. Anyway, I'd probably better get on with this before Maxine gets in.'

'Tell me about it,' said Hattie, rolling her eyes. 'Let's hope she's not on the warpath today.'

I turned back to my computer screen with a slow grin spreading across my face. Clearly being slutty did have its advantages. In fact, seeing as Maxine wasn't in yet, maybe I should work on said sluttiness.

I surreptitiously pulled open a new window and started Googling: 'how to have sex on top'. A *Cosmopolitan* article popped up. It was a Q&A from a girl whose boyfriend wanted her to 'master' the position. I read *Cosmo*'s sage advice: 'To assume the woman-on-top position, have your guy lie on his back and straddle him with your knees on either side of his hips. Or, if you prefer, you can squat over him with your feet flat on the mattress.'

Squat?? As though I was trying to pee without sitting on a gross loo seat in a public toilet? I really did not have the thigh muscles for that. How was this legitimate advice? I'd have to try to figure out how to straddle him with my knees flat on the bed.

'Start moving up and down to build momentum. Or you can rest your torso on his and sensuously grind him from side to side or in circles. But just because you're in the driver's seat, that doesn't mean you have to do all the work. To keep from tuckering out, have him wrap his hands around your hips and help you gyrate.'

'Sensuously grind'? What was this? Why couldn't they just write this in normal terms, and also, why were they assuming the average reader even knew how to grind—sensuously or not?

I sighed. At least the tips acknowledged that it was hard work, and Nick's trick of holding my hips was clearly a classic tip.

What about...a sixty-nine? I checked no one was behind my computer screen and quickly typed in: 'falling off a sixty-nine'.

The top entry was 'Man, sixty-nine, falls off a cliff'. Fantastic. Clearly nobody had ever fallen off a sixty-nine apart from me. Fuck it, clearly sixty-nines weren't for me and I should try something else. What about...'best positions to come in'?

Hundreds of pages popped up and I breathed out in relief. At least this was a popular search topic. One website had a list of the top positions:

Missionary. Tick. Although judging from the pictures, it looked as if my legs weren't going high enough above Nick's shoulders. How did these girls get their legs in these positions? I would have to get myself a gym membership ASAP. I made a mental note to call my mum for gym money.

Girl on top. Ugh. Yes, I knew it was a good position, if I could bloody manage it. It also suggested doing it backwards. That sounded even worse. I felt the familiar sexual panic rise inside me and tried to quash it. It didn't really matter if I had to practise 'reverse cowgirl' with him, right? Surely that was the kind of position girls weren't meant to be automatically skilled at?

Sitting up together. So I had to sit on him, thrust back and forth and up and down, whilst hugging him. This looked quite sweet. It reminded me of teddy-bear rolls from gymnastics at school. Maybe this is what they were trying to prepare us for.

Side-to-side. Right, so we lie side to side and he goes inside me, and I swing my legs over his thighs. Both of my legs? I craned my head to look at the diagram but couldn't figure out where the stick woman's second leg had gone.

Lying-down doggy. It was just like normal doggy but with me on the bed so that I could rub my clitoris against it. OK, I could do that, but wouldn't it be better to rub it with my actual hand? Maybe that could be managed.

I clicked on a different tab and was directed to a YouTube page. This was seriously NSFW, but it wasn't as if I was being paid to work there. Surely the intern could get away with a bit of extracurricular Googling? I pulled out my headphones confidently and stuck them in.

An attractive black man wearing tight Y-fronts came up on the screen. He lay down on the floor and a hot Spanish woman walked over to him. I felt my throat tighten—surely this wasn't going to be an actual porno? YouTube couldn't do that, could they?!

The woman was wearing underwear. Thank God. She climbed on top of the guy. 'OK, so this is a good way to have sex on top,' she said. She lay on top of him, with her legs on top of his and her hands clutching his. They were spread out like two Jesuses. Then she just lifted her body slightly and started humping him.

My mouth dropped open. She looked like a rabbit on speed. Were you meant to fuck them so quickly? I remembered my attempt with Nick, which had started off slowly. Maybe that wasn't what he'd wanted.

She swapped positions and did the teddy-bear hug. I relaxed as the couple hugged. It looked as if this would be a calmer position. And then she started rocking her body into his at the speed of light. What the actual fuck—was sex always meant to be so…fast? How did she even get her body to do that? It looked so spontaneous and natural but her rhythm was impeccable.

I looked up and saw Maxine walking towards me. Crap. I ripped out my headphones and closed the screen. By the time she got to my desk I was bright red and had a layer of sweat on my top lip.

'Ellie,' she said. 'Can you put in some calls for interviews, please?'

'Um, sure, but wait,' I cried out, as she started walking back to her desk. 'What interviews?'

She sighed loudly. 'We need some big interviews this month. So, just think of some celebrities you'd love to interview and get in touch with them. You know the kind of person we would be interested in.'

'Wait, I'd get to interview them?' I cried out.

'No, of course not. It would be Carla, the chief interviewer. I just meant you're young and our target audience, so try to think of the kind of people you'd like to read about and give them a call. Is that manageable?'

'Um, yes, sure,' I said.

Hattie and co. might want to hang out with me now, but I couldn't think of anything that would make Maxine be nice to me—or even pay me.

Thank God Nick didn't expect me to buy my own drinks.

* * *

A black cab pulled up outside the office and I jumped up from the wooden bench in excitement. The door opened and Nick got out.

'Hey,' he said.

He was wearing a suit and looked so fit it hurt. And he was smiling at me in the way guys did in romcoms. It felt surreal. Since when did I, Ellie Kolstakis, go on dates with hot guys who paid for cabs and looked at me as if I was Julia Roberts? I grinned back at him. If I was his Julia, then I'd better act the part. I gave him a kiss on the lips and climbed into the cab.

'So, you look pretty good in a suit,' I said flirtatiously.

'Thanks, you don't look too bad yourself.'

'That's what they all say.'

'Oh yeah, who? Do I need to get my macho guy on and mark out my territory?'

'You did not just call me your territory,' I cried.

'Oh God, here comes the feminist spiel,' he said, grinning at me.

I laughed and swatted his arm. 'If I wasn't convinced that you were kidding, then yes, you'd get the full lecture. But I have a bit more faith in you.'

'You do, huh?'

He leant in and kissed me. I bit my lip to stop myself from smiling like a loon. This was *fun*. Like, the exact sort of fun I thought I'd be having three years ago, but hey, better late than never, right? His hand stroked my hair as we kissed and I suddenly wondered what Emma and Lara would say if they saw us now.

They'd think I was falling for him. But how could you fall for someone you'd just met? This wasn't actually *Notting Hill*. That kind of stuff happened only in movies. Besides, I couldn't imagine Nick and I as a couple. He was so smooth and suave and I was this curly-haired mess. It was like when Bridget Jones tried to date Daniel Cleaver—it was doomed. They were better off as fuck buddies, just as Nick and I were.

'Oh, hey,' I said, breaking away from the kiss. 'I can see the Shard. We must be by you now.'

'Yeah,' he said. 'Pretty sweet landmark, eh?'

'Totally. I hear you can go up there for drinks and stuff, which is cool.'

'Yeah, my workmates go to the bar there a fair bit. Maybe we should go one day. It would be fun to take you.'

Fun. He was right. We were having fun and I was over-thinking everything. 'Definitely. Fun with you is good.'

He smiled. 'Yeah. Well, here we are.' He handed the cab driver a twenty-pound note and ignored my weak protes-tations to split the cost. Thank God he hadn't accepted or I would have been eating plain pasta all week. I followed him out of the cab into his flat. This time, walking in with Nick by my side, I felt as if I belonged. When Nick greeted the concierge, I gave him a small nod too.

'Home sweet home,' he said, pushing open the door.

I followed him in and hovered behind him. I suddenly felt shy. It had been fine bantering around in the cab, but being alone in his flat felt weird. Like, was he really going to make me a stir-fry right now? Did he even have the ingredients?

'So, luckily for you, I did a food shop yesterday,' he an-nounced. 'Which means we can make dinner whenever. Do you want a drink first though?'

I nodded in relief. A drink was exactly what I needed. 'I bought a couple of bottles too. Well, when I say bought, I mean stole from my flatmate Will.'

He laughed. 'Sweet. Well, let's drink the stolen brew, then.' He took it from my hands and squinted. 'Is that… sparkly?'

'Is it? Oh damn, I thought I'd picked up red. Do you mind? Typical Will, drinking sparkly pink wine. He says he's not camp, then he does shit like that.'

'No worries,' he said. 'I drink pretty much anything.' He poured out the Prosecco into two glasses. 'Cheers, to...to Will for providing the bevvies.'

'Cheers,' I said, feeling unnerved as he stared straight into my eyes. We clinked glasses and drank. I put mine down, hovering awkwardly. 'So, um...'

'Yeah, do you wanna just hang out a bit and cook later?'

'Sure,' I said, ignoring the gnawing hunger pains in my tummy. 'I'm barely even hungry right now.'

'Sweet.'

We sat down on the sofa and he switched on the TV. A *Top Gear* rerun was on. He didn't move to swap channels. I sighed inwardly and got ready for half an hour of chauvinistic car jokes.

'I just, like, hate Jeremy Clarkson,' I cried, three glasses of wine and two episodes of *Top Gear* into our night. 'And the other one looks like a hamster. Don't you think?'

Nick laughed. 'Mmm, if you say so. I'm pretty into cars though, so that's the main appeal for me.'

'Cars...no, can't say they interest me, sorry.' I put my glass down on the coffee table and wine sloshed over the side. 'Shit, sorry,' I said, realising that I was already drunk. I knew we should have had the stir-fry pre-alcohol.

I looked over at Nick. He was still wearing his shirt and looked hot. If we weren't going to eat dinner, the next best thing was a shag. I was kind of excited to practise reverse cowgirl.

I edged towards him and looked up at his face. He was engrossed in the programme and hadn't noticed. It was up to me to kiss him first. I had no idea why I was so nervous—especially because I'd just done the exact same thing in the cab—but I felt my heart race as I forced myself to make the first move and kiss him. I closed my eyes and thrust my face towards him.

'Whoa,' he cried, as my lips smacked into his chin. I flushed red and he smiled at me, taking my face in his hands. He pulled me close to him and kissed me. Phew. We were back on familiar territory. I kissed him as hard as I could and started pulling my clothes off. He took his off too, and within minutes, we were writhing around naked on his leather sofa.

Plufftttttttt.

He broke away from me. 'Did you just parp?'

'What?!' I cried out. 'No. It was my skin getting stuck to the sofa. And, seriously, *parp*? It's FART.'

'Oh-kay.' He grinned. 'You can calm down, Ellie. I don't mind that you *farted* in front of me.'

I blushed furiously. 'Ohmigod, I didn't fart. It's your sofa. Can we go in your room?'

'Sure.' He laughed.

I fled into his room and he followed. We stood there naked by his bed.

'So…' he said.

'Can you, um, lie down?' I asked.

He raised his eyebrows and lay down on the bed. I took a deep breath and walked over to him. I climbed on top of him, still facing him, and hovered nervously. He pulled me towards him gently and I kissed him. I took my right hand and reached blindly towards his penis. It was poking out of his tidy pubes. I tried to angle it into my vagina.

It didn't work.

'Agh, I can't… Can you?' I asked.

He tried to put his penis into me, but it seemed my cervix was well and truly closed. Fuck.

'Hey, I have some lube we can use,' he suggested.

'Um, if you… If you want to.'

'Yeah, let me get it out,' he said. He rolled over and opened a drawer in his bedside cabinet.

I froze in shock.

There were rows and rows of dildos. Small bullets, rabbit vibrators, hot-pink lumps of rubber. I closed my eyes and opened them again. They were all still there.

In the corner was a selection of small bottles. He picked one up triumphantly and waved it at me. 'Got it,' he said.

I stared at him in silence. I couldn't make any words come out. I just… What the fuck had I just seen?

'Ellie? Are you OK?'

'Mmm,' I rasped. 'Just, um, what are those?'

'Oh, my lightsabres?'

'Sorry?'

'My lightsabres.' He grinned. 'It's what I call my vibrators and dildos. We can have a bit of a play if you want. They're fun.'

I blinked at him in silence. I couldn't absorb anything he was saying. I did *not* sign up to shag Obi-Wan Kenobi.

'Ellie?' he asked. 'It'll be fun. Go on, lie down.' He gently pushed my torso and I obligingly lay back onto the bed. My whole body was rigid. I was scared shitless.

He parted my legs and looked straight at my untrimmed, unkempt vagina with pubes growing down my thighs. So much for me not letting him go down on me. He picked up one of his instruments and rubbed lube onto it. He pressed a button and it started vibrating. I craned my neck upwards and watched him move it towards my vagina.

He put it on my clitoris and I gasped involuntarily. I'd forgotten how good it felt to use a vibrator. I'd been too busy/stressed/lazy to do it lately and it felt good—except for the fact that I had no idea where the fuck his lightsabre had been.

I felt it move into my vagina and gasped. It was cold and slimy, creeping into me, and now all I could think about was it going into some other girl. Had he even washed it since?

I pushed his hand away and the vibrator fell to the floor. It buzzed in circles on the rug.

'What's wrong?' he asked.

'Um, I just… I'm not really in the mood for that. Can we just, uh, have sex?' I couldn't bring myself to use the word 'fuck' as casually as he did.

He shrugged. 'I'm all yours.' He pulled a condom onto his penis, then lay back down onto the bed and passed me the lube.

I held the tube in my hand and stared at it blankly. What was I meant to do with it? Should I squirt it straight onto his penis or into my hands? I assumed it was the former and rubbed it onto his rubbery dick.

He took his dick into his own hands and slid it into me. Luckily, it slid right in. But now I was facing the wrong way for reverse cowgirl. Should I swivel on him now, or later?

I turned my body around quickly without thinking. I didn't want to see his surprise, and then his confusion, when I would inevitably fuck up the rhythm and prove that I was as sexually inexperienced as a nun.

I used my thighs to push my body up and down and began wincing. I wouldn't be able to last long here. When would he put his hands on my hips to help me? Maybe I could ask, but wouldn't that kill the mood? Luckily, I felt his hands rest on either side of my arse. They guided me up and down and I tried to put my weight onto them.

Think light thoughts, Ellie, I told myself. *You are as light as a feather. You have strong thighs. You can do this. Just think of all the calories you must be losing.*

The thought of weight loss and a toned bod cheered me up and I managed to up the pace. But then I felt my left thigh muscle strain and I knew I had to stop. I put my legs straight out in front of me and used my arm muscles to push up my body.

This was so much worse. It was like a backwards press-up. Who ever said this position was enjoyable and *why*? How was I meant to come when my arms were on the verge of collapse?

I closed my eyes and tried to centre my strength in my core muscles as my Pilates teacher had taught me. But with my eyes closed, I could feel the sensations in my vagina more, and it was seriously stinging. I breathed through the pain and winced as Nick's penis went in and out.

I climbed off him, gasping. The pain was too much. He took this as a sign that I wanted to change positions, so he pushed me onto the bed and climbed on top. Good old-fashioned missionary. Maybe it would stop hurting now.

But as he thrust himself in and out quickly, my vagina burned up. It felt as if it was on fire. I closed my eyes tightly and prayed to God that he would come any second now. He didn't. Oh God, please, let him come. I bit my teeth together and groaned in silent agony.

I should tell him to stop. It hurt too much. But I just felt awkward saying anything. Besides, hopefully he would fin-ish in a second. *ARGH.* Why was this hurting so much? Oh my God, had he given me an STI from his lightsabre? Or was it cystitis? Lara had had cystitis before and said it was like peeing glass. It must be a UTI—but wasn't it meant to hurt mid-pee not mid-shag?

He came. I felt the condom expand inside me as his penis throbbed. I cried out in relief and pushed him out of me. The pain was still burning, but it calmed down as cold air went in.

'Are you OK, Ellie?' he asked.

'My vagina…is…on fire.'

'What? Shit, are you OK? Have I hurt you? You should have told me. I would have pulled out.'

'No, it, uh, wasn't that bad,' I lied. He was right though—I was an idiot for not asking him to get out of me. Why was I still so embarrassed to talk about sex during sex?! If I didn't tell him what I liked, and what I wanted, how was I ever going to come?

'Ellie? You don't look too good.'

'I'm… It's OK. It hurts, but I'm also a bit worried. It feels like something isn't quite right.'

'Shit, I'm sorry. Maybe you've had an allergic reaction. You're not allergic to latex, are you?'

'No, not as far as I know. I mean, maybe I have an un-diagnosed allergy?'

'I doubt it,' he said. 'They normally find that one with kids because plasters have it in too. Shit, maybe you're allergic to the lube.'

The lube. I searched wildly on his bed until I found the small pot. Durex, Heat lubricant. I turned it over to read the ingredients. There was just a list of chemicals; I could be allergic to *any* of them.

I paused. Why was this lube called Heat?

'Nick,' I said. 'Is lube normally called Heat?'

'Oh, no,' he said. 'You can get lube that has different effects instead of boring KY Jelly or whatever. This one has a heat effect so it makes you feel warm. It feels good on my dick. Wait, do you think...'

'You deliberately bought a lube that makes MY VAGINA FEEL LIKE IT'S ON FIRE?' I shrieked. 'How is that enjoyable? Oh my God, I thought I was dying, or had, like, AIDS from your lightsabre.'

He raised an eyebrow. 'What?'

I paused. 'I was, um, kidding. It's just... Nick my vagina really *really* hurts. Surely it isn't just this lube? This is not pleasurable. I honestly feel like I'm about to pass out from the pain.'

'Sorry, Ellie, I think it's just the lube. Hopefully it will die down soon.'

I closed my eyes and prayed for the pain to subside. Hours later, I was still praying.

Chapter 23

My vagina had been in agony the whole night and for most of Saturday. I had left Nick's king-sized, fluffy bed to come home and cradle my aching vag in my less fluffy bed. The only consolation was that he'd been texting me comforting messages all morning and clearly wasn't put off by my scalded vagina.

'Ellie, are you OK yet?' asked Emma, pushing the door open.

'Thanks for knocking,' I grumbled. 'I swear no one in this household believes in privacy. Even the mice watch me while I pee.'

'Ugh, can we not talk about the mice, please?' She shuddered. 'Lara and I have booked a restaurant for tonight, so are you going to be able to get your lazy arse out of bed?'

'Excuse me?'

'Sorry, I meant, are you going to be able to get your singed fanny out of bed?'

I threw my cushion at her, but it landed at her feet. She

picked it up with a sigh and perched on the end of my bed. 'Babe. Stop wallowing and the pain will subside. Does it even hurt any more?'

'I guess it doesn't hurt that much,' I admitted. 'But the humiliation still hurts.'

'What humiliation? It's not your fault his shitty lube burnt your vag.'

'I know, but it was all so awkward and he saw my hairy vagina up close and he had lightsabres and it probably smelt, and I was so crap at reverse cowgirl and...I feel like I'm never going to come in front of a guy. I swear I can only come in bed alone.'

'Lightsabres? Ohmigod, this sounds so exciting. Can you hurry up and get ready so we can hear all the juicy deets tonight.'

'I'm too mopey.'

'Ellie. None of these things are worth losing your Saturday night over. Guys don't care about pubes or smells— they're just lucky to be going down there.'

'Are you *kidding* me? Do you not remember my accidental Hitler wax? Or your reaction to Ben's Boyzilian? Pubes are still a thing.'

'Oh all right, but you need to get over it. I'm leaving in an hour and we're meeting Lara at Caravan. I expect to see you ready to go at 6 p.m.'

'Where is it?'

'King's Cross. I'll take that as affirmation you're coming. And please can you try to cheer up a bit? We don't want you dampening our Saturday night.'

I pulled the duvet over my head. Emma was normally so indulgent of my self-pitying days. Things had clearly changed since Sergio was out of the picture. I felt a twinge of guilt. My below-average Friday night and stinging VJ were really nothing compared to finding your long-term boyfriend in bed with an older woman. I remembered her tacky blue eyeshadow and forced myself out of bed. My problems were pretty pathetic in comparison.

Emma and I walked into the buzzing restaurant to meet Lara. She was wearing her hair piled up in a quiff at the front with dramatic make-up and a tight electric-blue top. She looked incredible.

'Ohmigod, amazing outfit,' shrieked Emma, as she enveloped Lara in a hug. 'Where is this new look from and why have I never seen it?'

'I have decided if I want to change my life and my luck, I need to change my look,' announced Lara, as she gave me a hug. Emma was as glamorous as usual in a black cotton and net jumpsuit with ankle boots and a leather jacket. She was showing less flesh than she used to and it suited her. I felt considerably underdressed in my jeans and the standard black top I always wore out. I probably should have brushed my hair.

'Yes, I feel so much better now I've bought a whole new wardrobe post-Sergio,' said Emma. 'It's my new angry/wounded look.'

'It's amazing,' I said. 'I hope you've made a playlist to match.'

'Naturally,' she said. 'What's your look called, Lara?'

'Um, my "I'm sick of being fucked around by a weed addict called Jez and I want to date someone worthy of me" look?'

'I think you need to work on the catchiness of the title,' I said. 'But apart from that, you look great too, Lar. So what's made you decide you want to ditch Jez once and for all?'

'Other than the fact that he's a pathetic arsehole?' she asked, pouring wine into all of our glasses. 'He left his Facebook logged on to my laptop. So obviously I read all his private messages and he has been messaging a bunch of random girls he's met online. They all have Russian-sounding names and their profile pictures make them look like prostitutes.'

'Oh my God, poor you,' cried Emma. 'I know exactly how you feel. It's just…awful, isn't it? You start questioning if you're even good enough for them and it takes weeks to remember that you're a million times hotter.'

'Well, it's a bit different,' I said. 'As in, you were with Sergio for months and it was exclusive, or meant to be, but Jez and Lara are pretty on-off. Besides, Lara, you did get off with Nick's mate the other day.'

'Thanks, Ellie.' She rolled her eyes at me. 'Although I couldn't even bring myself to go home with him because I'm so hung up on bloody Jez. It's like, I'm not pissed off that he was cheating on me, because, as you've said, we weren't official. It's more the fact that he sits on his arse all day doing fuck all and can't bring himself to take me on dates, but he has the energy to message other hos.'

'Don't call them hos,' I said. 'We're trying to be supportive of slutty girls, remember?'

'The woman who shagged Sergio is a ho,' said Emma darkly.

'Well, you're proving all the misogynistic men who view women as frigid or sluts completely right,' I said. 'You're basically giving them the licence to call women sluts.'

'Oh, shut up,' said Lara. 'You know we're normally the ones educating you on feminism. We both just realised the guys we were with are dumb arseholes. We're allowed to have off days. What's wrong with you anyway?'

'She's in a shit mood because Nick used heat lube and it burned her vagina. Also, because she thinks she's bad at sex and can't orgasm with a guy,' Emma informed her.

'Cheers, Emma.' I scowled. 'And you missed out the fact he has a drawer of lightsabres.' Lara raised her eyebrows questioningly. 'They're a bunch of vibrators and dildos he uses on girls. I may have an STI from one of them.'

'Whoa,' said Lara. 'That's so intense. I've never heard of a guy doing that. He must be pretty fun in bed.'

'Yeah,' said Emma. 'I love a guy with tools—especially if he knows how to use them. So you didn't come even with a vibrator on you?'

I shook my head glumly. 'No, and I don't know if I ever will. It's just…he can be doing it perfectly with the exact technique I like, but I just can't let myself go.'

'Does the whole trying to clear your head thing not work?' asked Lara.

'No, it just makes it worse. Even if I'm not really worrying about stuff and it feels nice, I just can't come. Also, he doesn't really last long enough for me to fully get into it. Even though I only need, like, five minutes when I'm doing it to myself.'

'Oh, babe,' said Emma. 'I wish I knew how to help. You've tried everything I would suggest. Do you try to imagine a scenario in your head?'

'What do you mean?' I asked.

'You know, like a fantasy. My favourite one is to imagine I'm lying on my back naked in an auditorium with loads of naked men around me. I'm touching myself and the men are all wanking over me and they try to climax as I do, and the goal is to get their jizz on my body—ideally into my mouth.'

Lara and I exchanged a glance and we heard a cough from behind Emma. 'Are you ladies ready to order?' asked the waiter. He was bright red.

We all caught each other's eyes and started giggling. The waiter backed away. I realised that meant we weren't going to get our dinner and quickly called him back. 'Can we just have three pizzas to share? Your best ones, please.'

'Which ones?' he asked.

'You choose,' said Emma, licking her lips. He nodded quickly and walked away as fast as possible.

'Oh my God, that was hysterical,' cried Lara. 'The waiter looked like he was about to die. But to be fair, I was dying a bit too. I mean, I have fantasies as well, but yours is hardcore.'

'Is it?' asked Emma, sipping her wine. 'I thought everyone imagined stuff like that during sex.'

'No,' I squeaked. 'I had no idea anyone visualised things.'

'Of course they do, babe,' she said. 'Women get off on fantasies during sex and masturbation, while men are way more visual. That's why they like hardcore porn and magazines, while we're happy with more of a storyline. Surely you imagine stuff when you wank?'

'I guess I do,' I said slowly. 'I just never realised that's what I was doing.'

'Well, what do you imagine?' asked Emma.

'Um, my favourite one is… Oh my God, this is so embarrassing. But I guess I like the thought of someone just coming up behind me when I'm in a crowd, and whispering that they want to shag me, and then, well, doing it.'

'That's a good start,' said Emma. 'But I reckon if you imagine more and really hone them, you can get some really fun ones. Some of mine even get a bit sci-fi. I swear I should be a porn director.'

'I kind of wish I could get spit-roasted,' said Lara.

I choked on my wine. 'Are you kidding me?'

'No,' she said, flushing. 'I don't know what it would be like in real life, but I love the idea of me giving head to one guy while someone else fucks me from behind. Especially two hot strangers.'

'That's totally normal,' cried Emma. 'But so is the bit about not needing it to come true. That's the whole thing about fantasies—they're just stimulation. Guys sometimes get weird if you admit that's what you're thinking about during sex, but, honestly, everyone does it. It's not like you wish the guy you were with was different, but they don't always get that.'

'How do you know all this?' I asked.

'*My Secret Garden*. It's a seminal seventies book about women and sexual fantasies. Have you never heard of it?'

'Um, isn't that a book about a little girl and a guy in a wheelchair?'

'No, Ellie, that's *The Secret Garden*. This book is a little bit more X-rated. It's just a collection of women's fantasies. There are hundreds. Some of them are amazing. They admit rape fantasies, bestiality, everything.'

I gaped at her. 'Am I the only one freaking out about this? Lara?'

'I haven't read it, but I've heard of it,' she said. 'It makes sense though, doesn't it? It's all forbidden, so it's already exciting, and it becomes this sexual taboo. It's like how men love the idea of schoolgirls or nuns because they're so forbidden. God, I wish I could do my thesis on this instead of property law.'

'Me too,' said Emma dreamily. 'I could read about sexual fantasies forever. Ellie, you should borrow this book—I have it at home. It's like porn for girls. Maybe it will help you imagine some things that you can hold on to while you're shagging. You have to concentrate on the fantasies so you can come.'

'Really?' I asked uncertainly.

'God yes, orgasms are hard work,' she cried. 'Men think they're the ones doing all the work, but really it's us in our heads making it happen. Don't you think, Lara?'

'Yeah, you definitely have to be in the zone,' she said. 'But, honestly, I think I might just be really lucky, because I can come quite easily during sex. Certain positions just do it for me.'

'Huh,' I said. 'I feel like there's so much to learn. There should be a class on this.'

'OH MY GOD,' yelled Emma. 'I can't believe I only just remembered. There *is* a class on it. They do it at the sex shop you went to in Hoxton when you got your first vibrator. I'm signed up to their email list and they keep emailing me about their orgasm lessons for women. You need to go.'

'Yes,' I cried. 'This could solve all of my problems. I can't wait! When shall we go?'

'Oh, I'm not coming with you,' she said. 'It's, like, twenty-five pounds and I reckon I'm more qualified to lead the class than whoever their sexpert is.'

I sighed. 'Fine. Lara?'

Lara rolled her immaculately made-up eyes at me. 'Oh

all right. Only you would make me go to things like this, Ellie. None of my other friends ever discuss lube or orgasms with me in the detail you do.'

'I literally have no idea how those girls survive life,' I said. 'If I didn't have you two to offload my sex problems onto, I think I would die a sad, miserable, paranoid death. I would just feel so alone if I didn't know other people freaked out about VJs and orgasms too. Ohmigod, did I tell you Nick said my pubes are spiky and coarse?'

'Yes,' they both groaned.

'Oh sorry,' I said sheepishly. 'Look, pizzas are here.'

* * *

The waiter put down the bill in front of us and scurried away. We howled with laughter again. We'd ordered two bottles of wine to go with our distinctly average pizzas and we were now officially pissed.

'Oh my God, eighty pounds?' cried Lara. 'How did we spend so much money? We're all broke.'

I felt the blood rush from my face. 'I don't think I even have twenty pounds.'

'More like twenty-seven,' said Lara.

'Uh-oh.'

'Sorry, guys,' said Emma. 'I feel bad because I chose the place. Maybe I should pay more?'

'Don't be ridiculous,' I said and put down my student debit card. 'I still have an overdraft. Let's do this.'

'I'm still a student,' said Lara. 'My loan's getting my share.'

'And I have a job that pays just above minimum wage, so I can cope if I don't eat for a week,' said Emma, chucking her card onto ours.

'We'll be fine,' I said. 'Let's just make sure we don't spend any more tonight. We can have wine back at ours.'

Lara and Emma nodded. 'Definitely.'

Chapter 24

We woke up the next morning with splitting headaches and memories of going to a bar after dinner. Lara and Emma were sitting in my bed drinking tea and nursing hangovers.

I was looking at my text conversation with Nick from last night, cringing more with every one I read. 'I just get more and more incoherent. I can't spell for shit. I have no idea why he kept replying. Maybe it's an NZ thing.'

'Maybe he finds it endearing?' suggested Emma.

Lara snorted. I rolled my eyes at her. 'Thanks, Lar. But you're probably right. If anything, he was probably just amused at how embarrassingly drunk I was. Oh shit,' I cried suddenly. I had an email on my phone telling me that my fifty-pound spend on orgasm classes was confirmed and it was starting in two hours.

'We're such idiots,' moaned Lara, reading the email over my shoulder. 'Why would we book an early orgasm class on a bloody Sunday?'

'With twenty-five pounds I seriously don't have, especially after dinner and the drinks we had in that bar.'

'Sorry about that, guys,' said Emma. 'I probably shouldn't have dragged us there and used Sergio as a guilt ploy. But in my defence, I did get those two rounds of cocktails for free when I flirted with the barman.'

I dropped my head into my hands. 'My mum is going to seriously kill me if she finds out I've been spending my moussaka money on alcohol and orgasm classes. That goes against, like, everything she believes in.'

'Ah, she won't find out,' said Emma. 'Besides, it was so worth it. I haven't laughed so much in ages. It was good to have an actual girls' night out without one of us going home with someone.'

'Definitely,' agreed Lara. 'Anyway, El, I reckon we should shower if we want to get our twenty-five pounds' worth of this class. I think our e-tickets say it starts at 12 p.m.'

I sighed loudly and climbed out of my bed. 'Fine. This had better be worth it. I expect to start orgasming the second I walk out. Hell, I want to be orgasming *during* this class.'

Emma started laughing. 'I would have paid money just to see that.'

Lara looked queasy. 'Just…go and shower, Ellie.'

'Yeah, go and shower and maybe start your orgasm practice there?' suggested Emma.

I threw a pillow at her on my way out of the door.

* * *

'Hi, girls, come in,' called the woman at the door of the sex shop. Lara and I nervously followed her into the hot-pink room. I had a flashback of buying my first bullet vibrator here six months ago. I still hadn't progressed on to another vibrator, but I was definitely keen to—especially after seeing Nick's collection.

'Have a glass of wine,' she said, handing us some sparkly Cava. We took one each gratefully and sat down on a pair of empty chairs. The rest were filled up with other women chatting amongst themselves. Everyone looked normal. I felt my shoulders relax and began to look around the shop. There was a twenty-inch dildo right in front of me.

'How do people fit these things inside of them?' I whispered to Lara.

'They don't. They're big massaging vibrators that you can put on the external bits of your body.'

'Oh, right. How do you know?'

'Ellie, that physically could not fit into a woman's vagina. Or a man's bum hole,' she added.

'I guess. But why would you want that instead of an actual massaging tool? Anyway, what's the time? I guess it's starting soon.'

On cue, a dark-haired woman in a kaftan sat down on a chair in the middle of the room. 'Welcome, everyone,' she said. 'Thank you so much for coming here today. My name's Veronica. Don't be nervous if you're a first-timer. This is a safe open space and you're welcome to say whatever you want.'

I glanced nervously at Lara. There were some things I didn't even want Lara to hear. She really didn't need to know about my recurring thrush.

'So, orgasms,' continued Veronica. 'We are all capable of having them, but every single person is different. You watch the movies and see woman orgasming left, right and centre. But that isn't real life.'

I stopped myself from crying out in agreement by nodding vigorously.

'What is real is women who find it difficult to orgasm. Women who only manage to orgasm in certain positions, places, or with certain people or even just alone. So, I'm going to help you understand your body today and give you some pointers that will hopefully get you to that special place.'

I grinned eagerly and looked at Lara. 'Isn't this amazing?'

'Um, it's barely started. But, yeah, it's interesting.'

'Right,' said Veronica. 'First things first—how to get there. You all need to practise alone. Masturbating alone is the key to getting an orgasm with your partner, or whoever you're sleeping with. It's like anything else in life—you need to put in the groundwork to get the results. The best way to do it is either with fingers or some of these vibrators that I'm going to pass around now. For most women, the easiest way to orgasm is through the C-spot, which, as most of you will have discovered, is the clitoris.

'But another spot is the U-spot, which is just underneath, around the urethra. All that area is sensitive and erogenous, so even though you will probably only climax through the nerve endings in the clitoris, you can get those good feelings from rubbing around that general area.'

She pulled out a model vagina and began stroking the bits around the clitoris. I stared in fascination. This was so true. I had definitely felt aroused after wiping my urethra rigorously post-pee.

'But the other area is that elusive G-spot,' she said. I jerked up in my seat. Were we going to learn the ultimate secret? 'It is just behind the front wall of the vagina, and if you put your fingers up there, you can feel it—but only when you're aroused. It feels like a small walnut when you're aroused and the more it gets rubbed, normally via penetration, the better it feels. Finally, we have the last spot.'

I looked up in surprise. I had no idea there were so many spots. 'The A-spot.' Whoa—was she going to talk about bum sex?

'The A-spot is at the very inner end of the vaginal tube between the cervix and the bladder,' said Veronica. She picked up a long, thin dildo. 'The best way to reach this is by depth. You need the penis, or dildo, to go right into the vagina to hit this sensitive tissue. So, that's it—the four main erogenous zones. Technically, you can all orgasm from these, but we must remember that everyone is different. Two-thirds of women have only ever orgasmed from their clitoris, so please don't feel disheartened if you can't climax from other places. It takes practice. And now for the tips.'

The rest of the class passed in a perfect haze. At one point, I lost all shame and pulled out my iPhone so I could take notes. I learnt that in order to achieve an orgasm I must:

1) Breathe deeply. Normally, I held my breath in just before an orgasm but Veronica said the best thing to do was take long, deep inhalations and exhalations throughout.

2) Practise everything at home. I needed to buy a couple of different vibrators to try them out and explore where my G-spot and A-spot were.

3) Try different positions. This was slightly more problematic as Nick and I didn't have any specific plans to meet up and I needed someone to try this out on.

4) Block off my thoughts. Veronica said when my mind starts trying to panic or go over unsexy things, I should tell it to shut the fuck up.

5) Try to feel the actual pleasure. I needed to focus on the actual physical feelings from sex and not the commentary going on in my mind.
6) Have a fantasy or image in my head. Emma was right. I needed to work on my fantasies and learn to focus on them when my brain started trying to think about the aesthetics of my vagina.

I went up to Veronica at the end of the class to thank her for her wisdom. Lara was too preoccupied rubbing large vibrators on her arms. 'They feel so good. It's like a free massage,' she said. I was more keen to put them inside me.

'Veronica, hi, I'm Ellie,' I said.

'Hi, did you enjoy the class?'

'Oh my God, it was amazing. I felt so bad because I've only ever come from clitoral stimulation on my own and I can't orgasm with a guy, but now after hearing all your tips, I can't wait to try.'

She smiled. 'Hey, I'm just glad I could help. I reckon you'll get there in the end. But try not to worry about it. The more you think about it, the harder it will be. Women are so different to men when it comes to climaxing—we're so much more complicated.'

'I know, I wish we could come in three minutes flat like some of the guys I know.'

She laughed and I glowed with pleasure. I was having sex banter with an orgasm teacher in a sex shop. Could my life be any cooler?

'You should buy some vibrators before you leave,' said Veronica. 'We have a twenty per cent discount today for you guys. I'd recommend one of our new flexible ones. They're perfect for getting into those tricky areas. Good luck.'

She left me staring at an array of vibrators. I reached out to touch them. There was a brand-new range and they felt soft. I picked up a bright purple one. It didn't look too threatening and now I knew how to use it, I desperately wanted it.

I grabbed one simple vibrating dildo with different speed settings, one new bullet and a tub of plain non-scented, non-heat lube for sensitive vaginas. I walked over to the counter to pay for my purchases. I could hardly believe that I had been exactly here about six months ago, nervously buying a tiny bullet. Back then, with my unbroken hymen, I had been scared to put these objects in me. I hadn't really wanted to lose my V-plates to a lump of plastic. Now I couldn't wait to shove it inside of me.

'Whoa, are you buying all of that?' asked Lara.

'There's a twenty per cent discount and I've never climaxed in front a guy. I'm as desperate as they get, and if this is going to help me, I'm ready to pay.'

'Fair enough,' she said. 'I'm pretty tempted by one of those massaging ones, but I can't think of a guy who would massage me with it. I'm starting to realise the depressing side of being totally single.'

'Why don't you just buy a normal dildo? That'll cheer you up.'

'Yeah, I could do.' She shrugged. 'But I don't know if I feel ready for it. It feels like I'm consigning myself to the single life by going out to buy myself a vibrator.'

'You're telling that to the wrong girl, Lara. I bought myself my first vibrator before I'd even broken my hymen. Look how well it has served me.'

'Erm, didn't you tell me you tried to put the bullet up your vagina and you panicked it was stuck in there?'

'For, like, two seconds. Anyway, I just bought a new one

that is attached to a remote control via a wire, so if I feel a desire to stick it inside me, I know it won't get lost up there.'

'Um, congratulations?'

'Thank you. Now I am going to take my purchases and go home immediately to try to locate my multiple alphabet spots.'

'Is that a polite way of telling me to go home?' she asked.

'Something like that. Oh hang on, my phone's ringing. Shit, it's Nick! I didn't know he was going to call.'

'Answer it, you idiot.'

'Hi, Nick, how's it going?' I said, walking out of the shop.

'Good, thanks. How's your, uh…'

'Vagina?'

He laughed. 'Exactly.'

'Much better, thanks. How's yours?'

'Ah, you know, very vagina-like. So, uh, what are you up to?'

'Um…just watching TV.'

'Cool. I was going to ask if you fancied going for a drink. I know it's kind of spontaneous and all, but I thought we could go to the Shard. Obviously if you're busy, it's—'

'No! I'd love to,' I cried, all thoughts of masturbating solo flying out my head. 'You'll have to excuse the fact that I look like shit though.'

'Ooh…you're not dressed to the nines? I think I might have to cancel.'

'Ha ha. Wait, you are kidding?'

'Yeah, of course. Shall I meet you at London Bridge?'

'Cool. I'll be, like, forty-five?'

'Perfect. See you then.'

Lara walked out of the shop. 'You ready to go home and play with your toys, then?'

'Change of plan. I'm going for a drink with Nick. My babies will have to wait till later.'

She raised her eyebrows. 'So you can ditch an orgasm for Nick and not me? I see how this is going.'

'I love you loads?'

'Damn straight. Come on, let's get out of here. The shop assistant keeps trying to make me buy leopard-print handcuffs.'

Chapter 25

'Hey,' said Nick, before giving me a kiss on the lips. I grinned up at him. I still couldn't get over having a public display of affection with someone so hot. I hoped there were tourists watching.

'Nice to see you so spontaneously,' I said.

'I know, I figured why not have a fun Sunday instead of watching Netflix alone in bed.'

'Um, there is nothing wrong with spending your weekends alone with Netflix in bed.'

He laughed. 'Oh, I'm not judging—that's what I've been doing every night this week. So, shall we go in?'

'OK, cool. I'm so excited. I can't believe this has been in London for so long and I still haven't been up the Shard.'

'Me too. So, I tried to reserve a table but you can't if you're just going for drinks. Is that OK?'

'Oh, of course,' I said, as we walked up to a glass door. 'I'm not a reserve-y kind of person. If I tried to reserve in any of my local bars, they'd probably laugh in my face. And tell me to get the fuck out.'

'Can I help you?' asked the doorman.

'Hey, mate, we're just here for a drink. Do we go straight up?' asked Nick.

'I'm sorry, sir, we're at full capacity, so unless you have a reservation, you'll have to queue.'

'What?' cried Nick. 'They wouldn't let me reserve when I called.'

'I'm sorry, sir, but you'll have to wait over there.' The doorman pointed to a group of well-dressed people gathered behind some large hedges. They were in some kind of pen hidden behind the strategically planted foliage.

'It's fine, don't worry,' I said, as we walked over to the line. 'We'll just queue for a bit. Thank God I put on actual shoes today and not just Converse. Everyone here's so glam.'

'I know. Hey, I'm really sorry we have to wait in line. I did try to book.'

'Nick, honestly, I really don't mind. I'm very used to queuing—I'm not one of those girls that the bouncer lets in immediately. Hey, maybe we should get snacks? I see a shop over there.'

'Why not? You're gorgeous,' he said, ignoring the question I was hoping he'd say yes to.

Then I realised he'd just called me gorgeous. Not even my mum had called me gorgeous. I gaped at him.

'What are you looking at me like that for? You must know how hot you are.'

I laughed nervously. I had no idea how to react to his compliment but it was the best thing anyone had ever said to me—it even felt too special to WhatsApp to the girls. 'Um, thanks.' I blushed. 'But I meant bouncers don't let me in because I'm just, like, not glam. I dunno, I feel like "those girls" are the ones in tight Herve dresses, not Primark.'

'You look "glam" to me. But I do love that you're not high-maintenance. My ex was and it really pissed me off. She'd always make me take her to the flashest restaurants, and it would take her hours to get ready.'

'Sara?' I asked, remembering the naked pube-less blonde girl from his photos.

'Oh yeah, sorry, I forgot you saw her that one time. Yeah, she was really appearance obsessed. It's nice going out with you—you don't seem that fussed about how you look.'

'Um, excuse me. Do you know how long it took me to throw together this casual chic look?' I cried in mock-annoyance.

'You told me earlier you didn't shower.'

Bugger. 'Well, there you go. If you want low-maintenance, here I am. I'm a pretty cheap date too.'

'Tell me about it. On our first date I only had to get you the one cocktail and you were ready to go home. I'm hoping for the same tonight.'

'Huh, on second thoughts, maybe I'll play at being a glam date today.' I grinned. 'I mean, we are going to a fancy bar in the new highest point of Europe or whatever. I should probably have quite a few cocktails.'

He laughed. 'Let's do it. We'll be the only people to get properly pissed up here. To be fair, I have saved us a bit of money already.'

'Oh yeah?'

'Most people pay to go up to the top to see the views. It's, like, twenty-five pounds though, so I figured we'll just go to the bar for free and spend that on booze.'

'Oh OK, you are definitely getting me drunk now.'

* * *

'This is so, uh, wow,' I said. We were standing in a bar with glass walls that looked out at the whole of London. I was drinking a fourteen-pound cocktail with coconut beer in it. The waitresses were wearing different floral dresses, depending on their exact role. It was the kind of place that most girls on dates would love.

Only, I wasn't most girls; I was unimpressed.

We were on the thirty-something floor of the building, but it didn't even feel as if we were that high up. I could see the whole of the city, yeah, but you could see that in the opening credits of *EastEnders*. And everyone was so obviously rich and glamorous that I just felt massively out of place. I would have preferred to be drinking three-pound beers in a Hackney pub.

'I know, it's amazing, isn't it?' said Nick. 'The views are stunning. How's your drink?'

'Good, thanks. Yours?'

'Yeah, nice, thanks.'

I smiled awkwardly at him. Now that we were up here, I couldn't think of anything interesting to say and my flirtation skills were seriously drying up. But then again, he had called me gorgeous. Maybe I didn't have to be so nervous. He'd seen me curl up in pain from a burning vagina—there weren't exactly many barriers between us now. It was kind of…comfortable hanging out with Nick.

'So, what have you been doing today?' I asked.

'Pretty much just been lying around the house feeling sorry for myself. My classic hangover act. What about you? Anything fun?'

I couldn't exactly tell him I'd been to an orgasm class…

'Um, same as you, really. I went out with the girls last night and we accidentally got pissed, so we've just been pretty bedridden today.'

'So we were both alone in our beds? Sounds like a wasted opportunity to me...'

'Well, there's always next weekend,' I replied. Who knew it would be so easy to have sex banter with a guy without feeling embarrassed?

He grinned. 'Cheers to that. So where were you girls out on Saturday?'

'Some dodgy bar near King's Cross. It was fun though. I think we were dancing till, like, 3 a.m. What about you?'

'Oh, we were out in Mayfair. Really great bar there, actually. Do you go out there much?'

'Um, not really. I have been, once, to Mahiki. Not a great night—although Lara enjoyed it. I guess we mainly go out in East London. It's a bit...well, cheaper. And I think I prefer the vibe. You know?'

'Yeah, I had a lot of fun at the place where I met you. It was the first time I'd been out round there, actually.'

'Really?! Oh wait...I forget you're a banker. I feel like your people tend to prefer the fancier parts of London.'

He nudged my waist. '"My people"? I feel like someone's being a bit judgemental here.'

'Hey, just speaking from personal experience,' I said, putting my hands up.

'Mm-hmm. Well, I'm not your average British banker.'

'That's very true. Bro.'

He laughed. 'That's more like it. You know, I reckon you'd love New Zealand.'

'OK, I think we might have some miscommunication issues going. I am not an outside-y kinda girl.'

'Do you mean outdoorsy?'

'See—can't even get the name right. I don't ski, snowboard, paraglide or do whatever it is you guys do there. I think I'd probably prefer Australia so I could hang out on a beach all day.'

He raised his eyebrows. 'You know we have beaches in NZ? Like, really stunning ones with white sand and turquoise water.'

'Seriously?! I thought it was all Hobbit-y with lots of fields and stuff.'

'Yep, I've heard that one before. You Brits really have no clue what's going outside of the UK, do you?'

'Hey, we're not that bad,' I protested.

'The Americans are worse, to be fair. They all think I'm from South Africa—even when I say I'm from NZ.'

I laughed. 'I guess the accents are pretty similar. Anyway, shall we get more drinks? I've drained this one and it's my turn to get a round.'

'No, I'm meant to be getting you drunk, remember?'

'Yeah, but I didn't mean it. Obviously I'll pay for the next round.'

'Ellie, no, it's my treat,' he said firmly. 'Same again? A ginger cocktail?'

'OK, thanks.'

I watched him walk off to the bar. He looked so attractive, and he thought I was gorgeous. How was this happening? This was the kind of date I'd dreamt about since I hit puberty, and by some miracle, I wasn't fucking it up. Maybe we'd even see each other more, like, outside the bedroom?

Oh God. I was officially doing what Emma warned me against—fantasising about dating the one-night stand. We were strictly casual, and that was a good thing. I didn't even want to date him anyway. He was too laid-back, and we were too different.

Besides, as much as I felt myself liking him more than I'd imagined, he wasn't what I wanted in a boyfriend. He was too flash, superficial and, well, blond. I wanted someone more like me, someone with more body hair than me and someone I could be a hundred per cent myself with. Nick was just too generic and hot. Mr Ellie Kolstakis he was not.

* * *

I lay in bed panting. 'That…was fun.'

'Give me ten minutes and maybe we can go again,' he said.

'OK,' I breathed out.

We were lying naked on his bed post-sex. It had been the best sex we'd had yet. Even though I still hadn't come. I didn't understand why. I'd tried doing the breathing the sex shop lady had recommended and it had helped, but just not enough. It made me feel kind of…sad. I'd made it into a bit of a joke for the girls, but they didn't really get it. They were both capable of orgasming on demand. I was the weird one. It wasn't fair. I wanted this. I wanted to feel like a proper woman. Instead, I just felt like a failure.

I closed my eyes and tried to make my heart slow down. Even though the sex hadn't lasted long, it had been pretty intense. I'd even found myself sinking my nails into his back when he came inside me—with a condom, naturally. It was part lust and part, well, jealousy. He got to come every single bloody time, while I had to lie there just hoping it would happen the next time. It wasn't even as if he'd particularly tried to make me orgasm.

Maybe every other girl he'd been with just came within seconds? Maybe I was the only one who couldn't come?

God, this was so stressful. What if there was something wrong with me? What if Nick could tell? Like, he'd obviously had way more sex than me—what if I was shit in comparison?

'Did you, um, was that… How many people have you slept with?' I blurted out.

He turned to face me. 'Hey. Where did that come from?'

'Oh, I dunno, just wondering. Not in, like, a weird way. I'm just…curious?'

'Huh… I don't know. I've never counted.'

Oh fuck. It must be hundreds if he couldn't remember. 'Like, roughly.'

'Definitely less than fifty.'

'FIFTY?'

'Maybe, like, forty?'

'Cool. Um, yeah.' I swallowed my saliva. This was fine. I mean, he was twenty-nine. He'd probably been having sex for, like, thirteen years. If you minused a few years for relationships, that was only about four girls a year. Oh my fucking God—that meant he'd seen at least forty vaginas.

'What about you?'

'Um, what about me?'

'How many people have you slept with?'

'Oh, like, not many,' I said. 'Just…just under double digits, I guess.'

'Less than ten? Really?'

'Yes, is that weird?'

'No, not at all. Sorry, I forget you're a few years younger than me. That's really cool. I like that you're not slutty.'

I smiled weakly. What the hell would he say if he knew the truth—that he was only number two. He'd probably be freaked out and think there was something wrong with me. Suddenly, I didn't feel like round two of sex. 'Can we turn the light off? I'd better get to sleep so I can wake up for work tomorrow.'

'Or...fancy going down on me?'

'Seriously?'

'You're just so good at them. Please?'

I grinned. Considering the fact that my first ever attempt to give head aged seventeen had ended with my teeth on James Martell's penis, it felt pretty good to be complimented on my skills. Finally, here was a sex act I didn't feel at all awkward about.

Besides, who cared if Nick had slept with way more people than me? I was only twenty-two. I had, like, seven years to catch up with him. And right now, he was the one begging me for sex.

I turned over and moved down the bed so I was face-to-face with his naked groin. Still smiling, I opened my mouth and lowered it straight down onto his very erect penis.

Chapter 26

NSFW

*R*elationships are meant to be romantic. That's a given that no one really ever questions. You're not meant to ask the details about the exes, or how many people they've slept with, because you love each other. None of that matters. It's all about the now.

But...what if you're not in love. Like, at all. And instead you're casually dating. Can you ask then? Are 'numbers' still a no-go, or are you allowed to request a written list of every girl they've ever shagged?

That was the dilemma I had last weekend. It was after my date to the Shard—told you he'd take me—but it was still only the third date, give or take. Was I allowed to ask him how many people he'd slept with?

Probably not, but I did it anyway. We were lying in bed and, out of nowhere, we had the chat. By 'we', I mean 'I', because obviously it was me who brought it up. He reluc-

tantly told me his number. It was more than five times the size of mine. He thinks it could possibly be even higher.

I don't really know why I wanted to know. I think it was just a way to get to know him better. But it was also probably a way for me to try to stop that little voice asking 'Why on earth is he with you?' Sadly, it didn't quite stop that insecurity.

But I don't regret my decision. Because it isn't as if we're in a relationship where I might freak out about that and wonder if we're compatible because he's so much more experienced than me. It's just casual dating, and, honestly, who cares if he's had more sex than me?

If anything, that's just incentive to start catching up.

I spent the rest of the week trying to avoid Maxine as much as possible, and then rushing home to see Nick. We'd seen each four times since the spontaneous Shard date, and when I wasn't shagging him, I was at home Googling tips on it. I still hadn't come, but I was definitely on my way. The fact that he was just a fuck buddy definitely helped. I didn't have to worry about trying to impress him—all I had to do was open my legs and occasionally provide some good banter. Honestly? I had no idea why Lara was bothered that Jez wasn't relationship material. Casual sex was the best of both worlds.

It was exhausting though. We'd drunk a bottle of wine last night and had sex in front of the TV. We'd even progressed to the kitchen, where he'd tried to fuck me on the counter—until I'd found dried cheese on my bum cheek and forced him into the bedroom. Ever since Will had nicked my hummus, I'd gone off the whole sex and food thing. In fact, I'd barely even seen Will lately. I felt a pang of guilt over the fact I hadn't replied to Emma's last WhatsApp. She'd wanted to go out over the weekend but I'd already promised Nick a shagathon. In the end, she'd gone home to hang with her family.

I pushed the front door open, yawning. It looked as if I'd have the place to myself until Emma came home this evening. Will was away with Raj and the lights weren't on in Ollie's room. He was clearly out too. I dumped my stuff in my room and collapsed on the bed. It was kind of nice to be home alone. It was fun spending time with Nick, but I still didn't feel as if I could a hundred per cent be myself in front of him. I hadn't farted in days. Also, it did kind of suck that he hadn't made me orgasm, especially because I was often so close to it. All I had to do was tell him to move his fingers a bit, or go faster, but I just couldn't bring myself to say it out loud. I just felt too awkward telling him what to do.

But now, I didn't really have that problem… I pulled my leggings down and started touching my clit. It felt so good to know I could bring myself to orgasm. I started the breathing Veronica had taught us, then I remembered—my sex toys. I'd gone straight to Nick's after the session and I still hadn't used them. They were probably still in the handbag I'd been using. I jumped out of bed and went to get the bag.

The vibrator was pink and soft. I cradled it, admiring its streamlined design and semi-resemblance to a penis. I pressed the hidden 'on' button and it glowed electric blue. It also began buzzing at full volume. I turned it off in alarm and switched on my radio so it would cover any sounds if the flatmates came back.

I had to do this properly. I'd need to do it with my breathing, my fantasies and everything else. I closed my eyes to try to drown out Jay Z rapping about his ninety-nine problems and slipped my hand down to my vagina. I stroked my clitoris gently and tried to create a fantasy as Emma and the sex teacher had suggested. I imagined Ryan Gosling standing next to me naked, but it didn't feel right. He was too famous for me to try to make him wank all over my naked body.

My fantasy man would have to be faceless—but with Ryan's body. I needed a setting. Maxine's office popped into my head. This was good. I could visualise a powerful male boss and use Lara's 'dominate me, please' fantasy.

'Come in,' he said.

I walked into the room. My boobs were bigger, more pert, and I had magically lost ten pounds. 'Yes?'

'Ellie, you have been very naughty.'

'I have?'

'I think you need to come over here and get on your knees.'

I groaned out loud. My fantasy was crap. It sounded like a bad porno—probably because I'd seen more sex on a screen than in real life. Screw solo foreplay—I would just get the vibrator back and shove it inside me.

It buzzed into action and I gently rubbed it against my clitoris. It felt similar to using my bullet and I started to gasp familiarly. I pulled it off and stopped myself before I came from my C-spot. That was the easy one—I needed to try to find the others.

I slipped the vibrator inside of me. I felt an uncontrollable urge to laugh at the buzzing sensation but stopped myself. Finding my A-spot was a serious business, let alone my G-spot, which was a whole new level. I forced myself to concentrate and pushed the vibrator deeper into me. I cried out. It felt as if it was jabbing into my ovaries. Nick had never gone this far into me—I didn't think his penis would be able to reach. Fuck, was this my A-spot??

I pushed the vibrator in further and it hit the same spot but I did not feel as if I was about to orgasm. I cheated and started stroking my clitoris again. I sighed in pleasure and wished girls could only come from their clits. This whole A–G-spot thing was getting stressful.

I felt my vagina lube up and took the vibrator out. I wanted to try to find my G-spot with my fingers. I slipped my right index finger in and tried to find this walnut that Veronica had been talking about. It just felt squishy and clammy inside. It was kind of gross. Why had James Martell been so keen to shove his fingers up here in Year Thirteen?

I sighed in frustration. I couldn't feel the walnut. Maybe I wasn't turned on enough. I closed my eyes again and tried to get back to being dominated by my fantasy man.

'Suck me,' he commanded.

I went over to him and took off the belt of his trousers. I went to throw it away and then changed my mind. This was my fantasy. I could do whatever I wanted. I took the belt, which suddenly turned into a rope, and tied him to the chair.

'No,' I said. 'I want you to suck me.'

I popped open my slutty blouse and shoved my boobs in his face. He started sucking my right nipple.

I felt my face heating up. It was fun getting into the fantasy, but I felt so embarrassed that I was dangling my nipple in a man's face. I hadn't realised shame could creep into fantasies.

I ignored the religious guilt my grandparents had tried to teach me and ripped off my man's clothes. I ran my hands over his body and grabbed his penis. He gasped.

I pushed his chair onto the floor so his little head was

bobbing up and I sat on his face. He obligingly started licking my clitoris—but then dream-me started freaking out
that it smelled.

'Fuck me,' I said.

His ropes vanished, and in a split second, he was thrusting into me from behind. I slipped my fingers into my vagina. It was fully lubed up now. The fantasy was working.
Who knew I was into dominating—although I was making
him do doggy. Wasn't that more being dominated? Oh, who
fucking cared, I'd just found my WALNUT.

It was on the front wall of my vagina, just as Veronica
had promised. It was like a tiny little knot. I rubbed it and
grinned. It felt good. But it still didn't feel orgasmic. Maybe
I needed the vibrator?

I shoved it in, but, annoyingly, I couldn't make it hit the
right spot. I grunted as I leant over to try to angle it in. It
was almost hitting it; I just needed to—

'Ellie?' The door burst open and Ollie was standing in
front of me. My open legs were in his face. I let go of the
vibrator and it buzzed out of me onto the bedspread.

'ARGH,' I screamed. 'What are you doing? Get out of
my bedroom!'

He stood frozen, staring at my vagina. I slammed my
legs shut and pulled a blanket over me. The vibrator was
still buzzing and glowing on the bed.

'Get out!' I yelled.

He blinked and ran out of the room. Oh fuck. This was
not good. The flatmate I seriously fancied had just seen
me in the most inappropriate position imaginable. My vagina had been in his face. Oh God, I would never be able
to face him again.

I turned the buzzing vibrator off and pulled on my knickers and some leggings. Should I go into his room and try to explain? But it had been pretty self-explanatory. I groaned and dropped my head into my hands.

There was a knock at the door. 'Who is it?' I asked nervously, knowing exactly who it would be.

'Ollie. Can I come in?'

Oh God oh God oh God. 'Erm, OK.'

The door crept open and Ollie was standing there looking apologetic. The sunlight from my window fell onto his perfect profile and I bit my lip with desire. I'd much rather have a night with him than my fantasy guy.

'Hey, Ellie, I'm really sorry I walked in on you like that.'

'Oh, no worries,' I said breezily. 'It's fine, whatever. Let's just pretend it never happened.'

'I did knock though,' he said. 'I think you just didn't hear me because of the music.' He gestured to the radio, which was now playing some kind of house music.

'Honestly, it's fine. I know you didn't mean to barge in.'

'OK,' he said. 'Hey, can I sit on your bed?'

'Sure,' I said, gesturing to a corner. He sat down and looked at me. We were about thirty centimetres apart because my bed was made for a child. 'What's up?'

'Just…thought we should talk.'

'Can't we just pretend nothing happened? I think I'm too embarrassed to relive what just happened.'

'What were you doing?' he asked curiously, totally ignoring my plea.

I stared at him. 'Are you kidding me?'

'I just… Were you masturbating?' he asked, looking straight into my eyes. His eyes were an insanely clear blue and it felt as if they were piercing straight into my throbbing clitoris.

I sighed. There was no point beating around the bush. 'I got a new vibrator today,' I said bluntly. 'I was just trying it out and thought I'd have a look for my A-spot.'

'What's that?'

'Erm, it's an erogenous zone that you can orgasm from.' I looked up at Ollie to see his face squirm or laugh, but he actually looked interested. Maybe he wanted to learn some tips to use on Yomi. The bitch.

He grinned at me. 'You were trying to orgasm?'

'That is generally the goal of masturbation.'

'Wow, that's... I haven't met a girl who's so open about this kind of stuff before. Yomi is not keen on discussing this sort of thing. I don't think she ever masturbates.'

'Really? I thought every girl did.'

'Nah. She's kind of...reserved when it comes to sex,' he explained. 'It kind of sucks. Seeing as we've been together for four years, I guess things are getting a bit stale.'

I stared at him in surprise. He clearly wasn't happy with Yomi. Maybe...maybe he would break up with her and shag me forever? 'That sucks,' I said, as sympathetically as I could. 'Have you, uh, tried to liven it up a bit?'

'Honestly, I think the only thing that could liven it up would be to sleep with someone else.'

I choked on air. 'Wow, right. That's pretty intense.'

'Yeah,' he said. Was I imagining this or was he staring straight at me? Like, in a very sexual way?

'So, um, are the others all out tonight?'

'Yeah, they're not coming back till late tonight,' he said. 'Do you want to have a drink?'

'Um, OK.'

He left the room and came back with a bottle of whisky and two glasses. 'I remember you like whisky, right?'

What was it with men trying to make me drink straight whisky? I sighed. 'Yep. Normally with a mixer, but, hey, why not.'

'Yeah, sorry, we don't have any mixers unless you want some Ribena?' I grimaced. 'Thought so. Here you go.'

I took the glass he offered me and sipped it. It was horrible. 'Ugh,' I said, as I drank more. 'Horrid but addictive.'

'Isn't it? Hey, Ellie, it's nice, you and me hanging out like this. I feel like we never get to do it.'

I blushed. It was so nice to hear my name coming out of his lips. His perfect— *OK, focus, Ellie.* 'Yeah, no, it's fun. I guess you're often up staying with Yomi, and I'm just always at work doing whatever Maxine says.'

'Yeah, or out on one of your internet dates. How are those going?'

'Oh, you know, just…shit. But I met a guy in real life, can you believe it, and I've been seeing him.'

'Hey, is this your one-night stand?'

I blushed again. It was so awkward that Emma and Will told Ollie everything. He would never fancy me—even if Yomi was out of the picture—now he knew every humiliating detail about my sad sex life. Oh, and the fact he'd seen my hairy vagina. 'Yeah, Nick. I've seen him a couple of times since. It's pretty casj.'

'Did you just abbreviate "casual"?'

'Do you mean, did I abbrev it?'

He shook his head and laughed. 'You're ridiculous. But, wow, sounds like it's getting pretty serious with this Nick guy. Emma said he even took you to some fancy bar for drinks and stuff.'

'Well, I mean, it's definitely still casual. But I guess I was a bit surprised he's wanted to see me so many times.'

'You shouldn't be,' he said. 'He clearly fancies you.'

I laughed awkwardly, trying not to go red again. Was it the whisky or was Ollie being pretty flirty? 'Who wouldn't?' I joked.

Ollie looked at me and suddenly pulled me towards him. My mouth was wide open in shock, and as my face collided with his, his lips kissed my top lip and half my nose. My whisky splashed onto my leggings. I broke away from him to dry myself down, then it properly hit me—what the fuck was I doing drying my leggings when Ollie Hastings was KISSING me?!

Without a second thought, I put my whisky down, threw my arms around his shoulders and started snogging him. It was incredible. For once, I wasn't even thinking about what my tongue was doing—I was just so excited to be kissing him.

'Oh God, Ellie,' he said, breaking away. 'I've wanted to do that for so long.'

Oh my God. Ollie had fancied me for ages. This was a miracle. 'Really?'

'Yeah, and then when I walked in here and saw you with your vibrator, it just turned me on so much. I love that you're so sexual and you touch yourself. God, it's making so horny.'

He started pulling off his clothes and then yanked my T-shirt off me. I was semi-naked with my tits out in front of Ollie. He stared at me as though I was a work of art and grabbed my boobs. This was actually happening. I was going to have sex with Ollie. Yomi's face popped into my head and I felt sick. Then Ollie pulled my bra off and groaned in appreciation of my naked body. Nobody had ever looked at me like that.

He pulled my leggings and knickers off too, so we were

both naked on my bed. His body was slim and as toned as I'd imagined, but he had a mass of pubes I hadn't expected. I hadn't realised boys' natural pubes would look so…wild. 'I've fancied you for so long, Ellie,' he said, as he kissed my neck. 'I've wanted to fuck you since we met this summer.'

I felt my clitoris throb and bit my bottom lip to stop a huge grin spreading across my face. Ollie—the most attractive man I had ever met—wanted to fuck me. I put my hand on his shaved blond head and pulled him towards me. I kissed him, long and hard. 'I've wanted to as well,' I said. 'But, Ollie, what about…'

'It's fine,' he said firmly. 'Forget it. This is what I want. It's just one night. We can get it out of our systems.' He started kissing my neck and talking in between kisses. 'You were just so dirty sitting there with your vibrator.' Kiss. 'It's so sexy.' Kiss. 'And you're basically cheating on that guy Nick.' Kiss. 'You're as bad as I am.'

I grinned uncertainly. I really wasn't that dirty—and I definitely wasn't cheating on anyone—but if Ollie wanted me to be dirty, I would oblige. I pushed him onto the bed and climbed on top of him. He gazed up at me in pure delight. It spurred me on in my role and I bent down towards his penis. It was thicker and shorter than Nick's. I took a deep breath, opened my mouth as wide as I could and descended onto it.

I sucked it, trying to make my mouth as saliva-filled as I could. He groaned loudly and I carried on.

'Wait, stop,' he cried out.

Oh fuck. A flashback to my worst memory came back and I wondered—had I bitten him?

'What?'

'You need to stop or I'll come. I want to fuck you. Let me get inside you.'

I gulped. 'OK, but do you have a condom?'

'Fuck,' he said. 'Are you not on the pill?'

'Erm…no. I'm single.'

He looked stressed and then jumped up. 'I think…I might have one in my room. Come with me.'

We ran stark naked to his room next door. He opened his drawers and started searching for the condom. I glanced at the wardrobe and saw the collage of him and Yomi. It had got bigger since I'd last seen it and now it was like a shrine to their relationship. I felt very sick.

'Here,' he said triumphantly. 'Got one. Get on the bed, Ellie.'

Oh God. We were going to have sex under Yomi's watchful eyes.

He slipped the condom onto his penis and climbed on top of me. I cried out in pain as he pushed himself into me. His penis was wider than Nick's and I wasn't used to it.

He moaned loudly and started thrusting really quickly. I bit my lip in pain and tried to breathe through the feeling that my hymen was ripping in half. Maybe Jack had never actually taken my virginity and it was happening now?

'This is so fucking good,' cried Ollie. 'Uhhhh.'

He pushed himself further into me. He was going so deep he might actually hit my A-spot, but I did not feel as if I was going to orgasm. It hurt too much.

'Let's change positions,' he said. 'Get on your knees.'

I nodded uncertainly. This all felt so weird. He pulled himself out of me and I breathed out in relief. But then he pushed me against the wall and started shagging me from behind.

I tried to enjoy my favourite position, but his penis was too big, I felt weird and YOMI'S FACE WAS STARING AT ME FROM HIS DESK.

'Ollie, get out of me,' I said.

'What? I'm about to come.'

'Get out,' I shrieked, lurching forward. He fell onto me and we collapsed onto his bed.

'What are you doing, Ellie?'

'Yomi's face is staring at me. I can't do this. I just can't.'

He sighed and lay back down on the bed. 'I can't believe you stopped when I was just about to come.'

I stared at him. 'Seriously, Ollie. You're more upset by that than the fact that you've just cheated on your long-term girlfriend?'

'I've slept with girls before. She doesn't know and never will. It won't hurt her. Anyway, El, let's forget it, please. I think you're so sexy.' He started rubbing my boobs and caressing my face. 'Seriously, you're stunning. All I want is to come inside you.'

I felt my vagina throbbing again. Why was it so irrational? I ran my hands over Ollie's brown body and rubbed his penis. It was smooth and— Wait, why wasn't it rubbery?

I sat up. The condom was gone.

'Erm, where's the condom gone, Ollie?'

'I don't know. I didn't take it off. It must have come out when you made me get out of you.'

I ignored the accusatory tone of his voice and leapt up. The condom wasn't on the bed, or the floor. It was nowhere to be seen.

'Are you sure it's not inside you?' he asked.

'What? Don't be ridiculous,' I cried. How could a condom get stuck inside of me—that never happened? It wasn't a tampon. Surely I'd be able to feel it if it was inside there—hang on, what was that? 'Oh my God. Do not tell me this is happening,' I shrieked. 'How is there a condom stuck inside of me?'

I squatted on the floor, hoping it would come out of me. It didn't. I shoved my hand inside to try to pull it out but my fingers couldn't find the condom. It was well and truly lodged up my vagina.

Chapter 27

'I don't know why we're here, Ellie. This is fucking ridiculous.'

I turned to stare at Ollie in annoyance. He was acting like a complete arsehole. It had taken all of my powers of persuasion—and eventually blackmail—to get him to come to A&E with me. He'd even refused to pay for a cab for us and had forced me to get a bus. Now we were sitting on uncomfortable white plastic seats, in a four-hour queue, and I had latex lost inside my vagina.

'Ollie, seriously, what the fuck? You're not the one with a condom inside of you. This could be really dangerous. How do you not *want* to be here?' I cried.

His brow creased and he turned to face me. 'You think I want to spend my Sunday night hanging out in A&E? What are you on, Ellie?'

'And you think I do? I have no choice. I could get, like, TSS or something. Do you know how dangerous that is?' I said. 'Besides, rubber could be way worse than tampons. I could get an *infection*.'

'Yeah, well, I doubt one night would really be that much of an issue. You could have just gone early in the morning. This is such an overreaction.'

My mouth dropped open. 'I just told you I could have an infection and you think that's overreacting? I could be pregnant, Ollie. Or, I mean, who knows, I could have caught something from you.'

A woman holding a child in her arms shot us a look of revulsion and turned around. An elderly woman winked at me. Oh God. We were officially having a domestic in the Royal London Hospital in Whitechapel.

'Are you actually saying you think I have an STI?' hissed Ollie. I looked down at the floor. It was pale green and looked pretty dirty for a hospital floor. 'Ellie?'

'I'm sorry,' I finally announced. 'I didn't mean it. I'm just stressed there could be something actually wrong with me.'

He sighed. 'OK. I don't want to fight with you, obviously. I just don't really know what to say.'

I closed my eyes. Neither did I. I had just slept with my housemate and helped him cheat on his girlfriend. It was meant to feel fun and empowering, but I just felt kind of dirty and depressed. Sex with Ollie was the first properly slutty thing I'd ever done and we'd ended up splattering blood on his walls and getting latex stuck inside me. If ever there was a clear sign something was doomed, this was it.

'Ollie, it's fine. Let's just forget it and hope we can get this all sorted ASAP,' I said. Fighting with him in this miserable waiting room was not going to make my night any better. Even though he was being a complete dick.

'OK, cool. I'm gonna go get a drink. Do you want anything?'

'I'd love a chamomile tea.'

'Erm, OK. And if they don't have chamomile?'

'Peppermint? Green?' He raised his eyebrows at me. 'Or…a normal tea?'

'Cool.'

He got up and I wrapped my jacket tightly around me. I wished I were drunk. Then maybe I wouldn't notice how everyone else here was really old or badly dressed. I felt like such a misfit. I shouldn't be in a shitty A&E with a condom stuck in me—I should be in bed with my herbal tea watching TV. How was this my life? I had a degree, for Chrissake, why was I in hospital on a Sunday night with a sex emergency?

I sighed loudly and put my head in my hands, no longer caring what anyone thought. I shouldn't have had sex with Ollie. I knew it was wrong. But he kept telling me how hot I was and I hadn't felt so pretty in ages. He was so out of my league—it was flattering.

Although, he was kind of proving himself to be a bit of a wanker. Had he always been so selfish? With a sigh, I realised that he probably had. I'd just never noticed because I was so blinded by how beautiful he was. Typical. I pulled out my phone. I needed the girls.

Emma: Ellie, where are you? I thought we were going to watch *Downton Abbey* together.
Lara: Maybe she's at Nick's place again…we've created a monster, Em. She's a sex fiend these days.

I laughed wryly; they didn't know the half of it. God, I missed them. I wished they were sitting here in A&E with me instead of Ollie. Maybe they'd come??

Me: Guys. Something crazy happened. I'm in A&E.
Emma: WTF!

Lara: ARE YOU OK?

Emma: Where are you? Will come now.

Me: Calm down, it's not horrendous. I just...have a condom stuck inside me.

Lara: Hahaha.

Emma: Oh, babe. Can't you just pull it out?

Me: I tried that. For an hour. So here I am.

Lara: Sorry, you can't get me out of Oxford to come to London just for some lost latex. Is Nick with you?

Me: Really didn't want to tell you over WhatsApp but something bad happened. It wasn't Nick.

Emma: ???

Me: It was Ollie.

The conversation went quiet and then Lara called me.

'Ellie, are you fucking kidding me?'

'OK, stop swearing at me, I'm in hospital. Besides, I can't really talk. He's going to come back in a second.'

'What happened? I can't believe you did that. What about his poor girlfriend? You know her.'

I sighed. 'I know. I feel really bad. But in a kind of surreal way. Probably because he's down the hallway. He was just so complimentary. I feel like he's fancied me this whole time too.'

She groaned. 'Of course he complimented you. He was just telling you what he knows you wanted to hear. He just wanted to fuck you, Ellie.'

'OK, thanks. Now I feel officially shit.'

She sighed. 'I don't want you to feel horrible, Ellie. I just... It's a huge thing. You saw how bad Emma felt when she saw Sergio cheating on her.'

'That was totally different,' I cried.

'How?'

'Well, they'd been together ages and he was regularly sleeping with someone. Ollie and I only happened once.'

'He's been with his girlfriend for, like, four years, Ellie. Besides, do you not think Emma would have been just as upset if it was a one-off than if it was regular?'

I felt sick. 'I guess. I feel bad now.'

'Also, do you think Nick would care?'

'What? No, we're really casual. Look, I'm going to go, Lara. I think Ollie is coming back. I'll call you tomorrow.'

Her voice softened. 'OK. Well, don't beat yourself up too much, El, what's done is done. I hope the condom stuff goes OK.'

'Thanks, see you later.'

I hung up feeling awful. That was the first time I'd ever lied to Lara to get off the phone to her—hell, it was the first time I'd ever wanted to get off the phone to her, full stop. But she had a point. I couldn't really pretend this was just typical millennial drama. I'd full-on cheated and ruined a four-year relationship. I was a horrible person. Emma must hate me. I nervously looked at my phone to see if she'd replied.

Emma: Please tell me that's not real.

Emma: Ellie??

Emma: Or at least tell me it was because he'd just broken up with Yomi??

Emma: Why would you do that??

Emma: Are you OK??

I officially felt like crying. I had done to Yomi exactly what Blue Eyeshadow had done to Emma. The only difference was that Yomi hadn't shown up with a surprise anniversary fiesta in hand and caught us à la Serge. I was a complete bitch. A bitch with a rubber lost in her fanny. Karma 1, Ellie 0.

'Hey,' said Ollie. He was standing next to me holding two foam cups. 'Sorry it took so long. The chamomile was pretty hard to source but I got there in the end.'

I took the cup from him gratefully and sipped it. It burnt my tongue, but the pain distracted me from wanting to cry. Karma 2, Ellie 0.

'Are we any closer to seeing a doctor, then?' he asked.

'Erm, I don't know. Hey, do you mind if I go and make a phone call quickly? I just need to speak to Emma.'

'What?' he cried. 'You can't tell anyone about this, Ellie. Yomi can never find out. Promise me you'll keep it quiet.'

'But why would Emma ever tell Yomi? Or even Lara? They don't know her.'

'These things always have a way of getting out unless neither of us say anything. I'm not kidding about this,' he said, staring at me with his intense blue eyes. For once I didn't feel weak at the knees.

'Ollie, it's my life too. I need to tell my friends,' I said, conveniently ignoring the fact that I had already told said friends.

'Please, Ellie. I really love Yomi. I don't want to ruin things with her.'

I closed my eyes briefly. Now I knew why people didn't have sex with guys who were already in relationships. It hurt like hell to know that they loved someone else more than you. That, actually, they didn't love you at all and probably barely fancied you. 'OK,' I promised. 'I won't tell anyone.' It was technically still a promise if I didn't tell anyone from now on, right?

He sighed with relief. 'Thanks,' he said. 'Hey, wait, where are you going?'

'I'm still going to call Emma. I just won't, erm, tell her,' I lied blithely, as I stood up and walked as far away as I could from the white plastic chairs.

The dialling tone kept ringing and Emma wasn't picking up. I bit my nails and dialled back again. This time she picked up.

'Hello?'

'I'm so sorry,' I wailed. 'I didn't think about anything. I just forgot how much it would hurt Yomi and I was so flattered he fancied me.'

Emma sighed. 'Ellie, you don't have to apologise to me, although I'm guessing this means he hasn't dumped Yomi. I'm not mad at you. I have no right to be. I guess I'm just surprised that you did it. It doesn't seem very…you.'

Why did everyone keep going on about it not being part of my personality?! 'But why not?' I answered with an edge to my voice. 'You guys are helping me be slutty and this just felt like the next step, you know? A one-night stand with the guy I fancy, and we would never speak about it again. It's the kind of stuff that always happens in movies—well, minus the A&E scene afterwards.'

'I think you've got the wrong idea about being slutty, Ellie,' said Emma quietly. 'It's not about having no morals and hurting people. It's just about having lots of sex and enjoying it. Did you even enjoy it with Ollie?'

'No,' I admitted, feeling shit and guilty again as the anger faded again. My emotions hadn't been so up and down since I was fifteen. Maybe the latex was interfering with my hormones? 'I guess… I guess I enjoyed the idea of it. I just…

Urgh, I feel like such a fuck-up. I should have just stayed a virgin. I can't even be a proper slut.'

'Babe, stop being weird,' said Emma. 'Obviously it's good you're doing what you want, and being sexually liberated and a modern woman, just…just go for the single ones, Ellie.'

I sighed. 'I know. I'm sorry. I miss you. I really, really regret what I've done.'

'I know. I miss you too. Go get the condom out of you and come home.'

'It's going to be so awkward with Ollie. God. I've ruined things for the whole flat too. He made me swear I wouldn't tell any of you, so can you just make sure Will doesn't find out?'

There was silence. 'Emma?' I asked. 'Don't tell me you've already told him.'

'I was emotional and it brought back bad Sergio memories,' she cried.

'You are not playing that line on me,' I cried. 'I can't believe you've told him. Tomorrow is going to be hell. What have I done?'

'Calm down and go back to Ollie. Just act cool and we'll deal with it all tomorrow, OK? Remember what Rhett told Scarlett.'

'That she was a selfish spoilt bitch?'

'That tomorrow is another day,' she said, and the line went dead. I walked back to Ollie feeling slightly better than I had after my chat to Lara. She'd hit me with the home truths the way only your oldest friend can, and, OK, it sucked that Emma was disappointed in me too, but at least she hadn't yelled at me. I could deal with this.

'Ellie, I've been trying to text you,' said Ollie. 'The doctor's ready to see you.'

'Oh shit. OK, let's go.'

We followed a nurse into a small green cubicle with a curtain. A man in a white coat and stethoscope walked in.

'Hi, I'm Dr Patel. How can I help you?'

'Hi, um, I have a condom stuck inside of me.'

His facial expressions didn't flinch and he pulled out a notepad. 'OK, when did this happen?'

'About four hours ago, I guess,' I replied, looking uncertainly at Ollie. He shrugged his shoulders.

'And have you tried to pull it out of you?' he asked.

'Yup, I tried for, like, an hour. I just couldn't reach it. Is it dangerous? Will I be OK?'

'It should be fine,' he said. 'Lie down and I'll have a look, but I think it's probably lodged at the top of your vaginal canal, near your cervix. It can't ever get lost, don't worry. We will be able to get it out. But it's good you came in, because if you leave it in there for a while, the bacteria can build up and you can get an infection.'

I shot Ollie a triumphant look. I knew infections were possible.

'Now, if your boyfriend would like to leave, I'll examine you,' said Dr Patel.

'Oh, he's not my…' I said, as Ollie started saying the same thing. We looked at each and I blushed. He walked out of the cubicle and I followed Dr Patel's orders to get onto the bed.

'Right, do you want to just take off your trousers and underwear?' he said.

I pulled off my leggings and pants. I flushed to see my pasty legs and hairy vagina exposed on the blue plastic bed.

Dr Patel didn't look fazed. He pushed my legs apart, got some gloves and came towards my vagina.

I closed my eyes and felt some things poke around inside of me. I winced, imagining them to be pointy metal scalpels. *Breathe, Ellie, one, two, three, breathe,* I told myself, trying to remember what the yoga instructor had told us the one time I'd made it to her class. *Find your inner core, ommm.*

The poking, and my meditative attempts, carried on for a while and then I felt something slide out of me. I opened my eyes and saw Dr Patel holding some metal tweezers with a saggy condom attached to them. I shrieked in joy.

'You've got it!' I cried.

'Yes, now let me just leave you with the nurse to finish things off. She'll explain everything else to you. Just be careful next time. Try to ask your boyfriend to hold on to the bottom of the condom when he withdraws and make sure it's the right size. OK?'

I nodded mutely.

'You might also want to take emergency contraception to protect against pregnancy. And I'd recommend having an STI test.'

I stared at him. I never thought I'd have to take the morning-after pill. That was the kind of thing actual slutty people did. The kind of people who slept with strangers in club toilets or…slept with their housemates when they were in a long-term relationship. I bowed my head. Dr Patel was right; I deserved the morning-after pill and everything else that came with it.

Karma 1 million, Ellie 0.

Chapter 28

At 6.45 a.m. my alarm went off. I grasped around for my buzzing phone and hit the snooze button. I'd had five hours of sleep—most of which was spent worrying about pregnancy, STIs and Yomi murdering me, and now I had to go to work. Oh God, work. Maxine. Monday. I had a full week of her constant bitchiness and demands ahead of me.

I felt a lump of dread appear in my tummy and closed my eyes tightly shut. I hadn't had enough sleep to deal with Maxine today. Maybe I could call in sick? I had been in A&E last night. But even the thought of avoiding work made me feel guilty. I pulled my duvet around me, wondering if I could have a ten-minute snooze, until I remembered that Ollie woke up at 7 a.m. I could not face seeing him—or anyone else. I pulled the duvet off me and ran straight into the shower.

Fifteen minutes later, I crept out of the house. My hair was still wet and I was wearing my comfort work outfit of black jeans and a baggy grey jumper sans make-up, but at least I'd managed to leave the house without seeing any of my housemates. Now I just had to figure out how to keep that up for the rest of the nine months left in our contract.

I kept my eyes semi-shut on the overground train to Highbury & Islington, and let myself be pulled along by the crowd onto the underground. I normally spent the tube ride thinking nasty thoughts about the passengers invading my personal space, but I was too depressed today. After what I'd done last night, everyone should be thinking bitchy thoughts about me. I was a horrid person.

I felt my eyes welling up and willed them not to leak tears. I just felt so damn guilty. Now that it had all sunk in, the whole thing felt even more sordid than it had in A&E.

Why had I done it?! OK, it was flattering that the hot unattainable guy I'd fancied for ages had wanted me, but he was just using me for a quick shag. I knew he had a girlfriend. How had lust trumped my morals? It wasn't even as if I'd particularly enjoyed the sex—it had just felt nice to be wanted so badly. I'd felt sexy and cool. God, what a pathetic reason to do something so awful. Blue eyeshadow lady had probably felt sexy shagging Sergio.

Even if Yomi never found out, I'd still altered their relationship forever. And if she did find out... I imagined her smiling face with the expression Emma had worn when she'd seen Sergio cheating. The thought of being responsible for making someone feel like that made me want to cry all over again. I no longer felt sexy or cool—I felt filthy.

* * *

I'd spent the entire day reliving Sunday night. By the time 5 p.m. rolled around, I was the first one out of the door and now I was almost home. Every time the bus got one step closer to the house I felt sicker and sicker. I was going to have to see Ollie again. What was I going to say?

The bus pulled up outside our place and I walked down to the house. I had to just grow up and do it. If I was going to be so stupid and sleep with my flatmate, then I was going to have to face the consequences. I pushed open the door and scanned the downstairs. He wasn't there.

I ran upstairs and saw his bedroom door was wide open. He wasn't home yet. Thank God. I heard a noise from Emma's room and knocked on the door. I didn't really want to face her either, especially as she'd been so disappointed on the phone last night, but I missed her, and right now I really needed a friend.

'Come in.'

I walked into her room. She was lying on her bed watching *House of Cards*.

'So, what's new?' she asked. 'You slept with Will?'

'What? No, of course not,' I cried. 'I… Are you mad at me about the Ollie thing?'

She sighed. 'Ellie. He's left.'

'What?' I cried out. 'What do you mean? Who?'

'Ollie has moved out. He must have taken the day off work and moved out today. All his stuff is gone and he left us a note saying that he's decided to move home to live with his parents in Bow for a bit.'

I stared at her blankly. 'Because…of me?'

She shrugged. 'I guess so. I can't think of any other reason why he would just bail without even saying bye to any of us. I mean, he's not a *complete* bastard, because he's left us with his deposit to cover next month's rent, but it does mean we have to find a new housemate. And, you know, the whole vibe of the house is fucked up.'

'I'm so sorry,' I whispered. 'I had no idea that would happen. I thought it would just be casual and...I don't know, like something on an episode of *Friends*, where they all get over it and it's not a big deal.'

'Life isn't a TV episode,' snapped Emma.

'I wasn't... I mean, I know. Have you spoken to Will?'

She let out a dry laugh. 'Erm, if by "spoken" you mean "listened to him rant about breaking a rental contract", then yes, I have. He's pretty pissed too.'

'Oh fuck,' I said quietly. 'I can't believe this. That Ollie has actually gone. I can't believe he didn't even say bye to me. After everything that happened.'

'Naturally your first thought is about you, and not the fact that our whole house situation is ruined,' said Emma, as she un-paused *House of Cards*.

I stared at her in surprise. This was so unlike her. She had never been angry with me before, and even when we'd spoken on the phone post-Ollie-sex, she hadn't been as pissed off as Lara was. She'd forgiven me—she'd even quoted *Gone with the Wind* at me.

'Emma, I'm really sorry,' I repeated. 'I'll find someone new to replace Ollie. I'll sort it all out.'

'Whatever.' She shrugged. 'I'm watching this.'

I bit my lip and walked out of the room. I wanted to call Lara, but I had a horrible feeling she was going to just repeat what Emma had said, but with a few more expletives and angry tones. I couldn't believe that Ollie had just gone. I needed to see it for myself.

I stood outside his room and pushed the door open. The room was bare, with just an old mattress on the bed and a wooden desk in the corner. For a second, I thought about moving my stuff into the room so that I could finally have a double room of my own, but then I remembered Emma's face. That probably wouldn't go down so well with her and Will.

All of the pictures of Ollie and Yomi had been pulled off the wall, and the off-white walls were now just stained with Blu-Tack marks. I stuck my head into my hands.

This was not how I imagined everything to turn out. Why was it all getting so complicated? I pulled out my phone to call Lara but couldn't bring myself to do it. I wished I could call my gay best friend, Paul, but he was living in the Czech Republic with his boyfriend, and this emergency wasn't worth paying £1.50 a minute for. My fingers hovered over Nick's name. Obviously he was just a casual sexual partner and I couldn't talk about my feelings to him, but I could maybe arrange to see him? That might cheer me up?

Oh fuck it. I pressed 'call'.

'Ellie,' he said. 'Good to hear from you. How are things?'

'Um, not bad, thanks. What about you?'

'Exhausting day at work. Really not looking forward to this week. So how was your Sunday?'

'Stressful,' I blurted out. 'My flatmate has just moved out without telling us, so we're kind of in the lurch.'

'Shit, that's so annoying,' he said. 'Do you know why he left?'

'Nope, no idea at all,' I lied. 'So weird.'

'Well, let me know if I can help.'

'Thanks,' I said. 'If you know anyone who wants to move into a cheap double in Haggerston, then that would be a huge help.'

'I'll ask around,' he said, 'but most of my friends are probably, erm…'

'Living somewhere a lot nicer?' I finished for him.

'Something like that.' He laughed. 'Hey, it's nice to hear from you. I think this might be the first time you've ever called me, you know.'

'Really?' I said. 'I guess, yeah, maybe it is. I'm not much of a phone person though.'

'Well, there's been a serious lack of texts from you too,' he said. 'I was hoping you'd suggest meeting up soon.'

I smiled. 'I could say the same.'

'You've got me there. But why don't you come over tomorrow night? I'd love to see you. Bring a change of clothes for work the next day and you can stay over. How does that sound? We can just hang out and watch TV or something.'

'Sure,' I said. 'That would actually be really lovely.'

'OK, great. I'd better go make some food, but I'll see you then.'

'See you later,' I echoed and hung up.

Nick had been unexpectedly nice. It was a relief considering none of my real friends were feeling particularly friendly towards me right now. Thank God I had a decent fuck buddy and not one who was going to blow me off when I really needed him.

I walked back to my bedroom feeling better until I bumped into Will.

'So the slut shows her face,' he growled.

I swallowed. 'Will, I'm so sorry. I didn't mean for Ollie to leave.'

'Yeah, well, he's gone now, isn't he? My best friend has bailed on us, without even fucking telling me to my face, and now we're all screwed.' I looked around to see if I could squeeze past him and head upstairs, but Will's broad shoulders filled up the whole corridor.

'I'm so sorry,' I said. 'Please don't hate me. I really didn't mean to fuck everything up.'

'I don't care who you sleep with. I don't care if you cheat,' he said. 'But I do care if you fuck my best friend and turn him into a wanker.'

'Maybe…maybe he was already a wanker?' I suggested. 'And we just didn't notice?'

'Maybe you brought it out of him.'

'Will, that doesn't even make sense,' I cried out. 'Can you just move so I can go to my room?'

'Fine, run away, Ellie, but I want you to know that I hold you directly responsible for this whole mess. Ollie loved Yomi and it's just you on your crazy slut quest who seduced him and made this happen.'

My mouth dropped open. 'Will, it was Ollie who was coming onto me. He kept telling me he'd been thinking about me and wanted to do it for ages. I tried to resist.'

'Hmm, well, you didn't resist very well, did you?' he said tartly.

I shook my head and walked past him to my room, feeling just as shit as I had before speaking to Nick. Somehow, one harmless little shag had resulted in one flatmate moving out and the other two hating me. I even hated myself for what I'd done. If it wasn't for the fact that things at work were looking up and Nick still wanted to see me, I didn't know what I'd do.

My phone rang and I glanced at the screen. Lara. I let it ring and then quickly pressed the mute button. I couldn't face a lecture from her right now. I'd rather lose myself in a Netflix marathon and pretend none of this was happening. It was either that or wallow in how much of a disaster everything was.

Chapter 29

I sat at my desk trying to write a column. I had no idea how to write something truthful and interesting without even touching on the whole Ollie saga. So far all I had was:

Sex can be messy. So messy that you end up in A&E.

I deleted it and sighed loudly. I needed inspiration. I pulled out my phone and checked the WhatsApp group with Lara and Emma. There was nothing new, and I had a sneaky feeling that the two of them had been messaging privately without me. Probably about me.

Me: Hey, guys—it's been ages since we hung out. Shall we do something this weekend?

Five minutes later, there was still no response. Not even an emoji. My friends were officially ignoring me. I didn't even know what I'd done wrong. Maybe I should try to call Lara. I grabbed my phone and wallet and asked if anyone wanted a coffee. This time Camilla looked up at me grate-

fully. 'I could murder a latte,' she said. I nodded, waiting for
her to hand over some coins, but she just mouthed 'thanks'
and looked back at her computer.

I rolled my eyes and walked out of the office to Pret. I
dialled Lara's number praying that she would pick up. It was
only yesterday I'd ignored her call, so she couldn't hate me
that much if she was still trying to get in touch.

The second she answered, I wished I hadn't called.

'Oh, finally, she calls,' said Lara. 'Feeling brave enough
to face me?'

How did she know? 'Maybe,' I said. 'I guess you heard
that Ollie moved out without a word, and Emma and Will
are furious with me?'

'Yeah, I heard. That's why I called you yesterday, to see
how you were feeling.'

I felt a pang of guilt for assuming she'd been calling to
yell at me. 'Really? I thought you would be mad at me too.'

'Ellie, you're an idiot and you shouldn't have slept with
him, but obviously I'm not pissed off with you. I just think
you're a bit, I don't know, lost at the moment.'

I felt my skin prickle at Lara's bluntness but remembered
that concern was highly preferable to her yelling at me. Besides, she was the only friend still talking to me. I wasn't
in a position to argue.

'What do you mean?' I asked neutrally.

'Just…everything. Are you OK, El?'

I burst into tears. 'I'm sorry, it's just…everything is a
massive mess, and now you're being nice and I presumed
you hated me.'

'Breathe, babe. What's up?'

'I just feel sick with guilt about the whole Ollie thing.
I keep having daydreams about Yomi finding out and it's

scaring me to death. I would just hate to make someone so miserable, you know?'

'Oh, El, there's no way she'll find out, unless Ollie grows a conscience, which doesn't seem likely, considering you said he's done it before.'

'I maybe even had a daydream about telling her…'

'Ellie. No. Just get that idea out of your head now.'

'OK, OK.' I sniffed, my tears drying up. 'I wasn't ever going to act on it. It was just a thought. But don't worry, there's no way I could put myself through watching her face fall like Emma's did when we caught Sergio cheating.'

'Poor Emma. I think this whole Ollie thing is reminding her of what it all felt like.'

'Great, let's add that to the list of things for me to feel guilty about.'

'Oh stop it, you know I didn't bring it up to try to make you feel bad. I just think maybe it would be nice if you hung out with Emma a bit, and maybe suggested a night out this weekend?'

'Ohmigod, what has she said to you about me? You've discussed it, haven't you?'

'I refuse to get caught up in this. All I'm saying is, call her. And get back to your bloody column.'

'OK, and thanks for not being mad. Love you, Lar.'

'You too, even though you're a massive idiot.'

I hung up feeling emotionally exhausted. Lara didn't judge me; she was just worried about me. And if she was on my side, Emma would eventually come round too. But I still felt so stupid for following my lusty vagina without a second thought.

Even karma was pissed at me. The fact that our encounter had ended in A&E just proved that. Hell, I deserved a latex infection after what I'd done. Poor Yomi. The only thing that was making me feel a tiny bit better was the thought of going to see Nick later.

Weirdly, I'd started to miss him in between dates. I was ninety-nine per cent sure I didn't want him as a boyfriend, and a hundred per cent sure that he didn't want to go out with me, so it didn't really make sense that I thought about him at least five times a day.

Then again, he was becoming a friend. It was about time we started living up to the 'buddy' part of our fuck-buddy relationship. And Nick was a nice guy—I bet he'd hang out with me in A&E without complaining if the condom got lost in me.

But, more important, he was single. We could fuck to our hearts' content without ruining anyone else's life.

* * *

'Hey, Ellie,' said Nick, after he gave me a long kiss on the lips.

'Hey, yourself. How's it going?'

'Pretty good, thanks,' he said. 'Come in, I've got a surprise for you.'

Oh God. Please don't say it was handcuffs or some kind of kinky sex. I mean, I was keen to experiment, but not yet. I'd been a virgin only six months ago, for God's sake.

The dining room table was set with plates, cutlery, candles and two dishes. My mouth dropped open in surprise. 'Oh my God. You made dinner?'

He laughed. 'Don't look so shocked. I do have a couple of basic skills, you know.'

It was official. Nick was the best fuck buddy in the world. Why did no one ever explain that casual shags cook you dinner, give you sex and basically do everything that boyfriends do, without being exclusive? This was ideal. I had all the benefits without any of the commitment stress. I pulled a lid off one of the dishes.

'Cannelloni!' I shrieked. 'That's, like, my favourite dish ever. How did you know? Ohmigod, this is so nice of you, Nick.'

He smiled and pulled me towards him for another long kiss. I wrapped my arms around him and kissed him back. 'I'm glad you like it,' he said. 'I remembered you saying you love Italian food. But you might want to try it before you thank me. It's been a while since I've cooked.'

'I'm so ready to try it. I'm famished,' I announced, as I sat down.

'That's what I want to hear,' he said, as he opened a bottle of wine. I felt a pang of guilt as I realised I probably should have brought a bottle with me—but his wine was definitely over a year old. That already beat anything I could afford.

'Cheers,' he said, raising his glass to mine. 'To meeting you that night in Drop and Pull, and to me persuading you to go home with me.'

'To the most successful one-night stand I've ever had,' I added, ignoring the fact it was basically the only one-night stand I'd ever had. Unless you counted Ollie, but with all the drama that had led to, I'd rather not.

We clinked glasses and I dug into the food. The meal was nice, but, more than anything, it was just amazing that he'd cooked for me. I couldn't even remember Sergio ever cooking dinner for Emma and they'd been together for ages.

'So how has your week been?' he asked.

'What, all two days of it?' I grinned. 'Not bad, thanks. My posh work colleagues are finally acknowledging me, so that's making life a bit better.'

'Oh yeah? What made them finally do that?'

I couldn't exactly tell him that it was because of my inappropriate sexual antics. Or that the bar he'd taken me to had helped. 'Um, I came in early one day. They approved of my newfound commitment to the job.'

'Cool,' he said. 'Well, uh, congratulations, I guess.'

'Thanks.'

'So do you have any weekend plans?'

'Nothing huge yet,' I said. 'Oh, except hopefully a big girls' night out. You remember Lara and Emma?'

'Yeah, 'course—but not as much as my mates do.'

'Hey, how come nothing came of that with either of them?'

'Aw, I dunno. I guess Myles and Cosmo were just looking for fun.'

'Fair enough,' I said. 'So what about you? Doing anything wild with the boys?'

'Well, actually, my parents are coming over this weekend from New Zealand. They're going to be here for a couple of weeks, but we're all going down to the Isle of Wight this weekend to see my brother.'

'You have a brother who lives on the Isle of Wight? I had no idea.'

'Yeah, he lives down by the sea. He's a surfer, so he's just doing some bar work and surfing whenever he can. He's got a girlfriend down there, so it's pretty chilled for him at the moment.'

'Whoa,' I said. 'That sounds amazing—I'd love to go to the Isle of Wight.'

'You would?' he asked. 'Well, why don't you come down?'

I choked on a lump of ricotta. 'What? With…you?'

'Well, my parents are renting out a cottage for the week—

it looks pretty big. We can all stay there. It will be fun. We can even have our own room.' He grinned.

I stared at him in shock. Was my former one-night stand inviting me on a weekend trip to meet his parents??

'Besides,' he added, 'then you get to see the Isle of Wight and tick that off your list.'

I smiled weakly. I barely had any idea where the Isle of Wight was, let alone a burning desire to go there. Why had I even said I wanted to go? What would I do there? How would Nick even introduce me—as the girl he's casually shagging? God, it would be so awkward; I should definitely decline.

'I'm not sure,' I said, and Nick's face dropped. He clearly wanted me to come. Maybe I should? It might not be that bad. Besides, it was technically a free holiday… 'Actually,' I said, 'I'm in.'

'Amazing,' he said. 'I'll go give my parents a buzz now. I'm sure they'd love to meet you. We'll hang out with them a bit, but we can go out on our own, don't worry,' he added, looking at my panicked face. 'We can sneak off without them.'

I nodded mutely as he went into the bedroom to call his parents. It looked as if I was officially going on a weekend away with my fuck buddy to hang out with his family in the Isle of Wight. Now I just had to figure out where it was.

I pulled up Google Maps on my phone, zooming out to the UK map. I scrolled to the right of London but couldn't see the Isle of Wight. I scrolled to the left and it wasn't there either. In a mild panic I scrolled down. I kept going further, and further, and eventually saw it semi-attached to Portsmouth.

I gulped. I wasn't just going out of the M25—I was leaving the mainland. I'd never been so far away from London in my life without jumping on a plane. What had I gotten myself into?

My phone buzzed.

Lara: Yeah a night out sounds nice.

Oh shit, she was replying to my suggestion for a girls' night out. I bit my lip as I wrote another message. Hopefully the girls would understand that a free weekend away didn't come my way often enough for me to turn it down.

Me: Can we do it the week after actually? Obvs still really keen but am actually going away this weekend! To…the Isle of Wight!
Lara: ?? With who? Why? Do you even know where that is?
Me: Obviously. It's near Portsmouth, south-east.
Lara: South-west.
Me: That's what I meant. I'm going with Nick!
Lara: Oh wow.
Me: And his parents. And his brother who lives there.
Lara: That's intense…well, enjoy.

There was still no response from Emma. I sighed but then saw my phone was buzzing again. It was a private text from Lara.

I'd just about persuaded Emma to forgive you and come out this weekend. You're a fucking idiot for bailing!! Fingers crossed she forgives you post-IOW…x

I closed my eyes and ignored the guilt creeping up my veins. Lately it seemed as if every decision I made backfired. Oh well. Emma would just have to understand. I always forgave her whenever she'd bailed on me to hang out with Sergio. She might not be used to me being the one with a guy, but now I was, she'd just have to do what I'd been doing for months.

* * *

'Tell me what you like,' whispered Nick, as he stroked my hair and kissed my lips. I pulled the duvet over me to cover my underwear-clad body and racked my brain for a suitable response. How did I tell him I wanted to dominate him as I did in my fantasies? It was too embarrassing to say out loud.

'Um, I like everything you do already,' I said.

'But what gets you the hottest?' he asked.

I paused, trying to think of a suitable response. 'You inside me?'

He kissed my neck and undid my bra clasp. I sighed in relief; it looked as if he was done talking. I closed my eyes and tried to conjure up a fantasy in my head as we kissed.

I was lying on all fours on a kitchen table, totally naked. Someone was licking my vagina and a faceless man with a huge penis was standing in front of me. I wanted his penis in my mouth but he wouldn't let me. He slapped my bum and then let me lick the tip of his penis. I started putting the virtual penis in my mouth and, in reality, felt myself getting wet as Nick stroked my clitoris with his fingers and kissed my neck. Nameless man shoved his penis deeper in my mouth.

I moaned out loud and Nick grinned at me. Oh my God, maybe I would actually come with him tonight? It wasn't exactly a penetrative orgasm yet, but it was definitely a step in the right direction. Only, his fingers were putting a bit too much pressure on my clit and he needed to move them upwards. I fidgeted and wondered if I should tell him.

I felt my near-orgasmic state decline. Oh God, no. I was worrying too much. *Clear your head, Elena Kolstakis,* I yelled at myself inwardly. Why had I used my full name? That was what my mum called me. Oh GOD, who thought about their mum during sex? There was no way I'd ever come now.

I had to go back to my fantasy. I closed my eyes and tried to imagine being on all fours again. OK, penis in my mouth, something licking my clitoris. Wait, surely it was someone not something? I zoomed my fantasy out, as though it was on a camera screen, and saw me on the table. A man had his penis in my mouth and behind me a big dark dog was licking my vagina.

I screamed out loud.

'Ellie, are you OK?' asked Nick. 'Did I hurt you?'

I opened my eyes wide. Nick's concerned face was hovering over me. I got off on being licked out by a dog. I was into bestiality. Couldn't you get locked up for that?

'Um, I'm fine. Sorry, it just felt sensitive for a second. Let's carry on,' I said quickly.

'OK, shall we do doggy?' he asked.

I gulped and closed my eyes briefly. It was a coincidence. He could not read my mind. He didn't know I had imagined a dog licking my clit. Besides, it would be better if he could fuck me from behind; I could keep my eyes screwed shut and try to imagine lots and lots of male tongues licking me—with no dogs in sight.

I got on all fours and he thrust himself into me. I winced in pain. My vagina seemed to have dried up the second I saw the dog. I sighed out loud as Nick came inside me and groaned. Yet again, I'd ruined my chance at an orgasm.

Chapter 30

I was standing on my bed in a state of mild panic. Clothes were strewn across every surface but the tote on the floor was still empty. I had no idea what to pack for my mini-break. Knowing where the Isle of Wight was barely even helped—I still had no idea what to expect. The only islands I'd ever frequented were off the coast of Greece and came with sand and see-through water. I doubted the British equivalent would offer the same climate.

I didn't want to be the girl who went on a country mini-break with heels and dresses. But did that mean Topshop dresses and flats would be OK—or should I go for leggings and knitwear? God, what if it was extra rainy there? Maybe I needed a windbreaker?!

I seriously needed Emma. I'd barely seen her ever since we'd had that awkward conversation, and whenever I texted her, she just sent me polite but distant replies. I took a deep breath and padded across the hallway to her bedroom.

'Emma?' I asked, tapping gently on the door.

There was no response. I rapped harder.

'What's up?' she said, as the door flung open. I fell against her.

'Oh, sorry, I didn't realise you were going to open the door,' I said. She gave me a withering stare. Shit. She was still pissed. Maybe it wasn't such a good idea to ask her for a favour?

'Oh-kay. What do you want, Ellie? Advice on your mini-break?'

'Of course not!' I cried. 'I just wanted to say sorry again. I hate this weirdness, Em. I really didn't mean for anything to happen with Ollie and I especially did not mean to fuck up the house situation.'

She sighed and her face softened slightly. I kept going.

'You know I only ever thought of Ollie as a totally unattainable crush. I had no idea he would ever consider sleeping with someone like me when he's, like, ten times fitter than me. I was just so flattered that I kind of just caved in.'

Her face hardened again. Bugger. 'You've already said all this, but I don't know why you have such low self-esteem, Ellie. You've basically got a boyfriend now.'

'Huh?'

'Nick,' she said, rolling her eyes. 'He's taking you to meet his family in the Isle of Wight. That doesn't exactly say casual.'

'What? He's only taking me so we can have a shag-fest in the cottage.'

She stared at me. 'Ellie, what are you on? I just… He's treating you so well and you're just going around sleeping with other people behind his back.'

'Um, one person. And we're not official. We've never even discussed being casual or not. Where is all this coming from, Emma? Sorry, are you trying to say I've cheated on Nick?'

'Not officially, fine. But if I were him, I'd be pretty pissed off to find out that you'd slept with someone else.'

'I don't really think he'd care,' I said.

'God, you're so naive,' she shrieked. 'Have you told him?'

'Um, no,' I whispered. I'd never seen Emma like this. She was normally so sweet and relaxed.

'Well, there you go. Sergio didn't tell me about that skank either. So, congratulations, you're just like him.'

She slammed the door in my face, leaving me standing in the hallway. I turned around and slowly walked back to my room. My open tote bag stared at me in accusation. I sat down on my bed with my back facing it.

Emma clearly wasn't over Sergio cheating on her and was just taking it out on me instead of him, but the Ollie thing had obviously upset her. Even Will seemed a bit hurt, instead of just pissed. I closed my eyes and tried to not think about it. Ollie had just fucked off back to Yomi, leaving me to deal with this whole mess. Leaving me in general. The guilt started seeping in again. Oh God, I couldn't deal with this again.

Right. Forget it all. Emma was just taking her misery out on me and she would get over it soon. I just needed to give her time. I forced myself to stop overthinking everything and stood back up to face my bag. I was going to the Isle of Wight straight after work tomorrow so I had to pack now.

There was no way I was going to be 'that' girl in a rom-com who headed down in heels and high-waisted dresses. No, I'd be going down in fleeces, jeans and thermals. Sod fashion. I was leaving the civilisation of London anyway, so it didn't really matter what I wore. It wasn't as if anyone in the Isle of Wight was going to understand colourblocking and my Celine-inspired look. I'd be better off in a North Face jacket and jeans.

Chapter 31

I stood nervously at Waterloo Station. I was wearing wellies and a waterproof coat, holding a blue bag filled with similar gear. I'd even left my work outfit back at the office so that I didn't have to drag heeled ankle boots and a smart dress with me on our weekend away. At least no matter what happened down there, no one would think I was a spoilt London girl.

'Ellie,' called Nick. I turned around and saw him grinning at me from across the station. I felt my vagina throb in response. He was wearing a suit—clearly, he wasn't as much of a forward planner as I was—and he looked good. His curly blond hair was brushed to the side, and when he came over to give me a kiss, I could feel the jealousy emanating from every other woman in the station. Little did they know we weren't even in love, we were just casual. I grinned even more at that; how grown-up was I, going on a minibreak with a casj date!

'Well, look at you,' he said, taking a step back. 'That is some serious industrial wear.'

I looked down at my black Hunter wellies and grinned. 'Well, when in Rome...'

'Is it meant to rain, then?' he asked.

'Oh, I have no idea,' I said, startled. 'I just figured every-one down there wore, um, wellies and stuff. Because it's so near the sea.'

He laughed. 'Fair enough. I'm sure you'll fit right in. OK, we'd better go find our train. Do you want any snacks first?'

'Sure.' We walked to the nearest M&S. I wandered off to the sandwiches aisle and found myself a meal deal. I met Nick near the tills. He was holding a bottle of wine.

'Ah, sandwiches, smart move,' he said. 'Maybe I should get one too.'

'I thought that was the plan. Is the wine for your parents? Maybe I should get them something too?'

'Oh, don't worry, they're not really like that. I got this for the train down. It takes a few hours to get there, with the ferry as well.'

'Ferry?' I cried.

'Um, how else did you think we were going to cross the Channel? I thought the name gave it away, but you know it is an island?'

I rolled my eyes at him. 'Yes, OK, I just hadn't really con-sidered the practicalities. I thought there might be a bridge, or... Anyway, why don't you go find a sandwich?'

He laughed. 'A bridge? You Brits are crazy. I'll meet you at the checkout.'

I clutched my meal deal close to me. Who knew what other surprises this trip had in store for me?

* * *

'Ellie, we're here,' said Nick, nudging me awake.

I yawned slowly before realising the train had stopped

and I probably had a line of drool down my face. 'OK,' I said, wiping my face and running a finger under my eyes to get rid of the inevitable smudged mascara. 'I can't believe I fell asleep.'

'Yep, before we started the wine. Which means now I get to bring a bottle to my parents and look like a good son.'

'Better late than never.'

'Hey, come on, we'd better grab our bags. We need to go find the ferry.'

I nodded sleepily and wrapped myself up in my coat. I followed Nick through the station to the ferry terminal.

'Have you got everything?' he asked.

'Yup, do we need to buy our tickets here?'

'Oh, don't worry, I've already sorted it,' he said.

I looked at him in surprise. 'Really? OK, well, let me know how much I owe you.'

'It's fine,' he said. 'Anyway, let me just find our tickets.'

'Cool,' I said. 'We don't need our passports, do we?' He stared at me and shook his head wordlessly. 'Right, no, obviously, we're still in England. It's just the only time I've taken the ferry before was to France, so I guess... OK, so you've got the tickets? Yep, good.'

We walked onto the ferry. It looked like a moving version of an old pub. The carpet was maroon, patterned and threadbare. There was a cheap-looking bar at the end, and in the middle, there was an empty canteen. It was officially the most depressing mode of transport I'd ever taken.

'So what do you think?' he asked. 'How does it compare to the France ferry?'

'It's a pretty, um, good carpet.'

He laughed. 'Yeah. Can I get you a tea or something to get you through it?'

I looked up at the desolate café. 'I'm fine, thanks.'

'OK. Well, cheers to our first break together, Ellie.'

Had he meant that to come out so intensely? I stared at him, but he smiled back as though nothing was amiss. 'OK, to…our first break together.'

He leant over to give me a kiss and I felt a small lump materialise in my tummy. I had no idea how, but it looked as if Emma might be right—maybe Nick did think of us as more than just fuck buddies?

But surely if he did, he would have mentioned it. Everyone knew that if a guy liked you, he'd tell you. That was the whole point of books like *The Rules* and all that 'he's just not that into you' stuff—if was he into you, he'd make sure you knew.

I was probably just overanalysing things as I always did. It was only a few months ago that I'd managed to convince myself that Jack the Deflowerer had liked me when he only wanted casual sex. There was no way I was falling into a similar pattern with Nick. Nope, we were just fuck buddies who were hanging out on the coast. End of.

* * *

'Ellie, so nice to meet you,' cried Nick's mum. 'I'm Linda.'

Linda was small, stunning and a redhead. She looked nothing like her lanky blond offspring.

'You too,' I said in a muffled voice, as she wrapped me in a huge hug.

'This is Mike, my husband,' she said, gesturing to the tall man next to her. He nodded at me and stuck out a hand. I shook it with an uneasy smile. 'But you'll be wanting to meet the other young kids, won't you? Chris is just through there with Holly.'

I followed her into the living room with a quick glance

behind me to check that Nick was coming too. He shot me a supportive smile.

'Bro,' said Chris, as he caught sight of Nick. He covered his brother in a huge hug and ruffled his hair. I swallowed, hoping he wasn't going to do the same to me.

'Shit, man, so good to see you,' said Nick, as he hugged his brother back just as heartily. 'And, Holly, looking good as always.' He walked over to the sofa to greet the tall, skinny blonde girl sitting there. She was wearing black leather trousers, a grey jumper, and was smoking a cigarette. Indoors.

'So, this must be the famous girlfriend,' said Chris. I looked at him weirdly. Why was he talking about Holly like that? 'Ellie, right?'

I stared at him. He was smiling at me, waiting for an answer. I turned to look at Nick. He was smiling too. What the fuck? Why wasn't he correcting his brother?

No one had spoken yet and Chris's smile was starting to wane. Holly looked at me curiously as she puffed on what I had now realised was an e-cigarette.

OH GOD. HE'D TOLD THEM I WAS HIS GIRL-FRIEND. Nick wasn't my fuck buddy at all—he was my goddamn boyfriend and he hadn't bothered to tell me.

Oh fuck fuck fuck. It was fine. This was a good thing. I could do this.

'Hi, yes, I'm Ellie,' I finally said.

Chris's face relaxed. 'Cool, nice to meet you. This is my girlfriend, Holly. Just…make yourself at home. We're all having some whiskies. You keen?'

I nodded mutely.

Chris poured me a drink and I took it gratefully, glad

to have something to do with myself while everyone was staring at me.

'So, shall we all sit down, then?' asked Nick. 'What's on the telly? Are the All Blacks playing?'

'It was on earlier, bro. You missed it. But we've got it recorded,' said Chris. 'Are you big on the boys, Ellie?'

Weren't the All Blacks another name for Converse? Or was that All Stars? Either way, there was no way I was going to guess and put my foot in it. I shrugged with a helpless smile, hoping Nick would save me.

He obliged. 'Ellie's not much of a rugby fan, are you?'

Ah. 'Yeah, I pretty much hate all sport,' I explained. Chris's eyes widened and Holly stopped puffing on her e-cig.

'Seriously?' she said. 'I have no idea how you're going to cope going out with a Kiwi.'

I refrained from pointing out that this was pretty much the first I'd heard that we were going out and instead poured the rest of the whisky down me. So far, the casual minibreak was not going as planned.

'Ah, I'm sure Ellie will be a true All Blacks fan after going out with me for a few weeks,' said Nick, putting his arm around me.

I smiled weakly at him, trying not to throw up the whisky I'd just swallowed. I, Ellie Kolstakis, now had a boyfriend. A bona fide partner who wanted to teach me to like his favourite sports. In a few months' time, we'd probably be bickering over watching rugby or trash reality TV. I'd never get to watch *The Only Way Is Essex* again.

I gripped the side of the sofa and tried to calm myself down. Nick was good-looking, successful, and HE LIKED ME. Surely the whole point of my slutdom was to eventually find a boyfriend? I'd just skipped ahead a few stages. I probably just felt so weird because I wasn't used to things happening quickly. I mean, it had taken me twenty-one years to break my hymen, for Chrissake. No one could have predicted I'd have found a boyfriend so quickly. Besides, it was midnight on a Friday. I was knackered.

'Hey, Nick, when's this game going to end? I'm kind of sleepy,' I said.

Chris turned to look at me in dismay. 'What? You can't go to sleep now—we just opened a full bottle of whisky. Besides, it's fifteen–twelve to the Wallabies and Richie's about to score a try.'

I stared at him blankly.

Holly sighed loudly. 'He means we could be about to take the lead.'

'Oh, right, OK,' I said. I turned to Nick to see if he cared that Richie was about to score, but his eyes were glued to the screen.

'YESSSSS!!' he screamed, jumping up.

'McCaw's done it again,' yelled Chris, as he enveloped his brother into another bear hug. Holly was jumping up too, punching the air. I wasn't.

'Ah, did you see that, Ellie?' cried Nick, as he wrapped me in a hug.

'Mmm, very good. So have New Zealand won?'

'Well, it's only half-time,' he said.

My mouth dropped open. 'Seriously?'

'Oh my God, Ellie thought it was over,' crowed Holly. 'Bless. There's still forty minutes left. More whisky?'

No, I did not want more whisky; I wanted to go to bed with a hot water bottle. But Holly ignored my mental pro-testations and filled up my glass with Jameson.

'Thanks,' I said through gritted teeth. It looked as if this was going to be a long night.

* * *

'So are your parents still downstairs?' I asked, as I sat on the bed pulling off my socks.

'Yeah, they'll probably stay up a while longer,' said Nick. 'They're pretty cool.'

'Oh definitely.' I nodded, trying to stifle a yawn. We'd ended up staying downstairs drinking whisky with the boys' parents for another two hours of rugby highlights. I hadn't even known Richie McCaw existed until 11.58 p.m. and now I never wanted to see his smug little face again.

'Do you like them? I reckon they're pretty keen on you.'

'Yeah, of course,' I said. It was true; they were great. Linda had even winked when Nick eventually led my shattered body upstairs. My mum would have crossed herself and done a Hail Mary if she'd thought we were going up to shag. She didn't even know I was here alone with Nick— I'd lied and said I was away with the girls.

Nick pulled his T-shirt off and came up behind me on the bed. He wrapped his arms around me and started nuzzling my neck. I grinned at the feel of his naked skin against my body and turned to face him.

'I've wanted to do this ever since I saw you at Waterloo in your weird little gum boots,' he said, kissing me and pulling my fleece over my head.

I kissed him back and took the rest of my clothes off, ignoring the fact he thought my wellies were weird. He did the same and we climbed under the covers. There was a thin layer of dust on the bed sheet and I tried not to think about the last time they'd been washed. Instead, I remembered

Nick basically calling me his girlfriend. Had I just totally hallucinated, or was I in a legit relationship?

'Nick?' I asked.

'Yes, gorgeous?'

Oh my God, he called me gorgeous. I felt a grin spread across my face, then stopped. I needed to double-check where we were at in this relationship, or whatever. 'Were you, um, serious before? Like, with what your brother said and stuff? You know?'

'I don't know what you're talking about,' he said, trying to manoeuvre his penis into my vagina. What had happened to *Cosmo*'s rule that girls need twenty minutes of foreplay?

I pushed his hand off his penis. 'Wait a sec. I just… Oh fuck it. Am I or am I not your girlfriend?'

Nick stopped trying to penetrate me and broke away from me. 'Yeah. Is that not what we're doing?'

Holy fuck. I had a boyfriend. An actual willing boyfriend who I hadn't persuaded/influenced/blackmailed into being with me.

'Oh my God.' I grinned.

He laughed. 'You Brits are so funny making everything official. I've thought of you as my girlfriend since our first proper date, Ellie. We've always been so open with each other—it's not like it was going to just be a casual fling.'

'No, no, 'course not,' I said, still smiling inanely at him.

'Good. So, you're happy, then?'

'Yes, of course,' I cried. 'I just never expected it.'

'Well, so long as you weren't shagging anyone else, I guess that doesn't really matter.'

Oh shit.

Emma was right and so was Ollie; I'd basically cheated on Nick.

I lay there frozen. My mouth carried on kissing him, but my brain was not OK. All my horniness had disappeared and I couldn't process anything that was happening. Had I cheated on the boyfriend I didn't know I had?

'What's wrong, Ellie?'

'Oh, nothing,' I said, forcing myself to act normally. I wrapped my arms around Nick's neck and said, 'I just want you so badly.'

He groaned and slipped his penis into me. I bit my bottom lip as he thrust backwards and forwards, without stopping him or telling him that, actually, things were not OK because I had shagged someone else. Who had a girlfriend of his own.

There was no way that tonight would be the night I orgasmed—I could barely feel any moisture in my vagina. It was so dry it actually kind of hurt. I winced. I had to bear the pain; it was my just deserts.

I lay there wondering when the hell my life had stopped being an endless rerun of PG cartoons and turned into this X-rated mess. I was having sex with my boyfriend, when I'd had another man's penis in me less than a week ago, and I had no intention of ever telling him.

I was worse than Sergio.

Chapter 32

'Morning, lovebirds!'

I groaned and rubbed my eyes. There was a bright white haze in front of me, but as my eyes adjusted to the light, it slowly turned into a smiling Linda wearing a white summer dress. I was about to sink back into the pillow when I remembered that this was my boyfriend's mother.

I pulled myself up and ran a hand through my hair. 'Hi, Linda.' I yawned. 'What time is it?'

'Just gone 10 a.m. Holly's just showering but I thought you'd like to go in next. I'm taking everyone out to have breakfast in the sun.'

'Oh, amazing. We'll see you downstairs.'

'Good luck getting Nick up—he hates the mornings.'

I smiled brightly as she left the room. Nick could sleep in, but if I wanted to beat Holly in the future-daughter-in-law scales, I had to up my game.

* * *

I stood in the hallway seriously regretting my packing choices. It turned out that November weather in the Isle of

Wight was not the Arctic rainy winter I had been expecting. Linda was in a summer dress, the men were in shorts and Holly was wearing very cool dungarees just like the ones I'd spent fifty pounds on last month and never worn because it wasn't warm enough.

I shifted uncomfortably in my jeans, plain black long-sleeved top and Converse. Compared to the others, I looked as if I was either allergic to the sun or going through a serious goth phase. The worst part was that these were the summeriest—and nicest—clothes I'd brought with me. So much for not trying to look like a London princess; now I just looked as if I was born without any dress sense.

'All ready, Ellie?' said Linda, looking anxiously at my lumpy black torso. 'Won't you be too warm in that top?'

'It's all I brought with me.' I blushed. 'It was kind of cold in London.'

'Oh dear,' she said. 'Well, you can always borrow something of Holly's.'

I looked at Holly's size-eight body and grumpy face. 'NO,' I practically shouted. 'Um, I'm, like…very cold-blooded, so I get cold really easily. I'll probably be the perfect temperature in this.'

'OK,' she said doubtfully. 'Let's go, then.'

We all traipsed out of the house into the blaring sunlight. I took a deep breath and reminded myself that things could be worse; I could have brought only my wellies and forgotten the Converse.

'So what do you think of the Isle, Ellie?' asked Chris. 'It's your first time here, isn't it?'

'Yeah, it's lovely. Very, um, warm. And it's nice to breathe the sea air.'

He nodded enthusiastically. 'Yeah, I love the sea. It's also pretty green though. Hey, you know what? We should go to the garlic farm. I've heard you can get garlic beer.'

'There's a…garlic farm?'

'Oh God, the garlic farm,' groaned Holly. 'I grew up in Portsmouth, so we had to go for pretty much every school trip. I know it like the back of my hand. We don't have to go, do we?' She pouted at Chris.

'I want to try the garlic beer. Shall we go after lunch?'

Mike nodded ambivalently. 'If you think it's worth it.'

'That'll be nice,' said Linda. 'We can buy some to take home. It just isn't the same in NZ. I really miss England when it comes to the food and herbs. Do you know what I mean, Ellie?'

'What, me?' I asked in alarm. I had no idea what she meant; the only herbs I'd ever seen were in little glass bottles in Sainsbury's. And I'd never been to New Zealand—how was I meant to know what the cuisine was like?

'Mum just misses British food,' explained Nick, coming up behind me. 'So, what pub are we going to?'

'Just the one round the corner,' said Holly, mid-puff on her e-cig. 'They've redone it so it has this huge terrace. It's perfect for this weather.'

'Yeah, I can't wait to get the pints in,' said Chris. 'Let's have a big one tonight. I haven't got on the drink properly for a long time.'

'We'll show you a bit of the Isle of Wight nightlife, Ellie.' Nick grinned.

'It's going to terrify the poor girl,' said Holly.

'I'm pretty sure it won't,' I replied. 'I've survived Tiger Tiger on a student night, so I reckon I can survive anything.'

'Isn't that up in Piccadilly?' asked Nick. 'I think my colleagues go there sometimes.'

'Are they sex pests? Cos it's a full-on meat market there. After a night there, I'm sure I can handle anything you've got going on down here.'

'Yeah?' said Holly. 'Can't wait to see it. Oh, just one thing, everyone dresses to impress, so you might want to ditch the thermals.'

I rolled my eyes at her back and followed the group into a nearby pub. There were a bunch of tables in the shade and one straight in the sun. I resigned myself to an afternoon of serious sweat patches as Holly led the group straight to the sunny table and thanked God that at least black hid sweat stains.

'This is nice, isn't it?' said Linda. 'We can get some cold drinks, some good British pub grub, and get to know each other better. Ellie, welcome to the family.'

Family? I smiled faintly and prayed it would rain.

'So what do you do, Ellie?' asked Chris, as he put his arm around Holly. I glanced at Nick and he grinned supportively.

'Ellie works for the *London Mag*, which is this really cool online magazine,' he said. 'She has her own column too.'

'Really? How exciting,' cried Linda.

'Yeah, it's cool, I guess. But it's still just unpaid, so it's not that big a deal.'

'I'm going to Google you,' announced Holly.

I sat up in alarm. 'What? No! Don't do that.'

'Why not?'

'Um, because they're, um, kind of private?'

'Nah, don't look them up, Holly. I don't know if us lads could deal with it—Ellie said they're pretty detailed. All about periods and stuff I really don't want to know about,' said Nick.

I shot him a look of gratitude. 'Yeah, exactly. Really

not lunchtime appropriate. The whole column is called "NSFW", but it's really not safe for any social occasion.'

'En esef what?' asked Linda.

'Not safe for work.' Holly grinned. 'It means Ellie's written a sex column.'

'What?!' I shrieked. 'No, no, I haven't.' Oh God. I was fucked. There was no way she wouldn't Google it now. This weekend was going from bad to worse.

'It's about sex?' asked Nick. 'I thought you just wrote about, like, periods and feminism or something. Fuck—am I in it?!'

Oh God.

I looked down at my hands with their chipped nail polish. Maybe if I ignored this whole situation, it would just go away?

It didn't.

'No, of course you're not,' I finally said, looking up at the table feeling my cheeks burn. 'Can we, um, please not talk about this? Please?'

'Oh, bless the poor girl, you're all embarrassing her,' cried Linda. I shot her a grateful smile and went back to staring at my hands. 'So, boys, when are you both coming back home for a visit? Magda and Cassandra miss you.'

'Dogs,' said Mike. 'Not their other girlfriends, don't worry, Ellie.'

I tried to smile at him but couldn't bring myself to engage in any banter. All I wanted to do was finish this brunch, get the garlic farm over and done with, and go to sleep in a very, very cold room. Preferably somewhere very far away from the Isle of Wight.

* * *

Chris parked the van up next to a tractor and we all got out. There was a small brick cottage in the middle of lots and lots of muddy fields. This was the famous garlic farm.

'So, um, where's the garlic?' I asked.

'In the ground,' said Holly.

'Oh, right, obviously.' I laughed. I'd imagined tall fields of greenery but I was clearly pretty far off the mark.

'This is literally all there is,' she said. 'I have no idea why we're even here.'

'For the beer,' cried Chris. 'Who's keen to go straight to the restaurant?'

'Oh, why don't we go for a stroll first,' suggested Linda. 'I'm keen to walk off that pie I just had.'

'We can get the tractor,' said Holly. 'They do tours for, like, two pounds each.'

'Two pounds? I reckon we walk,' said Mike.

I suppressed a sigh. I would definitely have preferred to sit in a tractor than walk around a bunch of muddy fields.

'How are you doing, babe?' Nick came up to me and gave me a kiss as I ploughed through the muddy path. 'Having fun?'

'Yeah, of course,' I said, feeling a wave of guilt come back over me. I wished he wasn't so bloody nice—it just made me feel worse about what I'd done with Ollie. 'Just a bit tired, I guess.'

'Yeah, this lot are pretty full on.' He grinned. 'Why don't we lag behind a bit and have a romantic walk of our own?'

'Yes, please,' I cried. This was the first suggestion I'd heard all weekend that I was genuinely glad to do.

'Cool. So what do you think of the Isle of Wight?'

'Really nice,' I lied. 'It's so good to get out of London, you know?'

'Tell me about it. I'm a farm boy, remember? I can't be dealing with the Big Smoke for too long.'

'Really? Do you think you'll go home soon?'

'Maybe, but I don't have solid plans. And, hey, don't worry—I'll take you with me if I do move back.'

I coughed loudly. 'Sorry, um, dust in my throat.'

'Are you OK, Ellie?' he asked, stopping in the middle of the field.

'Fine,' I said, trying to shift my gaze away from his intense green eyes. What the hell was I doing not jumping into his arms?

'Is it being with my parents? Or Holly? I know she's kind of, um, hostile to new people but she'll get over it. She's probably threatened by how gorgeous you are.'

Oh God, he was observant and thoughtful too. I was the worst person imaginable. He put his arm around my shoulders. Actually, maybe he was so nice that he would understand? Maybe I could tell him about the whole Ollie thing, then he'd forgive me, we'd be all good, and I could enjoy my wonderful boyfriend as I was destined to do?

'Nick,' I said, before I could chicken out. 'It's not Holly. It's something else.'

'What is it?' he asked with concern.

I looked around the fields. The others were well ahead and I could barely see Holly's pale yellow hair. I took a deep breath. 'OK, so I, like, didn't realise we were an official thing. Because we'd never spoken about being exclusive, you know?'

'Do you not want to be exclusive, then?'

'NO,' I shrieked. 'I mean, no, of course not. I definitely want to be. I just… Look, what I'm trying to say is that I thought we were casual. So, I…behaved casual.'

'Do you mean that whole thing where you took ages to reply to my texts? I'm kind of over that.'

Boys noticed that? Damn. 'No, um, not that.' I took another breath. 'Nick. I slept with someone else when we were dating. Like, pre us having our exclusive chat. That's OK, right?'

Nick's arm dropped from my shoulders. His face scrunched up in disbelief and he took a step back. 'Are you serious?'

Oh shit. This was not how I imagined this conversation was going to go.

'Well, yes, but it was ages ago.'

'Right, OK. When?'

'Um, a week ago?'

'What?! Ellie, we were dating and sleeping together then.'

'I know. But, honestly, Nick, it was a one-time thing. It didn't mean anything.'

'Fine, whatever. You're right. We hadn't had the chat. We weren't official. It's fine.'

'Um, I'm not really getting that many "fine" vibes off you?'

Nick looked straight at me. 'Honestly? You're right—you were allowed to do what you did, but it still makes me feel like shit. I thought I knew you, and now I realise I was wrong. I never thought you'd be the kind of girl to sleep around.'

My inner feminist started to waken. 'Um, sorry, what do you mean by that? Why can't I sleep around when I'm single—which, by the way, I thought I was, seeing as you never told me otherwise.'

'I just misread you. My bad. So who even was this guy?'

The lump of guilt came back. 'Oh God. So, it was my flatmate. Ollie.'

'I thought you lived with a gay guy and one who had a girlfriend.'

I took a deep breath. 'I do. It was the one with a girl-friend.'

Nick took another step away from me. 'What the fuck, Ellie? You cheated on me by making someone else cheat too?'

'I thought we'd established I wasn't really cheating on you.' He stared at me with disgust. Oh God. 'Nick. I'm really sorry. I didn't mean to—I feel so, so awful about it. It's the worst thing I've ever done, hands down.'

'I'm such a fucking idiot,' he spat. 'I brought you to meet my fucking family because I cared about you that much. But all the time, you're sleeping with your mate who has a girlfriend.'

'No,' I cried. 'I wasn't like that. I didn't…know you cared.'

He raised his eyebrows at me. 'I made you dinner, I told you how great you were, and I messaged you the whole time. What about that suggests I didn't care?'

I shrugged helplessly. How the fuck had I misread the past few weeks so badly? 'Nick. Please. I'm sorry.'

'Ellie, if you can do that, I don't know what else you're capable of. If you can fuck someone with a girlfriend while you're fucking me, then you're not who I thought you were— you're just another slut.'

My mouth dropped open. Had he actually just said that? How dare he call me a slut just for having casual sex. Isn't that exactly what he and I had done when we met—we had a one-night stand. Why was he suddenly convinced I was some kind of Mother Teresa?

'How can you say that?' I cried. 'That's so derogatory and…and cruel to women. If I was a guy, you never would have said that.'

'Yeah, I would have, because what you did was just cheap and shitty. I thought you were better than that but you're not.'

I didn't know whether to scream or cry. I chose the former.

'You complete asshole! You can't just call me a slut for sleeping with someone BEFORE you properly asked me out. You can't backdate the start of a relationship, Nick. And who I chose to sleep with before we were official is totally my business. You have *no* right to judge me for it.'

'Yeah? Then why are we even together?'

'God knows. You're the one who suggested it.'

'Well, maybe that was my mistake,' he said, walking away.

'Nick? What are you doing? We have the rest of the weekend here—how am I going to get home?'

'Should have thought of that before you acted like such a slut.' I stared at him in shock. 'You can get your stuff from the cottage—the key's under the doormat—and make your own way back.'

He walked off, leaving me standing in the middle of an empty, muddy field. He was actually going. I would have to go home alone.

What would Holly say? His parents? How the fuck was I going to get home? And he thought I was a slut?

I felt my knees shake and I dropped down to the ground. I started to cry. My dream weekend had turned into a relationship minibreak and finally morphed into hell, in less than twenty-four hours. What the fuck was I going to do?

There was a rustling behind me. Nick had come back. He'd forgiven me and it was all going to be OK. Thank God. I turned around.

A massive woolly mammoth with two horns was staring at me.

I screamed.

'Moooo.'

Wait. Did mammoths make that noise? It kind of sounded like a cow. I squinted at it and realised that, without all the fur, it was kind of cow-like. It didn't have any black or white patches but those were definitely udders.

I stared dubiously at the woolly cow before breaking down into tears again. My boyfriend thought I was a slut. He'd abandoned me in a garlic field and the only company I had was a furry mammal with nipples.

Chapter 33

I walked into my room and threw my Gap tote onto the floor. I was absolutely exhausted. It had taken four hours, one tractor, one ferry, one wrong train and then the Tube and a bus to get home. My feet were sweating in my wellies, my face was swollen from crying, and I had dark red indents on my shoulders from my bag's strap.

If I had more energy, I'd be crying. Because Nick thought I was a slut. In the mean sense of the word. And maybe he had a point.

Emma and Will weren't speaking to me, Lara was obviously disappointed in me, and my mum was appalled by my antics being plastered all over the internet. My first ever relationship had lasted twenty-four hours and now he thought I was an evil whore. This whole slutty phase had just started out as a bit of fun and a way to finally catch up with everyone and have loads of orgasms, but it had ended up becoming a full-blown disaster—without any orgasms.

I pulled off my wellies, waterproof jacket, fleece, jeans

and try-hard lace knickers. I just didn't understand how it had all gone so wrong. Everyone my age had casual sex and it was fine. But I had to go and do it with someone who wanted to be my boyfriend, and then someone else's boyfriend.

The only consolation was that Yomi hadn't found out. I couldn't deal with that. Watching Emma find out about Sergio was my most traumatic life experience to date and it wasn't even really my life experience. I felt tears pricking my eyes again. I'd broken a relationship and gone against my moral code, just for...what? Ollie's horny face popped into my head and I felt sick. I'd had sex with him just because he'd flattered me so much by making it seem as if I was this stunning girl he'd wanted for ages.

When really, he just wanted a quick shag and hadn't cared about me at all. Unlike Nick. Who had liked me all along, but I'd just been too dense to notice. Ugh, why hadn't he just told me?! I hadn't even known I was cheating on him. If he'd just made it clearer that he was serious about me, then maybe this never would have happened. From the start, he'd made it seem as if we were just fuck buddies. Hell, the night we first shagged, he'd been staring at his ex-girlfriend. He got with me only to make her jealous. I'd thought we were just using each other for sex.

I climbed into my bed and lay face down on the pillow. I felt officially shit. It was as if there was this unspoken code to being slutty and no one had bothered to fill me in. How was I meant to know what was too far? I thought the general rule was just to follow your instincts and do whatever felt right, but that hadn't exactly worked.

I just didn't understand what was and wasn't OK. Cheating was bad, obviously. But what if you didn't *know* you were cheating because your boyfriend hadn't bothered to tell you that you were in a relationship?! Forget not knowing whether that was bad or not—I didn't even know if it constituted cheating.

I reached for my phone. It had no messages, no notifications and not even an app update. My own phone didn't even need me. I chucked it back onto the bed and sighed. Everything in my four major life fields was totally fucked.

1) Work. I didn't have a salary and my boss was exploiting me.
2) Friends. Barely speaking to me and seriously disappointed in me.
3) Love. Non-existent. Twenty-four-hour boyfriend called me a slut.
4) Family. My mum was close to disowning me because of my sex column.

I closed my eyes. I wanted to sob hysterically and get all the stress out of me, but I was just too numb. This wasn't like my other big dramas where I was humiliated/rejected/ abandoned and could wail over wine—this felt so much bigger. It wasn't just one isolated incident that was the issue here; it was my whole life. It was my decisions, my lack of moral code and my selfishness. It was no wonder I was left here alone in my room.

I pulled on my dressing gown and walked downstairs to the kitchen in search of comfort. Naturally my shelves and quarter of the fridge were empty, but there was a tub of fresh ricotta on Will's shelf. It wasn't exactly the chocolate soufflé I was craving but it would have to do. I grabbed a spoon, shoved some jam into it as a last-minute addition and trudged upstairs. This was my life now: stolen ricotta and solitary Saturday nights.

* * *

'Ellie?'

I opened my eyes and saw two big green eyes staring at me.

'Nick?' I cried.

'Um, excuse me?'

I rubbed my eyes. Emma was leaning over me with her eyebrows raised.

'Sorry, sorry, I was half-asleep.' I sat up, yawning, wondering why my eyes felt so sore. Then I remembered I'd fallen asleep crying into the ricotta. All the feelings of hopelessness came back until I realised that Emma, one of my friends, thus one quarter of my life components, was talking to me. I bolted upright. I had to try to win her round with my charm and wit.

'So, um, how are you?' I asked.

'Hanging,' she said. 'I went out with Meely last night. I only came in here because I heard noises and I knew you were away, so I just wanted to check there wasn't, like, a burglar or something.'

'Oh,' I said, my spirits sinking again. I should have known she wasn't coming in to say things were fine again.

'So now I know it's you, I'd better get back on the internet and post some more ads about Ollie's spare room.'

She got up to leave but I pulled the sleeve of her hoodie desperately. 'Em, I'm sorry. I really am. Don't worry about trying to find someone to fill the room—I promise I'll do it. And if I don't, I'll pay the rent.'

'You mean your poor mum will pay the rent,' she said, rubbing her arm.

I forced myself not to pull the duvet back over my head. 'You're right,' I said finally. 'But I will get paid soon at work and I'll start paying my mum back, I swear. I know it's gone on long enough.'

'I was just saying,' said Emma. 'It's fine. It's your life. You can do what you want.'

'Please stop being weird,' I wailed, giving up on my calm and responsible vibes. 'I'm sorry for being so shit. I didn't mean for everything to become this total mess. I really, really didn't. I promise I'll fix it.'

Emma sighed. 'El, I'm not mad at you. I'm just not over everything. I just need some time and I'm sure we'll go back to normal.'

'Time? But what if you never do? What if I've fucked up our friendship for life?'

'Good to see you're as dramatic as ever.'

'But I'm serious, Emma. You and Lara are the only good things in my life and I'm done prioritising boys and sex over you. I know I have been doing that and I'm done with it, I swear.'

'Babe,' she said, in a tone more like her normal one. 'You know I'm never going to stand in the way of a good shag. I just feel weird since Serge and you've been acting weird and it feels like everything's, well, fucking weird right now.'

'I know. I never thought I'd say this but I kind of miss my virgin days where the only problem was no one wanting to go near my vagina. Now it feels like there's too many people down there.'

Emma laughed. 'You do realise you've still only slept with three people, El? That's, like, ten times less than I have.'

I grinned. 'I know. It's so weird—I feel like I've had the sluttiest few months imaginable, but, in the real world, it's probably what most people did before they'd even started their GCSEs.'

'Yeah, but it has been in quite a short space of time. And it's been messy.' She sat down on my bed and bit her bottom lip. 'I am sorry things have been so crazy for you, babe. I didn't mean to be pissed off with you for going away with Nick either. I just felt like you were bailing on me. When I needed you. You know?'

'Completely,' I agreed, nodding my head. 'I've been a total bitch. But karma has had its way, and things with Nick are over now. So, when I say it won't happen again, it, like, really won't.'

'What? What happened? Is that why you're back early? I had a feeling something was wrong.'

'No, Emma,' I said, raising my left hand. 'I'm not going to talk about it because then I'll make it all about me like I always do, and I'm done being selfish.'

'Oh, shut up, Ellie, and tell me the goss,' she cried.

'Even if it's depressing and it will make you hate me more than you already do?'

She rolled her eyes. 'I don't hate you. I just miss you. So stop being this girl I don't know who holds things back and *spill* already.'

'OK, fine, but you asked for it. So…it turns out Nick didn't think we were fuck buddies. He thought we were a couple. He introduced me as his girlfriend.'

'I knew it,' gasped Emma. 'This is so great—why aren't you pleased? You've wanted a boyfriend your entire life and you've finally got one. How is that a bad thing?' Then her face went pale. 'Oh shit, don't tell me you told him about Ollie?'

'I felt guilty—I had to! Besides, surely that's the right thing to do? Honesty and all that?'

She put her head into her hands. 'Have you learnt nothing from me, Ellie? You don't tell them the stuff they'll never find out—you just don't.'

'Well, I kind of did… And he went crazy and called me a slut and left me in a garlic farm.'

She moved her hands away from her eyes. 'Why were you in a garlic farm?'

'Don't ask.'

'How did you get home?'

'A tractor, a ferry, a train, a Tube and a bus.'

'Oh my God, that sounds so intense. Are you OK?'

'Um, shouldn't you be more concerned about the fact that Nick called me a slut and broke up with me just after I realised we were in a relationship?'

'Obvs I want to know about that. I just can't believe you had to get in a tractor.'

'Again, not the bit to focus on here.'

'OK, sorry, I just really can't imagine it. But, wow, so Nick thought you were a proper couple. What was it like before the slut drama happened?'

'Amazing,' I said. 'Well, actually…I don't know. Come to think of it, it might actually have been a bit shit. We were getting drunk with his family for most of the time, and then we had this majorly awkward brunch where I was sweating non-stop, and then the Garlic Farm happened.'

'No, but what about the feelings? Wasn't it exciting to be able to say "this is my boyfriend" and all that?'

I sighed. 'Honestly? I don't know. It took me ages to have it sink in and it still felt weird. I know it sounds really un-grateful, but I'm not actually sure I was that thrilled. I feel like it happened too soon, you know?'

'Yeah, but who cares? Bar the slut thing—which he to-

tally said in anger and will get over once you apologise—
he's great, isn't he?'

'Yes, I mean, he's smart, attractive and lovely. But, Em,
I don't even know how much we have in common. I don't
even know how sad I am. Like, OK, I cried all of yesterday evening. But is it just the rejection? Or do I really miss
him for him?'

'I don't know, babe. But from the sounds of it, you get
on really well. Like, you never had any awkward silences
on your dates, did you? And I thought you said he's really
funny.'

'He is. And I do love the fact that we get to have sex
whenever I see him.'

'Ooh, have you orgasmed with him yet?'

'Nooo.'

'Meh, it will come in time. Honestly, Ellie? I have no idea
what you're doing here in Haggerston. You should be in
the Isle of Wight right now begging him to take you back.'

'I'm not going to beg! He was such a dick to me and how
was I meant to know we were in a relationship anyway?'

'Look, you know I'm normally the first one to say you
should stand up for yourself and not be the needy girl, but
you are kind of, technically, in the wrong here.'

'His parents probably know I'm a slut by now and his
brother's girlfriend is a vaper and she hates me and I don't
care about the All Blacks and I never ever will,' I blurted out.

'I, like, have no idea what you just said.'

I groaned. 'It's just that I find the idea of an actual, full-
blown relationship kind of terrifying. What if we don't have
enough in common? What if he makes me watch rugby
and fetch him beers, and sit in a room with the girls while
he does laddy things? That is not what I want for my fu-

ture, Emma. I don't want to sacrifice my independence for a relationship.'

'Um, babe? No one said it had to be like that. Serge never made me do any of that.'

'He's European.'

'So?'

'It's different.'

'Ellie. It sounds like you've just got classic commitment issues.'

'Isn't that what men are meant to have, not women?'

'Uh, yeah, in romcoms. Nowadays it's men who are needy, haven't you noticed? It's always the guys trying to be all relationship-y, just like Nick was to you, and we're unbothered cos we're young and hot and know we can have everyone. Especially with stuff like Tinder. There's always someone within a five-mile radius, so you never have to be needy again. You know?'

'Yes, I do know. Hence I don't want to be in a serious relationship or I'll never get to go on an online date again and my slutty phase will be actually over. Although, after the stuff Nick said to me about being slutty, maybe that's a good thing.'

'Oh my God,' said Emma. 'We had a pact about the slut thing, remember? You can't re-appropriate a word's meaning if you keep switching back to the old meaning.'

'Is this not a special exception? I just got dumped by someone who used the word "slut" because he wanted to convey just how, like, loose I am. And don't give me that look—my mum uses the word "loose". I picked it up from her.'

'Wasn't saying anything, babe,' she said, spreading out her hands. 'Look, I get that it sucked he said that, but it only hurts because you're letting it. You could just imagine he was trying to say "You're someone who has a lot of sex, and your most recent shag was morally dubious, not to mention ill-timed." Does that hurt as much?'

I laughed. 'I guess not. I know you're right. I just feel like everything's kind of falling apart, you know? Nick was so brutal yesterday. And my mum thinks I'm some kind of brazen hussy and it's giving her extra grey hairs. And you and Will hate me for the Ollie thing, so that's a massive mess. AND I really, really don't want to go to work tomorrow or ever write another column. I don't even have anything NSFW to write.'

'OK,' said Emma. 'Let's fix this one by one. First, I don't hate you, because I never could and you're an amazing friend even if you did fuck our other friend.' I gave her a wobbly smile. 'Will will get over it, although he was screaming about a spoilt spinach and ricotta cannelloni this morning, so you may have a bit more apologising to do. Bar the whole Nick thing, it seems like the next biggest issue is your column, but how do you actually feel about it, El? Like, screw whatever anyone else thinks.'

I sighed. 'I don't know. On one hand, I love writing it and I don't really care if people know this stuff about me. It's not like I'm actually describing the sex—I'm just saying I have it. Besides, people find it funny and I love that. But the only problem is that every time I write it, I feel guilty because I know my mum's going to go crazy, and, well, what if I do fuck up my future? I may never get employed again.'

'Babe, we're the Facebook generation. We've grown up with the internet—public oversharing is just what we do. So long as you keep it vaguely appropriate and do it well, I doubt any future employer is going to care. Hell, if you stay in the same industry, I bet your next boss will love that you did this. The only potential issue is if you can't shake the guilt.'

'That's just it though. I can't tell if the guilt is because of what I'm doing to my career, or more just part of the religious guilt my mum taught me about never masturbating and all that. You know, like the female shame about using your vagina and daring to talk about it. I bet if a guy did it for *GQ* or whatever they'd laugh about him being a bit of a player. If I was a boy, I know my mum wouldn't care as much. This is SEXISM.'

Emma scrunched up her face. 'Um, maybe, but I feel like that's not the real problem here. Am I right in saying that you want to keep doing this?' I shrugged in response. 'Exactly— you do. And the only problem is your mum caring. But you have to stop letting that be a problem. Like, you can't always please your parents. OMG, someone Tweeted the best thing the other day about life being a relay race and your parents always giving you the baton—but there comes a point where you're like, why am I even holding this baton any more, you know? So you can just drop it and walk away.'

'Um, OK,' I said. 'I guess I see your point, but there is also the minor fact that I still don't actually earn a salary and am exploiting myself for no money.'

'So ask for one.'

'Do you not think I've already tried? Maxine is a psycho bitch who refuses to budge. I have tried SO MANY TIMES.'

'Well, this time, just make her an offer she can't refuse,' said Emma, crossing her arms with a grin.

'Do you have a plan? Please tell me you have a plan. I really need money to buy food.'

'Sorry, babe, I just say the motivational things. You've got to go and actually do them. Good luck.'

* * *

I was standing outside my office building at 8 a.m. Even Maxine wouldn't be in this early, but I needed the time to prep myself before the big meeting. Well, it wasn't a meeting per se because Maxine still didn't know it was happening, but it was going to be big. I was going to finally ask her for some money and it was going to work because I'd come up with a plan. I had something to offer that she couldn't refuse and it wasn't unpaid labour.

Emma's inspirational speech had helped. So had the fact that I'd basically hit rock bottom and had nothing to lose. I was angry and I was ready to fight for my rights.

I poured my flat white down my throat, relishing all £2.10 of it. I could do this. I could go in there, reclaim my life and stand up to that bitch. If Anne Hathaway could stand up to Meryl Streep, I could totally do it. I'd just have to try to do it in Primark's finest instead of Valentino—and try not to chuck my phone in a fountain.

'Loitering?'

I whirled around and saw Maxine standing there, arching her eyebrows at me. They put my home-tweezed brows to shame.

'Just on my way in,' I replied brightly, trying to regain my composure. This was not how I wanted her first sight of me to go.

'Come on, then,' she said.

I nodded weakly and followed her in. She padded along in her casual flats and I started to regret my heeled boots. I'd worn them to look powerful but they just made me feel clumpy and try-hard next to her.

'So, um, I was hoping to come and see you later,' I said. 'There's something I wanted to talk to you about.'

'Go on, then.'

'No,' I cried out. 'Um, not now. I wanted to do it, um, properly. In your office.'

She raised her eyebrows again and I felt my cheeks burn up. *Why* was I so bad at the 'you go, girl, reclaim yo life' thing? This was not how it would have gone in the movie version of my life.

'Fine. Come by at half-eight.'

I nodded quickly. 'Cool. Yep, will do.'

She ignored me and walked out of the lift straight to her office. It was fine; I could totally do this. I just had to be less Ellie Kolstakis and more Anne Hathaway.

Me: I'm freaking the fuck out.
Emma: Think of the $$$!! You can do it.
Lara: Don't freak out or you'll act weird and lose your high ground.
Emma: Yeah, stay strong, babe. You need to have your 'go gurl' moment.
Me: What if I bugger it all up?

There was a significant pause in the conversation before Lara replied.

Lara: Then you leave and get a different job. It'll be fine!

I sighed and put my phone down by the bathroom sink. It wasn't going to be easy but I had to do this. I looked at myself in the mirror. My hair was looking pretty good, my eyeliner was even, and the black chiffon shirt I was wearing looked smart. If I didn't know better, I would have thought I was someone with a paid job.

In the past few months, a lot had changed. I'd gone from being the girl who'd been penetrated only once, to the girl who fucked her flattie and had people—OK, one person— wanting to be her boyfriend. My adult life was finally starting—it was just a lot messier than I had anticipated. Either way, I needed to ride this wave before it went off without me and I was left wondering where my life went.

I grabbed my phone and walked out of the bathroom. I was done spending my days hiding in the loos. I would go and get my salary—even if it meant breaking my mum's heart. If she couldn't deal with her child turning into a sexual adult, then she shouldn't have had kids.

'Maxine?' I said, as I pushed open her glass door.

She pushed her black Chanel frames down her nose and peered at me over them. 'Ellie. Come in.'

I obliged and sat down on the chair in front of her desk. 'Thanks.'

'So what did you want to talk to me about?'

'Maxine, I want a salary.' Her face didn't move, so I carried on. 'I work nine to ten hours a day, I help everyone with content, I've secured really good interviews for the mag, and now my columns are bringing in thousands of readers a month. I can write more and I have ideas of how to expand the business through new content.'

'Ellie, I appreciate all the hard work you do, but budgets are tight here.'

I felt my heart sink, but then I remembered my leverage. I crossed my arms and sat back in my chair. 'I have a killer column for you, Maxine. I'm done hiding the details—I want to embrace this and make it my own. I don't want to write about my life any more—I want to tackle a new everyday woman's issue each week. Starting with losing a condom inside you. And slut-shaming.'

'Why would that be more popular than the current one?'

'Um, because confessional journalism is so over. Everyone my age wants to know about the general stuff—we don't care about making everyone into a celeb any more. So I can use bits of my life as a jumping-off point, but what I can really give you is an insight into what people my age want to know. Not posh people like Camilla and co., but actual, real, "how the fuck is this my life" twenty-somethings. I want to write about issues we all care about. I want to write about feminist issues in an acceptable way. But I'll only do it for £25,000 a year. No negotiation.'

Maxine took off her glasses. Oh fuck. I'd gone too far—I knew I should have asked for £20,000, although how anyone expected me to live off that I had no idea.

'OK.'

My mouth dropped open. 'What?'

Maxine looked amused. 'Let's do it. You're right—we're meant to be an edgy site and we need edgier people to work for us. I'll get a contract drawn up. You can start your new role now. Oh, and I'm only paying you £23,000.'

I knew £25,000 was too good to be true. But fuck it—I still had a salary!! And Maxine thought I was edgy. I bit my lip to stop a huge grin spreading across my face and instead nodded seriously. 'OK. I'll accept that. Thanks.'

'Thank you, Ellie. But don't let me down.'

I wanted to fall at her feet promising I wouldn't, but I forced myself to stand up tall. 'Thanks for the chance,' I said and walked out.

I had done it. I was going to get an actual salary, and I hadn't even had to use my backup plan and get on my knees and beg. Anne Hathaway had nothing on me, because I HAD A SALARY.

Chapter 34

NSFW

Ever since I started writing this column, my life has started living up to the title. I guess it proves Oscar Wilde right—life really does imitate art. But people have reacted in different ways to this obvious show of, well, sex.

For some, it's been the stamp of cool they've needed to respect me. For others, it's embarrassing but they're intrigued out of good old-fashioned curiosity. Others think it's awful. Not only am I, a young woman, having casual sex—I'm writing about it. I've even been called a slut.

It's why I want to finally deal with this, the S-word, because I'm sick of girls being slut-shamed. It's been going on for long enough, and it's time we took a stand against it.

I thought about what would happen if we banned the word 'slut'—but it won't work. Banning things just makes them more exciting, and there's that niggling issue called freedom of speech.

So my friends and I tried to re-appropriate the word 'slut'. We tried to give it a positive meaning and go back to the basic fact of it just meaning someone who has a lot of sex. We called each other sluts to get rid of the stigma attached to it.

But that didn't really work either. It got confusing, because not everyone was using it the way we were. When someone called me a slut—I forgot all of this rationale and I just felt sad.

It's why I've finally realised that when it comes to the S-word, all we can do is remember that's exactly what it is—a word. We're the ones who give it power and put meanings on it. Some might use it in a positive way— 'you're so slutty I love it'—but others are derogatory— 'yeah, she shagged him. What a slut'.

That negative use is just part of a wider social problem— as in the world is pretty fucking unfair. But as much as I want to, I can't change that. All I can change is my personal relationship to the word 'slut', so I've decided to finally accept it for what it is—a word.

I'm going to stop being so scared of it, and if someone calls me a slut, I'm not going to care. I have the power either to let that bother me or to ignore them and realise that's just their ignorance. I don't have to let that little syllable get to me.

I want to live my life the way I want. I'm going to be judged for it, because that's the world we live in and I can't control it—but what I can control is how I let that affect me. And there's no way I'm going to let someone else's stupidity stop me from living my life. So to anyone who wants to slut-shame me, go for it. I'll be too busy having fun to even notice.

I stood outside Pizza Express shivering in my thin pleather jacket. I was starving and the girls were typically late even though I'd given them two hours' notice before calling the emergency dinner.

I grinned to myself. Lara was on the train up from Oxford, assuming that I was still in breakdown ricotta mode. She was going to die when she found out I'd stood up to Maxine—and won. Now that I had a pay cheque I was even planning on treating them to the meal. They didn't need to know I had a twenty-five per cent off voucher.

'Babe,' called out Emma, as she tottered down the street towards me. She was wearing black suede leggings with seriously high boots. I hugged her happily, knowing she was finally getting back to her pre-breakup self.

'Sorry about the last-minute plans. I just really felt like seeing you guys.'

'No worries, I just really want to know what happened. God, Maxine is such a BITCH. What did she say to you, hun?'

'Oh, um, just, like, really bitchy things. I'll tell you properly when Lara gets here. I love your shoes by the way.'

'Really? I haven't worn them in ages because I'm trying to tone down a bit and be more adult, you know? But I didn't have anything else that would go with the outfit.'

'Somehow I can't believe that, but either way, they look great. And what's all this about toning down—that's just your personality.'

She shrugged. 'I guess, but my personality has kind of let me down lately.'

'Sergio's a wanker,' I cried.

'Um, I meant just with getting stressed at you for the Ollie thing,' she said, as people turned to stare at us. 'Not Sergio.'

'Oh shit, sorry,' I said sheepishly. 'But, Em, we've been over this—you were legitimately allowed to be mad at me. I kind of fucked up our flatshare.'

'It's true, you did, but…I might be able to persuade Meely to move in.'

'Really? That would seriously up our street cred.'

'Ellie, it's weird that you find her so cool. She's just like us. You're going to freak her out if you keep going on like that. But, yes, it's a possibility. So we won't all get kicked out for not paying the rent.'

'Glad to hear it. I really don't need to add "evicted" to my list of this year's events.'

'So true,' said a familiar voice. I turned around and hit Lara with my bag. 'Ow, can you be a bit more graceful, Ellie?'

'Sorry. Just glad you're finally here. Shall we go and get a table?'

'Fine,' she grumbled, and we walked inside. 'So have I missed the disaster recap, then?'

'Nope, we were waiting for you,' said Emma, as she sank down into a chair. 'All I know is that Maxine is as much of a bitch as ever.'

'*Quelle surprise.* So, you asked for money and she told you to get fucked?'

'It was worse,' I said, and they both looked suitably shocked. 'She acted like an actual human being.' I paused for dramatic effect. 'Which means I've either misinterpreted her this whole time, or she's having a breakdown.'

'I'm lost,' said Emma.

'Shut up,' cried Lara. 'She gave it to you?'

I grinned. 'Twenty-three thousand pounds!!!!! I mean, it's £2,000 less than what I wanted, but I get to write about actual topics and not just exploit myself for money. I've already done my first one about slut-shaming—it's going up soon.'

'Oh my God,' shrieked Emma. 'This is so, so good! Congrats, El.'

'I know,' I squealed.

'You deserve it,' said Lara. 'I just wish you'd warned me it was good news or I might not have come down from Oxford and actually stayed to do some revision for a change.'

'Revision's overrated. Besides, I knew you'd only come if you thought it was bad news.'

'I did think you'd be crying hysterically,' said Emma, as Lara nodded.

'Jeez, thanks for the faith, guys.'

'You do cry a lot,' pointed out Lara. 'Every time you have a mini crisis you sob hysterically. It's only fair we figured you'd be a mess.'

I rolled my eyes at them. 'Well, I'm not. I obviously had a bit of a cry on the weekend—because my boyfriend called me a slut and dumped me—but I've pulled myself together and now I have a *job* with *money* and my friends are my friends again.'

'We always were,' said Emma.

'I know, but still. I feel so much better, like I've sorted everything out. I've even come to terms with the whole Nick thing. I was factually slutty, and if he meant anything else by it, then he's judgemental and wrong. I deserve better than him.'

'Are you sure you don't miss him though?' asked Emma. 'He did seem kind of perfect for you, babe—bar the slut thing, obviously.'

'No!' I cried. 'He yelled at me and abandoned me to the cows.'

'Yeah, but you did sleep with someone else,' said Lara.

'BECAUSE HE NEVER TOLD ME WE WERE A COUPLE,' I cried, as the nearest waiter U-turned back to the kitchen. 'I'm not a mind reader—how was I meant to know?'

'Um, because it was obvious?' said Lara. 'He always messaged you, he called you the whole time, he suggested cool dates, he bought you drinks, he made you dinner, he cared about you and your life, he remembered your friends' names… Seriously, Ellie, one-night stands don't really do that.'

I sat back in my chair. 'Shit. I guess he did do quite a lot.'

Emma nodded. 'I did think he was getting quite keen, El. Didn't he always pick you up at work too, and the fact that he invited you on a minibreak was just the biggest give-away. Casual shags don't do that.'

'Do you think that he thought I knew he wanted to be more than casual?'

'Probably,' said Lara. 'Any woman with half a brain would assume the guy really liked her if he did all that stuff for her.'

'Wait, seriously?' I asked.

They nodded.

'Oh God. I'm an idiot. I just didn't see all the signs.'

'Well, obviously,' said Lara. 'Every other guy has always been a total bastard to you. You've read into it way more than they have and you've got hurt. It was your natural defence to see the worst.'

'She's right,' said Emma softly. 'Babe, they're not all like

Sergio. I got taken in but it doesn't mean you have too. You may genuinely have found the right one.'

I raised my eyebrows. 'Please. Nick is not The One. We have, like, zero in common and he thinks I'm a slut. He may have fancied me during our "relationship", but I think that ship has sailed.'

'No, it hasn't,' said Lara. 'You're just being dramatic.'

'You could save it,' said Emma. 'I mean, he is the nicest guy you've ever dated.'

'I've dated two men. Precisely two.'

'So? How many guys out there can you imagine doing all that cute stuff for you? Especially ones who earn so much and are attractive and normal.'

They had a point. He was pretty out of my league. 'Fuck,' I said.

'Exactly,' said Emma. 'In fact, I don't know what you're doing here—I'd be at his right now apologising for being such an idiot.'

I looked at her and then at Lara. 'Guys…'

'Oh my God, no,' said Lara. 'I've come all the way!'

'You can have dinner here and I'll pay for it, and then you can sleep in my bed.'

'The one where you and Ollie had sex?' she asked.

'No,' I cried. 'That was in his room. Mine's fine.' I stood up and rifled through my wallet, pulling out my one and only twenty-pound note. 'There you go, guys, dinner's on me.'

'That's it?' asked Emma. 'I think it's probably going to be a tiny bit more.'

'There's a voucher online. I'll forward it to you while I'm on my way to Waterloo, OK? Love you guys so much, have a good dinner, and WISH ME LUCK.'

I ran out of the restaurant before they could stop me. They were right; Nick wasn't like other shitty men—he was The One. Well, the right one for now anyway. I had to win him back.

* * *

I stood outside Nick's building. I'd raced on the Tube all the way to Waterloo and now I felt like a total idiot. The last time I'd seen him, I'd been standing in a muddy garlic field. He would have had to explain to his whole family why I'd been exiled back to London and why he'd fancied a psychopath. He probably still hated me.

But I still had to do this. I had to give myself a real chance of having a proper boyfriend. Nick was kind, attractive, generous and caring. Yes, he was a banker, and did call me a slut, but really I should be flattered that he'd even cared enough to be so pissed off. I couldn't imagine any of my other internet dates being remotely bothered if they found out I'd fucked my flatmate.

And you know what, Ellie, you do deserve Nick, I told myself. It was about time I ditched this teenage insecurity. It was driving me—and my friends—insane. Nick fancied me, so clearly I wasn't that unattractive. Even the other online dates had wanted to go out with me. I had amazing boobs and I was clearly good at my job or Maxine wouldn't have said yes. Besides, I was STRONG. I'd stood up to Maxine. No one did that. If I could handle her, I could damn well sort stuff out with Nick.

'Can I help you, ma'am?'

I whirled around in surprise. The concierge had come up to the door and was now holding it open for me. Oh fuck. He probably thought I was a stalker—or a prostitute. Then I remembered that, actually, I was a columnist for an online magazine. I stuck my chin in the air and walked through the door he was holding for me.

'Thank you,' I said. 'I know the way from here.'

'Very good, ma'am.' I shot him a look to check he wasn't hiding a smile, but he looked pretty sincere. I breathed out in relief and ran up the stairs to Nick's floor.

21B. The door was shut. I crept up towards it and put my head to the keyhole. I couldn't hear anything. Maybe he wasn't even home. I suddenly felt like an idiot. I'd just rushed over without even sending him a bloody text. He probably wasn't in and I'd have wasted my night and an Oyster card journey.

I heard a sound from inside. Oh God. He was there. This was so much worse than a wasted £2.40. He was going to think I was a nutter. I might have felt as if I was in an Audrey Hepburn movie when I was fleeing Pizza Express, but really it was more like a scene from *American Psycho.*

I took a deep breath and pressed the doorbell before I could run away. The door opened.

'Ellie,' he said, staring at me.

'Hey. You're in.'

'Um, did you not think I would be?'

'Wasn't…sure.'

'How have things been?'

'Umm, fine,' I said. Why wasn't he inviting me in? Shit, did he have someone in there?!

'Do you… Do you want to come in?'

I breathed out in relief and followed him into the flat, wishing I'd thought to take the lift so I could check my make-up in the mirror. What kind of girl went over to see The Potential One without fixing her mascara?

We sat down awkwardly on his sofa. He was still wearing his work shirt but had changed into tracksuit bottoms. He looked sexy. I felt the exact opposite.

'How was the rest of the Isle of Wight?' I asked.

He let out a brittle laugh. 'Uh, kind of weird. Everyone was freaking out that you left, and they made me try to find you. I traced you to a tractor but the driver said he'd dropped you off by the ferry.'

'You came to find me? Why didn't you call me?'

'I didn't really think you'd pick up the phone after the things I said to you in the field.'

I remembered how it had felt as if I'd been run over by that bloody tractor when he'd called me a slut. 'Hmm, fair enough.'

'But you got home OK?' he said, running his hand through his hair. 'I felt shit when you left. I was really worried about you.'

'You were?'

'Do you really think that little of me?'

'No, 'course not! I just thought you were too mad at me to care if I was being mugged en route home. But, no, I was fine. Sad, but fine.'

He sat back in the sofa and looked at me. 'Why are you here, Ellie?'

I stared back at him. Honestly, I had no idea. Was I really there to try to win him back so that he could be my boyfriend? Could I actually see myself being with him?

I opened my mouth to try to say something relevant but nothing came out. Crap.

He sighed. 'Ellie, I really like you. I'm sorry it got so weird on the Isle. I guess I just felt pretty shit that you'd fucked some other guy.'

I winced. 'It wasn't like that, Nick.'

'Yeah, I know. But it just made me feel like you don't really want something serious with me. And then...I kind of read your columns and I realised you thought I was treating you like a rebound.' I flushed in embarrassment. He now knew everything about me. This was horrible. 'But it was my fault. I shouldn't have spoken so much about Sara at the start. So I do have a vague idea of how you feel about wanting it casual. But now I'm telling you I do really like you. Do you... Do you want more?'

This was it. My opening to say that I did want something serious and please could we put all this behind us and go back to those ten minutes of being a cute couple.

I looked at him, with his tanned skin, floppy hair and hopeful green eyes. He was the ideal guy, but, for some reason, it didn't really feel as if he was the ideal guy for me. He wanted me to be his girlfriend; I just wanted to shag his brains out.

'Oh God,' I said eventually. 'I can't believe I'm saying this, Nick, but I think you're right. I don't want something serious.'

His face dropped, then he crossed his arms. 'Right. So you came here because...?'

'Because I really wanted you to be my boyfriend.' He opened his mouth, but I carried on speaking. 'No, let me explain. I just... I realised how much of an idiot I was last weekend, and how great a guy you are. But then when I got here, I...I think I've just realised that you're right. I don't want something serious. I don't feel ready for it, Nick. I really just want to be young and fun and single and, like, carry on dating guys and having sex—but only with the ones I like.'

'So I was right. You are a slut.'

'You're not listening to me,' I cried. 'I want to be single. If that means having sex with more than one person, then fine, yes, I want to be a slut. I want to have sex and feel good about myself. Is that a problem for you?'

He looked taken aback. 'No, it's… Ellie, it's fine. Obviously I get it. I'm a guy. That's all I wanted to do for the past ten years. But now I'm a bit older and I want more. Ah, fuck, I guess I've been pretty harsh on you. You're a few years younger than me.'

'I don't know if it's an age thing per se. I just haven't really been with many guys. In fact, my number is *seriously* unslutty.'

He smiled. 'I had a feeling it was. I think that's why I was so shocked about the flatmate thing—it didn't seem very you.'

'It wasn't. But to be honest, Nick, you don't really know me that well,' I said quietly.

'Fair enough. I wish I'd had the chance to though.'

'I'm sorry,' I said. 'I think I've just been all over the place. When you called me your girlfriend in the Isle of Wight, I realised how lucky I was. You're amazing. But I think if I agreed to be your girlfriend, I'd just be using you. You tick so many boxes it's so hard to say no, but, for some reason, I just don't think we're right for each other. I think you deserve more. And I guess I do too.'

'If this is meant to make me feel better, I'm not sure it's really working, Ellie.'

'Sorry. I'm rambling. I just want you to know that you're incredible and I would love to keep on casually dating you. I just don't want a boyfriend.'

'Really?'

'Yeah. How about it?'

He sighed. 'If you'd asked me a year ago, I would have thought you're the perfect girl and jumped at the chance. But, Ellie, I want a girlfriend. I'm getting on a bit and I do just want to settle down.'

I felt disappointment collect in my tummy. 'OK, fair enough. I guess I can't have everything.'

'I'm sorry. But we're all good though, right? Mates?'

'Yeah, mates.' I smiled.

He smiled back. 'I wish I could have more, but I think I'd rather have you in my life than out of it, even if it just means we're friends.'

'Me too. And if you do ever change your mind about the casual sex thing, just shout.'

He laughed. 'OK, and likewise with the relationship thing.'

'Deal. Hey, actually…before I leave, how about we say bye properly?'

'What do you mean?'

'You know…'

He stared at me blankly.

'Oh, for God's sake,' I said. 'Do you or do you not want to shag me for one last time?'

He grinned at me, shaking his head ruefully. 'God, you're amazing. I can't believe I'm letting you go.'

'Is that a yes or a no?'

'Fuck it—I'm still human. Let's go to the bedroom.'

'Or we could stay right here,' I suggested, ignoring the thumping nerves in my arteries.

He kissed me in response.

Chapter 35

I was lying naked on Nick's cream couch. My pleather jacket and mismatched underwear were scattered on the wooden floorboards. He was sitting astride me with his penis poking straight out at a ninety-degree angle. It was pale against his tanned skin and I could see the outline of where his swimming trunks had been.

'You're amazing, Ellie,' he whispered in between kisses.

I grinned and kissed him back enthusiastically. This was everything I wanted. It felt so right to be lying there naked with him, knowing that this was the last time I'd see him. He wasn't my boyfriend, I never had to watch a rugby game again, and—even better—from now on I was free to do this with any other guy who asked.

I lay back on the sofa and closed my eyes. He moved away from my mouth and started giving me little kisses on my neck. Then I started to feel the familiar anxiety. I opened my eyes and saw his perfect face up close to mine. He barely even had any blackheads.

The lights were on full and my very untanned skin was on show. He could see my body hair, tiny moles and lumpy skin. He could probably even feel the little hairs on my stomach that had grown there ever since I stupidly tried shaving them aged sixteen.

All I wanted to do was run and turn the lights off. Then I remembered—it didn't matter. I didn't need Nick's approval. I didn't even want him to be my boyfriend. We were just two human beings having fun together.

I felt myself relax and started to enjoy the gentle kisses. My mind wandered to the scene earlier in Maxine's office. She'd given me a job. I had the job I'd always wanted, and I was going to get paid for it.

I gasped loudly as Nick put my nipple into his mouth and sucked it. It felt good—and the fact that I was employed made it feel even better. I closed my eyes again and smiled. Things were OK. I wasn't a fuck-up. I might have been bitten, bled on and confronted with a Boyzilian, but I'd survived.

My friends still loved me. I had kind of ruined things with Ollie, but I hadn't been infected by the lost condom and I'd well and truly learnt my lesson: guys in relationships were off limits.

Nick did the same to the other nipple. I breathed out loud. It sounded sexy. Oh my God, I was finally having my film noir moment and it wasn't even deliberate. I probably did look like a French movie star lying on the sofa with a hot man pleasuring me. I grinned wider and settled into the role with a loud breathy gasp. I imagined Marilyn Monroe would have made the same sound when guys sucked her tits.

I threw my arms around Nick and snogged him back properly. I sat up and wound my legs around him so that our very naked bodies were stuck together. He reached across me and pulled out a condom, quickly opening it and sliding it onto his penis.

Remembering his previous requests for me to go on top, I pushed him down onto the sofa and got astride. I gingerly lowered myself onto his gherkin, biting my lip in anticipation of the pain that never came. He put his hands onto my hips and guided me into the rhythm. I went up and down while his face spread into a grin.

It felt good, but clearly not as good as it felt for him. I went faster and simultaneously tried to rub my clit. I tried to enjoy it but it was too hard multitasking. Nick started breathing heavily and I realised he was about to come.

Before me.

I pulled myself off him without thinking and inched up his body. I sat my vagina back down on top of his face.

'Mff?' he asked from underneath my pubes.

'I don't want you to come yet. I want you to lick me.' I did it. I'd told him what I wanted. I was owning sex.

He groaned and started rubbing his tongue against my clitoris. I cried out loud as he got exactly the right spot. I looked down at him and saw his little face moving as he tried to rub my C-spot. He was doing this for me. It felt good, even though my vagina was pubier than I would have liked and I hadn't showered since 6 a.m. Would he notice?!

Then it hit me—I didn't actually care. For the first time, I really, really didn't give a shit if my vagina didn't look like the perfect ones I imagined existed behind the lacy pants in Calvin Klein ads. My VJ may not look like a bald plucked chicken or smell like Jo Malone, but so what? It had a perfectly good clitoris attached to it and there was a very willing man beneath it.

I didn't even care about what number on my list Nick was. Or whether I was 'slutty' or not. That was all totally irrelevant. The only thing I cared about right now was how... oh God...amazing the sex felt.

I closed my eyes as he licked me faster. I forgot to breathe sexily like Monroe and made loud grunting noises. The familiar build-up feeling came and I gripped on to his shoulders. 'Faster,' I shouted.

I grabbed on to him desperately as the feeling built up in me. 'Oh God, keep going,' I cried out. He obliged. I could feel myself getting close to climax. Oh my God, was I actually going to orgasm with a real live male?

I felt the orgasm start to plateau and banished the thought from my mind. It didn't matter if I orgasmed or not, I was just there to enjoy myself. Although...if I did want to orgasm, I'd better start breathing more and get a fantasy.

I started picturing an enlarged penis hovering in the air and tried to do the yogic breaths I'd learnt off YouTube videos. 'Om... Om... AHHHH.'

I cried out loudly as I felt my body melt. I closed my eyes tighter as the feeling ran through my body and my vagina trembled. I breathed out slower as it subsided.

'That...was...amazing,' I said, opening my eyes.

Nick's eyes were screwed shut and he looked as if he was in pain. I shimmied down his body onto his chest. 'Um, are you OK, Nick?' I asked.

He ran his hand across his face and opened his eyes. There was a damp liquid clinging from his eyebrows to his eyelashes. With horror, I realised what it was.

'Ellie,' he said. 'You just came on my face.'

NSFW

It is not easy to orgasm.

I just need to put that out there because I don't think it's something that a lot of women hear that often. But it's true. About fifty per cent of women experience problems with orgasms, fact.

In movies, TV and pretty much all media, orgasms look easy. You see women having mind-blowing sex with a guy they've just met, or orgasming every time their boyfriend goes down on them. THIS IS NOT TRUE.

Which makes it a lie. Perhaps these media execs think it's a pretty harmless lie—maybe they even think it's em-powering to show so many women having great sex—but I think it can be pretty damaging.

It means that those of us who struggle to reach those few seconds of ecstasy feel shit. As if we're not real women. Or we're sexual failures. Friends have told me they've felt guilty when their boyfriends have spent hours down there and nothing's happened. So they do a When Harry Met Sally *and fake it à la Meg Ryan.*

It's partly to make their boyfriend feel better—but it's mainly so they don't feel like crap girlfriends. So they don't feel as if they've managed to mess up the one natural joy that God gave us.

But I think it's time we ditched that guilt and faced up to this taboo—it's fucking hard to orgasm. There's stuff you can do for it—all it takes is a quick Google or a trip to your GP—but at the end of the day, you're never going to sud-denly pull through in a blissful cloud of euphoria unless you accept there's a bit of a problem.

I wanted to keep this column a bit less 'confessions of a

twenty-something woman' and more 'serious issues women face' but...I may as well admit that I've struggled with this.

Alone in my room with my fingers, I was coming anywhere and everywhere.

Put me in front of a penis and I was doomed. But, dear lovely readers, I'm writing this minutes after I overcame that hurdle. In fact, he's lying by my side. He's not the love of my life, and, to be honest, I doubt we'll ever do it again (it's OK, he knows this). But it wasn't him *who helped me get there—it was me.*

I thought that the big hurdles to orgasming were actual issues—his skills, the state of my vagina, the real worry that it was too unattractive for him to spend too much time down there. But now I've realised that's all bollocks. The only real hurdle was my lack of self-love.

And the second I ditched the paranoia, the insecurity and the worries? A wet, sticky bliss. I've also learnt that nothing else matters. It doesn't matter if you're sleeping with number 2 or number 222, or whether they're The One or just a one-night stand—the only important thing is that you actually enjoy the sex and feel comfortable.

Fuck everything else. None of it really matters. Because when it comes to sex, all that matters is that you're having fun.

On that note, I'm off for round two.

* * * * *

Acknowledgements

I feel so lucky to have so many amazing people in my life. Thank you so much to all of you for supporting me—that's my parents, my wonderful friends and the best friend I've ever had.

Thanks to all of you for helping me work through the 'second-book doubts' and reminding me why I write. It means so much to me when you tell me how you snorted out loud on the train reading my first drafts and that you can relate to Ellie's problems—that's all I can ask for from my readers.

On that note, thank you so much to all the people out there who loved *Virgin*. I LOVE getting your messages about how much you enjoyed Ellie's story, and I love hearing your own stories—keep 'em coming.

And of course, thanks again to my amazing agent Madeleine Milburn who made all of this happen, and to my editors for all their hard work, and always believing in Ellie.